Bound
to the
Beasts

I0769395

A WHY-CHOOSE
fairytale reimagining

ARI WRIGHT

Published and formatted by Blue-Eyed Books

Bound to the Beasts, Royalverse Book 2

Copyright © 2025 by Ari Wright

All rights reserved.

No part of this book may be reproduced in any form or by any electronic or mechanical means, including information storage and retrieval systems, without written permission from the author, except for the use of brief quotations in a book review.

This book is a work of fiction. The names, characters and events in this book are the product of the author's imagination or are used fictitiously. Any similarity to real persons both living or dead is coincidental and not intended by the author.

ebook ISBN: 9781969660009

ISBN: 9798991446495

cover art: Sonia Garrigoux

graphic design: Blue-Eyed Books

*To everyone who finds themselves feeling more
like a thorn than a rose these days.
The ones who are meant for you will love your sharp edges
as much as they adore your petals.*

*And for Kelly, who made me read too many dark romances.
I hope you're happy, Kel.
This is all your fault.*

what is an *Omegaverse?*

An **Omegaverse** is an alternate universe wherein humans have evolved a biological hierarchy based on three individual designations: **alphas, betas, and omegas.** In an Omegaverse, every person falls into one of those three categories (or "designations") by the time they reach adulthood. Their **designation** then determines certain elements of their physiology, psychology, and physical appearance. The humans in this Omegaverse are not shifters.

Alphas are large, strong, dominant, possessive, and territorial. While civilized, they often struggle with the urge to use force or exert their dominance over others; particularly fellow alphas. Optimized anatomy makes them physically superior in many ways, including reproduction.

Male alphas have a "knot" at the base of their penises. This **knot**, much like the penis itself, becomes engorged when they are aroused and expands to its full size upon completion, "locking" an alpha into his partner. Female alphas have a "lock" inside their vaginas that perform a similar locking maneuver on their partners.

Alphas are biologically compelled to find compatible partners based on individual scents. They also tend to form **packs** with others. Omegas often become the center of packs because they are the only designation capable of creating **bonds** between others. There is rarely more than one omega in a pack. Once a pack bonds with an omega, all of their scents alter subtly. This shift helps protect bonded omegas from unwanted advances.

Betas remain the most similar to everyday humans. They do not have intense scents or the same biological compulsions that alphas and omegas share. Many beta-beta relationships resemble traditional monogamous partnerships. Because they cannot bond among themselves, they often choose to marry instead.

Omegas are smaller and softer in stature, naturally submissive, wary of violence, fearful, emotional, empathetic, and magnetically attractive. Omegas' bodies are built to endure the demands of an entire pack of partners, emotionally and physically.

Omega biology draws alphas in. When omegas are aroused, their bodies send nearby alphas a signal by **perfuming**. Omega perfume is a concentrated hit of their specific scent, intended to lure an alpha to their aid.

Alphas and omegas each have distinctive scents. Their bodies produce these scents at all times, but they are particularly strong when the individual is sexually aroused or emotionally distressed. Alphas and omegas can have very intense, all-consuming physical and emotional reactions to each other's scents. While uncommon, the phenomenon is called **scent-sensitivity**.

Scent-sensitive alphas and omegas are referred to as **mates**. By some twist of fate or biology, they are near-irresistible to one another. Separating from their scent-sensitive mates would cause an omega extreme pain and distress.

Omegas experience **heat cycles**. These "heats" are spurred by the biological imperative to mate/bond with an alpha (or group of alphas) who will provide for and protect them. When an omega goes into heat, he/she will experience intense physical pain unless they are knotted by their alphas regularly. Heats send omegas into a state of limited lucidity that is known as a **heat haze**. This haze makes them extremely vulnerable and unstable.

Omegas can take **suppressants** to lower their hormone levels.

Suppressants help make the pain of heats tolerable for omegas who do not have alphas. Unfortunately, over time, suppressants become less effective.

Unbonded alphas who encounter an unbonded omega can experience **rut**. Rut is a condition wherein an alpha loses his/her mental faculties and gives in to the biological imperative to knot/lock an omega. Rut is often dangerous for omegas.

Omegas **nest** in order to feel secure. An omega's nest should be a soft, round place that feels low to the ground and dark. Omegas take great pride in building their nests to their individual tastes and their alphas' approval. It is their alphas' duty to provide this space and the resources to outfit it.

Courting is the process by which alphas can press their suits with an omega of their choosing. It is generally a task undertaken by the entire pack in pursuit of their one chosen omega.

Neutralizers can eliminate scents. They allow alphas and omegas in certain environments to live/work without worrying about designation-related faux pas. These can be circulated through the air or worn on one's body. While effective, they are not 100% reliable and rely on specific, contained environments. Once an omega hits their heat phase, most scent-cancellers no longer work properly and omegas will be distressed if they cannot scent their alphas.

it's about to get beastly

CONTENT & TRIGGER WARNINGS

welcome to the Royalverse

I'm so glad you're here!

Bound to the Beasts is the second installment in Ari Wright's Royalverse and it is intended to be read as a *complete standalone*!

This is a why-choose Omegaverse romance. It includes lots of knots, tons of spice, and absolutely no choosing!

If you don't like grumpy alphas, swoony mates, and group sex scenes, this may not be the HEA for you <3

Warning: the following content/trigger warnings *do contain spoilers.*

CONTENT/TRIGGER WARNINGS:

BDSM, choking, collaring, stalking, dub con, scheduled sex, breeding, loss of virginity, violence, blood, weapons, torture (off page), injuries, burns, masked man, kidnapping, forced marriage, past abuse (off page), suicidal ideation (past), fire/burns (off page), slut shaming, praise and degradation, murder, "hate sex," DP/DVP, forced climax, bondage, Dom/sub dynamics, age gap, chasing/primal.

And our beastly billionaire would like you to know that it's Cillian (Sill-EE-an) with an "S" sound, not a "K" 🫣

Vigilante Shit — Taylor Swift
Bad Romance — Nathan Fields, NYLO
Castle — Halsey
Prologue (From "Beauty and the Beast") — Moisés Nieto
How Villains Are Made — Madalen Duke
Black Sea — Natasha Blume
Haunted — Beyoncé
The Devil is a Gentleman — Merci Raines
Venom — Little Simz
Mr. Sandman — SYML
Panic Room — Au/Ra
Swan Lake, Op. 20, Act 2: No. 10, Scene. Moderato — Pyotr Ilyich Tchaikovsky, André Previn, London Symphony Orchestra
Big Bad Wolf — Roses & Revolutions
Take as Old as Time (Belles Villain Song) — Lydia the Bard
Heavy In Your Arms — Florence + The Machine
One More Light — Linkin Park
lift me from the ground — San Holo, Sofie Winterson
November — Max Richter, Mari Samuelson, Konzerthausorchester Berlin, Jonathan Stockhammer
Daisy - Sorry X Version — Sorry X
How You Like That — BLACKPINK
Toxic — 2WEI
Vendetta — UNSECRET, Krigarè
Empires — Ruelle
My Immortal — Evanescence
DARKSIDE — Neoni
Everything — SMNM
Beauty and the Beast — Midnite String Quartet
Beauty and the Beast — The Rose

the
Blackwood Family
tree

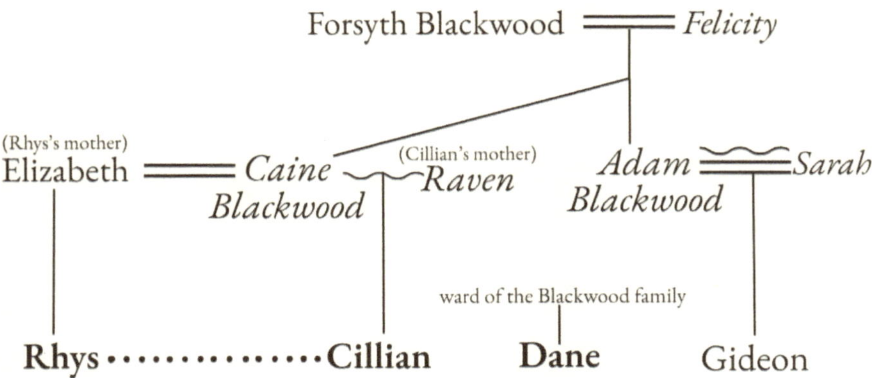

key

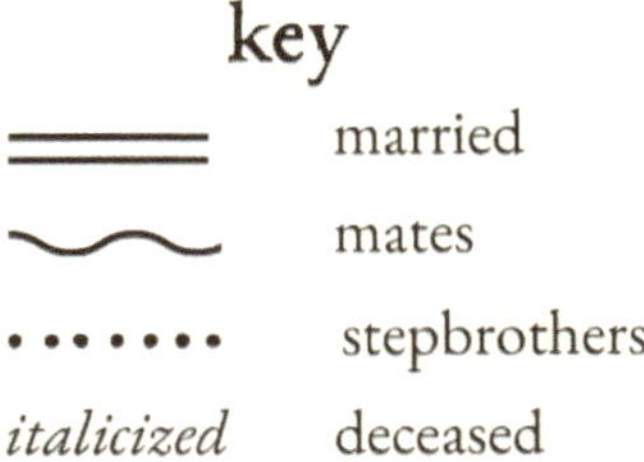

please note: some characters here are not named or
mentioned on-page... perhaps for good reason

THE DAMN THING STARED AT ME FOR YEARS.

Porcelain and painted, with ruby lips and the barest brush of blush, her ashen face blended to cream and roses.

Her dress was every bit as perfect. Fitted black lace. Layers of silk and crinoline. Delicate ballet slippers tied around her ankles.

I hated her.

And not just because my father called me and my sister his "little dolls."

That's what we were, though. Handcrafted from the finest materials, built to be objects of beauty.

Emphasis on *objects*.

Regardless of our unfortunate similarities, every day, the porcelain doll gazed and I glared. Loathing her for mocking my existence and constantly reminding me what I was.

Until one stormy night in particular, when lightning flashed white enough to blind and thunder rolled so deep no one heard the screams.

Not even me.

I woke up to an empty bedroom. And I *knew*.

Violet.

Someone had taken my sister. But they'd left that *stupid doll* on her bed.

Still watching. Witnessing the sale of my only sibling with a serene expression on her pristine features.

She'd seen it all. And the bitch was *still smiling*.

So maybe we weren't the same, after all, I think, staring at my reflection. *Maybe she was better than me*.

The mirror stationed at the corner of the bridal suite is a stately antique. Slightly warped glass, sepia tinged. It puts some color back into my complexion and casts an amber pall over my crimson pout.

I blink at it, trailing my green eyes over the ebony lace fitted precisely to my meager curves. Ironically, this gown might be the single loveliest thing I've ever worn. Long and form-fitting, with a lace train suited for royalty, a dark crystal belt, and a thick veil of dusky tulle.

I brush my fingertips along the intricate scallops trimming the blusher. It covers everything above the sweetheart neckline molded over my chest, obscuring the jut of my collarbones and the way the bodice tapers into elegant lace sleeves.

A black wedding gown.

Either the man I'm about to marry revels in the fact that our wedding ceremony is also a funeral for my dreams... or he has a seriously twisted sense of humor.

I'm not sure which would be worse.

But I do know that the girl in the mirror looks way too much like that damn doll.

A knock at the door sounds seconds after my elbow hits the glass. I stare into the shattered surface one final time, my image fracturing as I spin for the door.

Here comes the bride.

ONE

BRIAR

WHY IS THE DEVIL SO GOOD-LOOKING?

I thought he was supposed to be a *disgrace*. A corrupt angel, ripped from the lofty heights of heaven and shoved into some subhuman pit of heat and hatred? Surely, the ultimate fall from grace should *disfigure* a man—or at least rough him up a bit.

But no.

Somehow, all that evil turned him into something mythical. Wickedly beautiful.

Painfully so.

I would know; he's waiting for me on the altar of the Gothic chapel. Wearing a bespoke suit every bit as black as my dress.

And he's the one who lifts the dark lace veil covering my face.

Cillian Blackwood stands opposite me on the carved marble steps, his expression as grim as mine. The look seems just right on his stern, too-beautiful face. I scan over it, absorbing the clean-shaven, solid jaw that somehow manages to stand out alongside his sculpted cheekbones. Their slashing angles match the thick black brows over his ice-blue eyes.

The eyes of a wolf.

Because that's what he is.

And in this moment? I've never felt more like a lamb. His main course—or maybe just a sacrifice. I suppose I'll find out tonight.

The priest speaks. I'm not sure why he's here. Or why *we're* here, really. In an actual *church*. We could have done this at a courthouse.

Or an asylum.

That would have been fitting.

It isn't as though this exchange has romantic undertones. I've never even *spoken* to the man whose hand ends up in mine, his left ring finger angled for the solid gold band clutched between my pointed nails.

I have to swallow the urge to gouge him as the priest leads me over my vows. I regurgitate them, playing my part. Staring up at Cillian's face and slipping that hateful ring into place.

Well, staring at the bridge of his nose anyway. I refuse to look into his eyes for this.

He can have anything he thinks he wants, I whisper to myself, *because he'll never have <u>me</u>.*

Those words have become my mantra. And as he repeats the same timeless promises back to me—*in sickness, in health; for richer, for poorer; for better and for worse*—I find I barely hear him.

I'm too busy chanting the words that have become my solace. The one real promise I make today. My only true vow. To myself.

I'm not his.

I'm not anybody's.
I never will be.
And this devil?
Can go right back to Hell.

HELL, AS IT TURNS OUT, IS A BIT CHEESY.

Gazing out at Blackwood Manor, I repress the unladylike urge to snort.

Because, I mean... *really*?

Did he hire an architect and show them every stupid villain's lair and evil king's castle he could find for inspo?

In the backseat of his Rolls-Royce, Cillian flicks me a brief look of exasperation. His deep voice rumbles like thunder. "What now?"

Somehow, I've managed not to speak apart from the words I was forced to repeat at the altar. As a former performer, though, I find it remarkably easy to get my feelings across without voicing any opinions out loud.

I've made sure he knows exactly how I feel about all of his choices. This glossy, chauffeured car, his odd choice of wedding venue, the ungodly expensive meal we sat through with my snake of a father and two other old men whose names I refused to learn.

I turned my nose up at the fancy red wine and champagne, harrumphed when presented with caviar, wagyu steak, and priceless fish dishes. The only thing I deigned to accept came in the form of my "wedding cake"—an individual chocolate torte that looked too scrumptious to turn down.

Especially since, at that point, I'd been starving for damn near four days.

My eyes scan over the mansion's facade, hunting for a lit

window to peek inside. *The kitchen—I need to be able to sneak into the kitchen.*

It will have to be after hours, when he sleeps.

If he sleeps.

Some monsters don't.

"Briar."

I hate the way he says my name. The soft rasp of his voice over the first syllable—the slight vibration under both Rs.

I hate that he says it *at all.*

I preferred being Miss Brynn. Though, given the alternative is now "Mrs. Blackwood"...*Sure, buddy, call me Briar.*

Snapping a pissy glare at him, I raise my brows. *What more do you want, asshole?*

I'm here.

I'm—ostensibly—his.

What else is there?

My body is quick to remind me, tightening in all sorts of inconvenient ways and places. I growl at the instincts moshing in my middle.

My Omega could not be more conflicted. On one hand, she's been desperate for attention from any alpha for as long as I can remember. But, on the other, she's a girl's girl. So when I made it clear we could not *ever* find this particular alpha male attractive...

Well, let's just say she's doing her best, okay?

Not now, I remind her, clamping my inner muscles into stillness, hoping to avoid perfuming. *We're in a <u>situation</u> here!*

As per usual, around Cillian, she feels distinctly dazed. *Dazzled,* really. My father's constant crusade to keep me pure and chaste for whoever wound up being stupid enough to buy me—spoiler alert: Cillian Fucking Blackwood—left me lacking the presence or proximity of alphas for my entire adult life. I've only been around the bonded ones at the ballet and they all smelled distinctly like Back Up Bitch.

Since I designated at sixteen, my Omega has gone a little loopy whenever we have a chance to share air with *any* alpha. It's not her fault that she's gone a smidge psycho after six years without more than a few moments' proximity to everything her pitiful heart desires.

It will be fine, though.

She's on my side here. Not *his*.

As soon as I make it clear to her that we are *not* touching this man with a ten-foot pole—and find some way to learn his schedule so I can avoid him indefinitely—she'll settle down.

Honestly, it should be easy. He's only one man. I can avoid *one man*, surely.

My three contractual demands when I agreed to this insanity were pretty clear: my own room; no bonding, *ever*; and I absolutely *refuse* to let him touch me—sexually or otherwise—without direct permission.

I threw that last element in behind my father's back, stealing the paperwork from his desk before it was couriered to my future "husband." I never expected Cillian to *agree*.

Because, let's face it: if I'm not here for sex, why the hell *am* I here?

He must take promises made in triplicate seriously, at least, because he hasn't so much as accidentally bumped my arm since we left the altar. I also noticed that his de-scenter is nearly as thick as mine. Meaning I, mercifully, don't have a prayer of figuring out what he smells like, let alone collapsing into some sort of embarrassing omega meltdown over it.

"*Briar.*"

He says my name again, this time with the edge of a bark. *Rude.*

My teeth grit as his silent command tickles my throat, forcing a reply I don't want to give. "*What?*"

He gestures at the car's window and the enormous, Gothic-style estate beyond. "Do you object to our house somehow?"

Our house.

Because it is ours, *now*, I remind myself. *Mine and his.*

Thinking this, I turn in my seat to get a better look, swallowing another smirk. It truly is comically large. Obviously intended to be imposing, with its pointed spires and intricate curls of stonework, all dipped in an ebony finish.

It would be pretty, maybe, with some landscaping. The dark-gray storm rolling in over the sea in the distance doesn't help.

"Are we on a cliff?" I ask instead of answering him, noting the jagged rocks tucked around the back of the manse. "Over the ocean?"

Cillian brushes at his spotless suit pants, clearly peeved not to get a straight reply. "Yes."

I flinch, hating the way my mind automatically catalogs that detail as a last resort. *It would look like an accident... or not,* if I really wanted to spite him.

No, I tell myself, stern. *No. I promised Violet.*

Cillian's cool eyes narrow. "Whatever you're thinking," he begins, his voice all black silk to match his shirt. Before he sticks a new knife in me, barking a final command sharper than any blade. *"Stop."*

His order gets obeyed, whether I like it or not. My thoughts fling themselves away from the churning gray water, snapping back to the here and now.

At my answering glower, he sighs once more. "Let's get inside and make our introductions, shall we? There's a fair bit for all of us to work out."

All of us.

The words roll around my skull like a marble in an empty bowl.

The alpha—*my* alpha—adjusts his sleeves, casting me a raised eyebrow. "Surely, my pack will want to meet my new wife."

H—

His—

His pack?!

I thought he lived alone. Everything he's ever said and done—from our marriage contract to showing up solo at the church today—promised a *lone* predator.

When Cillian sees the horrible realization dawn, he flashes a pointy grin. The smile of a wolf, alright—but not necessarily one who operates alone. Which would make me the prey he chased right into their den.

"Did I not mention my pack, Briar?" He tilts his head, all stoic amusement. "How rude of me."

two

RHYS

KILL ME.

I clutch my temples and slump onto the plum-velvet sofa, in what used to be my very favorite room of the manor. My pack-mate, Dane, glances over, frowning.

I shouldn't be able to tell, given that the lower portion of his face is obscured by the mask he wears these days. The black titanium monstrosity stretches from the hollows of his cheekbones, along his ravaged jaw and up to the bottom part of his nose. Mesh covers his mouth, allowing him to speak—and, I suppose, breathe. Though he doesn't often take advantage of the former.

"Silent but deadly" takes on a whole new meaning when one

looks at Dane. He's enormous and always has been—a hulking hunk of honed muscle, half-covered in sharp, curling ink patterns. If that wasn't enough to warn anyone off, his uncanny eyes and the total fucking hatred he exudes usually does the trick.

Failing that?

People die.

I don't like to know the details. Makes my job as our pack's lawyer a hell of a lot harder when I do.

Dane sets his phone down and cocks a thick brown brow at me. A silent question. Asking if I want him to turn my music on.

Sometimes, when my headaches get so bad that even *silence* feels like shards of glass scraping the inside of my skull, we blast classical pieces as loud as the speakers allow. It's difficult to describe, but having a *source* for the pain piercing my temples helps me block it out.

With a grunt, I throw one arm over my eyes and wave the other at him. Wordless as ever, he rustles around for the surround-sound remote. A dramatic score gradually swells into the room.

I breathe through my nose, feeling it tingle uselessly. The pressure pressing into my skull swells higher. I do mental gymnastics to block out the noise—and, therefore, some of the ache.

Fuck me, it *hurts*.

Most people who look at me and Dane probably assume that poor bastard got the worst injuries. Which is fair. Part of his face burned off and had to be molded back together like melted clay.

But is there a *screwdriver* sticking out of his *head*?

I think *not*.

I can't smell him, but, if I could, I bet I'd find his oaken scent burnt to shit. I've known the guy practically my entire life—from the godforsaken day I moved into this haunted house and realized I was probably never going to get to leave it.

He didn't, either, but he never really had many other options. It was being a ward of the Blackwood family, or being shipped back to the orphanage Cillian's father yanked him out of.

Honestly? If I were Dane, I might have taken my chances with the bunk beds and communal showers.

Gritting my teeth against a flash of pain, I force my eyes open and peer across the room. Our friend-turned-packmate stands in front of the window like a sentry, staring through the crack between the velvet curtains.

Dane's first words today rasp behind his mask, his voice rougher and lower than anyone else I know. "They're here."

I lurch to my feet, but nausea seethes in my stomach. Anxiety loops through my mind while I slow my movements, gradually trudging to the window and forcing myself to adjust to the gray light.

Fuck this stupid plan. I told Cillian not to do this. I fucking told *him I couldn't do it. Why didn't he* listen?

For months, we argued about his plot to marry a suitable omega. Which is *bullshit* given the fact that our pack had decided never to take an omega. Mostly because Dane and I refused to be tied to one who wasn't our mate. And Cillian refused to take one who *was.*

He has his fucked-up reasons for that, and I have mine. Agreeing to forgo the entire issue was the only way for us to move past it.

Until now.

My sort-of stepbrother is an asshole of the highest order, but he's usually good for his word. So Dane and I were both blind-sided last month when he told us he planned to turn some random girl—Briar Rose Brynn—into his *wife.* And then refused to discuss it with us at all.

It makes sense now, though. The second I see her.

She steps out from the back of the Rolls with a dancer's grace. Breathtaking. *Unholy* beautiful.

A pretty little ballerina, with enough poise to wound... and looks to kill.

She hasn't danced in months, according to Cillian, but her skill is clear. The turn of her foot, the arc of her neck. She's still wearing that gown; a Blackwood family heirloom. Our pack alpha insisted on it, probably to make a fucking point. Or maybe he was telling the truth, and he's only doing this so our pack can take over Blackwood Corp once and for all.

Either way, message fucking received.

He's the alpha. And this is *his* call. Because Dane and I only have the Blackwood name thanks to *him*.

Dick.

The damn dress still seems remarkably morbid to me. Which is some *shit*. Because, trust me: if *I* think it's morbid...

It doesn't matter, though. Even if I liked her, my Alpha has made it very clear we won't have anything to do with her. Although, in my mind, where no one will ever hear, I can almost admit I *may* get the appeal.

She looks like a dark angel in that goddamn dress. Or a seductive sort of curse.

The kind that might just kill me.

But damn. What a way to go.

three

BRIAR

As I glide up the shiny stone steps to the house, the final crescendo from Tchaikovsky's *Swan Lake* crashes around me.

It takes me a moment to realize it isn't just in my head. It's coming from inside.

The song cuts off as soon as Cillian swipes at a hidden keypad beside the door. The metal slab falls away, revealing the wide, rounded foyer.

My eyes don't know where to leap first. There are so many carvings, curls, and detailed fringes. Then there's the décor, all gloomy and sumptuous. Berries, purples, and, of course, Cillian's signature black.

We won't dwell on the fact that black is also, coincidentally, my signature color...

I drag my focus from the pitch-colored floor over the grand staircase curved along the wall, up to the amethyst chandelier hanging from the center of an intricate dome.

The ceiling is covered in dark designs, devoid of any light, giving the entryway a gloomy, forgotten feel. The candles don't help, flickering uselessly on a large marble entry table. They cast menacing shadows over everything nearby, the shapes squirming in their own weak light as thunder claps outside.

Great.

Fantastic.

Candelabras. Gothic architecture. And an arranged marriage.

It's the fucking fourteenth century in here.

I shoot Cillian a sideways look, playing off the panic squeezing my insides as I mutter, "Can't afford the electric bill?"

The alpha is not amused. His jaw flexes. "My packmate gets migraines. The candles are for his benefit."

I try not to let that make me feel bad. Violet used to get migraines, too. It was part of my father's excuse for "sending her away." That, and her designating as a *beta*.

Perish the thought.

While I do my best to lock my face into utter stillness, my lungs run out of oxygen. For a moment, I consider just passing out. Because, honestly, I do *not* want to taste the air in here and determine just how much my Omega will be wigging out for the foreseeable future.

Also, fuck this guy.

But that word—*fuck*—is the one reason I have to stay alert.

I may not be formally educated, but I'm not stupid. The second he mentioned the pack he kept under wraps all these weeks, I knew exactly why he hid them.

Cillian promised not to touch me.

But *they* did not. And the moment I breathe, for one horrifying beat, I'm *glad*.

Dear God, yes.

Let them touch *me.*

Let them tear me to tiny pieces with their teeth.

Let them bend me over this cold marble table and rut into me until my shitty, half-ruined legs don't even work anymore, <u>*please*</u>—

But wait. What am I smelling? Because it seems like...

Nothing.

The air is pure. Damp and tainted with the room's general musk, but otherwise scentless. Locking my trembling knees together beneath my gown, I toss my Omega some side-eye. *Uh, babe? You good?*

She blinks blearily, replying with the equivalent of a nod. *I thought we'd be able to scent them*, she admits, sheepish. *Sorry.*

I forgive her easily, focusing on my relief. *Thank God.* There are faint traces of alpha-ness in here, but she's right—they're nothing special. Something wooden. A spice. Maybe some herb?

But it's okay. I can breathe, at least. With any luck, my dark cherry scent won't hit any of them particularly hard, either.

Shuffling footsteps echo on the second-floor landing. Which means there's exactly zero time for me to process before I glance up again.

Good fucking night.

Holy shit.

Luckily, I have a ton of experience repressing my reactions. I can refuse to give these alphas the satisfaction of knowing I'm afraid, the same way I refused to react to my father's punishments over the years.

It's second nature to turn to stone, dropping any facial expression altogether.

Unfortunately, *their* faces are crystal clear.

And just about as beastly as they come.

four

DANE

I HOPED SHE'D BE HIDEOUS, FOR OBVIOUS REASONS.

Stupid, of course. Cillian told us how lovely she was. But part of me held out, thinking *maybe...*

Maybe I wouldn't have to be the monster in this story.

But of course I am.

I'm the monster in everyone's story.

And she's stuck with me, the poor thing. Bound to us, legally and in the eyes of whatever church Cillian paid off.

The little omega doesn't display a shred of emotion. Her stillness reminds me of the marble goddess in our garden—ethereal beauty and cold, unblinking stone. Polished and pretty.

Jesus. Too pretty.

Now that I'm standing here, looking at Briar Rose Brynn—or *Blackwood*—I'm not sure which of us this will be worse for: her or me.

There's an obvious sort of cruelty in it, for her. She's beautiful; I'm ugly. The lack of symmetry would pain anyone in her position, but it's also particularly cutting for me.

I am *ugly.* And she is *beautiful.*

I'll never be able to show her my face. Or who I am.

I'm not sure why that simple thought puts a cramp in the dim, hollow space behind my ribs, but the realization hits hard before sinking into my center like an anvil. Cillian must sense it; he turns his cool eyes on me.

"Dane, would you show my bride to her room?"

Heartless bastard. I'm obviously the scariest alpha among us. He's dropping her into the deep end of this nightmare, forcing her to follow *me* into the bowels of an unfamiliar house.

I don't know which of us he intends to punish—most people never know with Cillian—but it's effective either way. I direct a low growl at him while Briar recoils, as if he's struck her.

Or I have.

Fuck, did that sound *scare* her? Her scent isn't strong, to me, but I get the distinct sense that something has soured. The fine hairs on the nape of my neck rise and tingle, distress streaking down my spine.

I grit my teeth and step backward, averting my gaze so I don't have to see the fear on her flawless face. Cillian's voice edges toward a bark. "*Go*, Briar. Dinner will be served at seven."

I don't want to glance up again, but my damn instincts have been honed over decades. When her head snaps sharply to the right, I find myself back where I started. Staring.

She cuts our pack leader a disdainful look. "What do you call the five fucking courses I just sat through with you and the Alliance of Evil?"

Shit.

The air in the foyer goes still.

No one speaks to Cillian like that. Not even us.

But what is he going to do? Kill her? He *married* her. Briar is ours now, and soon, all of polite society will know.

The Blackwoods are American Royalty, after all. Which makes *her* a newly minted queen.

"I call it you being an abominable brat," our alpha replies, smooth and unruffled. "You only ate dessert. Perhaps you'll consume something other than pure sugar this time around. If not, we'll try again at breakfast."

Her green eyes flash. "I am not a child."

Beside me, Rhys snorts, muttering under his breath, "Aren't you?"

Fucking hell. I forgot he was here, which does not happen to me. My situational awareness is unparalleled. Too keen, in most cases.

But no one can fade into the shadows quite like my packmate. Despite the shock of silver-blond hair on top of his head and the ink curled under his clothes, Rhys has always had a knack for blending in seamlessly. Even when he's standing in plain sight.

Cillian pretends not to notice our youngest packmate's jab. He steps toward Briar instead, posture rippling with deadly intent. My muscles swell, adrenaline pumping as I resist the insane urge to throw myself in front of her.

Goddamn omegas. Awakening all sorts of urges I should not have for our *prisoner.*

Because that's what she is, basically.

The suited alpha slowly backs her into the wall at the base of the curved staircase. He comes as close as he can without touching her, his ankles pressed into the pooled lace train of her gown.

Calculating blue eyes roam over her face, but he speaks to me. "Dane? Show our omega to her room. *Now.*"

I grit my teeth against the command, my Alpha chuffing a frustrated snort.

I have to agree with the voice in my middle: this woman is a lot of things.

But she definitely isn't *ours*.

IN ANOTHER LIFE, BRIAR ROSE BRYNN WOULD HAVE made an excellent assassin.

She moves as soundlessly as I do. Slippered, dainty feet eat up silent steps while I stalk down the second-floor hall, grunting one-word explanations behind my mask.

"Bathroom."

"Closet."

"Gym."

Cillian's bride may loathe us, but she's curious. Her wide green gaze darts into every room we pass, blinking to capture mental pictures. She thinks I can't see her cataloging her surroundings, because she waits until I face forward after every cracked door. Clearly, she doesn't realize my peripheral vision is unmatched.

It helps to see people coming if you don't want them to kill you.

Although, at this rate.

I pause outside the room nearest to the double doors at the very end of the floor. My knuckles tap it softly as I hesitate, questioning how much to say.

"Cillian's study." My throat scratches as I swallow. I swear I haven't spoken this much in months. "You never go in here unannounced. Trust me."

Her answering snort is completely deserved.

Because—*hell*—did I just say *trust me*?

Yes, delicate, beautiful omega; trust the huge, masked alpha you've literally never met who's dragging you around this horror-show of a haunted mansion as his literal prisoner.

I rub the nape of my neck as it heats with chagrin. I didn't agree to this, damn it. I *told* Cillian this was a bad idea. I begged him not to marry a pretty omega, told him I didn't think it would solve our current issues. Especially since she isn't scent-matched to us.

Let's be honest—a mate is the *only* way anyone could ever tolerate a melted face like mine. Or Rhys's *personality.*

Briar pauses a good four feet away when I get to her suite. *Smart girl, staying out of arm's reach.*

Her pretty eyes loop over the doors. Looking for an external deadbolt or some sort of lock bar, I assume. She shouldn't be relieved not to find one; this isn't where we keep our usual hostages.

Just, apparently, the ones Cillian marries.

With a silent sigh, I depress both polished brass handles and fling the carved doors open.

The room isn't bad, as far as prisons go. I haven't been in this house's Omega Suite since we bought the place, but, clearly, Cillian had it prepared. Coggins must have spent weeks cleaning in here.

It's the only white room in the whole damn house. All the same Gothic architecture and pomp that Cillian and Rhys prefer, but, in here, the etched curls and fine details are dipped in ivory.

Snowy wainscoting and stonework make the bed especially dramatic. Draped in every feminine shade from deep plum to rich, raspberry red, it's clear the four-poster wrought-iron frame was designed with certain sorts of activities in mind.

Just looking at it conjures about forty different ways to tie a person up.

Or down.

I turn away, ignoring the rumble that starts low in my lungs as I step aside to give Briar more room.

She glides to the center of the ornate rug, her black-lace gown trailing over the Oriental pattern. Intelligent eyes roam past the white vanity and its matching stool. Up to the enormous smoked-crystal chandelier casting gray light that doesn't quite reach the room's shadowy corners.

One of those holds built-in bookshelves full of tomes that match the colors on the bed and the rug. Another has two perpendicular doors—one for her closet, one for her lavish bathroom.

Part of me hopes she'll walk over and peek inside. The rest of this room may be as ominous as it is beautiful, but I remember the bathroom's impressive luxury. All white marble with onyx veins and brushed gold fixtures.

She might like it, I think, taking in her dark, heavy eye makeup and the thin gold chain strapped around her right wrist. *Or at least appreciate having a door that locks.*

The bedroom doesn't.

Believe me—I checked.

She doesn't ask about the nest and I'm grateful. All I know is that no one has been in there for a long-ass time. I'm pretty sure there are two ways to access it, one from this room and one from Cillian's...

Instead of heading for the mystery nest or the safety of the en suite, Briar drifts toward the balcony opposite the room's entrance. Her dark, flawless brows crease as she frowns at the view through the French doors, confused.

I gust out another deep breath, stepping closer without really meaning to. Planting my feet more than a yard away, I nod at them, urging her to open one.

It squeals on its hinges, but Briar doesn't seem to mind. She pulls the painted wood out of her way and steps onto the rounded platform beyond... jerking into complete stillness.

"*What—*"

She doesn't need to finish the question—it's obvious. And one I've wondered a few times myself, looking up at it from the outside.

Because the entire balcony has essentially become an atrium. Only, instead of glass to enclose the view of the ocean and the cliffs below, the iron railing is completely ensnared in a *wall* of roses.

Dark crimson and pure white, the budding blooms hang from a tangle of thorny vines at least six inches thick. Layer upon layer of rose plants, all about to reach the height of their season.

Briar runs her gaze along the overgrown railing, the completely obstructed view...

And I see the moment she understands.

These weren't here before.

They're here for *her*. To keep her *in*.

It's the one thing that gives me pause about Cillian and his supposed plans. Because he approached us with this marriage strategy a couple of months ago. Out of *necessity*...

But he had these roses planted over a year ago.

Dozens of them.

Two stories below.

Did he know they'd grow to this height by this specific time? Was he always planning to lock an omega in here? And did he know it would be Briar?

Briar *Rose*?

The same questions reflect in the beautiful woman's eyes as she turns to me. I stare at the glowing green, anticipating one of the inquiries I wish I'd bothered to torture Cillian for answers to.

Instead, she murmurs, "How long until the roses die?"

Because then it will just be a tangle of thorns.

A wall of death.

"Two months, probably," I husk.

Her nod is absent, her voice light and faraway. "Figures. My heat is in two months."

And now she'll have to watch these roses bloom and wither, knowing every fallen petal brings her that much closer to the three of us descending on her like wolves to a carcass.

The knife in my gut wrenches viciously. The storm beyond

the wall of thorns sends a clap of thunder over the sea. Briar shivers.

And we both watch as a blood-red petal floats to the cold stone floor.

five

RHYS

W E D O N ' T T A L K A B O U T I T .

For as long as I can remember, here in this house, that's been the rule. Our unspoken agreement.

Cillian and I don't discuss being two sides of the same fucked-up coin. And Dane doesn't remind either of us.

Not that we hate the thought of being pseudo-brothers so much. There have been times—though I'd never admit it—when Cillian was just about the only thing that kept me from the edges of cliffs.

Because, like it or not, he's here.

He stayed.

27

My mother didn't. Once Cillian's father decided to swallow the business end of his own Glock, she ran as far and as fast from the Blackwood Family Freakshow as she could. And left me behind.

Which makes sense.

I had to get my brains from somewhere.

God knows they weren't from my own father. The man who spawned me is some sort of criminal.

And the man who tried to raise me? Is in the dirt.

Caine Blackwood wasn't a genius, either. My former stepfather only had to marry my mom—a disgraced high-society omega with a bastard son—because he was damaged goods, too. Years before, he defied his father's orders and ran off with a mistress after knocking her up. Then he decided to keep his mistress and son here with him after he married my mother and indirectly adopted me.

Yet the guy expected all of us to be one big, happy family.

See? *Stupid.*

That kind of delusional optimism might fly for the general population, but the Blackwoods aren't *people*. Hell, sometimes I wonder if we're even human.

Cillian stands at the base of the foyer stairs, staring up at the hallway where Briar and Dane disappeared. The tilt of his head, the flash in his pale eyes; he looks more animal than man, especially when his lungs rumble ominously on a slow exhale.

Something in my center pricks. The same indefinable instinct that tells me where bodies are buried.

Figuratively.

Of course.

I grit my teeth against the painful pulse inside my skull. It's dimmed just enough for me to think, processing the scene with renewed clarity.

"Tell me what the fuck is going on."

Cillian absorbs my demand with a slow blink. If possible, his square, impassive features smooth into something even less readable. "A marriage of convenience," he replies, toneless. "You know this."

Yes, I know the *story*. Grandfather thinks his time is coming and wants his legacy secured by an heir. Either from our pack or our cousin's. Meaning we *need* an omega.

But, of course, a "true heir" doesn't just require a willing pussy.

It requires a *wife*.

Cue Briar Rose Brynn—only daughter of some lunatic inventor who happened to actually invent something after *decades* of failure. According to Cillian, Brynn developed a chemical weapon worth billions, but hadn't quite figured out its worth—so striking a deal with him quickly was essential.

The old loon probably still had dollar signs in his eyes when he mentioned that he was also trying to find a "suitable match" (aka purchasing party) for his obnoxious prima ballerina daughter.

And, hell.

Cillian needed a wife anyway.

So this was simply good business.

Better, certainly, than letting the crazy man know exactly how much money his product would make us—or, God forbid, another firm. Not to mention what it will go for on the black market.

Illegal dealings are our pack's specialty. While Cillian's cousin, Gideon, and his pack run Blackwood Corp's *legitimate* holdings, we make the *real* money. Selling our company's weapons to groups that would, let's just say, not look great on the Christmas card list.

But, hey. A guy's gotta eat.

And no one defies Grandfather's orders.

Besides, who better to run the family's *illegitimate* holdings than Cillian, Forsyth Blackwood's one and only *illegitimate* grandson?

People don't think about that enough. How much our high

society circles judged Cillian for his very existence. How smart and ruthless my almost-brother must have been to rise through the ranks of his twisted family anyway. Not to mention taking on the most lucrative portion of the business, running it seamlessly, and never getting caught.

Anyone who isn't afraid of Cillian is as good as dead.

But Briar isn't. And when our pack alpha told us about this plan, I assumed his marriage of convenience included a *willing bride*. Now that I've met her, I don't know what the fuck he's trying to pull. Or why he would ever want *an enemy* in our house.

Where lesser men would quail under the ice in my gaze, our pack leader merely cocks a brow. "If you have something to say, I'd rather you did so now."

As opposed to misspeaking in front of Briar.

I return his arch expression with one of my own. "Does *she* know why she's here?"

His gaze flickers, heat licking through his irises. "If she doesn't already, she will tonight."

Six

CILLIAN

THE BLACKWOOD GROUP CHAT

DANE

Briar says she won't come down for dinner

CILLIAN

And we say she will.

I wonder who will win.

RHYS

You're a sick bastard.

This is all a joke, right?

Cillian?

CILLIAN HAS SILENCED NOTIFICATIONS.

RHYS

Motherfucker.

Cillian

THE BLACKWOOD CREST LOOMS OVER MY DESK, ITS stone scales as dark as the damask wallpaper behind it.

I lean back in my chair, rolling a crystal tumbler of scotch between my hands. Low light sifts through the amber liquid—a golden blur in my periphery.

Years of absolute control have taught me every edge and corner of my mind. I know I can't flick my gaze from the sculpted seal hanging over my desk. The same way I can't cross my ankle over my knee.

If I move a single muscle, I'll stand up.

If I stand up, I'll walk out of this room.

And if I walk out of this room...

No. I squash that seed before it germinates, grinding the grain under my heel.

Not yet.

I've built my entire life on those two words. Holding off, holding back, holding *in.*

If you stay still long enough, people forget you can move. You become a *fixture.* Something decorative instead of something deadly.

Which is when you strike.

I flex my fingers around the carved crystal in my clutches. *Not yet.*

There's a plan in play here. I knew carrying it out would be damn difficult, but I underestimated just *how* torturous it'd be to have Briar in our house. Let alone on the other side of my study's wall.

This wall.

I did that the same way I do everything: on purpose. Hanging our family crest where I knew I would see it each time I dared to glance in her direction. A reminder of the past. An omen for the future, if I'm not careful.

But I'm *always* careful.

My eyes slide over its shining onyx grooves. Scales. Precisely etched over a thick, coiled tail. Spread all the way up the forked body. Covering both of the snake's hissing heads. Sometimes, when it's late and I've been at my desk for hours, they almost seem to slither.

The battle-axe buried in the creature's shimmering body isn't nearly as interesting. Flat and lifeless by comparison—the rough-hewn stone is carved into an obvious token for our family business.

Weapons. Destruction. Death.

But Grandfather's words wind through my mind like a curl of smoke. *"Most people think the axe is there to symbolize us. Our company. But it doesn't. The snake does."*

Because a blade tried to sever the beast's head. And instead of dying, it grew another.

A keen observer might also note the Blackwood family tradition of producing two sons. No one knows how or why, but every generation of Blackwood men had two sons for nearly a hundred years, even if they had to cobble a family together the way my father did.

The result was the same.

Two sons.

One victor.

And one who wasn't so fortunate.

Normally, staring at the two snake heads, their identical fangs bared, reminds me of my father and his brother. Today, with

Rhys's suspicious gaze burned into my brain, I find it hard not to see the parallel.

I decided we would be different a long time ago, though.

And what he doesn't know can't hurt him. Much.

Dane, on the other hand...

Our right-hand-man-turned-packmate appears in my doorway. From the time we were eight, he's had a special gift for silence. My father once told me that's why he selected him to be a ward of Blackwood Manor—and learn to be my bodyguard while we were still children.

It was a twisted plan, but one that seemed to suit everyone. Dane enjoyed not living in an orphanage. He got to go to all the same schools Rhys and I did, provided he agreed to take any stray bullets that came our way. It turned out to be a paranoid over-precaution on my father's part, but over time, Dane became my best friend. And when I was old enough to defend myself, he took his talents to the Special Forces.

If anything, he came back more silent and steady than ever. To this day, he doesn't even let the doorjamb click when he turns the antique knob to my office.

My most dangerous packmate suddenly just *appears*, glaring stonily over his half-mask.

He doesn't need that goddamn thing. We've all tried to tell him. The burns that melted the skin along his right jaw and cheek have long-since healed. And his facial hair covers a lot of the scars, save for a few that were so deep they obliterated his thick brown hair permanently. Those climb toward his right eye, a mottled patch just visible over the edge of his metal-and-mesh muzzle.

I've known Dane long enough to read the disapproval in his golden eyes all the way across the dim room. "Like I said; Briar won't come down for dinner."

Of course she does. Exasperation whips through my middle, melting into a puddle of begrudging admiration.

"She's a touch on the defiant side," I drawl, setting my tumbler on my desk with calculated movements. Holding myself in my rolling leather chair with every speck of control I possess. "I'll have to train that out of her."

Something fierce blazes across Dane's visage. His deep voice drops even lower. "So you're going to start right away? You won't even give her *a day* to adjust?"

Technically, she has my word that *I* wouldn't touch her without permission. I never said anything about the others, though.

"No," I clip in return, noting the time—*fucking hell, we have to go*—and stiffly pushing to my feet. "But I will give her a choice."

Instead of ripping the cursed family crest off the wall separating me from the omega, I force innocuous motions. One hand slides into my pocket while the other buttons my suit jacket.

I make for the hallway, keeping my gaze well away from the double doors to her room. Rhys can fetch her if Dane refuses.

I'll control myself. For now.

Not yet, I think again, turning toward the stairs. Swallowing the urge to snarl. *But soon.*

SEVEN

BRIAR

MY PERP-WALK—OR "TOUR"—WITH DANE TAUGHT ME one thing for sure: the footsteps rushing toward my door? Definitely don't belong to the silent, bearded beast.

God knows what that man is hiding under his mask, but I saw enough of his sideburns to know he has pretty thick facial hair under there. I've amused myself by scrunching my nose over how hot and itchy wearing that thing must be. Doing my best to avoid thoughts of where I am or how Cillian will react to my refusal of his dinner "invitation."

When I hear a deliberate patter arrow toward my doors, I

instantly bolt upright. My gaze drops to my bare belly and legs, widening.

Shit.

I ripped off my stupid wedding gown the second I was alone, only to realize I have no clothes or other belongings in here. There are plenty of options in the closet Dane showed me, but I couldn't bring myself to put on any of the garments intended for *Mrs. Blackwood.*

Somehow, the silky black kimono on the back of the bathroom door felt safer. Like something I was borrowing, the way a person wears a hotel robe. I threw it on with every intention of replacing it with my own as soon as possible and decided not to tie it before I lay on the big berry-and-amethyst bed.

That was dumb.

Scrabbling with the sash, I barely get the damn thing closed before both doors fly open.

Because, *yeah.* They don't lock.

A trim, lanky figure in a light gray uniform comes barreling into the room, followed closely by a slender woman in similar attire. It's traditional garb for a valet and a maid, I realize—all proper and layered with starched white details. A stiff collar for the man, a frilled apron for the woman.

I blink at their intrusion, my shock doubling when the woman reaches over and smacks the back of the man's head. "*Louis!*" A French flair accents her hiss. "You cannot simply waltz into the *madame's* room anymore. She *lives here* now!"

The gangly man stops just past the threshold, a look of absolute horror draining the color off his thin, handsome face. He turns toward me with both hands raised.

"A thousand apologies," he says in a matching drawl. Then he coughs, turning red before adding a winsome smile. "*Mon Dieu,* I've certainly made a terrible first impression."

My open mouth snaps shut, but I can't form words. A whine from my Omega tangles in my throat as I hold my robe shut and fight to hide my tremors. The man's expression falls.

"Truly," he goes on, "I apologize for barging in. Master Cillian requested I come collect you for dinner, and Fiona here was curious…"

He gestures to the pretty brunette maid beside him. She's an omega, if I'm not mistaken. And so is he.

That fact has a bit of the tension slipping from my shoulders. "I'm Briar," I manage. "Cillian's"—*hostage, prisoner, purchase*—"wife."

Gah. The *taste* of those words. The way all my muscles clench when I say them. Even the ones between my hips.

Please, I beg my Omega. *You have to hold it <u>together</u>, girl. You're all I've got left.*

She nods briskly, muttering to me and herself. *Right, right. Sorry.*

The male omega seems to know I'm losing my mind. Apparently it's amusing, though, because his lips quirk in a mischievous smirk. "I'm Louis, the jack-of-all-trades around here. Valet, server, sous-chef. This is my sister, Fiona. She's your maid. You'll meet our chef, Mrs. Porter, if you're ever brave enough to interrupt her cooking. And then there's—"

Louis cuts himself off with another choked cough. His sister snorts, rolling her eyes. "Monsieur Coggins, the butler and chauffeur. I suspect he'll have a word or two about your arrival when you meet him, too."

Great.

Perfect.

Gossiping butlers and interfering maids. This isn't the fourteenth century. It's the eighteenth.

Do you think there's a guillotine around here somewhere? I honestly wouldn't even be surprised.

"Joy," I reply, drenching my voice in sarcasm. "Listen, I'm sure you're all *lovely*, but I'm sort of in the middle of a crisis here. I won't be making any friends in this house and I most *definitely* won't be going down for dinner. Ever. So you can tell that pack of motherfucking *monsters* that I—"

Fiona's doe eyes bug out. "Shhh," she interrupts, her hands fluttering anxiously. "Madame, he will *hear* you."

She must mean Cillian. But I'm not afraid of him—not *really*. He had ample opportunity to use excessive force against me today and I'm still in one piece. Though he did look pretty murderous when I turned down four courses in a row during our dinner.

Our *first* dinner.

Dane wasn't horrifying, either. Scary-big, for sure. Too bulky for me to have a prayer of fending him off. And tense in a mysterious way I didn't *love*, but...

No, the only alpha in this house I think I may actually *fear* is the too-pretty, silver-blond one. Not because he appears any stronger or more dominant than the others, but because I saw *malice* in every dark flicker of his eyes.

"Who will hear me?" I ask, scoffing. "Because if it's either of those dumbass brutes—"

My words die as slow, long-legged paces approach from the hallway.

Where Rhys has been standing all along.

Waiting.

THE ARISTOCRATIC ALPHA IS EVERY BIT AS LITHE AND graceful as he looks.

Before I can draw a startled gasp, he closes in on the ornate king-sized bed. I only get a brief glimpse of his feral gaze and the taut, angelic lines of his face before he snaps his hand out and grabs my forearm. With one rough yank, I stumble to my feet.

"Wha—I—"

"*You,*" he barks, silken and steel all at once, "will *shut your fucking mouth.*"

His command instantly registers. My Omega squirms under its weight, trying to free me from it. But my lips seal themselves shut as he snaps a furious look at the gawking staff members. "*You*," he repeats toward them. "*Out*."

The two omegas scurry from the room, leaving mine crying, *Wait! Take me with you!*

A whine ekes up my throat instead. The loathing on the blond alpha's face flickers, then turns to malicious glee.

He spins me effortlessly, tangling our legs until I'm forced to walk backward. Into the wall.

He cages me there, paying no heed to my personal space the way Cillian did. Unlike his pack leader, this alpha invades every way he can, flattening his lean strength into my pitiful body, pinning me with my wrist held fast beside my face and his other hand locking my left arm at my side. His grin is hard with rage.

Downstairs, in the dim foyer, he didn't look like this. There, he was a shadow. But here, in the light? He's a fallen *god*. Some evil deity, carved from cold, unyielding alabaster by a master sculptor.

His face is a celebration of masculine beauty—the highest cheekbones, a perfectly straight nose, the loveliest aqua-gray eyes and dark blond lashes. A jaw sharp enough to *slice*. And the same chiseled sort of lips that make Cillian's mouth magnetic. Only *this* alpha twists his in malevolent delight.

When our position and his expression register, instinctive fear gives way to fury. I bare my teeth in a growl of my own, thrashing against his hold. A spark ignites in his dark eyes.

"Oh, baby." He chuckles. Somehow—*impossibly*—more handsome in all his wickedness. "You don't want to fight. That will just make me hard."

He presses his groin into my belly, showing how serious he is when I feel an iron ridge against my nearly bare skin.

Shit. Fuck.

I'm still in a *robe*.

A frantic whine escapes this time. If anything, it only kicks his maniacal smirk higher. "There's a good girl," he taunts. "Already halfway to tears. You'd cry real pretty for me while I choked you on my cock, huh?"

His gaze floats over my features, as if considering my worth. Concluding his assessment with a careless shrug. "Too bad I don't fuck Cillian's *whores*."

The words sink into my center. Rage roils to a bubbling boil.

And I will be *damned* if this *utter asshole* thinks he could put his dick *anywhere near* my mouth without *losing it*.

"*Pwt!*"

The venomous alpha rears back as a thick glob of spit splatters across his rich-boy nose. I use his shock to my advantage, ripping my wrists from his hands and jerking my bent knee upright. Into his crotch.

It connects with the hard knot and softer scrotum under his erection. He roars a growl, but I hold my ground, shoving him away. "Call me 'good girl' again," I dare him, "and you'll no longer *have* any balls for me to kick."

Satisfied, I spin for the door. Intending to run and hide in whatever corner of this creep-tastic castle I can find.

But Cillian is there.

Working his cool gaze down my body in a winding loop.

He suddenly flings it away from me, landing a steady glare on his packmate's face. "*Rhys*," he barks. "*Downstairs*."

Rhys, I repeat internally as he mutters to himself and storms out of the suite. It's much too good a name for such an asshole. Maybe I'll just call him "venom" instead.

Cillian watches the vicious alpha stalk off before pinning me with an equally intimidating stare.

"Dinner is served, wife," he adds. "*Come along*."

eight

DANE

DANE

WHAT IF SHE DOESN'T EAT MEAT? I MUSE, EYEING THE steaming platters Louis spread over the length of the dining table.

It would be unfortunate. Our chef and her assistant make incredible roast chicken. And the beef carpaccio is usually delicious, too.

Rhys grumbles as he stomps into the room and dramatically flings himself into a chair. With a grimace, he drops his head back and pinches the bridge of his nose. Whatever pain he's in doesn't stop him from muttering, "Fucking bitch."

I raise my brows, silently asking for an explanation. He spares me the barest of glances before full-on scowling. "She kicked me in the balls."

She...

A tangled sound tumbles up my throat. Too gruff to be a scoff and too smooth to be a growl.

I think it might be *laughter*.

"Seriously?" I snort. "She's, like, a hundred pounds."

His eyes narrow. "She spit in my face first."

This time, a true guffaw scrapes out of me. The rumble is hoarse and unfamiliar, which is sobering. *I never used to be like this.* Before the fire—the *attack*, Rhys calls it—I loved to laugh. It didn't happen *often*, but...

This is the first time in months that something has struck me as *funny* instead of darkly ironic. A notion that promptly evaporates when Briar comes shuffling into the room with her shoulders hunched up by her ears.

Wearing a robe.

Good God.

How long has it been since I saw so much of a beautiful woman's skin?

Too long, apparently. Because it only takes four steps—four slices of her pale flesh peeking from the silky edges of her kimono —for my cock to rouse.

Christ. First laughter and now a *hard-on*?

The woman is resurrecting pieces of me left and right.

Which is inconvenient, considering the hatred seething behind her expression when she flicks a look at Rhys and me.

Briar slinks into the chair Cillian pulls out at the end of the table, her lush pink mouth puckered in a disgruntled pout. Our pack alpha gently pushes her seat in, his mood shifting from cool disapproval to something foreign as he stares at the shiny raven hair on her crown.

When he straightens, his face flips to impassivity. He clips to the head of the table and nods at me. "Would you serve Briar her meal? Some of *everything*."

She flinches at his not-so-subtle emphasis, rocking in her seat. "I'm not hungry."

"You are," Cillian returns. "And you'll eat your meal here with us every night—or dinner will become breakfast, lunch, *and* dinner."

Briar's verdant gaze snaps, her fire hot enough to singe, even given the considerable length of our antique table. The piece seats sixteen, so the fact that I can *feel* the residual sting of her glare from five places away...

She's a fighter.

I never would have guessed that when I watched her swan out of the Rolls-Royce. A dancer, yes. A damn wet dream? That, too. But never a fearsome opponent.

I see it now, though. I've underestimated her.

And I don't think I've ever underestimated *anyone*.

That's worth at least a little bit of respect in my book.

So when the tiny omega turns toward me and mumbles, "Small portions. You might eat enough food for ten regular men, but I—" She squirms under the weight of three stares, ducking her head and mumbling the last part to her lap. "It's been a while since I had to clean my plate, okay?"

I resist the urge to question her about that. From where I'm sitting, it looks as though she's never cleaned her plate in her entire life. Or perhaps even *had* a plate to clear.

What the hell was that crazy scientist *doing* with her? Surely he knew he had to *feed* her? Or is this maybe something to do with her dancing? Trying to stay rail-thin for ballet, despite her career-ending injury?

Cillian briefed us on her history. She became a prima ballerina at the age of nineteen, only to lose her place when she fell during a performance last winter. Dancing was the last vestige of freedom the girl had, apparently, because as soon as she lost her spot, her father decided to make a proper match for her. According to the details I managed to dig up, Dr. Brynn was desperate for funding to continue his "research," and decided to sell his daughter's hand to the highest bidder.

Cillian's never been one to lose an auction.

Or anything, really.

Which is how we ended up in this godforsaken mess in the first place.

Here in the low candlelight, Briar looks like skin and bones. I usually like women who are fuller figured—and as pretty as she is, I can't stop noticing the prominent jut of her clavicles, the protruding hinges of her wrists as she slips her crimson napkin from a gold ring and drapes it over her lap.

Thank God for that. Her musky-tart cherry scent is subtle, but I don't trust myself if her perfume makes an appearance. Given the hard bulge pressing into my fly and the tension pulled taut across my shoulders, who the hell knows what I'm capable of at this point?

My Alpha's been spoiling for a fight all damn day. If he doesn't settle down soon, I might have to find some unfortunate fuckers to kill after dinner.

Gritting my teeth, I carefully spoon decent portions of each dish onto Briar's porcelain plate. When I set it in front of her she sighs and mutters again, "Gee, thanks, Cujo."

She's quick-witted. It takes my mind a moment to catch up, processing the reference, realizing she's basically calling me a rabid dog.

Because I'm wearing a muzzle.

She isn't *wrong*, though. I start to chuckle to myself before a cold wash spills over my guts.

Shit. The mask. I have to take it off to eat.

It's been a long time since the guys have seen me without it on. We typically take our meals separately—or not at all, when we're in the middle of a "project." It never occurred to me that a *wife* would mean proper dinners.

She isn't my wife, I remind myself. *Just Cillian's.*

His grandfather insists on "legitimate" heirs, but any member of our pack could have legally taken her as our bride for it to be official. Our alpha insisted *he* be the one to go through with it for reasons he didn't deign to share.

Although, given how Rhys is wincing and shifting in his chair, maybe Cillian made a good call.

God knows if *I* had shown up at the altar, we would have had a runaway bride instead of a scantily clad newlywed shooting daggers over a platter of roast chicken.

Briar picks up her fork and begins poking at her food while my packmates fill their plates. I sit still, staring at the rose-and-dahlia centerpiece, contemplating how to get away with not eating. Until a pointed *thunk* pulls me back to reality.

It's Cillian, setting my own dish in front of me. Filled to the brim.

The thunderous look on his face speaks for him—informing me that we're *all* going to eat so she will. Whether we like it or not.

A silent sigh stoops my shoulders. *Fucking hell.*

I was hoping to avoid this for as long as possible, but I suspect Cillian might be correct once again; it's probably better to rip the stitches and expose the wound. While she's already disgusted by us.

Given the way we're positioned—with her at the foot of the table and me in the middle portion to her right—she won't be able to see the worst of the damage. The left side of my profile looks fairly normal, especially in flickering light like this.

I'll have to make sure to keep all the lights off if we're alone together.

It's an insane thought because we *won't* be alone together. She only has to choose one of us to make an heir. And she has two much better–looking prospects here.

Not that Cillian would ever cede the honor to Rhys.

She is *his* wife, after all. They'll have to consummate their union at some point.

I focus on that fact and the odd sense of grieved relief it gives me. *No, I won't have this omega. But she also won't have to look at me any more than strictly necessary.*

I unlatch the leather straps of the titanium mask, letting the metal and mesh fall into my palm. It's a relatively subtle motion—and as silent as anything else I do. But I still feel Briar's attention fly to my recently exposed face. Searching for the damage she can't yet see.

I shovel food into my mouth, barely tasting it. *The sooner I finish, the faster I can cover myself up and get the hell away from this woman. She's probably scared half to—*

"What happened?" Briar asks, her voice steady. "To your face?"

I'm so stunned, I almost whip my head in her direction. Instead, I catch myself at the last second and freeze, sliding my gaze to Briar without moving.

Cillian clears his throat and begins to cut his meat. "We had a fire at one of our offices a couple of years ago," he explains brusquely.

It's a lie of omission. We didn't *have* a fire. We were *set* on fire. By someone who knew Rhys and I used that innocuous strip-mall office as a front for our real work.

Flames flash through my memory. They were just that, at the time—flashes of blinding heat. Too bright to look at, even through the choking black smoke that accompanied burning gasoline.

I smelled it first. Rhys was too *in the zone*, the way he tends to get when we're closing in on one of our targets. I recall him muttering incoherently as he stood over his maps and satellite images, backlit by the "storage" closet where I had an informant tied to a chair.

I was distracted, too, trying to get a specific name out of the fucker. Ironically, I got it, but couldn't remember it later. After.

That night marked one of a few select occasions when Cillian Blackwood got blood on his hands. He generally leaves that to me, but when he found out we'd been targeted while dealing with certain cartel members, he drove straight to their Manhattan safe house and annihilated everyone there.

That didn't surprise me. Cillian is a cold, calculating bastard, but I never doubt that we're his family. I've been his best friend for as long as either of us can remember—and, even for all their estrangement, he thinks of Rhys as his brother. He would never let our permanent injuries go unavenged.

I would trust either of my packmates with my life or just about anyone else's.

Except maybe this omega's, given the lethal way Rhys glares when she asks, "Why?"

It's an intelligent question. *Why*—not how. Meaning she correctly assumes foul play.

"None of your goddamn business, you nosy little viper," Rhys starts, his carved features creased with outrage. "You think we're going to make you a *real* member of this pack just because you come in here wagging your wedding ring and your golden pussy around—"

"*Enough*," Cillian interrupts. Cold fury fills his face. "Briar is my *wife*. She can ask any question she wishes."

And he can refuse to answer all of them.

Anyone who knows Cillian would hear the fine print implied in that statement. It appeases Rhys, who plucks up his wineglass and swallows three large mouthfuls as he seethes.

"Eat your chicken, Mrs. Blackwood," our pack leader goes on, rough and smooth at once. "We have important matters to discuss."

ninε

BRIAR

Okay, okay.

The food is good.

Loads better than whatever I managed to scrounge together for myself in recent memory. In fact, I can't seem to recall the last time I had anything *hot*...

I chew a bite of roast chicken, focusing on the temperature so I don't moan at the taste. God forbid any of these assholes think I *enjoy* a single facet of this this elaborate—unfortunately legal— abduction.

My *husband* said he had something for us to discuss anyway.

I'll think about how much I like the food—and how desperately close my Omega is to melting down—later.

I level Cillian with a gaze, trying to keep my squirm subtle as slick slips into my panties. "What the hell," I grumble flatly. "It's not like I have anywhere else to be. Fire away, *Mr. Blackwood*."

Dane flinches at the mention of fire and I almost feel bad. But then Rhys growls under his breath and vindication swoops through me.

Fuck these guys.

Just... not literally.

You hear me? I holler internally. *NOT LITERALLY.*

Got it, my Omega agrees, panting. *Got it.*

For fuck's sake. When my heat comes, I am *toast*.

Or whatever beasts eat.

I bet they eat pussy, my Omega offers. Which... is maybe the first time she's ever used that word. I'm not sure whether I should be proud or appalled.

I settle on the latter, needing all the starch I can muster while I stare the pack alpha down. Something seethes in those light irises every time I snag his focus. I wonder if he's used to omegas not being able to look him in the eye.

Well get used to it, asshole.

He slowly sets his utensils down, regarding me with cool intensity. "I presume your father explained our need for an omega."

I stab a piece of asparagus, purposefully dropping my gaze to hide the bolt of panic blocking my gullet. "An heir or something?"

"Yes," Cillian intones. "We need to produce an heir in order to take over the company. As alphas, an omega clearly represents the best odds of achieving this goal."

I roll my eyes while I chew, once again ignoring the burst of brown butter on my tongue. "And you need your evil spawn not to be a *bastard*. So one of you had to *marry* me first. Yeah, I've heard. I can read a contract, you know."

Cillian's weighted pause forces my attention back to his face.

"Yes," he replies, dry. "I am aware. And I know the contract only mentioned me, but you have my word that none of us will touch you unless you allow it."

It can't be true... but a stupid strand of hope winds around my lungs anyway. I narrow my glare, waiting for the catch.

Which comes immediately.

Cillian sips from his drink, his icy eyes twinkling. "However, you may want to reconsider your position on that. If you want your freedom back."

Utter silence rings through the room as everyone freezes. My mind catalogs that detail—*the others are as shocked as I am*. They didn't know he was going to say that.

But why would he keep something like this from them? Or are they pretending to be surprised?

"My freedom," I repeat. The manic urge to laugh tickles my throat, but I settle for a smirk. "*What* freedom? In case you haven't noticed, I don't have any here; and I wasn't exactly swimming in options before our little ceremony today, either."

Cillian arches one thick black brow. "Would you like options, Briar? Because we can give you anything you want. Money, your own home, revenge. You just have to give us what we want first."

Money.

My own home.

Revenge.

That last word sparkles through my center, sinking into secret places I didn't know I had. But why? And how the hell does this bastard know when I don't?

"And you want... what?" I guess dully. "For me to spread my legs every hour until you get an heir?"

That slashing brow kicks a bit higher. "There are many ways to produce a child. If you don't want to *spread your legs*," he says with a slight snarl, "we could always go down a more clinical route."

He waits for that thought to germinate, images of test tubes and syringes swirling. I recoil internally, scrambling back from the searing memories of my father's laboratory and the fear I felt every time I peeked inside.

Cillian's wolf-blue eyes see everything. They gleam as he absorbs my expression. "But I don't think my wife likes that idea."

My wife.

It's my turn to flinch as his words sink in. Too true, damn him.

He's underestimating how spiteful I can be if he thinks a few well-placed bribes and one threat will have me rolling over, though. I scoff.

"What makes you think I would *ever* give you what you want? You treated me like property today; so, in my mind, you're just as bad as my father."

It isn't true. No one could ever be as bad as my father because he's the reason I lost my sister. But Cillian doesn't know that.

I glower, concluding with, "You gonna take revenge on yourself, too?"

Rhys opens his sneering mouth, but Cillian holds a hand up toward him, still gazing at me while he replies, "I suspect your revenge against our pack will come in the form of financial damages."

Money.

These assholes are American Royalty. They have *a lot* of money. Enough for me to move far away. Buy myself a house, a security team, a full roster of alphas for my heats. A private investigator to find out what happened to Violet.

I bite my lip, glowering at him while I consider.

Dane's raspy voice interrupts, once again stunning the room into stillness. He won't turn his face toward me, but fervor snaps through the one golden eye I can see.

"No one here will touch you without your permission, Briar," the giant alpha vows, glaring at the tabletop.

Huh. So the big guy has a soft spot for chivalry. That may work in my favor.

I don't have the heart to tell him his packmate already

manhandled me off the bed earlier. Though I'm tempted when Rhys snorts, "Yeah, sure. Tell us *no* all you want for now. But when your heat comes? You'll be running around here naked, *begging* us to fuck you."

I've been sedated for all my heats, courtesy of Dr. Brynn and his fanatical obsession with keeping me "intact" for whatever pack he conned into buying me. So I don't know for sure if Rhys is correct... but the unfortunate state of my panties seems to underscore his point.

Shit.

Cillian and Dane seem equally troubled by that notion. While Rhys gloats with an arrogant, gorgeous smirk, his packmate frowns mightily. And their alpha wears a softer, more ponderous scowl.

"She still doesn't have to do anything," Dane argues, staring daggers across the antique table.

Cillian interrupts them. "No, of course not," he puts mildly. "But on the likely chance that Briar does want alphas for her heat, she may prefer to have *experience* with each of us beforehand. To make her more comfortable."

"*She* is right *here*," I snipe.

Cillian nods, infuriatingly calm. "The answer seems obvious to me," he says, blinking blandly. "We all do what we can to produce our heir as quickly as possible. That way you're free of us sooner rather than later. Your heat gives us the best odds, biologically, but a lot can be done in two months."

God. *Of course* this man knows exactly when my heat is due.

I bet he has a chart somewhere. Though, of these three, Rhys actually strikes me as Most Likely to Graph Sexual Potential for some reason.

But I know something none of these assholes do.

With careful casualness, I toss my hair back and tilt my head. Going for a blasé kind of curiosity. "And what happens if I do all this and still don't produce your precious heir? I'm just stuck here for eternity? Sounds like a bad deal on my part."

Cillian's eyes trace every line of my face. And, for a moment, I could swear his mouth *almost* twitches.

"An excellent point, Mrs. Blackwood. If we're unsuccessful by the end of your heat, our pack will furnish a separate residence for you. Hired cars, security, a generous allowance. You'll be free, for all intents and purposes. We'll only expect you to return for high-level social events and your heats. Otherwise, you can do whatever you wish." A warning note bleeds into his voice. "Within reason."

Ooh, he's possessive, my Omega swoons. *Or maybe just protective. Either way—*

I toss her an exasperated look. *Seriously?!*

I'm just <u>saying</u>, she cries. *Those are good traits during a heat!*

I've never really had one before, so I'll have to take her word for it. Besides, at this point, what is my alternative? Rhys has a point, damn him—I can't go into heat alone. And I *really* don't want my first time to happen when I can't understand what's going on.

But—*God*—what would agreeing mean? Would they share me? At *the same time*? Or turn this into some sort of twisted Sex Chore Wheel so they can take turns coming to my bed every night?

And no, that concept is *not* making these stupid, useless panties *wetter...*

Let alone the clenching flesh under them.

Shit, shit, *shit*.

"I need time," I decide, spinning my panic into forcefulness I do not feel. "To decide."

Cillian picks up his wineglass, slowly sipping. Regarding me with the cool command of a king. Or a god. "Two days."

"Two *weeks*."

"*One* day," he tosses back, eyes shifting again.

I bare my teeth in a snarl, gritting, "One *week*."

That time, his half-smile truly does break free. "Deal."

ten

RHYS

WHAT—AND I CANNOT STRESS THIS ENOUGH—*THE fuck?*

Louis keeps his eyes averted as he carries away the last of our evening meal. Cillian was correct; our bitchy little viper did, in fact, clear her plate.

It took her a while to eat the tiny scoops Dane served her, so by the time she stands and sashays out of the dining room, I've had nearly half an hour to stew.

I pick up my knife, weighing it in my palm for a moment, then flick my wrist. It goes flying for Cillian, who lifts his hand and snatches the hilt mid-air.

55

Across the table, Dane once again has his mask on. He huffs, silently scolding me for my technique. If *he'd* thrown a dagger, no one would have seen the blade until it was sticking out of his target.

Show off.

I slump into my chair, fighting the painful pulse behind my brow. It got marginally better while I ate, but now it rears up as quickly as it died down. I don't let the throb stop me from glaring at our pack leader, though.

"You gonna tell us what the *ever-loving fuck* is wrong with you?" I ask. "Or do you want us to start guessing?"

Cillian swirls the dregs of his wine. His tell.

He doesn't *really* have one, but I've noted that holding his glass and rolling it between his fingers is usually a sign that his mind is busier than usual.

Dane notices, too. "Something else is clearly going on here," he grunts. "We could have had our pick of a thousand omegas."

That much is true. Two years ago, before we agreed not to take one on, Cillian spent at least an hour each week actively arranging courtship opportunities with wealthy, titled heiresses. Hell, he even managed to make inroads with a shah trying to marry off his only daughter.

So why Briar?

And why now?

Dane goes on, asking for me. "This woman clearly hates us. Why choose someone who will fight this every step of the way?"

I know the reason *I* would have chosen her. But our pack leader doesn't share my fucked-up proclivity toward fighting with women before we fuck.

No, Cillian has always *wanted* a wife. He didn't have any desire to go down the same, scent-matched road to ruin his father trod; but a pretty, boring little omega who would get on her knees every night and follow the commands he issues in that kinky bedroom of his? Someone to submit and swoon behind closed doors; and hold her head high for all of polite society in public? A *proper lady*?

Yeah, he was into that.

Not a vicious little brat with daddy issues.

That's *way* more my type.

If I had one. Which *I do not*.

But fuck me, she looked hot with angry tears in her eyes.

Cillian spins the knife I threw before flinging it right back at me. So quick, I barely dodge left. The blade sinks into the upholstered chair back beside my right bicep.

I gape, draw a breath to shout obscenities at him, and deflate when my pack leader casts me a chilling stare. His voice matches the blue flames there.

"*Never* put your hands on my wife without permission again."

Indignant ire floods my middle. "*Your* permission or hers?" I scoff.

Cillian's growl is low enough to raise the fine hairs on my nape. "*Both*."

It's been years since I heard Dane bark, but he musters a strong pulse of alpha power, a command cracking from behind his mask. "*Stop*."

We both look at him, absorbing the slightly manic set of his golden eyes. He shifts under the attention, always uncomfortable to be stared at. Casting his gaze to his lap, he scrubs his fingers through his overlong hair, muttering to Cillian.

"We're already at each other's throats and it's only been three hours. Rhys and I deserve an explanation. Why *her*? We could have bought her father's patent for a fair price and still made record profits off of it. *Why* did you *marry* his daughter? *Why* would you saddle all of us with an omega who fucking *hates us*?"

It's unlike Dane to have an outburst that doesn't involve putting a bullet in some evil bastard's brain. I can tell his tirade has gotten our pack alpha's attention. Cillian regards him for a long beat.

"You make the mistake of thinking I had a choice," he says cryptically, standing. "None of us ever really did."

ELEVEN

BRIAR

I'LL GIVE CILLIAN BLACKWOOD THIS: HE NAILED THE whole "evil resides here" aesthetic.

Really. Black marble floors, carved, shadowy archways.

Top notch.

He's just lucky I happen to like Gothic vibes.

We won't tell him, I grumbled to myself this morning when the wardrobe I stubbornly avoided last night finally won. After I discovered that the two suitcases I packed hadn't made it to the manor and were "mysteriously" missing.

I figured I'd better get over my aversion to letting my *husband* provide my clothing. You know, unless I want to attend *all* of our meals naked.

This dress is far too beautiful to spend its life hanging in an armoire anyway. The close-cut silk is ruched around my torso in delicate ripples, its folds and stitches so fine I wonder how on earth it could possibly fit me. This—along with all the other lace-and-silk confections filling my new wardrobe—feels like the sort of thing a seamstress would spend hours tailoring.

Its short train whispers against the stone floor chilling the soles of my feet. The gorgeous dress was one thing, but *shoes* seemed like a supremely stupid choice. After all, this is a stealth mission.

A failed one.

But still.

I tried to open Cillian's office door first. It was locked and didn't even have a keyhole to tamper with. The rest of the second floor is infuriatingly... open.

Every. Single. Room.

Almost as if Cillian is taunting me. I can practically hear the bastard. *Come in and look around, wife. What's mine is yours.*

After creeping around for a half hour, I more or less have the lay of the land. The house is built in the shape of a semi-circle, with the Omega Suite as an end-cap to the right side of the curved hallway.

By the time I've scouted the rest of the floor, I'm curious to see which room sits parallel to mine. If the house makes any sense, it will be Cillian's—though that wouldn't explain what takes up the space *between* our rooms.

Could it be the nest?

Is *that* what's behind the one and only locked door in my suite? And if he wants to breed me so bad, why the hell did he lock me out of the one place that's most likely to tap into my omega instincts?

Goddamn riddle of a man.

I lift my hand to clasp his heavy antique doorknob. It turns easily, which somehow still catches me off guard.

He even left his *bedroom* unlocked? Jesus, if he's already willing to be *this* transparent with me, what the hell does the guy have hidden in his office?

A small giggle interrupts before I can push the thick wooden slab open. I startle, jumping as I find the maid smirking at me from what appears to be a threshold to a back staircase, tucking into the dark corner next to Cillian's double doors.

Fiona raises her elegant brunette brows, speaking with an amused accent. "I would not do that if I were you. Mr. Blackwood is normally still asleep at this hour—and he does not wear pajamas."

I drop the handle like it seared my palm. Fiona chuckles again. "Yes, it's quite a show. Also, his bedroom is... different. I'm sure you'll see eventually."

Blazing hell. What does *that* mean?

Taking a cautionary step away, I cast the closed portal a dirty look that earns me even more bemusement. Fiona points above us, to the third floor. "The others will likely still be asleep in their rooms, too. They all stayed up very late. Arguing."

Arguing?

Over what?

Me?

Could it be that, perhaps, the pack alpha doesn't have *absolute* control over the others?

I file that piece of information away, keen to examine it later, and clear my throat, gesturing at the narrow back staircase. "I'll just... go downstairs, then."

Fiona nods, stepping aside. "Very good, Madame. I will send Louis with your breakfast tray. He meant to bring it up earlier, but had a slight meltdown when he realized he didn't know if you preferred tea or coffee. And then couldn't decide between scones and bagels..."

She shakes her head fondly, exasperation twisting her lips. The way only a sister would.

A phantom knife slides between my ribs, sending a silent gasp of pain to my heart. I swallow hard, my voice coming harsher than I intend. "Tea. And toast."

Fiona blinks, then drops her head in a practiced curtsy. "Right away, Madame. I'll have Louis find you as soon as it's ready."

She hurries down the hall, and I watch her go, slumping dejectedly into the nearest wall. *Shit.* I don't want to be "Madame." And I definitely don't want the only other female omega in the whole house to think I'm a raging bitch.

I should try to... make her like me?

Christ on a cracker. I have literally no idea how to do that.

My whole life has been two things: my father's oppression and ballet. Years of being made to stay inside our decaying house, forbidden to so much as look out the curtains without his permission. So many nights spent in his basement laboratory, enduring his experimental procedures, all designed to make me a "healthier" omega.

Because not being one was never an option, according to him. As if he had gotten some golden guarantee from God himself.

I never figured out why, mostly because asking questions about how Violet and I came to be and why we were so different only earned me punishment. "Time to think," he called it.

Even now, my mind automatically recalls the sound that accompanied that measured reprimand—a rusty key scraping a rustier lock. The punch of a deadbolt. Violet's whispered voice under the crack in the unlit closet.

Knock twice if you're okay, Rosie.

I was never okay.

I always knocked twice.

Of all the horrible things I felt after they took her, I remember silence the most. Sitting in that damned closet, knowing that no whispers would come. Lying in bed, staring at the ceiling, listening to the wordless quiet of an empty room. My own chewing echoing in the dingy breakfast nook. Because Violet wasn't there to hum anymore.

Between the two of us, she was actually the musical one. Supremely talented with our ancient piano, always warbling soft nonsense lyrics under her breath. Until she sat down to play... and then, magically, they weren't nonsense at all.

That's how I started dancing—as a joke. A way to good-naturedly poke fun at her hobby. She played, and I threw my body into exaggerated leaps and twirls, doing anything I could to make her laugh.

We didn't know our father was paying attention... or that he would try to hone those rare light moments into "ladylike skills." All the better to attract "proper" packs when he was ready to collect on his investment.

Namely, us. Our lives.

He didn't expect Violet's body to betray his carefully crafted plan and designate as a *beta*.

He didn't waste much time, then, either. In fact, I think that horrible stormy night came just a couple of weeks after the initial bloodwork. In less than a month, he traded in on Violet's "meager" value and shifted all his hopes to me.

For the first time in my life, I wasn't just *allowed* to leave our house. I was *forced*. Pushed into auditioning for the prominent city ballet, made to practice until my toes bled and my body felt like it might crumble to dust.

But I liked the pain. I *loved* the music. And every time I launched myself into arcs and spins, I could pretend, for half a second, that I might never land. That I could float away. *On.*

Freedom, maybe, is the word.

Or *was* the word.

Sniffing, I shake off the memories and move toward the back stairway. Curiosity is as good a cure for dread as anything else. Definitely better than the desire to drown myself in a bathtub with my curling iron.

My Omega glowers, and I smirk at her. *Too dark?*

She harrumphs, not deigning to give my morbid humor any attention. She's practical that way, just like Violet is.

Was.

Jesus. *Is it too early for a cocktail? Surely Snobby McSnobberson has some decent booze around here some—*

Oh. Holy. Shit.

The back stairs drop me into another impossible hallway. But instead of more random rooms, an enormous set of double doors hangs open right in front of me. Revealing an absolutely breathtaking *library.*

twelve

BRIAR

THE CAVERNOUS ROOM COULD BE A CATHEDRAL.

Three stories high, with endless curved *walls* of books. Thousands. Or *tens* of thousands.

Like my suite, it's another rare room of pure white, apart from the ceiling and the circular atrium at its core. Overhead, the snowy stone is carved into large, overlapping scales, their edges gilded with flaked gold paint. The dome over the center of the cross-shaped space has a matching golden frame, filled with stained glass.

Smoked gray, ruby red, the darkest pinks and lightest greens.

Rose patterns, cosmic swirls of stars. Crescent moons and thorny vines.

I slowly step below it, turning in a circle as I admire the slant of morning sunlight through kaleidoscopic color.

Wow.

It's incredible. Beautiful enough to rival the world-renowned basilicas and castles I've studied in books.

Violet used to make fun of me for that. She claimed I was the only person in the world who could spend twelve straight hours bent over a book and not even notice time passing.

She wasn't *wrong*. Before I started dancing, escaping into fictional worlds or travel guides was my one way out of my father's prison; the only time I felt the wild joy of being *free*.

I could live a thousand lives if I wanted to. Sure, they would exist in my mind, as ink on paper. But it was better than that dark closet.

And later, when I was all alone? The characters in my books kept me company at night. Especially once I got old enough to use an eReader I found abandoned in the ballet's Lost & Found and started downloading whatever free romance books were featured on it...

I wonder if there are any of those in here. There must be. It's statistically impossible for there to be so many books in one place and not have a single one with—

"Fuck."

A low, vicious curse echoes from the farthest part of the library. My gaze leaps from the atrium above to the back wall, where a matching window spans all three floors.

I see him a second later, on the second-story's curved landing, beside the great window. A flash of white-blond that blocks the rosy light.

My body freezes as Rhys groans, abandoning his prostrate position on the dark-purple chaise lounge. He's still in his clothes from last night, the dress shirt rumpled and halfway unbuttoned when he sits up.

The venomous alpha doesn't see me, thankfully, as he squeezes his eyes shut against the sunlight and bends over his knees, burying his face in his hands.

Pain, I realize. *He's in some sort of terrible pain.*

Without lifting his head, he reaches behind himself and fumbles with something against the wall. I hear a bell trill in the outside hallway.

"LOUIS!"

His enraged shout has me diving for cover. I scurry around the corner, flattening myself into the shadows at the north side of the room. Thankful, once again, that I decided not to wear any shoes.

The omega attendant comes panting into the room, a silver tray rattling in his hands as he quivers. "Coming, sir!"

Shock stabs my chest when Louis casts me a quick glance, half apologetic and full of warning. I heed the caution there, shrinking until I'm hidden against a shelf of encyclopedias.

Louis clambers up the stairs tucked into the southern alcove and appears at Rhys's side within seconds. "Tea and toast?" the alpha grunts, not bothering to move.

When Louis nods, he lets out a low growl, clutching his head. "Fuck me. Fine. Just set it there and leave me."

Louis lays the tray at the end of the chaise, hesitating. "Sir, would you like me to call—"

Rhys roars, "I said *leave me. Now.*"

Louis immediately scrambles back, but Rhys gives another pained groan, snapping his hand out in a universal gesture for "halt."

"Never mind," he snarls, shoving to his feet. "I'm going upstairs. No interruptions. Especially from *her.*"

"I understand, sir," Louis replies, dipping into a bow while Rhys stalks past. There must be an exit I missed up there, because he doesn't come down or catch a glimpse of me before I hear a heavy door slam.

After a long pause, Louis releases an audible breath. "Coast is clear, now, Madame!" he calls, collecting the silver tray. "I have your tea!"

I clutch a hand to my chest, still trying to recall how to inhale as I drift back to the center of the enormous space. Louis descends the stairs, rolling his eyes with a friendly smile. "*Mon Dieu*, that man. He's lucky he's so fun to look at, no?"

At the moment, I can barely recall what the vicious alpha's face looks like. I meet Louis at a small reading table positioned close to the southern stairs, leveling him with a deadpan look.

"No," I repeat flatly.

He chuckles, setting down the breakfast tray with a flourish. "This was always meant for you, but I'm afraid the whims of our Mr. Rhys tend to come before all others. Or else."

Frowning, I reach for a piece of toast and savagely rip a bite out of it. My eyes flick to exit Rhys just disappeared out of. "What does he *do*, anyway? Is he actually as smart as he thinks he is or just pretty?"

I may have blown it with Fiona, but her brother seems as keen to share his gossip as I am to hear it. His warm eyes sparkle as he sits on the other side of the chaise, keeping his gaze on me while he pours my tea.

"Oh, he's smart, alright. Smart and mean and absolutely *lethal*." The valet extends a steaming cup of tea, his smile conspiratorial. "I know it probably seems like Dane is the one to watch, with that terrifying mask and all the scars... and I'm fairly sure he does handle most of the dirty work... But Rhys is another kind of danger altogether."

Dirty work. A shiver streaks down my spine. A strange coil of heat settles low between my hips. "And Cillian?"

Louis's grin widens. "Is the master of every single person in this house."

Including you.

He doesn't say the words, but he doesn't really need to. I'm here, after all. Under Cillian's command. Because he manipulated and moneyed-over everyone in both our lives to get me into his greedy clutches. To get his *heir*.

A child to inherit the company that made Dane into a mask-wearing probably-murderer and Rhys into some sort of evil mastermind. A *weapons* company, Father said. And conspicuously did not add any details.

I do my best to act innocent while I sip my tea. "All of them work for Blackwood Corp?"

Louis takes the bait, leaning forward eagerly. "Officially?"

I force a swallow, my brows arching. "Um... yeah?"

He glances toward the doors and drops his voice to a whisper. "*None* of them do, except Mr. Cillian."

I feel my brows leap. Louis nods, his eyes just a bit too bright to match the solemn line of his lips. "He's technically a vice president, along with his cousin, Gideon. They both manage the company's biggest contracts, but the rumor is..."

He trails off, nervously looking around once more before his voice drops even lower. "The rumor is: Gideon and his pack handle the corporation's big government and private sector clients... and Mr. Cillian handles their *other* clients. The ones no Fortune 500 company would want on their books."

I'm embarrassed to admit that it takes me a full minute to understand what he means. Because aside from militaries and private security personnel, who else *needs* weapons?

Other than *criminals*?

My eyes widen. "So when you say Dane does *dirty work*, what is he *doing*?"

Louis purses his lips to the side. "We do not know. Only that he's a mountain of a man who moves more silently than wind. And he used to be Special Forces, back when Mr. Cillian went off to college."

"Ivy League?" I guess, "Business degree?"

Louis smirks as he nods. "Yes. Both Blackwoods went to Yale. Though, Mr. Rhys has a law degree."

Great. The bastard really *is* as smart as he thinks he is.

And soooooo hot, my Omega adds. *His face is insane. We should sit on it.*

I nearly jerk in shock. My Omega has *never* talked like this before. Of the two of us, I'm usually the one lusting after alphas and their knots while she squirms with awkward shyness.

It's like Invasion of the Pussy Snatchers in here! I practically scream. *WHO ARE YOU?!*

She settles down, embarrassed, and mutters, *I'm just saying...*

"He's the one I'll need to be careful with, then," I say out loud, casting my gaze into my tea.

Louis pauses just a beat too long. A quiet sigh escapes before he reaches over and cups my free hand.

I blink at him, thrown by the solemnity covering his face. "You need to be careful with *all* of them. But *especially* Mr. Cillian." Utter sincerity fills his handsome scowl. "If you think you know him, I promise you do not. And if you think you can outsmart him, then you are nowhere near smart enough."

His words are harsh, but his voice is soft. He's truly worried about me and trying to be helpful.

But he underestimates me.

They all do. And I have to use that to my advantage.

Being beautiful helps. Not because it will win these men to my side—because it *distracts* them.

A shiny flash of gold. The rainbow glitter of diamond. So pretty, they don't notice the gold is a hilt and the diamond is a *blade*.

I'm not a sparkling bauble. I'm a *knife*.

And if they're too stupid to see past all the glitter?

Their funeral.

I need my freedom and the means to find out what happened to my sister. But they want *an heir* in return...

That can't happen for too many reasons to count. I have a birth control implant no one else knows about, for one. And I refuse to go from being a virgin to being pregnant in the space of a couple *months.*

Even if I *wanted* to have a baby, I certainly wouldn't make one with these monsters. God knows how many people they've hurt. How many lives have been lost because they sold weapons to evil people?

Not to mention whatever fresh Hell they just purchased from my father.

No. I can't *actually* give them what they want. But I could *pretend*.

It would be dangerous to try to fool them, I know. Louis is right—they are as sharp as they are ruthless. *Deadly.*

But this was my sister's last wish. And I will do whatever it takes to make good on my promise.

Which really just leaves two questions.

"If I make a deal with Cillian," I ask Louis, "will he keep his word? Is he honest?"

Louis gives my hand a final squeeze before he stands. "He will keep to his word," the man says, shooting me what can only be described as a warning look. "But he doesn't have an honest bone in his body."

thirteen

BRIAR

"ROSIE? CAN YOU HEAR ME?"

The phone feels hot in my hand. Its glass screen stings my ice-cold ear and nips at my chilled fingers, but I clutch it harder, glancing around the gray alleyway.

My heart slams into my ribs, thumping unevenly as the hairs on my neck prickle. I whip my head around, making sure no one followed me out of the ballet theater. The staff must be suspicious. No one should have any way to contact me here—this is only my audition.

Father insisted on bringing me. According to him, it didn't matter that I was sixteen and virtually untrained. It's time I *made myself useful; and getting into the prestigious ballet academy will afford him opportunities to rub elbows with wealthy investors.*

I was shocked when he told me to get ready to leave our house. It had been months since my last outing—and this one came with a steady stream of threats.

Before he dropped me off, Father made it very clear what would happen if I tried to speak to anyone at the theater about my circumstances. He told me he would lock me up, send me away like he did with Violet, or make sure whoever had her would punish her in my stead...

If she were still alive.

I believed him. Any doubts I had about how deranged the man who made us may be went out the window when he disappeared my sister. Without a trace. In the dead of night.

"Parents" aren't permitted to attend auditions, so I've settled for keeping my mouth shut and haven't so much as made a peep outside of polite small talk with the director. When an assistant came scurrying in holding a phone and announced that I had a call... every conditioned alarm bell went off, begging me not to take it.

Who on earth would be calling me—and why? What if someone mentions it to my father when he picks me up?

So what if they do, a despondent voice in my mind asks. The one that's been appearing more and more.

After two weeks alone, with no word on what became of the one person I love, I've started wondering how much I truly care about Father's threats.

Am I honestly going to come here every day and not tell someone how heinous he is? Or try to run? So what if he hurts me or locks me up or ships me off? Do I really care what happens to me anymore? Does anyone?

"Rosie," the voice hisses again. "I don't know how much time I have."

My lips move, but I can't make words. All the questions I want to ask—is it really you, where are you, are you going to live—*trip over each other.*

In the end, I only manage to croak, *"Violet?"*

"It's me," she whispers, and the words are so soft and reassuring, I know it must be her. No one else has ever spoken to me like that.

I start stammering half questions. *"Oh my God—where—who —what happened, Vi?!"*

My sister's voice quiets and sharpens all at once. *"Listen to me, Rosie—you have to* listen, *okay? I don't have time to explain. But just—trust me. You trust me, right?"*

I think of all the other ballerinas—their vicious glares and pinched sneers. How they seem torn between hating me and looking for holes to use for sabotage. The director, with his predatory smile. And my father. His laboratory. His "health shakes" and padlocks and cool detachment.

Violet is literally the only person I've ever trusted.

"Yes," I rush to reply. *"Of course, Vi, but where—"*

"I can't talk," she snaps, more fervent than I've ever heard her. *"But* listen, *Rosie."*

It's almost impossible, but I seal my lips together. Violet rushes on. *"You have to do everything he says, Rosie,"* she begs, her voice low and urgent. *"Every. Thing. Don't question him. Don't try to make plans. Don't go near his lab or look into his research. Just... do what- ever he wants you to do."*

My mouth falls open in shock. Of the two of us, Violet was always the one hell-bent on figuring out what our father was up to so we could stop him. Or at least get away.

"B-but, Violet, I can get out *now. He left me here alone and—"*

"No," she interrupts. *"It does not matter how safe you think you are or how well you plan—promise me you won't disobey him. Promise me you won't try to run or hurt yourself."*

Her words end on a quiet sob. When she continues, she sounds even more intense. *"Promise me, Rosie. Please."*

Cold air rips through the alley. But it feels warm compared to the dread crystallizing in my lungs. "I—Violet, what did he do to you? Where are you?"

I hear a whimper. My sister repeats her command, speaking faster. "Promise, Rosie. Anything he says, you do it. Please."

My gut wrenches, nauseous tingles enveloping my middle. The deepest, most visceral form of fear wraps its talons around my heart. "I—Okay. I promise."

I hear the relief in her voice, even as she rushes to hang up. "Good. I love you, Rosie. Whatever else happens, just remember that, okay?"

I feel her slipping away. Panic rears up in my chest and I blurt, "Violet, wait! Where are you? What are they going to do to you?"

The line goes dead for so long, I think she must have hung up. But then I hear her whisper, the last words she'll ever say to me.

"Nothing good."

A FROZEN STAB OF FEAR IMPALES MY MIDDLE. STATIC rings in my ears and I bolt upright, wailing. The horrified sound echoes off the too-large, too-empty suite and barrels back into me. I scramble into the oversized bed's headboard, clutching my head in both hands.

Oh God, oh God, oh *God*.

My breathing stutters as I sob. Wishing I could pacify myself with lame platitudes like "it was just a dream."

It wasn't a dream, though.

It was a memory that likes to haunt my sleep.

Really, it shouldn't bother. That one phone call already stalks my every waking hour, dragging all sorts of unanswered questions around with it.

Why did she want me to obey the evil man who created us?

What did she think would happen if I didn't? And how could it be any worse than surrendering?

I pant into my palms, trying to remember how to breathe. But a new wave of terror crashes over my head when I suddenly *feel* someone watching me. My head snaps up, vision blurring behind my tears.

The room is empty.

Everything looks the same, down to the French doors on the right side. The wall of not-quite-budding roses shivers against a gust of wind. Casting sinister, thorn-filled shadows over the empty stone floor.

fourteen

DANE

THE BLACKWOOD GROUP CHAT

RHYS

Alright assholes

Who's been in my library?

DANE

I'll give you one guess.

RHYS

That bitch.

I'm missing FOUR novels and there are FINGERPRINTS on my shelves

CILLIAN

Jesus Christ.

DANE

You have way too much time on your hands.

RHYS

Not as much as you, apparently.

Are you still lurking outside Briar's door like a damn dog?

DANE

Fuck you.

CILLIAN

Not so fast, Rhys.

How do you know Dane is there? Unless you* wandered down near her room?

RHYS

Fuck you.

CILLIAN

Good talk, gentlemen.

"SHE TAKES HER TEA THERE EVERY MORNING."

My back snaps straight. *Shit*.

Our valet raises one glossy eyebrow, smirking at me as he balances a silver tray on his arm. I've got to hand it to Louis—it's fairly difficult to sneak up on me. Then again, I might be in a bit of a trance.

Oblivious to my observation, Briar tilts her head at the book in her lap. Her toes point elegantly when she crosses her ankles, resting them on the railing of the Omega Suite's balcony. Leaves from the tangle of rosebushes brush the soles of her feet and she flexes them absently, turning a page before flipping her hair to her other shoulder.

I watch, oddly fascinated. Why would she choose to sit on a balcony that doesn't have a view? Does she like the rosebushes after all? Or is it simply as close as she can get to the gardens below?

Guilt squirms in my gut. I know Cillian forbade her from stepping foot outside because she's a flight risk. I hate the notion of keeping her prisoner, but we're not exactly anonymous figures. If she tried to bolt and the wrong people got hold of her...

More fuckers for me to kill.

Still, Cillian posting extra security at *every* exit to keep her locked in here feels wrong. There are also cameras. Like the one currently trained on Louis and me while we peer through the crack in her bedroom doors.

Briar sighs, her shoulders rounding when she reaches the end of the book in her hands and makes a face at it. I try not to notice how damn cute she looks with her nose scrunched. Not to mention the flawless flash of her thigh when she sits up and tosses the tome onto the small table beside her.

Hell. She moves like ink on water, all striking elegance and sensuous fluidity. I can't make myself look away. Which is becoming a real goddamn problem, given the way I spent last night.

And the night before.

And every night since she got here last weekend.

My teeth grind, a fresh tide of shame rising. I really didn't mean to start allowing myself into her room each night. And I definitely didn't intend to let watching her sleep become a habit.

The first time, I only went in because I had to. My Alpha was climbing the walls inside me, pushing pure *urgency* into my bloodstream. I finally got up and went down to her room, certain I'd find the little omega held at gunpoint or something.

But no.

She was *asleep.*

And she was...

Enchanting.

I admit the word to myself, watching the way she sits forward, finding a small bald patch between vines so she can gaze out at the garden. Or perhaps the cliffs beyond.

That thought puts a growl under my next exhale. Louis gives me a pointed look as he bustles past. "Careful, sir," he teases. "Your humanity is showing."

This cocky omega is one to talk, considering how patently obvious his feelings for our alpha butler are. I don't think anyone else has noticed, but stealth and observation are second-nature to me. I've seen the way Louis turns red every time the two men interact.

When I cross my arms over my chest and glower at our valet, he chuckles nervously. "Apologies, Mr. Dane. I'll make sure Madame doesn't know you're out here, um, checking on her?"

He's right to stick a question mark at the end of that statement. I have one in my own mind. *Am* I checking on her? Or is this something else? A compulsion? Blatant attraction?

All I know is, despite her scent being a pleasant tease instead of an overwhelming addiction, the voice in my middle wants me near her. And he was in a blind *rage* after whatever nightmare she had last night.

It was obviously agonizing. I had to force myself to leave to avoid intervening and giving my position away. Even then, distance from the omega didn't help calm me down—I wound up in our gym, beating the shit out of a punching bag until well after dawn.

But it doesn't matter how much my stupid cock or my stupider Alpha lust after this woman. She's made it clear none of us are welcome to touch her—and she's taking her sweet time deciding how she feels about Cillian's proposed "deal."

That's probably for the best. How would any of us sleep with her on a regular basis without developing unhealthy attachments?

Says the guy sneaking into her room while she sleeps and stalking her while she drinks her tea.

Louis reads my mind somehow. His wry expression implies such a thing might be good for me. But I know better. Having any sort of emotional investment in Briar would only end in ruin for any of us—most of all me.

Because I'm fairly sure, if I ever got my hands on her, I'd never let go. Or kill myself trying to keep my distance.

God knows this house is haunted enough. We don't need another ghost.

fifteen

CILLIAN

Dane once told me that the only effective way to deal with torture is to find some greater lesson in it.

The first week of having Briar under my roof is a special kind of hell, but at least I've used the time to learn a few things.

For one, my wife enjoys the library. She drinks tea, not coffee. Prefers red wine over champagne. And always, without fail, chooses a black dress.

They look like sin and salvation on her. Underscoring her luminous skin, complementing her shining dark hair. The fabric is stark and crisp against her pale flesh; as sharp as the lines she draws onto her emerald eyes and their thick kohl lashes.

I watch them flutter as her eyes slip closed on a swallowed moan. Stabbing the desire to shift in my seat, I ignore my hardening cock and stare as she scoops a second bite of mushroom risotto past her plump little lips.

This time, she can't quite conceal her hum of approval.

Given that this is our fifth official dinner as a pack, I should probably be used to watching her eat by now. But there's something about witnessing her satisfaction and knowing I've provided it that turns me on to no end.

I've been observing her carefully, reviewing every scrap of footage captured on our home's security system. Familiarizing myself with the way she twirls her hair as she drinks her tea, always poring over a book and chewing her bottom lip absently between sips. How her feet have forgotten how to walk without a subtle point. The minute expressions on her face—typically veiled by a put-on air of apathy she barely maintains.

Until someone angers her.

Namely, me.

When she glances up and finds me watching, all indifference falls off her features. Poison darkens her green irises. "*What?*"

Fuck.

I hold myself still, pinning my natural reaction down. With a practiced shrug, I gesture at the two empty seats between us. "You could at least wait for the others."

Briar scoffs. "And have *three* of you eyeing me while I'm force-fed? No thank you. I think I'll take advantage of the fact that your asshole packmates clearly don't know how to tell time."

Goddamn it.

This is a losing battle.

I've been coming to terms with that thought for forty-eight hours. Trying to figure out how to accelerate my timeline, alter the plan...

Before she destroys me.

I won't last much longer if she keeps talking to me like this.

And neither will the guys.

They both appear on the threshold of the dining room, having clearly heard her latest insult. Dane ducks his head and shuffles to his seat, while Rhys opens his mouth to launch an answering attack.

My sharp growl cuts him off. I nod at his seat. Pure rage fires his light eyes, but he slides to his place and plops himself down, immediately draining his wineglass and snapping his fingers for more.

Briar watches with ill-disguised disgust. Louis lurches into action, hustling to refill the crystal goblet. I notice that my bride purposefully waits for my packmate to take a large mouthful before unceremoniously announcing, "I've made a decision about our deal."

Rhys instantly chokes on his wine, sputtering all over his white dress shirt and his steaming bowl of risotto. Briar's eyes sparkle. "Oh," she adds, blinking in faux innocence, "Sorry. I didn't mean to startle you."

Good God.

Is she trying to kill me?

I swirl my wineglass so I don't drag her over my lap and press my erection into her belly. *Her ass would look good propped over my knee, especially given the cut of that dress.*

This one is strapless, with a tight bodice down to the middle of her thighs and a gossamer skirt floating to the floor. I knew she would like it; I also knew it would put her mouthwatering chest and shoulders on display.

The elegant expanse glows under the light from the amethyst chandelier. All that's missing are jewels.

Emeralds would offset her irises. Rubies would match her lips.

She waits for Rhys to finish coughing, a tiny, evil smile playing at her mouth. When he notices the expression, his eyes *blaze* with rage.

If there's one thing Rhys can't stand, it's embarrassment. Leave it to Briar to figure that out after just a handful of meals in his presence.

I wonder what she's learned about Dane. Or me.

I clear my throat. "A decision?" I repeat, eyeing my wife across the table. Admiring the graceful tilt of her head and working to keep any expression off my face. "Do tell, Mrs. Blackwood."

Her eyelids lower minutely, casting me a quick glower before she corrects herself, affecting a pleasing expression. It's clearly one she's practiced; the demure sweep of her lashes, a pretty purse on her lips.

Hmm. I've only been married for five days, but I already know this can't be good.

I arch my brows expectantly. She rises to the challenge, tilting her chin to meet my gaze. "I want the whole deal in writing. My own house, the money, the promise that I'll get to leave after my heat. With or *without* your heir."

I have to work to keep pride out of my voice. "Of course."

Her eyes narrow slightly, suspicious of my acquiescence. "And I want that signed agreement filed with a lawyer of *my* choosing. *And* locked in a safety deposit box that only *I* have access to. It's at a bank in town. One of you will need to take me there to lock it up and none of you can ever tell my father about it."

I'm genuinely surprised. My background checks and recon work were very thorough and should have turned up a safety deposit box if she had one. I wonder how she managed to keep it a secret from both me and her father. Either way, I'm impressed.

"Alright," I determine aloud.

Rhys will take her. They'll both hate it. But I'll cross that bridge after she gives me what I want.

Briar nods, satisfied. Her preening posture returns, though she carefully avoids eye contact with any of us. "No one touches me unless I say. No one comes into my room except when I want them to. And you all *better* know what you're doing."

More pride swells in my chest. But Dane goes utterly still and Rhys snaps forward, snarling, "Listen here, you little bi—"

I pick up my knife, spinning it in my left hand. A clear

warning that Rhys catches in his periphery. Falling silent, he sits back with a new scowl.

"Like I was *saying*," Briar goes on, all attitude, "I reserve the right to change my mind any time, any way I want. And you sorry assholes are going to be motherfucking *gentlemen* about it."

My palm tingles and my cock kicks. "If you want a gentleman," I rumble, "you will speak to me like a lady. If you prefer to be a brat, I have other methods for dealing with those."

Briar's lips press flat as she exhales through her nose. "*Fine.*" Her teeth grit. "*Sir.*"

It's almost impossible to hide my reaction to that honorific. So much so that I fail, my fingers visibly tensing against the stem of my glass. Briar tracks the movement, her throat bobbing on a swallow.

"I—" She almost stammers but stops herself, tossing her hair back to brazen it out. "I've made a schedule."

Rhys nearly chokes on his merlot again. "A *schedule*?"

Briar thoroughly ignores him. Which is another surefire way to drive him insane. *Bravo, little wife.*

"You'll each get a night, once a week, and no one bothers me otherwise. Oh, and you'll each have thirty minutes."

Fucking hell.

She's adorable. And brilliant.

"Thirty minutes?" Dane repeats, oddly toneless. He's left his mask on, peering over it in Briar's direction.

"Yeah." She only flicks him a quick look, equal to the one she graces Rhys with before turning back to me. "Thirty minutes."

Rhys sneers, opening his mouth to argue again. I hold up my hand, unable to completely hide my next smirk.

"You know it doesn't work that way, Briar. If you expect us to perform in such a short amount of time, you're going to have to let us have you the way *we* like. Not just on your terms."

Briar stills, blinking. When she finally moves, I sense the subtle squirm of her lower half. Probably pressing her thighs together.

Indecision flickers in her cat-like eyes. Across the length of the table, I can't quite tell if she's confused by what I said or by the fact that it *intrigues* her.

Possibly both.

Suspicion fills her features. "What would that mean?"

Rhys snorts and takes a glug from his goblet. "She's a fucking prude, too. Figures," he mutters, shooting me a glare. "You sure know how to pick 'em, Cill."

I reach for my knife again, not planning to miss this time, but Briar snaps her own reply. "Spoken like a guy who can't last thirty *seconds*, let alone thirty minutes."

Rhys's mouth drops open. My wife completely dismisses him with a flip of her dark hair, spearing me with another pointed look. "I deserve to know what I'm agreeing to here, don't you think, husband? Especially since I wasn't given that courtesy on the day of our *wedding*."

Strategically calling me "*husband*," tapping into any guilt I might harbor about our ceremony. Like I said: fucking brilliant.

Another small smile pulls at my mouth. "Of course, *dear*. But no one can know exactly what they'll be in the mood for. So if *efficiency* is important to you, you're going to have to agree to take whatever we want in the moment and give us permission to follow our impulses."

Rhys scoffs. "As *if* she could *ever* handle my—"

I growl, low and quiet, but the damage is done. Briar's face fills with indignation. She exhales through her nose and tosses her hair back one final time. "Fine. I'll do my best to be *flexible*. But you all better make it snappy."

"Thirty minutes. You have my word," I tell my wife. "We'll buy you a stopwatch if you'd like."

Briar drums her fingers along her own glass, ignoring my jab and shaking her head. "No time for that," she says. "We're starting tonight."

sixteen

RHYS

If there's one thing I thought I understood, it was the depths of my hatred.

But this? Now?

Staring across our corner of the dining table, I realize the loathing I feel for Briar is a whole new beast.

It's so big, I can't even see the edges of it anymore. Can't measure or pace it out. Is it mine? My Alpha's? I don't fucking know. I just know I've never felt such vehemence about anyone.

Except maybe my parents.

And whoever tried to kill me in that fire.

I know it doesn't make sense for Briar to be on that level, but

I can't explain the fury that roars in my blood every time I see her. My Alpha wants his *mate*, damn it. That's the only thing he's ever cared about. Now, not only is *this* omega here, reminding us of everything we don't have...

But she's fucking *gorgeous*.

So *smart*.

And she keeps *stealing my books*, goddamn it.

Not to mention looking for ways to piss me off. Like making me dribble wine down my chin with her little "announcement."

What will I do if she picks me? I wonder, glaring at her self-congratulatory smirk.

After fighting about it all week, I told Cillian I would play this little game. Breed his wife, get our heir so we can end this feud with Gideon's pack as soon as possible.

I thought I was finally resigned to it. Our company is hanging in the balance; the stakes are a hell of a lot more important than whatever *feelings* I have.

But, fuck me. I have no idea how I'll be able to convince my feral Alpha to *breed* her.

All the women I've slept with over the years have been a *battle*. He wanted to tear them to shreds, punish them for daring to touch what rightfully belonged to *his mate*. I usually had to talk him into keeping his violent urges to himself.

Now, though? I don't know where to fucking start.

That fire—losing my ability to scent omegas and recognize a mate—pushed him off the deep end. The headaches that stem from fighting him usually incapacitate both of us, but ever since Briar arrived, I've had to wrestle him off the edge of a rampage *every day*.

He might not even *let me* put my dick inside her.

You know, if I wanted to.

Which I *don't*.

Because she's obviously an uppity bitch who thinks she has a golden snatch. I don't care how much she resembles my type. Or how much fun it would be to fuck her into submission.

She's only getting my cock because I have to give it to her.

The wordless animal crouched in my core snarls, his tone accusatory. If he could still speak to me, I think he'd be calling my ass out. Something like, *Then why do you feel so smug about her possibly choosing you first? Do you <u>want</u> her to?*

I deny it, but there's no way to ignore the sick swirl of excitement fogging my logic. I shake my head internally, explaining, *It doesn't matter. Cillian, Dane, and I agreed we would do this.*

So I'm at this little omega's mercy.

Which might just be the most valid reason for how much I despise her.

DANE

TONIGHT.

As in this night? The one happening *right now*?

I don't think I've ever seen Cillian stunned before. In nineteen fucking years, the guy has never let his jaw fall slack the way he does after Briar issues her edict.

Because that's exactly what it is: a royal decree. A queen telling her men how they'll perform. And when.

Hell. Now is *not* the time for a hard-on.

Well, maybe it is for Cillian or Rhys. Or *will be* after our plates are cleared.

Envy blazes low in my gut. It doesn't make sense, given the

last thing I want is this little omega having to *look* at me. Or touch me.

But somehow, *knowing* she won't choose me stings.

This isn't new. It's been over two years since I had anyone in my bed, but my packmates pick up beautiful women all the time and it never affects me.

Why would I be jealous now?

I distract myself by weighing them up, trying to guess who she'll select. Cillian is the obvious choice. He's her husband, after all. And undoubtedly more respectful.

Something tells me Briar won't choose him *because* he expects her to, though. She seems keen to keep our alpha on his toes.

Rhys is better-looking, but, to be fair, Rhys is more handsome than most men alive. Almost uncomfortably so. I should know— I've spent years working next to the fucker.

I know he's been rude to her, but she must have noticed his face by now... Though, if she picks him, I'll probably have to station myself outside the door to make sure they don't kill each oth—

"Dane."

When my eyes snap up from my plate, they seem to be the only things in motion. The rest of the room has frozen. Watching me.

Once again, Cillian seems thrown. His eyebrows crease as he glances between me and his wife while Rhys openly gapes.

"Please," Briar adds, quieter.

I've never felt so stupid. Please *what*? Why did she say my name? What is she asking me for? And what is this *feeling*, squirming under my diaphragm? Like I would literally do *anything* to pluck the splinters of fear from her eyes?

A blush heats her cheeks. Realization drops into the center of my mind like a boulder.

Is she... *choosing me*?

"You—" Words trip over each other in my throat. I cough to clear them, mesh muffling my grumble. "You don't want that.

Trust me. You'd regret your decision pretty fucking fast, little girl."

She doesn't react to the gruff, sarcastic way I address her. Which is unlike Briar, given how much she hates Cillian calling her anything other than her first name.

Knowing my features are covered, I turn to search her face; expecting hatred or disgust—maybe even mockery.

Come to think of it, a prank is the *only* explanation that makes sense here. She's clearly already figured out Rhys and Cillian's buttons—why *wouldn't* she scorn me the same way? Making my disfigurement into a punchline, trying to give me false hope that she might actually want me in some way.

It's a smart move. Exploiting my worst nightmare.

But the poor thing doesn't know I stopped hoping for shit a long time ago. I don't even remember *how* to hope anymore. That much is clear, given the whistling emptiness expanding where my thoughts should be and the nauseous lurch stabbing my stomach.

If I'm honest, there's *yearning* there, too. Rooted so fucking deep it hurts.

All her jokes aside, I'm not sure I've ever *wanted* anything this badly. As a general rule, longing seems stupidly impractical for a man like me. I may have gotten in with a wealthy pack, but I had the kind of upbringing that made it clear I will always be poor— even if only deep down, where it counts.

I don't usually let myself covet beautiful things. Because people like me are designed to break them.

Which makes this aching pull anchored in my middle a fucking problem.

Tell that to my Alpha, though.

I can't remember the last time he spoke to me. Normally, the bastard only nudges me once in a blue moon, and typically not with any sort of urgency. Now, though...

She's scared.

The thick, scratchy voice accompanies a sharp bolt of anger— directed at *me*.

I can't understand why, until I meet her eyes. *He's right.* Fear has filled the sparkling green orbs, overflowing into the rest of her body. Stretched through her shoulders. Blanching her knuckles. Trembling on her lips.

Fucking hell.

Is it possible she *isn't* kidding?

Cillian seems to think so. He slides his icy eyes from Briar to me and back again, nodding slowly. "Alright, then."

He stands and slowly buttons his suit jacket, clutching his glass of wine as he abandons his meal and strides toward the exit. Issuing one final word in his wake.

"Tonight."

A confirmation. Or maybe a command.

Either way, it will be the end of me.

eighteen

BRIAR

IT COMES AS NO SURPRISE THAT THE DEVIL KNOWS HOW to dress a slut.

The red silk I found among a drawer-full of similar negligees barely covers my tits... and definitely doesn't cover my ass. It's still more fabric than any of the other strappy, frilled contraptions in there, though, so I pluck it out and slide it on after showering.

I have no idea when Dane is going to show up. Or if he will at all. Probably not, if the way he shoved up from the table and stalked after Cillian is any indication.

I didn't bother sticking around after that. I'd heard enough of

Rhys's taunts and the seethe in my stomach made dessert seem like a supremely bad idea.

This nightgown isn't feeling much better, honestly.

It's cruelly ironic how much I *like* the pieces these beasts bought for me. Tonight's dinner ensemble was gorgeous. And this deep, rich crimson silk, trimmed in the most delicate lace...

Why does it have to be so *beautiful*?

Just like my stupid husband. And his stupid house. And his stupid pack.

Dane probably won't care how I look, anyway. He may be the one alpha in this house who wants to be here less than I do. Which is one of the reasons I chose him.

I haven't let myself examine the other reasons too closely.

My fingers trace the hem of the negligee as my mind races. Images of the hulking alpha, always in dark jeans and an equally inconspicuous shirt, fly through my mind. His silent steps. The taut awareness in every muscle stacked onto his thick body. The surprisingly warm color of his eyes...

And his mask.

Why does a tremor dart down my back at the thought of it?

I feel perfume seep between my bare thighs, the essence sweet and dark. Tart, sugared, black cherries.

The tiny, insecure corner of my heart that actually cares about the opinions of alphas pinches in anxiety. None of these men have reacted to my scent in any major way. My reflection bites her lip. *What if they don't like it? Won't the aroma only get stronger once we start—*

A low tap sounds against the suite's double doors. My eyes fall shut on a shaky exhale. I squeeze tightly, forcing my breathing to level out before I reopen them. In a pitiful attempt to hide my trembling knees, I lower myself into the cushioned stool at the scrolly white vanity.

"Come in."

I don't hear the handle turn or the door swing open. Nor can I detect any sound from Dane's thick-soled boots as he steps over the threshold. But I watch him in the arched curves of my mirror, waiting while he warily glances into each corner of the room before settling his gaze on the reflection of mine.

He stares, waiting. Projecting tension. His gold irises shift and his chest heaves subtly.

My spine snaps straight. The wetness collecting at my core thickens into true slick. I only manage to half swallow the omega whine tickling my throat.

If possible, his eyes get even sharper. The fingers hanging limp at his side twitch.

"You wanted me here," he husks behind his mask, "so here I am." His suspicious gaze burns brighter. "Just get it over with."

Is he talking about sex? I thought Cillian made it clear that I was going to be following their leads. I was secretly thankful for that, on a practical level. Since I have no idea what to do with a manly specimen like this alpha without some guidance...

I swivel on my velvet stool, facing the darkly clad mountain of muscle across the room. "What do you mean?" I ask, hating how breathless I sound.

Dane lumbers forward. It only takes a few of his big, soundless steps for an unholy image to flash through my mind. *Me, racing down the shadowy halls in this house. And the huge masked man. Hunting me.*

Goosebumps break over my skin, hardening my nipples. He freezes, those all-seeing eyes tracking the quiver that rolls over me.

I can't see the lower half of his face—just the cold slate curves of metal and the mesh that allows him to breathe. But, somehow, I get the distinct sense that he's scowling. Thick walnut brows crouch over his gaze.

"I won't hurt you," he grunts, almost exasperated. "But I'm not thrilled about your game, either. So just do it."

He crosses his arms. Grapefruit-sized bulges flex under his navy Henley. My focus lingers on his biceps for a second too long before I blink, shaking my head. "I don't know what you're—"

Dane growls at me for the first time—a deep, ragged sound of pure fury.

Or... maybe not *pure*. Because it sounds the slightest bit *pained*, as well.

"You want me to take off all my clothes first? Stand here naked before you tell me this is a ploy to humiliate me? I get it, little girl; this is a shit situation and you want to hurt us back. But I don't have to make it easy."

My lungs snag, then squeeze. *He thinks I picked him so I can reject him.*

The jaw muscles at the edges of his mask flex, his dark facial hair rippling as the tendons in his neck pop. He takes another slow step toward me, dripping deadly intent.

"I may not be a smart-ass like Rhys." Another step—*oh God*. "Or as powerful as Cillian."

One more pace puts him close enough to touch. I crane my neck back, staring up with wide eyes while my insides flip. Lightning flashes in his gaze as it rolls over me, assessing the way I quiver.

Slowly, he leans over me, pressing his palms into the edge of the vanity. Caging me between his broad, rumbling chest and the thick bars of his arms. I gasp, instinctively arching into the antique dressing table.

Dane takes the final step separating us, bending to put his masked face inches from mine. "But I'm *dangerous*, little girl," he finishes, snarling. "More than either of them could ever be."

I *believe* him.

And I'm *gushing* slick.

So much, my eyes flit from his searing stare to the way my nightgown has ridden up, the delicate crimson lace barely skimming my pussy. The fabric there has darkened where it molds to my pale skin—a veil, hiding the parts no one else has ever seen.

He notices, deliberately skimming his attention down my torso. When he clocks the mess coating my inner thighs, a snarl catches in his chest.

The sound dies quickly as the scene sinks in.

Him, accusing me of faking this entire thing just to make him suffer. Trying to scare me. Me, wet and wearing an obscene scrap of silk without any panties.

I watch the gears in his mind grind, disbelief creasing the space between his brows. My throat thickens, watching awe and wariness fight for space on his face.

No, I tell myself. *We do not feel bad for this man. He's only marginally better than the other two.*

But that's the thing, isn't it? It's going to be one of them. So why not make it the least evil of the three?

A masculine, wooden scent floods the room. Releasing a shuddering breath, I carefully lift my hand to the sliver of space between us. He audibly grits his teeth, that same hunted skepticism flaring in his eyes as he forces himself into stillness. I swallow hard, gently skimming my fingers over the left cheek of his mask.

It's warm, I think, dizzy. Body-temperature titanium kisses the sensitive skin of my fingertips, sending snaps of electricity up my arms. My nipples stiffen into painful points, the modest swells around them tingling with a heavy sensation I've never felt before.

The same feeling pulses in my core. Tightening, aching, melting. Pounding in time with the fluttering beat of my heart.

We need him, my Omega whines, threatening to project the noise for the alpha to hear. *We need him now!*

I hate that she's right. That's what this thick heat coursing through me means—my body craves what he can do to me. It wants all this *strength*, his warmth and weight and width. Covering me. *Filling* me...

"Please," I murmur, searching his eyes as I coast my fingers down, over the place where the metal mask meets his strong jaw. To the puckered scars covering the side of his neck. When I touch them, he flinches, panic and shock expanding in his eyes.

I let my lashes fall shut and exhale shakily, submitting just enough to put myself at his mercy one last time. "Please, Dane? I really want it to be you."

nineteen

DANE

IF YOU DROPPED ME IN THE MIDDLE OF A DESERT WITH nothing but a ballpoint pen, I would have dinner on an open fire within an hour.

If someone kicked me out of a sky-diving plane without a life vest, threw my car into an ocean, or tied me to the back of a feral gorilla—I would find my way to safety before anyone even noticed I was missing.

I can kill a man with a paperclip. A penny. A cell-phone case. Give me a fork and I'll kill three at once.

My life has prepared me for every type of unthinkable scenario.

But it takes standing over Briar Rose—hearing her offer up sex and submission like gold-wrapped truffles—for me to realize: nothing ever prepared me for *this*.

Something *good*.

A dream. Or fantasy. Hell, maybe even a wish.

Or all three, given that she looks like a goddamn *goddess*. And somehow smells like summer nights and Christmas mornings, all rolled into one.

Fucking hell, she is *gorgeous*. The tilt of her coal-lined eyes. Her shimmering jade irises. That luscious pink pout.

Do the stiff little nipples under this red silk match her mouth? Does she taste as tart and sweet as she smells?

What is *wrong* with me that I'm staring at her instead of finding out?

I came in here with a clear goal: tell her I understand how pissed she is about her situation, but make it clear I won't be the punchline to her jokes.

Now she's gazing at me, eyes full of the purest form of entreaty:

Fear.

Briar blinks to clear the mist glossing the verdant green, but it only reappears a second later. She glances away, clearly embarrassed. Something in my center loosens.

She doesn't have one damn thing to be embarrassed by. Her father threw her to the wolves. All she's done is try to survive with some sort of future for herself. And this, here? This is the moment she has to give up part of herself to get what she needs later on.

I don't see any weakness in these tears. Only bravery.

The fact that they exist, that she's letting *me* see them. I've underestimated her yet again.

That's impressive. Especially when she exhales through her dainty nose and tosses her hair back, meeting my eyes while crystal droplets fall from hers.

It reminds me of the way she acted at the dinner table,

ordering us around like bordello boys who live to service her. My lips flicker into a rueful smirk she can't see, amusement and lust sparking in my veins while something heavy and thick scrapes my throat.

I cram the tangle of emotion down, focusing on the uncertainty spinning through her pretty irises. *I can fix that.*

I don't know why her put-on confidence makes me hard, but she deserves to know. With a quick flick of my hand, I balance on my left arm and snatch her palm with my right. Before she notices I have her fingers in mine, I guide them to the inseam of my jeans, resting her touch against the ridge of my cock.

"Is this what you're after, little girl?"

I watch her carefully, absorbing every flicker across her features. When I walked in, I didn't much care what she wanted or didn't. I thought she was mocking me and figured any sex between us would be an awkward chore.

Was I truly resigned to that just five minutes ago?

Because now, I won't let her touch me unless she really *wants* it.

And I don't know why.

The fresh scent of sugared black cherry makes it harder to think. Especially when she closes her fingers around my length and gives a careful squeeze.

"Yes," she whispers, eyes blazing through tears. "I want it."

My Alpha rages against that reply, concern pouring from him. I feel my forehead crease as I frown behind the mask. My hand finds the curve of her cheek, cupping her fine bones and porcelain skin. *So breakable.*

"Hey. Look at me."

She already is, but I watch surprise leap in her gaze as I lean closer, lowering my voice to a stern murmur. "We don't have to do this, Briar."

She opens her mouth, but I pinch her chin softly, searing my stare into hers. "I mean it. I'll leave right now and tell the others whatever you want. If you want me to go, I'll go."

Briar's eyes bounce between mine. I can't fathom what she's thinking but her fear seems to shrink, leaving the glistening green pools warmer.

They trace what she can see of my face. Her tongue slowly swipes her lower lip as she reaches up to touch the titanium molded under my cheekbone.

"Will you take the mask off?" she asks, quiet but steady. Lust sparks in her gaze. "Or leave it on for me?"

Fucking—

My control doesn't just snap. It *dissolves*.

My arms spring closed, ripping her off the velvet stool and into my panting chest. Briar goes limp, submitting and softening the second her nose finds the base of my throat.

She inhales my smoldering scent. And *moans*.

Fuck. Why isn't she afraid? Doesn't she know a man without control is just an animal?

I've never felt more like a predator than I do when she trembles and a burst of tart perfume floods the air. My canines pulse, a dizzying surge of pure carnal need shooting through my veins. Razing everything in its path, lighting every nerve.

I spin and haul her to the bed. Its enormous frame creaks when I tackle her onto the duvet. More of her scent wafts off the dark berry–colored covers rumpled under her.

Briar gasps and I rear back, an instinctive clench snapping at my stomach. But when I scan her face, I don't find any pain—and I feel her press her naked core to the bulge running along my right thigh.

Holy God. Even through the worn denim, she's hot and *soaking*. My chest rattles on a growl as my fingers follow my gaze, sliding down her silk-covered hip to trace the bare pussy lips shining in the room's low light.

Her slick feels every bit as smooth as the fabric draped across her torso. It glides under my touch, beckoning me to the fluttering entrance gushing for more. My erection aches and my pulse pounds faster.

I dip one finger into her wetness. Feeling it clasp at me, begging for more. "Jesus, Briar," I husk. "Is all this for me?"

The omega looks as dazed as I am. Her dark lashes flutter as she bites her lower lip. "I—yes."

She's shy like this. I didn't expect that, but it's the only other thing that could make me as hard as her queen-like confidence. The combination of one so soon after the other has me half-feral.

I clutch her hips and tug her closer, pressing the line of my cock against her slit. When I rub, she shivers under my palms and tugs at my shirt. A tentative question swirls in her eyes.

Hell.

"The scars on my face aren't the worst of them," I rough out. "You want me to keep the shirt on, little girl. Trust me."

Her sexy-as-hell regal expression reappears. Telling me *no*, she doesn't trust me. And she already knows *exactly* what she wants.

Pushing onto one elbow, Briar uses her free hand to reach past my shoulder and pull the Henley over my head. I don't stop her, but my guts seethe. I clench my teeth. Bracing.

She's about to scream. Struggle to escape. Get away from the beast as fast as possible.

Instead, her glimmering eyes gently roam over the wreckage, pausing on the more obvious burns. Puckered, swirled skin. Thick bands of mottled pink, darker splotches of discoloration that will never fade. And, eventually, the black ink tattooed over my unscathed left arm. Scars of my own design.

I already had half a sleeve before the accident; but, after, my body felt disturbingly uneven. I gradually wound up having everything from the left side of my collarbone to my wrist covered. Hoping it would restore some balance.

Briar lingers over every detail. The sweep of her gaze, touching parts of me no one else has in years... My stupid, desperate cock *jerks*. Like she's ever going to want any of *this*.

"You're so—" Briar stops and swallows. Icy arrows of dread swoop through my stomach. "*Strong.*"

My fingers curl tighter, dimpling her flesh. Disbelief spirals behind my sternum, landing in my middle with a hard *thud*. My eyes burn into hers. "*What?*"

"Your body," she whispers, hesitantly placing her palm on my ravaged shoulder. "The muscles. The size. The tattoos. Even the scars. You just look... indestructible."

I have to remind myself to keep breathing. *Is this really her reaction? No screaming or squirming? Not even a* wince?

I watch warily, waiting for everything to sink in. But she only glances lower, where I'm wedged between her creamy thighs. A shimmer gilds her gaze.

"You're the biggest," she murmurs, biting her lip. "Maybe I should have thought about that."

It's the second time I've felt the urge to chuckle because of her. Instead, I smile behind my mask and thumb the bitten curves of her mouth. "It will fit. Trust me."

Briar flashes a small, beautiful smirk, sitting up. "You keep telling me to trust you," she breathes, reaching for her hem. "It's a little late for that, don't you think?"

But she peels her nightgown off in one smooth motion, tossing it away. Leaving her naked under my touch. And completely at my mercy.

twenty

BRIAR

THE ENORMOUS MASKED BEAST STANDING BETWEEN MY legs visibly loses his breath.

I watch the wide, scarred expanse of his chest stutter. Candlelight dances across his tattoos and catches in the cut lines of his abs when his torso clenches. The thick length pressed into the seam of my thighs twitches beneath his jeans.

They're soft. Worn denim that doesn't chafe as I hook my calves over his hamstrings, arching my back.

If there's one thing ballet taught me, it's the importance of posture. I make sure mine is pretty, poised to show him exactly what I'm offering.

Dane's ocher eyes remind me of a fire pit. The golden warmth smolders and seethes, flames licking in their depths. He looks *dangerous*. Huge, stacked in strength, covered everywhere with evidence of the trauma he's survived. Pain endured and inflicted.

And that *mask*.

My body shivers, perfume spilling from my pussy as it tightens on air. A pang of painful longing spirals through my core. My Omega whines, the sound escaping along with more slick.

Dane's dark brows snap together. His deep growl pricks my nipples. My back arches more, presenting my aching breasts to him. Not knowing what I need or why but praying—*please, God* —that he understands. That he'll know what to do.

The alpha gives a low snarl, his focus flickering to my tits. With measured intent, he places the tips of his fingers against my sternum and slowly skates them down. Tingles ripple from his touch, tweaking the pink nipples to the point of pain.

He watches them stiffen, gliding his hand to the right one. Cupping me in his huge, raspy palm. When he gives a solid squeeze, my lungs stop working.

His fingertips pump the sensitive swell before closing around the tip. Pleasure pours through my torso, bubbling heat echoing in my pussy. The exposed nub at the top of my slit throbs in the cool air, sending goosebumps across my thighs.

"Responsive," Dane grunts to himself, eyeing my core. His cock visibly strains while he starts to unclasp his belt. Those melted honey irises snap back to mine.

"Last chance, little girl," the alpha husks. "Once I'm inside you, I won't stop until you come all over this cock."

My pussy tightens and his jaw hardens under the mask. Dane's voice drops lower as he roughs, "Maybe not even then."

He means it as a warning, but it feels like a promise. Especially when he rips his fly open and snaps his hand to my hip. Sliding it to the heat between my legs, cupping the molten, melting softness. He teases my opening with two fingertips and rests his thumb at the top of my clit.

I mewl and buck. Intensity darkens his eyes. "Ask me."

The command barely registers before I obey. "*Please.*"

His tongue clicks. He gently rolls his thumb over the bundle of pulsing nerves and watches me choke on a gasp. "Mmm," he hums. "You're going to be a good little girl for me, aren't you? I didn't expect that."

Honestly, neither did I. But something about him—the way he observes me, weighing every move with the careful grace of a trained predator—makes me feel less safe and more protected than ever. It's a heady combination; adrenaline racing in my veins, the solid warmth of security anchored in my center.

Dane grasps my chin, using his other thumb to trace my lips. He locks his gaze onto mine, peering into me. Seeing too much, damn him.

But at least he's looking. Trying to understand.

It's more than anyone else has ever given me. And it's enough, for now. For *this*.

I spread my legs wider, tilting my pelvis to show off my wet slit. He gives my chin one last squeeze before breaking our stare. His attention leaps down to my pussy, heat flaring over his visible features.

"Okay," Dane murmurs, surprisingly tender. "You can have it, baby."

I whimper as he gives my clit a final brush, moving to yank his gray boxers out of the way. An impressive cock bobs free, the thick erection roped with veins and glistening at the tip.

It's hard to see his knot in the dim room, but he clasps his dick in his hand, stroking down to the swollen flesh at its base. Squeezing hard enough for the muscles in his tattooed forearm to pop.

My jaw falls slack, perfume and arousal gushing out of me. Dane rumbles his approval, eyes tracking the thick, liquid desire.

"That's it," he encourages, rasping. "Make more slick for this big alpha cock."

Oh *fuck*.

My core feels so hollow, I could cry. A wild whine rips from my throat, spurring the enormous alpha into action. A feral gleam fills his gaze as he peers at me over the metallic edge of his mask. "Does it hurt, little girl?"

I pant, trying to muster any sound aside from a moan. All I get is another whimper.

Sparks fly through Dane's eyes. "I can fix that for you."

With one smooth punch of his hips and a deep groan, the alpha buries half of himself inside me. Pleasure pulls taut through my lower belly. Everything between my legs clenches against the burning stretch. I try to gasp, but my lungs shudder uselessly, eking out a pained squeak as my eyelids squeeze shut.

Dane is frozen. Bent over my lower half with one palm flat on the mattress and the rest of his body locked into utter stillness. Air finally flows down my scratchy throat. The bridge of my nose tingles from a sudden rush of tears.

I'm not sure what's worse—the pain or the thought of this alpha ripping himself away. My hands fly out, instincts screaming. Needing to hold on to him.

I wrap my fingers around his biceps. His gaze flicks to mine instantly, the gold seething with horrified disbelief. When he sees my tears, his brows knit. "Briar—"

Frantic, I shake my head, digging my nails into his rounded muscles. "P-please," I beg. "I—I want it to be you."

I've said that already, but now he knows *exactly* what I mean. The words hit him as visibly as a slap. Some of the outrage drains from his expression, softness blurring the surprise. Consternation colors his tone. "You could have told me."

The tears come faster, vulnerability welling under my diaphragm as I whisper the one truth I have left. "I can't tell anyone anything."

Dane stares hard, thinking. My insides clutch him, and a

garbled growl catches in his chest. I hook my heels around the backs of his knees, crying harder.

"*Please*, Dane. Just—take me."

The menacing alpha pauses for a long beat, then sighs. Nodding. With a gentle tug, he lifts my hips from the bed. "Come here."

The world blurs before my swimming eyes. I blink, realizing he's flipped us. Now the big man is lying on the mattress below me. One huge hand guides my face to the curve of his neck while the other clasps my waist, repositioning my burning core and his throbbing cock.

Our bare torsos collide. Dane goes rigid. His skin heats, burning my belly while he gasps. The stinging stretch in my core ticks wider. Fuller.

"*Fuck*." He exhales hoarsely and pulls in another deep breath, soothing, "Shhh. It's okay. You're alright," when my body tweaks tighter.

Slow, languid caresses slide over my side. Thick, calloused fingers tangle at my nape. They rub soft, tingling circles and my wet lashes flutter. Some of the stiffness seeps from my spine.

"That's a good little girl," he murmurs, gruff. The palm spanning my waist slips down to my hip, carefully guiding me through a small thrust. "Like this, okay?"

It still burns, but I'm so wet that the top half of his cock easily dips in and back out, until the wide, rounded head is the only part in me. The friction seems *right*, somehow. The deepest parts of me ache for more while my clit buzzes.

"You're going to move however feels good for you," Dane says. His deep voice rumbles under the scarred skin pressed into my breasts. Solid alpha energy smoothes the dizzy dread in my middle. "I want you to learn."

My stomach flips and my body clenches. He grunts, the sound reverberating in his throat. My Omega pushes to the surface and I find myself nuzzling his hot skin, wanting his deep, woodsy scent all over my face.

When my lips skim his pulse, Dane's fingers tense against my scalp. The rattling growl in his chest smooths into a sound I've never heard before. Something calming and sonorous. A hypnotic hum that loosens all the tension coiled in my muscles.

He's purring, my Omega whispers in wonder. *For us.*

I let her answering moan tumble out, burying it in the crook of Dane's neck. He turns his head to rest his chin on my crown, lifting my hips in a roll. Showing me how to move on top of him.

My tight muscles burn, but by the third rock of his body into mine, the girthiest part of his shaft rubs a circle of nerves near my entrance. Euphoria flutters into my belly. Everything deep inside stutters, aching to clamp on to the thickness. I cry out, the sound edged with desperation.

"Right there, huh?" Dane pants. "That's where this sweet little pussy will take our knots. Once you're used to this, I can show you that, too."

I picture the knot expanding at the base of his cock, locked into the flexible ring of pure bliss throbbing for more. Slick squelches from my pussy, and my hips do a swivel all their own, seating him farther than ever.

Dane hisses, but his purr projects pure approval. "That's it, little girl. Use this alpha cock. Rub your clit all over it or pull it deeper. Whatever feels good."

His mask muffles the words slightly, but I hear them echo in his chest. I nestle closer and he purrs louder, until the rattle vibrates all the way into his cock. And my pussy.

The remaining pain unspools around his buzzing erection. The burn dissipates, leaving a molten puddle of *want*. It melts the straining muscles, relaxing them as fresh slick dribbles onto his knot. He curses, the hand on my hip clamping tight to reposition me slightly.

When the warm swell of his knot rubs my clit, I gasp, "*Dane!*"

He growls, his cock rubbing in a slow-but-steadier rhythm. "Good omega. Just like that. Grind your clit into my knot while this pussy takes my cock."

I thought I knew what an orgasm felt like, but this is something completely different. The sensations swarming my body are stronger than anything I've ever experienced. More delicious and addictive. Overwhelming in the best possible way.

He's *everywhere*. Flexing strength underneath me, fingers scraping my scalp. The tug of my hair, the rattling purr prickling my nipples. Hot skin grazing my slick clit on every. Single. Glide. His thick cock. So fucking *full*. Bursting. *Bliss*—

I cry out as a wave of pleasure swallows me whole. My body spasms, tugging his girth as deep as it can while I clench around it. The tension in my core detonates, shattering into a thousand tiny shards. Catapulting glitter into my veins.

Dane's body bows and he *roars*, the sound so raw and unfiltered that renewed rapture rolls through me. My toes curl, my pussy locking down on his pulsing length for one perfect moment before he tears out of me.

Savagely palming his knot, Dane aims the torrent of pearly white cum surging from his cock. Painting my thighs and lower abdomen in washes of white. Melding his release into my paleness. Making a mess of me.

More of a mess of me.

Dane's tightly laced abdomen flexes, holding his body in a half-curl. He pants through his mask, his chest heaving as he watches himself mark me with those uncanny gold eyes.

Seeing the evidence of what we've done, the way he very much did *not* use this vulnerable experience to try to get his pack an heir...

The big man looks directly into me. And I swear I still hear the words he doesn't say.

We won't tell anyone.

I don't notice the blood until Dane barks a low curse.

In a blink, he's flipped us back around and silently dropped into a crouch. I have no idea how someone his size moves so gracefully, but my mind can't really ponder much of anything at the moment. It's too busy absorbing the euphoric warmth singing in my bloodstream.

Dane uses his discarded shirt to wipe me clean, thoroughly examining everything between my legs until I blush. His gaze is frank and his fingers are gentle, carefully probing to make sure I'm not injured.

"I feel okay," I murmur, resisting the urge to squirm. "Can I —would you hand me my robe?"

Dane rises to his feet, brows folded together. He nods without a word, those heavy boots disturbingly soundless as he ghosts to the closet door and takes the lacy black confection off its hook.

Instead of tossing it to me, he comes back to the bed and holds it open. My cheeks and chest turn pink. I duck my face and slide to my feet.

He settles the delicate fabric on my shoulders, his fingers briefly lingering along my collarbones. I hear a quiet purr, but by the time I turn around, he's gone. I blink, thinking he's abandoned me, until I hear the bathtub thunder to life.

Does he... want to clean himself off?

Why does that make me want to *cry*?

The big man reappears on the threshold of the bathroom a second later, though. Still in his mask, jeans, and boots. Shirtless. Littered with burn scars, healed slices, and bulging muscles. He's tied his hair back, showing off the carved lines of his massive shoulders and the thick, stubbled neck I couldn't stop nuzzling.

Dane crosses his arms, jaw ticking as he nods at the bath. "Epsom salt bath. That will help. So you don't get too sore."

Oh.

I bob my head and lick my lips. Something tugs at my middle.

The voice there whines, willing me to cross over to him. Maybe slide my arms around his waist.

And do what? I ask my Omega, a sudden wave of despair swamping me. *It's not like I can* kiss *him. And, clearly, he doesn't want to cuddle.*

The thought shakes me out of my melancholy moment.

Because, *honestly? Cuddling?* What the fuck is *wrong* with me?

I force my shoulders back, not bothering to tie my robe's sash before striding toward the open bathroom door. He observes, a new glimmer filling his gaze. Just before I reach the en suite, a thick, muscled forearm bands around my waist, halting me.

Dane steps into my side, capturing my cheek with his free palm when I whip my head to face him. He strokes his thumb over the ridge of my cheekbone, burning his golden beams into my eyes.

My resolve softens. Unexpected gratitude floods my chest, rising to block my throat. "Thank you," I manage, nearly croaking. "For not— For—" I release a deep, weary sigh. "Just... thank you."

Dane listens, nodding slowly. Instead of replying, he skims his attention down my exposed body, lingering in ways that have me perfuming all over again.

When he senses my arousal, the bastard has the audacity to chuckle. His dark amusement should outrage me—but it only sends a fresh flutter through my belly.

"I'd offer to stay," he murmurs, bending to briefly brush his forehead against mine. When he pulls away, a new kind of light shines in his eyes. "But my thirty minutes are up."

twenty-one

RHYS

THUNK.

Our butler, Coggins, sets a silver tray on the coffee table in front of me and raises of his graying eyebrows. Darting a pointed look between me and the toast.

Dear God.

Now even *the help* is giving me grief?

Is there no depth I refuse to sink to?

"Last I checked, you weren't my fucking mother," I groan, sitting up and cracking my neck.

Coggins may be the one asshole in this house who's allowed to talk back to me. And that's only because he practically raised me and Cillian. With a dour scowl, he scoffs, "No, sir. *You* clearly didn't have the benefit of a mother."

He's not wrong, but I lift my hand and flip him off anyway. The older alpha rolls his eyes. Sniffing, he points to the morning meal. "You'll eat it or I'll lock the liquor cabinet tonight."

Meddling son of a bitch. He's just made the one threat that will give me pause. And he knows it.

Glaring, I snatch up a piece of toast and stuff it into my mouth. Without my sense of smell, the flavor barely registers. I only get a slightly charred taste and a hint of the butter's unctuous texture.

I swallow the bland wad and reach for my tea, gulping it down in four chugs. Coggins offers a slightly appeased chuff, turning on his polished heel and striding from the music room.

As soon as he disappears, I slump forward, scrubbing my fingers through my hair. Tearing at the roots with my fingernails. Wishing I could claw out the dull ache swelling under my skull.

My headaches dissipate occasionally, but those "good" days are getting fewer and farther between. Now, I can't even sleep in my own bedroom without risking migraines. I've been reduced to collapsing on whatever couch is closest when I'm tipsy enough to fall asleep.

What the fuck did I even drink last night?

The empty bottle beside my feet looks like some good shit. Fancy red wine. Squinting at the label, I remember choosing the nicest vintage I could find. It felt appropriate to celebrate Briar fucking one of us for the first time by pouring Cillian's hard-earned money down my gullet.

I set it in the middle of the coffee table, chancing a look outside. Before our "accident," I used to love opening up this room. Our house has stone eaves carved over each window exterior, which meant I could always have fresh air, even when it rained.

I preferred the rain, actually. Those were the afternoons I

spent reading or playing my favorite pieces on the upright piano positioned between the wide windows.

The flash of lightning, cool gusts, and billowing curtains. It felt *good*. Like abandon.

Now, weak sunlight hovers behind thick gray clouds. I squint into the searing light, wishing I could have just one afternoon as my old self. A single day to appreciate all the things I once took for granted.

I only hear Dane approaching because he chooses to be heard. We do that, sometimes, as a courtesy. God knows neither of us wants to surprise the other when we're in the middle of a fucked-up reverie.

That's how people lose an eye.

My packmate drops into one of the leather club chairs facing my sofa. His gold eyes snap to my tray, a question clear in his arched brows.

"Yes, I'm eating breakfast," I grouse. "Fucking Coggins."

Dane nods. His focus sails to the doorway, sensing our alpha seconds before I do.

"Good. We're all here," Cillian says smoothly as he enters, striding to the other club chair. He folds his body into it and reaches for my platter, helping himself to the empty teacup and steaming pot.

Clutching the porcelain in one hand, our pack alpha eyes Dane over the painted rim. "How did last night go?"

I balk, snorting. "For fuck's sake. We're doing *check-ins* now? Am I going to have to get those weird-ass wooden positioning dolls and reenact the whole scene for you? Are there punch cards involved?"

Cillian ignores me. Dane grunts, dropping his gaze to his lap. "It was fine," he mutters, muffled by the mask. "She did every-thing I told her to."

Somehow, I seriously doubt that.

Dane doesn't notice my glower, though. He's too busy

burning a hole in the Persian rug. I feel something new brewing in him and decide I don't like it.

"Are we sure there's no other way?" he finally adds, toneless. "This is it?"

Cillian's blue eyes take on an unfamiliar intensity. "No," he says slowly. "There is no other way."

I'm still waiting for a goddamned explanation on that. Why is there no other way? Did our grandfather mandate this shit or something?

And why is it starting to feel like I don't recognize my pack-mates anymore?

Suspicion winds its thorns around my throat. A growl rattles low in my lungs. "Cillian, I swear to—"

He stands without hesitation, buttoning the navy pinstriped jacket covering his white shirt and tie. "I have to go into town for a meeting," he announces. "I likely won't be home for dinner, so Rhys?"

Our gazes collide—mine full of loathing, his bemused.

He smirks. "I guess it's your turn tonight."

THE GREATEST TRICK THE DEVIL EVER PULLED?

Convincing the world he didn't exist.

And the Blackwoods do that better than anyone.

Our office is about an hour commute from the manor's strip of pristine North Shore real estate, at the very heart of Manhattan. So civilized, with its panes of smoked glass and sleek steel beams. Priceless modern art graces the walls of our lobby. And the building's security personnel dress like they're working the door at Bulgari, not the world's top manufacturer of death.

It takes a trained eye to peer beyond the facade. The average person wouldn't notice how Raul—the middle-aged "security

119

liaison" working the elevator keypad—holds himself with the bearing of a trained mercenary. They would miss that the soles of his shiny black loafers are about a half-inch thicker than they should be; designed to conceal the knife hidden in the toe.

All this art? It's beautiful, but sometimes I wonder if anyone ever questions how we acquired the pieces, given that many of these artists don't typically work on commission.

Even the skyscraper itself. It was built in less than six months. Defies several zoning laws. Broke multiple city codes. And no one has ever so much as questioned it.

The signs are all here.

Is it our fault if no one ever bothers to look at them?

The elevator glides open on the fortieth floor. Two more mercs stand sentry on either side as I exit onto the executive level.

Most of this space was designed with appearances in mind. Large windows and opaque glass walls offer natural light and city views. A conference table sits in the middle of the marble floor, always with a lovely floral arrangement at its center. Somewhere, a secretary's phone chimes.

So innocuous. A pretty, placid office.

I ignore it, striding to the row of rooms built into the farthest wall. Their black stainless steel doors are on par with the aesthetic, but I know they're actually bulletproof. And fire-proof.

Without bothering to knock, I press on the handle and let myself in. As I suspected, Grandfather sits behind his executive desk. It's a French antique from the nineteenth century. An heirloom.

For nearly three hundred years, Blackwood patriarchs have sat at that desk until they drop dead. Which means, one day, it will either belong to me... or the other fucker in the room.

"Gideon," I chip, repressing a smirk at the shock splitting my cousin's features. I drop my head in a respectful nod. "Grandfather."

Forsyth Blackwood sits at the helm of his empire, wearing a two-thousand-dollar golf shirt. It's part of the illusion, I know.

He's supposed to be semi-retired, so he shows up here dressed like he's hitting the links later. Which is stupid, in the city, but people buy it.

The same way they fall for his over-bleached veneers and the Botox holding his face up. A pretense of vanity, intended to distract from all the true evils this company perpetrates.

Apart from the false trappings of an eccentric old man, Forsyth looks like my father—and, by extension, me. A familiar scowl creases his square features. The thick white hair on his head doesn't move as he tilts his head slightly, considering me.

Grandfather is many things, but slow isn't one of them. He snaps together the reason for my unexpected visit within half a second. Begrudging esteem fills the space around his frown. He waves a weathered hand at the other seat opposite his desk.

I unbutton my suit jacket and sit, casting Gideon and his sour expression a brief glance before focusing on my cufflink. Adjusting my sleeve as I murmur, "Apologies for my tardiness. I assume my receptionist forgot to add this meeting to my agenda."

We all know that's a lie. My cousin has been gunning for this secret meeting for weeks, trying to scrape together any possible advantage in our race for an heir.

I don't hold it against him. Some people don't have the spine or the sense to accomplish a goal without help from on high.

Or so it would seem.

I don't need to say a word. We all know how embarrassing this is for him. I'm married, with a new bride who—for all they know—might be growing my baby as they speak.

And Gideon's pack can't even *find* a suitable omega.

Neither of them knows I have sources inside their penthouse, reporting the latest updates to me. They think I buy their bullshit story about courting an omega "abroad."

In reality, Grandfather is fast losing his patience with their pickiness. Though, according to my sources, Gideon's packmates are the real issue—apparently, they have various objections to this race for an heir.

Mine would, too, if I'd given them the opportunity.

Crossing my ankle over my knee, I carefully flash both men sharp, expectant looks I hope seem believable. As far as Gideon knows, I'm unaware of his agenda. I need him to continue thinking that.

My cousin may not rule his pack with an iron fist, but he isn't an idiot, either. "We were just discussing the party this weekend," he casually replies, standing and ambling to Grandfather's omnipresent bar cart. He pours us each a tumbler of scotch, the early hour be damned.

Gideon slides back into his chair, muddy gray-blue eyes—also similar to mine, but different—jump over to me. "You're still hosting, right? Giving us all a chance to meet the new ball and chain?"

My molars grind, but I keep my tone neutral and shrug. "I assumed so."

More like *they* assumed so. I'd rather keep Briar hidden for the rest of eternity. But she's supposed to be a show of strength. And what good are those if you don't actually display them?

Besides, I suspect observing me with Briar is the primary reason our grandfather is attending this "family gathering." He usually doesn't like parties, which makes his next statement all the more pointed.

"It will be nice to see the whole pack together," Grandfather intones, his sharp gaze flickering at me. "I look forward to it."

Fucking hell.

My whole life has been a series of tests and this is no different. He's pushing at the edges of this arrangement, looking for loose screws. Ensuring his investments in the future are churning up dividends.

I keep my expression smooth, nodding. "If you wish."

Grandfather doesn't seem appeased, though. He huffs a discontented sound. "Just keep that brat of yours on a leash. Important people are joining us and I won't have her pouting over her meal like she did last weekend."

My lips roll together for a long moment before I take a slow sip of scotch, forcing my features into a bored expression. "Consider it done."

Gideon's gaze bores its way into the side of my face. "Must be easier to get a firm grip, since you paid good money for her."

I find the Blackwood family crest emblazoned on the wall behind Grandfather's desk. My brief glance helps me hold my tongue.

Not now. Not yet.

"She's been fine so far."

A lie, but one so dull they don't detect it. Gideon's eyes narrow. "Fine, not good?" He scoffs. "If you'd held out for a mate, maybe you wouldn't be fucking a corpse every night."

No. Not yet. Not now.

"It's true, she's not our mate." I swirl my scotch, inhaling the rich, bitter scent. "But we're doing our best with what we have. To fulfill Grandfather's wishes."

They both nod, my grandfather looking as appeased as Gideon does dour. I swallow a smirk, knowing I've already met my goal for today.

This is the way I've survived a life that was never meant for me. Take the beatings. The blame. The short end of every stick.

Do it respectfully. Nod your head. Memorize the words: *As you wish.*

Take every menial task. Do them so competently, no one can question you.

Move in silence. Build your traps. Wait. Wait. *Wait.*

Gideon sneers in his scotch. We've been rivals our whole lives —I'm sure a large part of him is over the moon about me missing out on matehood and settling for a mail-order bride. Even if it puts me ahead in this game between us.

But his petty emotions don't interest me. So I let him think I don't see the look that passes over his features.

Because the greatest trick the devil ever pulled?

Has nothing on the plans I've made.

twenty-three

BRIAR

THE CUT-CRYSTAL CLOCK ON THE FIREPLACE MANTEL ticks quietly. The long hand crawls past the twelve.

Which officially makes it after midnight.

He didn't come. My Omega's dismay is a whole different flavor than my own. She's nervous and tearful. I'm absolutely *enraged.*

This motherfucker thinks *he* gets to reject *me*?

After everything these assholes put me through: lying to get me here, locking me up, manipulating me into becoming their own personal breeding vessel...

How dare Rhys not even bother *showing up*?

"The hell does he think I am?" I mutter, strapping on a strategically placed garter. The rich emerald silk matches tonight's negligee. Another barely-there piece trimmed in black lace. I throw the coordinating kimono over it and storm out of my suite.

Where are we going? my Omega frets.

I show her a mental picture and get a cringe in return. *Won't he be mad?*

A feral rush of vindication floods my chest. *Oh, I hope so.*

IT'S COMICALLY EASY TO FIND RHYS'S BEDROOM.

The third floor is smaller than the second, for one thing. That makes sense, given the Gothic architecture—I suppose the higher up I go, the narrower things will become.

I take the back staircase near Cillian's suite. His room is dark and empty. The door hangs ajar, which is tempting; but my fury won't allow me to wander into a side quest.

I need to find Rhys Blackwood and rip him a shiny new asshole. Now.

My first impression of the third floor is a humorless laugh. *Damn, these guys really know how to drag out a point.*

Black carpeting, dreary damask wallpaper, and onyx-lacquered doors line the rounded corridor. It looks like a haunted house out of a cartoon. I half-expect a suit of armor to leap from one of the empty alcoves carved between doorways.

The room directly above Cillian's obviously belongs to Dane. A faint thread of his too-warm-to-be-wood, too-earthy-to-be-anything-else scent winds through the air outside the closed doors. I inhale the dark aroma and my belly dips, tingles erupting between my thighs. Chasing the bit of soreness I've spent hours pretending not to relish.

Our alpha, my Omega pants. *Can't we just go to him instead? He was so good to us.*

She's been fixated on the masked mountain *all day*. Waxing poetic about every move he made last night, from yanking me into his arms to coming across my skin instead of going off inside me.

Why did he do that?

And why did he brush his forehead against mine before he left?

It was a scent mark, my Omega huffs. Exasperated with me. *Obviously.*

God, I hate it when she's right. Almost as much as I hate the achy tug sprouting from my sternum. Trying to lure me closer to the sound of Dane... working out? I hear grunts. The quiet kind that men in movies make while they do push-ups or whatever.

They also remind me of last night... and the wet throb in my core reminds me why I'm up here now.

Right. Rhys.

I continue on my search, tiptoeing past open doors. There's another gym up here, this one fully equipped with a small boxing ring and multiple punching bags. To my surprise, I also find a music room.

It's unused, of course. A tomb, actually—with a white tarp draped over an upright piano the way coroners usually shroud corpses. Similar images bob to the surface of my memory, fuzzy pictures of Violet's out-of-tune piano, covered in a blanket of dust.

By the time I drag my eyes away from the abandoned studio, I know where I'll find Rhys's room. In the most logical, unfortunate place, of course—right on top of mine.

It's also impossible to miss the eerie red light emanating from the crack under his doors. Like the whole damn place is as radioactive as his personality.

I'm so pissed, the color doesn't even give me pause. I march right up to his door, pounding my fist four times.

There's a groan, but no one answers. I knock again, louder, before outright banging with my open palm.

An ear-splitting roar rocks me back a step. The doorframe rattles and Rhys appears, snarling, "*Do you want to die?!*"

Rage flashes in my eyes as I hold my ground, squaring my shoulders. Before I can open my mouth to reply, the venomous alpha steps into my personal space. Threatening, "Because I can think of *no reason* why you would *wake me up,* aside from a fucking *death wish.*"

Self-preservation kicks in. I shove him with both hands, flashing a menacing sneer of my own.

"No reason?" I shout. "*No. Reason?!* I'm offering myself to your pack of dogs like a tailor-made incubator and you can't even *bother* to show up? What's the matter? Does your dick only work if you're scaring the shit out of some poor innocent socialite?"

His flinty, soulless eyes ignite. "Mouthy little bitch," he growls, backing me into the wall with two long strides. Caging me with his stupidly long arms. "Maybe you *need* someone to scare the shit out of you."

I move fast, grasping the knife strapped under my garter and raising it to his throat.

He wasn't expecting that and I don't blame him—I'm sure they had one of their henchmen toss the Omega Suite for weapons before I moved in. But I stole this particular switchblade from Dane last night, when it fell out of his pants during our... whatever that was. He left without making sure he still had it, and I took full advantage.

Vindication swoops through me when Rhys's features leap in surprise. It only lasts half a second before he bares his teeth, hissing, "*What the fuck* are you doing?"

"I believe it's called 'making a *point,*'" I snap, pressing the tip of the blade into the place above his pulse. "Cornering me won't work again, venom. I learn my lessons the first time."

He starts to sneer, but I don't wait to see what he has to say. My wrist flicks. Blood wells along the edge of the steel tip.

Red. Huh.

"I thought demons bled black," I smirk.

With a low bellow of outrage, Rhys leverages one hand to push off the wall and clutches his cut with the other. Backlit by that odd reddish light, his silhouette stills. He blinks at the crimson smeared across his fingers. Casting me a wide-eyed, utterly feral look as a growl rasps in his lungs.

My Omega scrambles, panic ballooning behind my chest. I suppress a shiver, gripping the hilt of my dagger until my knuckles blanch.

Rhys doesn't take his eyes off me for a fraction of a second. Somehow, they only get more intent the longer he stares, ignoring the trickle of blood seeping into his open shirt collar. Ruby soaks the starched white fabric as I force down my Omega's whine.

"Tell me why you didn't come downstairs," I demand, breathless. "We made a *deal*. And I'll be damned if your psycho pack alpha uses your refusal as an excuse not to hold up his end. So tell me what your problem is."

Emotion moves across his gaze. A flash of something deep and raw. Realness I've yet to witness from him. It intrigues me, especially when it disappears as quickly as it came.

Rhys locks his expression into a more familiar, indolent look. His off-hand tone scares me more than any aggressive one could. "You know," he says, calmly taking one step closer. "I think I was right about you, viper. And you were wrong about me."

I glare, holding the knife where I know it will catch the light. "Is that so?"

"Yeah," he grits, angelic features set in menacing lines. "I didn't come down to your room tonight because I refuse to be treated like a goddamn stud horse. If you want me to fuck you, you're going to have to get over yourself, fall to your knees, and prove your pussy will be worth my while."

It should be the most insulting thing anyone has ever said to me...

But it feels like a lie.

I can't quite determine how I know he's full of shit. Because, damn. He's a good liar. Maybe even as skilled as Cillian.

Self-doubt creeps in as bottomless aqua-gray eyes work a slow path down my body and back up again. "Clearly you don't have what it takes. Guess my instincts were correct."

His perfectly etched mouth ticks into a humorless smirk. Again, some internal alarm goes off, telling me the expression is an act.

What is he hiding?

Figuring it must be some predictably tasteless sexual desire, I roll my eyes, waving the dagger. "Let me guess, you were hoping I'd cry and beg for mercy? Because if that's truly what you like, I *was* wrong; you're even *more* pathetic than I thought."

Rhys's lips stretch into a maniacal grin. And there's nothing fake about it. *Shit.*

"That's where you're mistaken, baby." He takes another measured step. Advancing. "It isn't fear I'm after—it's *fury.*"

Oh.

Is that really all it is? He wanted to piss me off? Or wasn't interested *until* I got pissed off? It feels like I'm still missing a critical piece—one that would explain the coldness under his darkening expression.

But his light eyes spark. "I want to feel you *fight*. Tear into me. Make me bleed. Make me *earn it*. So I know, when I finally get you on your back, I've conquered you in a way no one else can."

My mind spins, trying to understand.

Wanting... to *believe*.

Because, God, I am so fucking *angry*. I have been for as long as I can remember. Burning from the inside out. Lost in flames I didn't light, but feed with every fantasy of revenge.

And right now? I'm not just furious. I'm *enraged*.

Is it possible for someone to *desire* that?

Does Rhys?

I lower the knife just an inch. "Well, if that's what you like"— I scoff, breathing hard—"then you missed out on the night of your life. I could stab you again, though. If it would help."

All the amusement falls off his gorgeous face. Cold, colored light fills the hollows under his cheekbones and pools in the carved space between his clavicles. I realize, somehow, that we're standing just inches apart.

"You shouldn't tempt me," he warns, a growl rumbling under the words. "I would love nothing more than to teach my asshole brother a lesson by *ruining* you. If you're smart, you won't give me a reason."

He already knows how smart I am, though. So his taunt feels more like a test.

My eyes skim across his exposed flesh. So flawless, compared to Dane's. Less muscled, too, but Rhys is leaner and every bit as tall as the big man.

The only marks he has are there on purpose. Ink as dark as his fucked-up desires, emblazoned across his pecs.

Three words, to be exact, written in fine-line small-caps.

DEATH BEFORE DISHONOR.

I like it. And I hate that.

The phrase is a summary of my darkest hours. The siren call of those jagged cliffs, Violet's plea through the fuzzy phone line. The feeling of flying into a *jeté* and letting myself fall—like maybe, for a moment, I didn't exist. And, perhaps, that might be better than living as a porcelain doll. Created, bought, traded, shelved.

Rhys's eyes are smoldering coals in the dim hallway. He watches, assessing my reaction, waiting for his test results.

Will I heed his warnings? Run back to my room like a scared little omega? Let him win?

Death before dishonor.

Maybe Rhys and I have something in common after all.

twenty-four

RHYS

THE ONE ADVANTAGE TO HAVING A FUCKED-UP childhood is how prepared you are for the horrors of reality.

I've always known the world was a shitty, backwards place. So other people? Rarely surprise me.

This woman, though.

This *snake*.

I can't unriddle her from one moment to the next. Two days ago, she was practically crying when I cornered her. Tonight? She drew blood without a shred of remorse.

We can reflect on how fucking *hot* that was later.

For now, I need more information. This omega reads me *way*

131

too easily. It won't be long until she gets to the heart of how fucked up my Alpha is. Unless I figure her out first.

She slithered into our pack and took this deal for a *reason*, damn it. I'll never be able to beat her at her game until I figure out what it is.

I just wish I could find a way to care while my cock is rock-fucking-solid.

But since I can't think or judge or fucking *breathe* while she's looking up at me like this...

My Alpha roars, enraged. But my knot pumps fuller, so I ignore him. Making a decision I might hate myself for later.

"Alright, viper," I dare her. "Get on your knees."

Maybe I'm losing my mind—or I'm foggy because she woke me out of my first real sleep in weeks. Either way, my stomach lurches when she hesitates. But a second later, as she sinks to the carpeted floor? I find myself *wishing* she would make good on the violent gleam in her green eyes.

But just in case wishes *do* come true, I hold my hand open, curling my fingers twice. "Give me the knife."

She grumbles, true disappointment weighing her thin black brows. Another surprise. *Was this woman seriously going to hold me at knife-point while she sucked my cock?*

Jesus. That really shouldn't make me harder.

Briar doesn't surrender the dagger, but she does slip it back into her garter. The frilly scrap is practical, clearly, but it's also an aesthetic piece of this fetching little ensemble she has on.

Normally, lace and satin don't do much for me. Once you've fucked enough women, such charms begin to feel redundant, at best...

But this set suits Briar. The dark green color and thick bands of intricate lace; it almost looks like snake skin. The sort of beautiful markings that signal piercing fangs and vicious venom.

Perfect for the omega slowly poisoning our pack.

Or for *me*, if you believe the nickname she so lovingly bestowed.

Dainty fingers fly to the seam of my pants, cupping my balls too tightly. I whistle through my teeth, and she bares her white snarl with an answering hiss.

"Tapping out already, venom?" Her fist torques tighter. She feels my body stiffen and flashes a beatific smile. "You sure you want to play with me? You said you like anger, but I've got to warn you—I'm *pretty fucking mad.*"

I can see how true that is; feel it in her careless roughness.

My cock twitches, growing fuller.

She blinks at it. A swoop of vindication soars through my chest when genuine surprise swirls in her emerald irises.

The feeling is short-lived. The second she catches my mouth curling upward, Briar claws open the front of my trousers and practically rips my dick out.

Oh shit.

Why am I so *hard*?

I can't remember the last time I leaked pre-cum for anyone. Possibly never? But before my cock finishes bobbing in front of her face, I'm already producing thin, pearly drops.

Briar notices. Her tongue darts out, wetting her plump, pink lips as her focus slides down my shaft, to the knot underneath.

Which is also about to *burst.*

Seriously? *Fuck me.*

A victorious flash of bemusement sweeps across her face. Some of the tension drops off her shoulders.

But that's fine—I have an easy solution to regain the upper hand.

My belt rasps through its loops as I whip it free. She stills, gaze widening, something almost like fear expanding there.

The monster in my middle growls. She hears him and quivers. I find myself petting the smooth skin of her cheek... in a gesture that just might be reassuring.

"I'm not gonna hurt you," I mutter, looping the belt's tail through its metal buckle. "But I will use it to control you. If you can handle it."

Briar's pert little tits stutter as she represses another shiver. Likely fighting herself over how much the thought of ceding control turns her on.

I can't smell her perfume, but I'm not *blind*. I see how her thighs squeeze together. Despite that, I only get a brief nod, her eyes as wary as ever.

At this point? With my pulse pounding in the base of my dick like it's trying to beat its way out of me? I'll take it.

Dropping the loop around her head, I pull her hair free, ignoring how the silken smoke slides through my fingers. Instead, I instantly tug on the loose leather strap. It slips through the open buckle, forming a collar around her unmarked throat.

My pissed-off Alpha rumbles again. I roll my eyes at him. *No one is bonding anyone. It's just a little <u>leash</u>,* I argue. *Sheesh.*

He tries to fight back, but I cut him off with a snarl of my own, earning a sideways glance from the omega on her knees. The same *what-the-fuck-is-your-problem* look she's given me countless times.

I definitely do *not* find it *amusing*.

Just to prove a point—to her or myself—I pull the belt harder. She gasps, hands automatically seeking purchase on my covered thighs. Pointed black nails prick me through the fabric.

This time, I really do smirk. "What's the matter, viper? You tapping out already?"

Having her own taunt thrown back at her does the trick. She casts me a look of pure disdain, glorious fury shining through the golden streaks carved into her jade irises. An exhale tickles my scrotum—her slight hitch the only indication she's off-balance.

And then she swallows me.

Fucking FUCK.

Wet heat forms a velvet seal behind her lips. The plush cushions slide halfway down my length before she hums, flashing an appreciative look at my groin. Almost as if she wasn't expecting to enjoy the feel of me.

Is she—She has done *this before... right?*

I don't have the capacity to make a determination, since I'm currently *fighting for my motherfucking life*.

Jesus Christ. Has head always felt this *good*? What the hell am I doing with my life? Working? Wasting free time on food and sleep?

The error of my ways seems crystal clear as Briar's tongue slips up the underside of my cock, swirling over the head in a fluid loop. More pre-cum seeps out and she *moans*.

The sharp sound is like a dart to the balls. They draw up, my knot pulsing fuller. It feels incredible... until Briar wraps her hand around it and *twists*.

Oh fuck.

It hurts in the best possible way. Sensation radiates through my base. A growl rips up my throat when she presses harder. My wrist snaps to the right, tightening her makeshift collar until she wheezes around my dick.

"I can go rougher," I warn.

My little viper eases up on her fangs, unlocking her grip and moving to lightly scratch at my balls with her pointed nails. She glares the whole time; I smother the sparks igniting behind my sternum, stabbing a swell that registers dangerously close to *fondness*.

This woman literally cut you, I remind myself, watching as she takes my length deeper. *Made you bleed.*

Yeah, but she's also about to make me come.

And I've barely started with her.

My fist clenches around the belt. This time, I pull slowly, letting her feel each incremental addition of pressure.

She *likes* that. Her spine snaps straight. Her thighs clamp closed. And her perfume must be *extremely* potent, because I manage to catch the edges of it this time.

Something tart and dark. My mouth waters, imagining the taste of her slick fresh from the source.

The thought has me pumping my hips, stuffing my girth

farther than she's taken it before. Briar gasps again, arching her neck to accommodate the thrusts. She can't, though.

And isn't that my whole point? Breaking her down? Proving her pride is foolish? Showing her how thoroughly I would wreck her?

I don't fucking know anymore. Because when a sliver of fear lodges itself in her features, my rhythm slows.

Briar doesn't approve. Instead of taking the reprieve, she doubles down. Mind-bending suction tugs my throbbing erection past her lips, cramming my cock halfway into her throat.

Goddamn motherfucking—

I groan, shoving deeper on instinct. Wanting more of the glorious fury that flares in her gaze. She starts to gag again, but this time, her sharp nails dig into my hips, holding on. Making it clear she *wants* this.

Who the hell knows why? Perhaps she realized she was enjoying it a bit too much and wanted to reel herself in. I get that.

But it's too fucking late for me.

The sloppy trail of saliva dripping down her chin is mesmerizing. I swipe my thumb through it, pushing past the corner of her mouth, rubbing the sensitive pad along her canine. When I press and she gags, I know it's aching as much as mine are.

So her Omega must be as batshit crazy as I am.

My Alpha rages, shoving wordless need at me. Yearning for his mate, hating that I'm doing this with someone else.

I drown him out by bucking harder and faster, choking Briar on every plunge.

She takes it with a garbled moan, shimmery tears gathering in her eyes. Glossing the gorgeous anger and helpless pleasure clashing over her features.

"Fuck, that's it," I grunt, my body spinning out of control. "I knew you'd look hot as fuck with my cock in your throat and tears in your eyes. Such a pretty baby, gagging for my cum."

Briar pulls off long enough to gulp one last breath, releasing a desperate whine before she sinks her swollen lips all the way down to my knot in one go. The second the plush pink curves graze my taut, hot skin, cum sizzles up my shaft.

With a roar, I tear myself out of her mouth and grip my knot, milking it. Shooting a blazing layer of white across her chest. Up the infuriatingly unbitten column of her neck, to the proud jut of her chin.

As soon as it ends, Briar drops back on her heels, panting, and I fall forward. Catching myself against the wall with one palm while the other...

Winds up in her hair.

Petting her head.

Jesus Christ. I have to get out of here.

Briar beats me to it, though. My fingers are still drawing slow circles on her crown when she blinks out of her hazy-eyed stupor. Horror slowly fills her face. Without a word, she suddenly rips my abandoned belt from her neck and bolts to her feet.

I watch her run, tears and spit still streaming from her face.

Which should mean I won.

In theory.

twenty-five

BRIAR

A HARSH WIND RATTLES THE ROSEBUSHES surrounding my balcony.

In the pre-dawn dim, I can barely make out the buds. Most of them are still green, but a few early bloomers shudder in the cold autumn breeze. A handful of white petals fall to the stone floor.

I turn away, grumbling obscenities as I pound a fist into my pillow. It's no use, though. I've been trying to sleep for more than four hours.

The slick heat between my legs refuses to ebb. And *I* refuse to touch myself while thinking about Rhys Fucking Blackwood.

Absolutely not, I say for the millionth time, cutting off my Omega's beseeching whine. *We hate him.*

Even if his cum tasted like an herbaceous version of literal *heaven*.

Well, what little of it he deigned to give me, anyway. Instead of coming in my mouth, he chose to paint my front.

I washed him off with a cold shower. Somehow, that only seemed to highlight just how hot and ready my pussy was. And no amount of deep breathing, self-scolding, or mindless reading has helped.

It isn't just the arousal. A staccato buzz beats in my veins, fighting its way to the surface of my skin.

The sensation started when Rhys wound his long fingers into my hair. Or, if I'm honest, the night before—the moment Dane grabbed my chin and turned my face for a scent-mark.

I'm not stupid. I know touch starvation is basically a given, at this point... I just refuse to admit it.

My Omega, on the other hand...

We could always—

She doesn't get a chance to finish the thought before I shove upright, fumbling for the robe on the nightstand.

Screw this.

If I stay in bed any longer, I'll give in. And I won't be able to live with myself if I get off to thoughts of a man who choked me out with a belt and his dick simultaneously.

Dear God, why does *that* memory make me perfume *every time*?

I'm losing my mind, I decide, stomping to the suite's double doors. *There's no other possible explanation.*

Honestly, in my current state of emotional exhaustion, a little mental breakdown sounds a lot like a vacation.

But I suppose it's worth at least *trying* a snack and a glass of water first.

"Going somewhere?"

I jump a foot in the air, gasping so hard it makes me dizzy. A shadow near the hallway's curve melts off the wall. Forming a shape I'm all too familiar with.

My husband steps into the faint glow of a nearby sconce. Unlike Rhys, he hasn't undressed at all. His pinstriped suit and stark white tie are every bit as pristine as they looked yesterday.

Not that I noticed.

Cillian's stance remains casual as he slides a hand into his pocket. But his bright-blue eyes *glitter*. So stupidly handsome, I feel a fresh burst of slick slip from my core.

"Y-you're up early," I stammer.

His lips curve ruefully. "Never went to bed, I'm afraid."

I remember Fiona saying they often work late and sleep in. For some reason, my chest gives a strained pinch. "You shouldn't stay up this late," I scold, my hands finding my hips. "It isn't healthy."

For the first time since he lifted my veil at the altar, my husband actually smiles. It's brief, and somewhat reluctant, but the sincerity of it scrapes my very soul.

He shrugs as if he didn't just dazzle me within an inch of my life. "Guess I need better motivation to come to bed, *wife*."

This time, my core clamps so violently, I swear he must be able to *hear* the wet squelch of my pussy. Especially when the genuine delight falls off his face, leaving unreadable intensity in its wake.

His gaze flickers to my center, then slowly climbs back up my torso. It pauses on my hand. "I've noticed you don't wear your ring," he murmurs, icy eyes snapping back to mine. "Do you not like it?"

It's as genuine a question as any I've ever heard him utter. So much so, the odd pinch in my chest blooms into a full-blown ache.

I hate it. And I hate *him* for causing it. Almost as much as I hate that I *do* like the stupid ring he picked out. Enough that I hid it from myself the moment I got here and very purposefully tried to forget about it.

I scoff, still a bit too breathless to sound blasé. "*Like* it? The ring I received when I was *forced* to marry you? You're fucking kidding me, right?"

It isn't a *lie*. He, of all people, can appreciate omitting the truth when it suits you.

Still, I find myself inexplicably leaning forward when he opens his mouth to reply. Physically hanging off his every word—or, in this case, simply the *possibility* of hearing his thoughts.

But a different sound interrupts.

The haunting strains of a lone violin.

Cillian turns to stone, listening. After one melancholy movement tumbles into another, the pack alpha's head snaps back, bright eyes flying to the ceiling.

Because the music we hear is definitely coming from the forlorn music room I discovered upstairs.

And it's *beautiful*.

Cillian listens for a long time. Whole minutes. When he finally turns back to me, his expression has a new emotion woven through its impassivity. His voice rasps, betraying an undercurrent of urgency. "You saw Rhys tonight? He came to you?"

Oh shit.

Is that *Rhys*? And does Cillian think *I* have something to do with this?

Wait.

Do I have something to do with it?

Damn. Did I break venom already??

When I manage a lightheaded nod, Cillian's jaw clenches. The first song ends, the notes climbing to a frantic crescendo before Rhys launches straight into a new melody. My husband glances up again, true bewilderment crossing his features.

"He hasn't played the violin in *years*."

I'm not sure if I'm even supposed to hear the words, but they shock me. I've always loved music—it was one of the few subjects our father allowed us to study and, after Violet was taken, the one way I felt connected to her. Not to mention my time in the ballet.

So I feel fairly confident when I whisper, "He's incredibly talented."

Cillian's shoulders drop slightly. "Yes," he answers, equally quiet. "He must be—" The alpha cuts himself off, shaking his head.

"It's very late," he notes, almost as if chastising himself. "Now isn't the time for discussions. Besides, you and I will have plenty of time together tomorrow."

Oh God. He's right.

My husband starts to turn away, but pauses, roaming his gaze over my body more intently. "I'll leave something out for you to wear," he adds, his chest rumbling on a slight growl. "In the meantime, you might want to see if Dane can help you with *that*."

He jerks a final nod and disappears, leaving me alone as a damning drop of slick slides down my thigh.

twenty-six

DANE

I WAKE TO A QUIET HUM.

Before the sound finishes registering, I have my gun in my hand, pulling it from the back of the mattress and flipping off the safety.

My eyes fly open. I instantly toggle the switch back to safety mode and drop the weapon to my lap.

Briar.

The little omega is burrowed under my worn gray duvet, drooling on my pillow. Wearing one of my undershirts?!

What—How the hell did she sneak past me? And why is she here?

The soft morning light filling her pretty features reminds me that my own are uncovered. *Fuck. Did she see me when she came in?*

I set the gun on my nightstand and rush to slap my mask over my face. I have the first latch done and the second one pinched between my fingers when she mumbles, "I'm going to see you eventually, big man."

Pausing with the last strap halfway fastened, I slide wary eyes in Briar's direction. Praying she isn't already looking.

But she is. Black lashes flutter over brilliant green, the verdant color somehow softer and more luminous in the gentle dawn. A quiet emotion brews behind her gaze, tugging the corners of her lush lips down.

Sadness, I realize.

I thought I was used to reactions like these. Usually from old ladies and the occasional doctor. They notice the edges of my scars and give me plaintive looks that quickly curdle into pity.

I brace, waiting for her features to crease into an inevitable wince. But, instead, she nips the swollen curve of her lower lip and slowly extends one of her hands.

It lands on my chest—the spot over my sternum where the burns on my right smooth into the unmarked flesh on my left. Delicate fingers trace the jagged line, stroking carefully.

Tingling prickles break over my skin, spreading faster than goosebumps. Sinking deep in an unfamiliar way. They wrap around my heart and *squeeze* until the charred, black organ flips. My pulse stutters and speeds.

I stare at Briar's hand, half-bemused and wholly uncertain.

What is she doing?

Why does it feel like this?

And why is my Alpha *moaning* like she just pounded herself onto my knot?

Briar must read some of the wariness in my eyes. Her sorrowful expression quirks into a grieved smile. "You too, huh?"

I still don't know what she means. Does she feel this, too?

Whatever it is, I know it feels *good*.

Better than good. *Necessary*. Like a deep drag of oxygen after drowning half to death. Or a glass of cool water sliding down a raw, scream-torn throat.

Like the answer to a problem I didn't know I had.

Briar knows, though. She comes closer, slowly rising onto her knees, shuffling toward me. With a stunned blink, I realize—*Jesus*—she has *my* knife strapped to her thigh.

Cunning little girl *stole* it.

And she's wearing one of my T-shirts. The thin white cotton doesn't do much for her pale skin, but it clearly shows the outlines of her puckered nipples as her small breasts bounce.

The temptation to reach out and palm them is almost too much to bear, given I stroked off three times last night to the thought of feeling her body again. My fingers fist in the covers.

When she reaches my side, Briar blows out a trembling sigh. I freeze, waiting. Wanting. Breathing around the shape of something dangerously close to *hope*.

She places both palms on my bare torso, sliding them down to the tense ridges of my abs. Then back up to my mottled, half-melted pecs.

Fuck.

Sensation sweeps through my bones. The simplest kind of pleasure floods my veins. Every synapse snaps. My cock instantly jerks in my sweats. I groan before I can help myself, my head lolling back.

Craning my neck, I pant as I glare over my heaving chest. Silently accusing the little omega of witchcraft.

She smirks, her fine features utterly luminous. "There's nothing wrong with you, big man. You're probably just touch-starved."

Those words swirl through my muddled mind. Before I can process them, Briar moves again, swinging her leg over my torso and settling her weight right above my navel.

Hell and damnation.

Warmth bursts inside my body. A wave of euphoria swamps my stomach, tingles frothing into my lungs. Another deep, serrated sound snags in my lungs. I try to clamp down on it, but that only turns the hoarse groan into a purr.

Briar's pupils bloom. Her hands grow bolder, razing a heated path from the bottom of my ribcage to my shoulders.

Christ. The sun is coming up—she can see *everything.* All the discoloration and rippled scars lost to the darkness of her barely lit bedroom. Now on full display.

Her wide eyes rove over the marks. My stomach seethes.

But her expression only softens. "Here," she murmurs. "Let me try something."

Muscles coil as she begins sliding her hands toward my face. For a second, I worry she'll try to unclasp the mask. Instead, she sinks her fingers into the hair at my nape, rubbing slow circles.

Good God.

It feels incredible. My teeth grit. Warm wetness seeps from the throbbing head of my dick as my eyelids grow heavy. The tendons in my neck bulge and she adds pressure, letting her long nails scratch gently.

Fucking—

My hips buck. I force them back down, hating myself for how powerful this is. How much I need it.

Briar must feel the frustration in my body, because she hums again. "It's okay," she soothes. "I won't stop."

Why the hell is she so damn sweet to me? Choosing me to be her first, seeing how fucked up I am and calling me *strong.* Coming in here, last night. Putting on my shirt and curling up at my side like I'm not a literal *monster* with *blood* smeared all over my soul...

I can tell she doesn't have any answers, either. Confusion creases the space between her brows while she continues her ministrations, massaging the tension at the back of my neck.

I drag in deep breaths, focusing on her face. Remembering her sad smirk and muttered lament. *You too, huh?*

Did she mean she's touch-starved, also?

It would make sense. Touch starvation is supposed to be an omega thing; a way for their bodies to tell their alphas they need more affection and attention.

Until today, I didn't even know this could happen to an alpha. She did, though.

I'm not surprised. So far, the one constant with Briar is how consistently she blows my expectations.

My knuckles are numb from the desperate way I've been clutching my sheets. I uncurl them, slowly flexing my fingers before settling them on her hips. Briar's lips part, pure bliss flitting over her face.

God. So fucking *gorgeous*.

Too elegant to be a ray of sun; too bright to be a candle's flicker. Briar is all midnight light and magic. Soft and lovely. Warm, but mysterious. A constellation, or—

A moonbeam, I think, watching her milky skin glow.

My fingers press with more intent, sliding under her stolen shirt. By the time I reach the warm curve of her waist, slick has seeped into her panties.

I resist the urge to slip past the waistband or cup her breasts. Taking her example, I focus on kneading her lower back, feeling the way her body loosens when my purr grows louder. She whimpers, grinding her soaked center over my abs.

Hell, I know the feeling. Rueful amusement kicks my covered mouth into a half-smile. I redouble my efforts, snaking one hand up to her nape. Palming her blank throat. Caressing down to the place where my oversized shirt shows the valley between her breasts.

I press there, wondering if the firm pressure will feel as good for her as her weight on my middle. Briar moans until the sound breaks into a true omega whine.

My Alpha snaps to the surface, yanking my body's reins from my grasp. My purr roars. Before Briar can finish her stunned blink, I have the stolen switchblade in my hand. Slicing the front of my shirt down the middle.

Closer, my Alpha demands. Drooling. *All of her.*

I barely have a choice—but even if I did, I think I would still decide to roll us onto our sides and pull Briar's body flush with mine. Her naked chest molds tightly to my pecs. One of my arms hooks around her while the other guides her knee over my hip.

Once she's situated against me, I tuck her weapon back into her garter. Briar notes the exasperated amusement in my eyes as I finger the blade's pearly hilt.

She gives a breathless, genuine laugh. "You could warn a girl before you pull her own knife on her, you know."

She really *is* funny. Something about her sharp intelligence and dry wit makes me want to laugh—and this time, I let myself.

The raspy chuckle rumbles under my purr. Briar's green gaze warms as she traces the visible parts of my face. Her brow kinks.

"Dane," she whispers. "If you won't take off this mask... how am I ever supposed to kiss you?"

It's a real question. She holds my eyes as she asks, waiting with the sort of patience that implies true empathy.

As she stares, I realize I haven't spoken yet this morning. Not one word. And she's still shown me more kindness than anyone else ever has.

With a sigh, I reach for the strap holding my mask in place. "Close your eyes, moonbeam."

twenty-seven

BRIAR

My lashes float down, following my masked alpha's command.

Or *request*, really.

Because the burning entreaty in his gold gaze was far too desperate to signal demand. And he called me *moonbeam*. Which is somehow the cutest and most devastatingly romantic thing I've ever heard.

Dane waits, his burned, built body so still. When I've shut my eyes, his purr deepens. Vibrating against my peaked breasts, stimulating the stiff nipples that graze his chest.

My breath catches. His rough palm cups my cheek, a warm

touch tracing the curve of my lower lip before I feel him shift, looming closer.

Curiosity gets the best of me. I manage to keep my eyes closed, but my fingers float up to his uncovered jaw, feeling the hard angle. Caressing the short facial hair there.

Dane stills. For a moment, I worry I've crossed a line. But then his cock twitches against the inside of my thigh and he rests his forehead on mine.

The big alpha's scent-mark is slow and deliberate, this time. Unmistakable.

My throat tightens, bittersweet soaking my soul. I want to open my eyes and look at him. I want to shove him away and run from whatever this blossoming connection is. I want to dive into it and let it swallow me.

God, *why*?

How?

A second later, it doesn't matter.

Dane's mouth grazes mine. A slow brush, at first, but then he settles. Pressing firmly. Letting me feel the prickle of his short beard, the soft, dry warmth of his lips. Giving me time to adjust and *learn*. Just like he did when we had sex.

His fingers tense, pulling me closer. When I gasp, his tongue glides against mine. The slow, slick sensation lights my body up. Nerves sing in my stomach, flutters curling into my squelching core and stretching to my pebbled nipples.

Dane gives a masculine hum over his purr. His approval heats my blood as he delves his tongue deeper, rubbing our lips together in ways that feel illegal. My Omega whines, and I let the sound spill into the alpha's mouth.

That earns me another rasped groan. Dane's free hand palms my ass, petting the seam between my thighs. More wetness gathers there, and he snarls, abruptly breaking our kiss.

I keep my eyes shut, but it's a struggle. Panting, he curses, dropping his forehead to mine with more force. Hot, desperate breaths feather my lips.

"Just do it," he finally croaks, quietly desolate. "I keep hoping the thought of you seeing my face will get easier. But the more we —it keeps getting *worse*. So look now. *Run now*. While I can still keep myself from chasing you."

My heart twists, sending a scratchy lump to my throat. "Dane—"

I feel him shake his head. "No. Please. Just... fucking look. See what a goddamn mess I am so we can go back to whatever the fuck we were before we—"

Had sex? Slept next to each other? Tried to heal the cracks our touch starvation had carved into us?

God, we really have done all of that, haven't we? Me and this big man. This beast.

Dane might not be beautiful, but he isn't a monster like the others, either. Is it really possible that his face will scare me so much I forget that?

He wants to find out. And I suppose he's right—we need to know now. Before this ache where my heart should be gets any harder to ignore.

Holding my breath, I set my palm on top of his calloused hand. His fingers flex against my scalp when I clutch on to him, needing an anchor. Without another word, I open my eyes.

His face blurs and I blink. When it comes into focus, I feel my empty lungs shudder.

He wasn't exaggerating. The right side of his face does look completely different.

If his left side is a strong, masculine monument, then the right is a ruin. Craggy and uneven. Pocked and scorched.

A large scar curls up toward his gold eye, stretching along his jaw in a solid, dark-pink arc. The slice of cheekbone above his dark beard is mottled, the skin patchy, outlined by an uneven, raised ripple.

His facial hair is clearly intended to cover the worst of the damage. It papers over a lot of it, I'm sure, but I still see the permanent splotches. Swirls and lines. Patches where they tried to stitch melted flesh back in place or cover it altogether.

Oxygen spins into my chest as I blink a second time, working to absorb his entire face as one. It takes a moment. Like gazing up at a half-moon and retraining your brain to see the side wreathed in shadows as part of the whole.

But I do. And I like it.

He looks tough as hell. And under his scarred skin, his features are still *strong*. Ruggedly handsome, with a wide, even bone structure.

The sheer *size* of his bulging jaw and straight nose lend an undeniably attractive air of manliness. I lift my hand from his, carefully resting it on his cheek.

Dane's body convulses. He exhales hard, a hunted look leaking into his warm irises even as his cock kicks between us.

I back off right away, quickly removing my palm. But he grunts, low and sharp. "No." I watch his perfectly etched lips form words for the first time. Those bottomless gold-brown eyes spear mine. Burning. "I want it to be you."

I want it to be you.

My soul cracks open, pain and promises pouring from the darkest parts of me. I drop my chin as my eyes water, but nod, skimming my fingers along his scars as I repeat the two simple words he uttered when I had the same request.

"Come here."

Dane shudders when I press our lips together, purposefully sinking my gaze into his. He releases a harsh breath, disbelief blooming around his pupils when I trail a kiss up to his scarred cheek... and scent-mark him there.

I don't know what I'm doing and I'm sure it shows. But Dane's hands clasp me tighter than ever, as if he's suddenly afraid I'll float away. Or dissolve like a mirage.

Still staring steadily, I hunt for words. "If my opinion counts for anything... I like your face better like this." I add a smirk, hoping to ease the deep grooves bracketing his mouth. "Although the mask is fun in a kinky way."

My little flirt does the trick. Pure shock replaces the pain on his features. I watch them ripple, mesmerized by how much I can see now that he's here with me, unmasked, in the daylight.

"Are—" He shakes his head, visibly forcing a stern scowl. "Briar, you don't have to—"

Quick as a flash, I tackle him onto his back. I only manage it because he's so distracted, but a surge of victory still thrums through my middle when I land on his center, straddling his bulky body.

His loose, overlong hair tickles my wrists as I plant my hands on either side of his head and bend low, putting us face-to-face. "I know I don't *have* to," I whisper. "I don't have to do *anything* I don't want to, remember? That was the deal?"

Unmistakable lust flares in his richly colored eyes. "Yeah," he rasps. "It was."

"Alright, then." I try to sound tough, but my bones liquefy when he restarts his rusty purr. The vibration of it presses into my soaked panties, stimulating my slick core. When I wobble, he makes a soft noise and clasps one hand at my waist, holding me steady. The other guides my forehead down to rest on his.

I nose at his cheek and he catches my gaze, understanding saturating his. Without saying a word, he clamps his massive hand around my hip and guides my body down. I hear the snap of his waistband before his hot, hard length slaps my backside.

This time is quicker and dirtier. Dane doesn't even let me take my panties off—he just thumbs them aside and impales me.

All my carnal need from last night floods in, tingles swarming the space between my hips as my pussy melts around his girth. It barely stings at all—a pleasant sort of soreness that dissipates by the third plunge. Within seconds, I'm riding him with a ferocity that might be embarrassing... if the big man weren't staring up at me like some favored goddess.

"Is it good?" he rumbles. "Do you hurt?"

"It's—" I break off on a moan. *"Dane, harder! Please!"*

My internal muscles squelch at the lust burning in his eyes. His lips fall slack, and I can't resist bending over him for a slow, licking kiss.

"Briar," he gasps into my mouth, bucking underneath me. "Fuck, little girl. You make me want to wreck this sweet pussy."

I'm about to dare him to do it, but thick fingers find my aching clit, rubbing it in fast flutters that send me sailing into a climax before I can stop myself. Dane groans, his head tipping back while he savors the feel of my body clutching his shaft. The second I finish, he lifts me and comes right between my thighs, painting me with his release.

We both pant for breath as I collapse on top of him. His calloused hands start out rough, clutching me close, but soon smooth into comforting strokes up my back. Without a word, he removes the torn shirt I'm wearing like a vest and cleans between my spread legs, purring for me.

My eyelids start to feel heavy, but a different kind of rumble suddenly joins the one shaking his lungs. I chuckle before I can help myself. "Hey, big man? What's your favorite breakfast?"

Dane shifts under me. I know he's still hard, but the rest of him feels looser, somehow. The thick bar of his muscled arm melts along my spine as he brushes my hair over my shoulder.

"Breakfast?" he mutters, distracted by the slight indentation he clocks at the base of my throat. Evidence of Rhys's belt.

God, what is my life?

I distract myself by sitting up, grinning wider when I note the confusion on my big man's face. "Your stomach is growling almost as loud as your purr."

Dane gives one of his quiet smirks, snatching my hand and skimming his nose at the side of my wrist. Nuzzling me? Or trying to get a deeper read of my scent?

"I don't know," he replies, and for a second I worry he's read my mind. Then he says, "A breakfast sandwich, I guess. Extra cheese."

I thump on his solid, ink-covered shoulder to punctuate my point. "I would have guessed a dozen raw eggs."

Dane gazes up at me. I know I have carnal appreciation all over my face. He skims his eyes over my exposed breasts, their visibly aroused nipples. The wet spot at the front of my panties. And, I swear, the big man *blushes*.

"What about you?" he asks, all gruff and adorable. "You should eat something."

I should also probably find another shirt. And my own room.

Instead I fall onto the mattress beside him with a sigh. I don't tell him I'd been reduced to eating toast for most of my meals by the time Cillian swooped in, avoiding my father's dubious "health shakes." The food in this house has been a revelation—hot meals, full of different textures and flavors.

Dane watches me fidget with his sheets, biting the corner of my lip. He moves with his usual silent grace, his reach barely detectable until a phone appears in his hand.

It rings through the speaker, and Coggins picks up, sounding positively *startled*. "Mr. *Dane*?"

I slap a palm over my snort. Clearly, the butler has never received a phone call from this alpha in his life.

"Yeah," Dane grumbles, his exposed cheeks darkening. "I need breakfast in my room. French toast, eggs Benedict, Belgian waffles, chocolate chip pancakes, and two of those breakfast sandwiches Mrs. Porter makes me. Tea and coffee, too. Uh. Please."

Oh God. Oh *no*.

Is Dane... *cute?*

"Absolutely, sir. Right away!" their butler crows, genuinely delighted.

Dane catches me covering a grin with the edge of his duvet and rolls his eyes. But now that he's removed his mask, I see the way his lips quirk as he adds, "Bring two forks."

twenty-eight

RHYS

IN THE END, I HAVE TO KNOW.

The ancient clock in the hallway ticks in time with my foot-steps. I pace them that way on purpose, hoping to sneak up on the unsuspecting omega. Loving the idea of scaring her almost as much as I love the thought of seeing her face again.

Goddamn it.

God *fucking damn it.*

What is happening to me?

I hadn't picked up a bow in nearly a decade... and last night it was all I could do to hold on while years of pent-up emotion poured out of me, into the instrument I used to love.

But it didn't hurt.

It. Didn't. Hurt.

So I kept going. Playing harder, faster. Then softer, and with more intent. Until night bled into morning and the bright light burnished gold for afternoon.

Now it's nearly evening.

And I *have* to know.

Was it her? Did this random omega unlock the pieces of myself I'd hidden away? Or was it just having some form of sex after so long without it?

I find the door to her bedroom ajar. An ominous blend of rage and interest rolls through me, along with a very specific type of certainty.

Almost... *instinct.*

The library.

It feels empty, when I stride in. And, of course, I can't pick up her scent. That simple, bitter truth puts a snarl in my voice. "*Viper!* Who the fuck said you could be in *my* library?"

Instead of a fearful squeak or a whine, I hear rustling pages and a sigh. The noises draw me across the round, second-story landing. Over to the travel section of my stores.

Sure enough, there's the little viper. In her usual black—fishnets and shorts, today—coiled around a pile of books about Europe. Sharp green eyes snap up to mine, some blend of irritation and wariness.

"Can I *help* you?" she demands.

The sight of her is enough to make my blood roar. And *I hate it.* I hate *her.*

Am I insane? There's no way this bitch is the reason I've suddenly been able to play again. It has to be something else.

Baring my teeth, I growl, "Yeah. Get the fuck out."

Briar trembles slightly, but plays it off as a twirl of the dark, loose braid hanging over her shoulder. "No can do." She shrugs, turning back to the borrowed book in her lap. "Some talentless lunatic won't stop murdering violins on that side of the house."

I ignore the bolt of amusement that sticks in my throat, willfully focusing on the outrage bubbling under my lungs. "Fuck you," I spit.

Briar exhales, casting me another exasperated glower. "Well you *could have*, venom, but you never showed up."

Christ, am I holding a *laugh* in my lungs? I truly am losing my shit.

Tracing her unbothered expression, noting all of the delicate features that form her unholy beauty... A dark realization hits. "You're really not afraid of me, huh?"

Briar snorts, flipping another page. "Please, venom." Her slicing stare stabs mine. "There are way worse things to be afraid of than *you*."

The words—so calm and matter-of-fact—are clearly born of experience. My rage cools a bit as my mind spins, trying to imagine what would put such a somber, unimpressed look on her face.

I hate it almost as much as I loathe her. So I lift my foot and tap the toe of my loafer against her porcelain cheek.

Green flames burn in her eyes as she jerks back. "Didn't your mother teach you *manners*, cretin?"

A black mood rolls over whatever humor I felt. "She couldn't, really, considering she *left me here*," I snap in reply. "Coggins was basically my mother after that."

I'm not sure why I expect sympathy, but I don't get any. Instead, Briar huffs. "Well, my mom was a test tube. So."

God, does she have to be so *funny*? This time, a rusty laugh creaks in my throat before I can stop it. "Okay, viper. You win."

Her eyes swing up to my face, slowly absorbing my reluctant amusement. "Can I ask you something?"

I almost snort. "Sure, what the hell?"

A spark of bemusement touches her pretty gaze. She tilts her head. "Do you hate me specifically? Or are you always this charming?"

twenty-nine

BRIAR

RHYS TRIES TO FIGHT A GRIMACE AND FAILS.

Even cringing, he's absolutely beautiful up close. Amber light highlights his carved cheekbones, underlining them in shadow. Slashing brows crouch low over his bottomless sea-glass eyes.

And he has *slutty little reading glasses* tucked into the front V of his shirt.

I am so fucked.

Even more so when his striking features arrange themselves into a look of genuine introspection.

"I *used* to be charming," he mutters without sarcasm. "I took

159

tons of meetings for Blackwood Corp. Ran our legal teams. Had friends in the arts. Went to every opera and symphony."

Memories seem to flicker across his face. Pictures from another life. "But that fucking fire," he growls. "Whoever lit it knocked me out first. Dane found me, carried me to safety. You've seen what that cost him. He saved my life, but when I woke up, I still had insane smoke inhalation. It ruined my sense of smell and part of one lung. They fixed that, but I still can't—"

Understanding snaps inside me. "You can't smell anything. Not even omegas."

He releases a deep breath. "No. I can't."

I ponder that for a moment, leaning my head against the nearest shelf while I peer up at him. Whatever made him loathe me so much from the beginning isn't just about my scent. He can't smell Fiona, either—and from what I've seen, he essentially acts like she doesn't exist. No antagonism or boiling rage.

"What else?" I whisper.

Rhys cuts me an annoyed glare. "Well, you're too damn smart, for one," he gripes. "But..."

The blond alpha flings his focus to the heavens, blowing out a long sigh. "Cillian *married* you. Bound you to our pack. And you're not—"

His laugh is humorless, but not cruel. Just... hollow. "I always had this dumb idea that I would—I wanted a scent-match, okay? A *mate*," he spits.

My lungs freeze, my lips falling open. *Of all the things for us to have in common.*

Then again, I seem to share more similarities with this alpha than I'd ever want to admit. Surface things, like books and music. And the stuff other people can't see—pride, dark humor, bitter memories.

Before I reply, Rhys blazes on, his eyes shifting with slightly defensive fervor. "It was all Cillian's dad's stupid fault," he grumbles. "Caine married my mom, but it was a marriage of convenience for both of them. She had inherited her parents' tech company and didn't want to run it. Cillian's grandfather wanted to absorb it, so he had his son marry my mother. And implied there would be severe consequences if he didn't."

I listen, trying to picture what these people looked like. I imagined Caine as a more distinguished version of Cillian. And Rhys's mother surely would have been a great beauty, fair-haired and fine-boned.

"They were never happy," Rhys snorts. "But Caine was always good to me. Better than my real dad ever was."

I hear the undertones and subconsciously wince. Rhys flips me a devastatingly handsome half-smile. "He was a cold bastard. I guess that probably doesn't surprise *you*, given the way I am."

I do everything I can to seem unaffected, shrugging loosely. "You *do* suck."

Rhys chuckles, more handsome by the second. "Yeah, yeah, viper. We both know you love a good fight."

"And you don't?" I accuse.

Rhys makes a rough sound. "Another thing I come by honestly. After my mom left my dad, he wound up in and out of jail. He was still there, last time I checked."

It's a sad story, especially since… "Your mom didn't love Caine?"

The alpha's gorgeous face twists into a bitter smile. "Oh, she did. But Caine was already spoken for. Madly in love with his *mate*."

"Cillian's mom," I recall, picturing the scene. "Oh."

"Yeah." The corners of his mouth kick higher, but his eyes darken wistfully. "Oh."

Dane told me that Cillian and Rhys grew up here. Did that also mean… "Wait, if he had you here… and Cillian… did he also have both of *your mothers* here? At the *same time*?"

Rhys's gaze swirls, cool eddies of chaos and anguish. "They each refused to leave. Eventually, Cillian's uncle realized Caine was being groomed to take over the whole company. He waited for an opportunity to get Cillian's mom alone... and he killed her."

My head spins. Pain pierces deep, anchoring itself in my middle. "Cillian's mom was *murdered*? By his *uncle*?"

Rhys nods, the motion absent. "Yes," he says, toneless. "It was a brilliant way to eliminate Caine, actually. Poor bastard offed himself like two weeks later."

Holy fuck.

Cillian.

He watched his father mourn his mate so severely, he couldn't stand to *live* without her. No wonder he married me—he probably didn't want anything to do with a mate.

For all the same reasons Rhys *did*.

He had to witness his mother long for an alpha who could never love her. Because his soul belonged to someone else. I'm sure any young alpha would be determined to save his heart for the right person after *that*.

Even someone with a battered, blackened one like Rhys.

"What did your mom do?"

Vicious bitterness stains his angelic features. "She left, like I said. Packed her shit and shipped out. I was nine."

Shit. I never really had a parent, but somehow, this sounds worse. Because, at some point, Rhys knew what it was like to have love and stability... and then he learned what it felt like to lose it. Or find out it wasn't real in the first place.

No wonder he's so venomous.

Wounded creatures are always the most deadly.

Rhys clocks the wavering pity in my eyes. His smirk hardens into a sneer. "Awww, viper, don't get soft on me now."

His nickname used to infuriate me, but this time it pinches my stomach. Almost as if hearing him jeer it at me... *hurts*?

I draw my knees up to my chest, glaring as I fold them over the ache at my center. The blond alpha watches with those too-intelligent eyes. One corner of his mouth droops slightly.

A gasp sticks in my throat as he suddenly drops into a fluid crouch. Silver-pale hair falls over his forehead as he snaps his arm to the side, finding a thick book with a leather cover and plucking it from the shelf. When he drops it onto my pile, I blink in pure astonishment.

Is he—

Did he just—*recommend a book*? For me?

"Only this once," he claims, standing and scowling. Fidgeting with the sleeves of his dress shirt before he starts rolling them up. "Don't get used to it."

I watch as he creases the fabric over his lean, veiny forearms. Revealing one that's as flawless as his marble face and the other, which—

—has a tattoo.

Black, like the simple ink letters carved into his chest, but this one depicts an image rather than a phrase.

Onyx scales. Slithering up his forearm and bicep.

I reach out and touch it before I can stop myself, sure I must be hallucinating. Warm skin slides under my fingertips. The tattoo doesn't shimmer or ripple, proving it's not a hallucination.

It's really there. Slightly faded black ink; which means he's had it the whole time I've known him.

Rhys doesn't jerk his arm away, even when I whip an accusatory gape in his direction. His crooked, taunting grin should be illegal. "What?"

"Your tattoo," I snap. "It's a—"

His eyes practically glow, but his shrug is casual. "I called you viper," Rhys starts as he steps back, turning to walk away. "I never said I didn't like snakes."

thirty

BRIAR

"Of all the kinky, fucked-up bullshit—"

My muttering goes undetected as I stomp down the front staircase. Wisps of sheer tulle swish around my hips, flouncing with each step. I glare at the dove-gray leotard. Fresh rage rolls over my dismay.

Rhys would love me right now, I think dryly.

My Omega gives a forlorn sigh. She's still bummed the venomous alpha didn't appear at the dinner table two hours ago.

None of them did. Even after Dane and I spent half the morning lying around, stuffing our faces.

While we ate, I carefully plucked details out of him. How he came to be part of this pack. The way he grew up in a home for children and never had any other family. What it felt like to lurk in shadows behind the notorious Blackwoods.

I thought, after hearing all of that, that maybe we might be... bonding. Or something. But then he explained he had "work" to do tonight and refused to tell me what that entailed. It definitely changed the mood between us, though, and he left soon after, pointedly strapping his mask back into place.

His departure was a chilling reminder—I don't really know these men or what they do. And I may never be able to trust any of them.

Not even my big man.

My Omega whines at that, but I shush her. She only whimpers louder, flashing a sulky image from dinner.

Okay, so, fine. Eating alone at that big table was slightly humiliating. I knew Cillian and Dane wouldn't be there; I'm not sure why I expected Rhys to show up.

Of course he took the opportunity to humiliate me. *Nothing* between us changed last night or this afternoon, aside from me proving I could handle his depraved, delicious brand of domination. And make our deal "worth his while."

The prick.

He can absolutely *never* find out how much I like that book he recommended...

Cillian's car pulled up thirty minutes after I abandoned my lonely meal. He must have had Coggins place this outfit on my bed while I was pushing peas around my priceless plate.

Of course he also had the butler leave out my wedding ring.

And a note.

Eight p.m., the slashing scrawl read. *Meet me in the ballroom, Mrs. Blackwood.*

I debated chucking the entire thing into my fireplace. Five-carat diamond, new tutu, and all.

But Rhys's hauntingly lovely violin had finally stopped. And the sudden silence that pressed all around me was worse than any other sort of torture.

Knock twice if you're okay, Rosie.

I couldn't stomach sitting in my room *one minute longer*. Eight hours of wondering where Dane was and if Rhys's music had anything to do with me—starting last night, stopping after this evening—was *enough*. I *refused* to sit around waiting for either to come back.

So here I am.

Dressed like the prima ballerina I used to want to be.

Wearing the world's most beautiful, *hateful* ring.

Walking into the belly of the beasts.

Well. One of them, anyway.

Fiona hovers at the base of the grand foyer staircase. Her feather duster pauses when she notes my attire, a startled sound of bemusement greeting me.

I can't even blame her. I look ridiculous.

Crossing my arms over my chest, I glower. "Where is he?"

She titters again, pointing to the archway on my left. I march through it, eating up the rounded hallway to get to the light at the end.

I stop short, arrested on the threshold. My anger dissipates.

Oh my...

I've never seen such a beautiful room. Every shade of opulence, with gilded edges of silver and gold. The mixed metals cover the walls, shimmering foil wallpaper patinated to resemble the mercury glass laid into the dozens of arches carved along curving walls.

Flawless black marble shines underfoot, shot with streaks of gold and silver-white. The enormous dome above it matches the one in the library—rose, amethyst, and dark, smoky blue.

But none of those things are the reason I can't breathe.

No.

That would be the hundreds of candles flickering on the floor.

And the shirtless man standing in the middle of it.

I DON'T RECOGNIZE CILLIAN AT FIRST.

For one, he's backlit by what feels like a thousand individual flickers. And secondly, he's half-naked. Standing loosely, holding a glass of amber liquor by the tips of his fingers... *wearing sweatpants?*

Correction: absolutely *ruining* sweatpants for all other men.

Soft charcoal fabric hangs on his hips, showing off the chiseled lines carved into his pelvis. Tight rows of abdominal muscles ripple in the low light. A line of dark hair trails from his navel to the low-slung waistband, balancing the small smattering between his impressive pecs.

Truly, there isn't one damn thing wrong with him. His body is perfectly proportioned. Elegant and strong. Cut like a precious stone, polished to shine. Molded into the sort of masculine beauty that makes a masterpiece.

And he's *wearing sweatpants.*

Okay, I coach internally. *We can handle this. We do <u>not</u> find our husband attractive. That <u>cannot</u> happen. So...*

My Omega blinks owlishly, waiting for me to develop some grand plan. But, really, *is* there any defense against the way those loose cotton pants cling to the outline of Cillian's semi-hard cock?

I don't think so.

I try anyway, letting my focus roam over his face. Searching for things to dislike.

Unlike Rhys's sharp angelic beauty or Dane's rugged looks, Cillian has the sort of features that are easy to forget. Solid and square. Almost *too* handsome, I decide—he gives the impression he could have stepped off any billboard. Out of any rom-com.

He doesn't have Rhys's shock of white-blond hair or Dane's scars. I decide not to like that. *I bet it makes it easier for him to be shady, operate under the radar.*

If anyone were ever asked to describe my husband, what would they say? The one who's too handsome for words? An absolutely perfect specimen? The guy with a soul as dark as his hair, his suits, and his spiced scent?

But, shit. I am *screwed*.

Because as I look longer, I *do* notice some flaws. *Charming* ones.

The thin line sliced through the very tip of his left eyebrow. A tiny indentation denting the top of his right cheek. The way his five-o'clock shadow seems thicker on the sides of his jaw than it does on his chin. Sparse threads of silver woven into the glossy black hair at either temple.

Our gazes meet—and I see the one thing that will always set him apart. The wolf living in his icy eyes.

Did I dare say he looked forgettable?

The rest of his face seems impassive, but the blue fire in his irises is a beast all its own. Razing that apathy to ash. Climbing up his gaze in slow, seething licks.

There's power there, but weakness, too. A piece that sees me and sets itself on *fire*.

Why?

Does he hate me that much?

Is all of this just another way to break me? Take the thing I once loved and make a mockery of it? Here? In this beautiful room?

Maybe he chose it on purpose. Something else he gets to ruin for me when he rips this leotard from my body and forces me into whatever compromising position he's conjured up.

I banish the tears that sting the bridge of my nose, stepping over the threshold with my head held high. Repeating the vow I made to myself on our wedding day. *He can have anything he thinks he wants. Because he'll never have me.*

But we're here, my Omega whispers. *He's winning.*

Cillian seems to echo that sentiment. The corner of his

mouth kicks up as he glances down at the outfit he chose. And the ring on my finger.

This bastard.

He's a monster.

A liar.

A thief.

My *husband*.

And hell-bent on making sure I know it.

thirty-one

CILLIAN

I'M NOT SURE I THOUGHT MUCH ABOUT HOW IT WOULD feel to have her here, like this.

I couldn't. Not without risking this carefully constructed house of cards.

But tonight...

I circle Briar slowly, absorbing every fine detail of her form and the fabric hugging it.

This leotard is one of dozens. She doesn't know that yet, though. I've stored them in my closet, along with scores of evening gowns, sexy dresses, and accessories I've chosen or had made for her.

Which reminds me.

I take a slow sip of my drink, letting it unwind some of the tension stretched across my shoulders. My free hand slides into my pocket, fisting the gift I want to present to her.

Though, perhaps not while she's glaring.

There *is* a knife notched into her waistband, after all.

Instead, I lean down and brush my lips along her cheek. "Hello, wife. It's nice to see you."

Briar glowers, lifting her chin to the maddeningly stubborn angle that drives me wild. Her body quivers, but her voice does not.

"Why did you bring me here?"

The truth springs to the tip of my tongue. For a moment, I consider allowing it. What would happen, I wonder, if I admitted this is my favorite room in the manor? Or if I told her about the nights I watched my mother and father twirl around this very floor?

But, no. I've already decided what her story for tonight will be.

And this plan is still in progress.

Keeping my stride loose, I leave her alone at the center of the ballroom, moving to the lone dining chair I carried in here. There's a remote sitting on it. I set my glass beside it and turn back to her, asking, "Do you know where I saw you for the first time?"

God, if I could freeze time, I just might do it at this moment. With Briar standing under the stained-glass dome, surrounded by warm licks of light.

The candles dip and flare, casting their glow onto the gilded walls behind her. And it doesn't matter that she's dressed like a dancer. She looks like a queen.

I knew she would from the first moment.

That's why we're here.

Some of Briar's animosity dissipates as she considers my question. Her lips and brows turn down. "At the church," she replies. "On the altar."

She's wrong, but so stubborn about it that I feel the side of my mouth twitch. I come back to her side, circling until I stand at her back, admiring the elegant arch of her neck as she turns her face.

It takes every ounce of my control not to touch her. Instead, I step into her personal space and lower my voice. "I will remember watching you walk down that aisle until the day I die. But it wasn't the first time I saw you."

Shock stiffens Briar's body. She tries valiantly to hide it, keeping her eyes on the black marble floor.

I loom a little closer, inhaling the rich tartness of black cherries. "I was at the performing arts center," I rumble, memories flying through my mind. "Some luncheon for important donors."

Before the accident, Rhys was very involved in funding for the arts. He never asked me to go that day, but I knew the symphony meant a lot to him, so I attended anyway.

It was deathly dull. Three hours of nauseating self-importance and pseudo-intellectual drivel. I amused myself by imagining how much Rhys would have loved it.

When the interminable meeting finally came to a close, I took the shortest possible path to the parking lot. Which meant walking past the main hall. And the rehearsal inside.

"You were practicing," I recall, her image still crystal clear in my mind. A black leotard with gossamer ribbons of tulle instead of a full tutu. Worn satin pointe shoes. Her thick hair coiled into a tight bun, flawless skin on display. "*Swan Lake*."

This time, she can't help the surprise filling her face. We both know when she did *Swan Lake*.

And it wasn't recent.

The bitter tang of fear leeches into the air. I feel my canines ache, saliva welling as I nod. Intensity swarms my bloodstream, turning my next confession into a dark rumble.

"I watched you."

The smallest gasp trembles from Briar's lips. Her scent changes, the fear sharpening. Melding with something new. Deeper and more delicious.

My wife is a fighter, though. She claws for her dignity, forcing her chin into a haughty angle as she tosses me a narrow-eyed glance. "Is *that* why you bought me? Because you'd seen me dance?"

For a moment, I fall into her swirling green eyes. Wanting nothing more than to give in to the tide. Let myself drown there.

But she asked me a question.

This is dangerous goddamn territory we're treading. I choose my words carefully, pairing them with a slow nod. "And your father's patent."

An acerbic smirk pulls at her pretty lips. "Not sure why you wanted *two* of his failed inventions." She scoffs, quiet but strong. "I hope you didn't pay too much."

I would have paid anything. I didn't have to, because that idiot, Brynn, thought his daughter was an incorrigible brat and believed the story I told him about his new weapon technology being astronomically expensive to reproduce.

They weren't *lies*. The tech is costly—enough to push most other firms out of the market.

But not Blackwood Corp.

And as for Briar?

Well... the same is true.

She *is* an incorrigible brat. But she'll soon learn that *nothing* is too rich for my blood. Including whatever it takes to tame her.

"For you, wife?" I return her barbed smile with one of my own, fingering the single lock of loose hair that's fallen from her stage-worthy bun. I tuck it behind her ear. My mouth curves higher when I feel her answering shiver. "Never."

Briar's eyes darken as she jerks away. The prettiest shade of rose floods her high cheekbones.

So lovely, my little rosebud.

She huffs, smoothing her skirts and casting me another glare.

This one more suspicious than anything else. Like she can't quite believe I'd lain in wait for so long. "*Swan Lake* was nearly *two years ago.*"

As if I haven't counted each individual day.

"Yes. It was," I reply, burning my gaze into hers. Letting my answer and all of its implications sink in before I add, "Do you remember the steps?"

Briar blinks, the motion laggy. Probably from trying to process so much at once.

"Yeah," she murmurs eventually, looking at the floor. "Of course. But I don't have pointe shoes. And I can't do the leaps anymore."

Her injury. I clench my molars, breathing through the rush of pure fury that scorches my center. When the burn is manageable, I nod at the mirrored sideboard beside the entrance.

She turns and sees the shoes there. I know she's sharp enough to notice that they aren't new—that they're *hers*—but she doesn't ask how I got them. Perhaps she doesn't want to know.

Dismay colors her features for a brief moment. I expect more of her attitude but instead her chin trembles. "No," she snaps, watery. "I won't wear those while we—No. You have me here, Cillian, and I agreed to do what you want, but I won't get all dressed up and prance around just so you can fuck me."

I can tell the thought of dancing—her *art*—being used as tawdry foreplay *hurts* her. My gritting teeth grind harder.

Not yet. Not now.

Soon.

"I would never ask you to do that," I reply, my tone brusque enough to straighten her spine. "I won't fuck you until you *want* me to. We agreed on that in our contract. And I won't ever break any vow I make to you."

Her eyes bounce between mine. I see her mind spinning. Likely recalling the promises I offered at the altar.

To honor and cherish.

In sickness, in health. For richer, for poorer. For better and worse.

Until death do us part.

Briar's posture loosens as her brows pinch. Some of the ire drains from her irises, replaced by cautious confusion. "Then... what do you want?"

So many goddamn things.

But *not yet.*

So I simply gaze at her for a long moment, projecting sincerity. "I just want to see you dance again, Briar. That's all."

For tonight.

Our relationship, I'm realizing, is more about the things we *don't* say to one another than the things we do. As if proving my point, some unexplained emotion flares, deep and true, behind my wife's eyes.

But she only nods. "Deal."

It takes enormous willpower to move to my chair. I call on years of practice, stalking to the seat without allowing myself time to linger. With one punch of the remote's main power button, the soft strains of Tchaikovsky's melancholy melody float above us.

Briar stands at the center of the ballroom, listening. For a second, I worry she's changed her mind—but then, slowly, she assumes her first position.

God. She's fucking beautiful. A silhouette of grace, bathed in candlelight.

My wife only pauses to look over her shoulder at me, asking one final question. "The day you first saw me... was that the only time you watched me?"

I swirl my scotch and lounge back in the chair, sprawling with my legs open and my drink in one hand. Forcing my shoulders to stay loose when I shrug. "Of course."

Another untrue fact. It—*all* of this—*was* technically one time.

Because I started watching her that day. And I haven't ever looked away.

thirty-two

BRIAR

A DULL BUZZ SNAPS UNDER MY SKIN AS I SHUFFLE INTO the foyer.

I've always loved this feeling—the weight of physical exhaustion and the mental clarity that somehow accompanies it. My body is tired, but content. The aches in my joints aren't painful so much as reassuring.

I'm still here.

I can still dance the way I used to, for the most part.

And, if Cillian's rapt attention through every twirl and dip is any indication, I haven't lost my touch.

He watched until the candles started to burn themselves out, silently spectating as one song bled into another. And another.

After what felt like hours, I glanced over and found he'd disappeared.

I stood in the center of the grand, gilded ballroom, breathing hard in the rose-tinged moonlight. *What the hell just happened? Why didn't he try to take me?*

And why am I... disappointed?

My fingers rub at the satin slippers he left for me, noting a familiar scuff on the side of the left one. The slight fray to the ribbon on the right. And there, inked on the worn soles. BRB— my old initials.

And new initials, too.

Did he like that? And how the hell did he *get* a pair of my old pointe shoes in the first place? How long has he *had* them?

A frisson runs down my spine, interrupting my brooding. My head snaps up. The mystery of Cillian Blackwood fades to the background as a new puzzle steps out of the shadowed corridor opposite the one I'm lingering in.

Dane.

I notice the mask first. After spending the morning with access to his whole face, the metal and mesh feel like a fence in front of a garden.

It's doubly cruel, I think, because he has his hair tied back. But instead of the strong angle of his jaw, I only see titanium and gold, blazing brightly as he stares across the foyer.

He looks different. Aside from the intensity beaming from his eyes, the rest of him seems... empty. His broad shoulders slump forward as his hands twitch at his sides. I find myself disgruntled when I note that his dark green Henley covers his scarred and inked arms.

Worry worms into my middle. *We should go to him. Make sure he's okay*, my Omega whispers.

I start to, but Dane suddenly *snarls*. "No, Briar."

The command halts me immediately, but I can tell he feels

guilty about it. Especially when his tone softens. "Seriously. Don't."

I blink, trying to understand. He *liked* being touched earlier. And he looks *wrong*. Doesn't he need me to—

The big man shifts on his feet. A shaft of cool moonlight grazes his shirt, revealing several smears on the dark fabric.

My body shakes off his bark immediately, rushing closer. "Dane, is that *blood*? Are you *hurt*?"

The alpha growls, his brawny hand intercepting mine before I can lay a finger on him. He squeezes my wrist, the motion just to the right side of painful. Golden eyes seethe at me in the semi-dark.

"I said *no*," he repeats. Quieter and more deadly. He shoves me back gently, his brows folding. "You need to go, little girl. *And stay the fuck away from me*. Got it?"

The quiet bark is somehow more devastating than any shout could be. It hits my heart like a flaming arrow. A sharp stab, followed by a hot flare of humiliation.

He—he's rejecting us, my Omega sniffles. *But why? What did we do wrong?*

I suppress the urge to recoil, holding my ground. Cataloging every flicker of feeling on his half-covered face. "What happened, Dane? I thought we were—"

Friends?

That word sounds so stupid, even in my head. So I'm not sure why a deep wash of pain floods my chest when his face reflects the same sentiment, creasing into a look of pure disgust.

The masked alpha leans closer, his motions controlled. So careful around me, the way Dane always has been.

But his chest heaves like he's just run a marathon. Our eyes lock and something there softens... before shattering.

"None of us should be your *friends*, little girl," he murmurs. "Least of all me."

I can't stand the fractured feelings all over his face. And only being able to see half of it?

I reach for the leather strap on his mask, unlatching the buckle. Dane breathes harder, the ragged sound audible, now. Mesh and metal fall away, revealing his scars. But I don't notice them. I only see the pain pulling his lips into a grimace.

"I'm not safe for you, Briar," he rasps, the words a whispered confession. "I'm not safe for anyone."

I hear what he's saying—and I believe him. This alpha is enormous. Emotionally damaged. *Wearing someone else's blood.*

But I can't quiet my Omega's chants. Her promises that he *is* safe.

So I put my hand on his cheek. "That's a choice you make, big man. I think you'd be the safest alpha in this house if you decided to be."

His golden eyes bounce between mine, absorbing my words. The woodsy scent rising off his throat swells, its undercurrent damp and dark. "We never should have—" He shakes his head, the tendons in his neck bulging when he grinds his jaw. "We never should have done this. I'm so fucking sorry I let them take you."

I don't know if he's referring to Cillian and his grandfather purchasing me in the first place, or letting his packmates have their respective nights with me. Either way, I find myself shaking my head right back at him. Scraping bitter words up my throat.

"This house is no worse than the one I grew up in."

I have hot meals here. A library and the freedom to read about anything I desire. There are gardens for me to gaze at. And the ballroom Cillian just shared with me... the fact that he set it up so I could dance again...

Black memories circle ominously, like crows. My father's laboratory. The empty dresser where Violet's things used to reside. That stupid porcelain doll. The closet with the padlock.

Knock twice if you're okay, Rosie.

A shiver rolls over me as realization hits.

In a lot of ways, this life is actually *better*.

But I won't say that out loud. I barely let myself think it.

"It's so much less than you deserve," Dane rumbles. His

calloused hand starts to reach for a stray tendril of hair that's escaped my bun. We both notice the dark stains around his fingernails at the same moment.

The big man drops his hand to his side, fisting it as his teeth grit. I swallow hard, a potent blend of fear and something equally as arousing, but much more thrilling, swirls through me.

He really killed someone.

Why the hell aren't I *afraid* of him?

I'm not sure. But I know one thing: as he lumbers back a step, putting distance between me and the danger, my heart somersaults.

The big man turns to go, his thick boots treading silently toward the stairs. A hard twitch moves through me, tweaking the taut muscles low in my belly. Curling my fingers around—

His mask.

He forgot I had it. Somehow, that thought puts a small smile on my face.

"Dane?"

He pauses at the bottom of the steps, angling his head to listen without turning around. I toss the metal piece anyway, knowing he'll catch it. When he proves me right, his brawny hand snapping out to pluck it from thin air, I truly grin.

He looks so... *cute.* Hovering on the bottom step, blinking at his mask like he can't quite believe he left it behind.

"You're really not as scary as you believe you are," I muse.

Dane finally turns to me, then. His striking eyes work their way over my face. "Yeah, I am," he says. "You're just stronger than you think."

thirty-three

BRIAR

Maybe it's my years of experience as a literal fucking captive, but it hasn't taken long for me to learn who's coming into my room based on the way they approach it.

Fiona will give three quiet taps, Louis two. Coggins usually clears his throat first.

I know it's Dane when I don't hear footsteps before the solid raps. And Rhys tends to mutter curses before his fist even hits the door, giving himself away with some sort of taunt or jeer... though he's only come down here twice, both times because Cillian forced him.

Dane showed up for breakfast this morning, arriving with a

blush on his face and a rolling cart full of food. Today's choices were different than yesterday's, and it pinched some of the air from my lungs to think of him brainstorming new foods for me to try. Especially after last night.

He didn't stay, though, and seemed to have a hard time looking me in the eye before his silent footsteps carried him back to his room.

Which means the smooth, measured footsteps now aimed at my door—and the four knocks I don't recognize—must belong to my *husband*.

I watch my reflection freeze in the floor-length mirror, a dark red lipstick hovering halfway to my mouth. My ruby gown slides around my legs, the thigh-high slit parting as I spin to the side, scowling warily. "What?"

Cillian chuckles, the sound muffled by the door. "I have something for you. May I come in?"

I only say yes so I can tell his arrogant ass where to shove whatever he's brought me. But the second he sweeps into the room, all the oxygen in my body evaporates.

Good. Fucking. Night.

A tuxedo on Cillian is, quite simply, devastating. The white collar of his shirt makes his skin seem more golden; the spotless dark fabric matches the thick hair combed back on his crown. It gleams subtly under my bedroom's dim lights, along with his otherworldly blue eyes.

The devil looks *good* in Armani.

My spine tingles as perfume slips into the air. I *pray* he can't sense it or see the way my spine straightens. But the slight quirk on his stern lips reminds me: the devil doesn't answer prayers.

He does, however, come bearing gifts.

The flat leather box in Cillian's hands looks as expensive as he does. I track it with suspicious eyes as he approaches, coming to stand close behind me.

My Omega pants, whining shrilly. *Can't we please just let him—*

I start to say, *No, we can't, absolutely not*, but...

Our gazes meet in the mirror's reflection. And his is *soft*.

"You look enchanting."

I've only heard him this sincere one other time. The words sift through my mind while I sink into his ice-blue stare. *I only wanted to see you dance again, Briar.*

He *meant* that. And he means his current compliment just as much.

Why? Has he finally decided to try to make things right between us? Or is this all some new manipulation?

There's only one way to find out. So, I force a raspy whisper. "Thank you."

Some strange magnetism sucks up the air between us. Cillian comes closer and I find myself leaning back, drawn to his broad, dark silhouette. Neither of us looks away from the picture we make—Mr. and Mrs. Blackwood. An impossibly beautiful demon... and his *bride*.

I shouldn't like it.

Not even a little bit.

It shouldn't make it harder for me to breathe or send a warm prickle to the space between my hips.

But tell that to my Omega.

He took me, I remind her. And myself. *We hate him*.

For the first time ever, she isn't nodding along. I feel her hesitance, holding a pivotal piece of myself back.

Because she *doesn't* hate him.

She might even *want* him.

I know she can't help it. Longing for an alpha's care and approval is what makes omegas tick. But she was all I had left. My only loyal friend.

A deep stab of betrayal hits my heart, forcing my eyes from the mirror to the floor. *I'm sorry*, she whispers.

It's not your fault. I turn my head, hoping Cillian won't see the tears I blink back. Outside, the rosebushes obscuring my view have formed a hundred tiny buds. The white and red florets quiver, their thorns casting ominous shadows against the balcony floor.

Cillian distracts me, reaching around my body to present the jewelry box in his hand. "This is for you."

I start to shake my head. Push it away.

But his thumb flips the lid open.

"Oh my—" The words fall from my lips before I can help it. Cillian tilts the box, letting light hit the black diamonds set into the sides of the heart-shaped gold... padlock?

Entranced, I watch the small, iridescent rows glitter and reach for them without meaning to, dragging my fingertip from the shimmering stones to the beveled edge of the keyhole carved into its center.

It's a lock, I think, strangely dizzy. *And a chain?*

Yes, in fact; the heart-shaped lock is nestled into the velvet case and surrounded by a gleaming gold curb chain with a ring on either end. One is a larger O-ring, clearly intended to have the chain fed through it, and the other is smaller. The perfect size for the shackle of the lock.

My mind races as I mentally snap the piece together, realizing it's... a collar. With a literal lock.

Realizing... *I love it.*

"Just for tonight," Cillian murmurs. "To show our enemies who you belong to. If you'll allow it, Mrs. Blackwood."

I feel light-headed—and he isn't *really* asking for my permission, is he? I tell myself no. Because it's the only excuse I can give for the dazed nod he receives in reply.

His second hand joins the first, arms brushing my sides as he removes the necklace from the box and discards the case on my vanity.

Large hands lift the heavy chain to my throat, settling the shiny links in the exact configuration I pictured—a tight loop around the base of my throat, with the smaller ring fed through the large one. It rests against my sternum, waiting for the lock that will anchor it in place.

"This only has one key," Cillian says, producing the gold sliver from his pocket. "But it belongs to me."

Sensation streaks down my spine—a potent, unholy blend of fear and arousal that leaves my panties soaked with slick. Cillian snaps the pendant's shackle through the small ring, resting the diamond-encrusted heart between my breasts.

I track his gaze in the vanity's mirror. Fanatical. On *fire*. So hot, I swear it will heat the lock he's staring at and burn a heart-shaped brand into my chest.

Then, for the first time since our wedding day, Cillian *touches* me.

Warm fingertips skim my collarbone, tracing the chain until his hands rest over the sides of my neck. Brushing my throbbing pulse points as my heart flips, pumping hot and thick through my tingling veins.

"Lovely," my husband says, transfixed on the reflection of my breasts in the mirror. "I thought the black diamonds would stand out nicely against your complexion. I was right."

His touch lingers, sliding to my bare shoulders. He turns his head, gazing down at my skin under his hands. Unreadable intensity swirls in his eyes.

"I swore I wouldn't touch you until you asked me to," he husks. "But—in case you haven't figured it out yet—I'm not a very good man."

I'm less and less sure what kind of man he is, actually. But when sheer, animalistic need flares over his features, I know one thing: he's *dangerous*.

And part of me *likes* it.

The same way I do with Dane... and Rhys.

I try to swallow the sound that climbs my throat, but Cillian feels it vibrate in my vocal cords. A whimper. Or even a whine.

He suddenly moves, snapping his hand up to hold my jaw as he crashes his lips into mine.

He never kissed me, on the altar. When the priest told him he could, he simply brushed his lips over my cheek.

Now I know why.

The pent-up passion he pours from his mouth into mine is the sort of thing that would set a church on fire. Slick heat and gliding tongues and a growled groan that plunders all on its own.

I melt and moan, pointed nails clawing for purchase, digging into his tuxedo-clad arms. He bites my lower lip, the harsh sting enough to distract me when his free hand slides between my breasts to fist the locket. And *pulls*.

I gasp, trying to suck air into my throat, but the solid chain is too tight for anything more than the barest taste of oxygen. Pure need spirals through my core, pooling in my pussy with a heavy, heated pulse. My hands start to skim lower. Wanting—*needing*—him. But—

The collar around my neck constricts again. The barest edge of pain snaps me back into my body long enough to tear myself away, dragging labored breaths past the gold chain... and the weight of Cillian's focus.

"*Tonight*," he starts, dominance personified, "*you will not touch me and you will not look at me unless I tell you to.*"

It's a bark; I have no choice but to obey, baring my teeth in a snarl as I rip my hands from his arms.

Asshole.

With my eyes averted, I can't see his face as Cillian heaves out a deep breath. Strong fingers slowly release my jaw and the lock pendant as he takes half a step back. Lingering just long enough to softly brush his lips over my cheek.

He disappears as quickly as he came, leaving me with stupid tears in my eyes and the imprint of his chain along the base of my throat.

Yet as I stare at the open doorway, I can't help but feel the echo of my husband's parting kiss.

And the way it felt like an apology.

thirty-four

RHYS

BLINDING SUNLIGHT POURS INTO THE MUSIC ROOM, rousing me from a dead sleep...

On top of the piano?

Discordant notes echo against my face. I jolt upright, bracing for the skull-shredding pain that I know will follow.

But it doesn't come.

A month ago, if you'd told me the sudden absence of the headaches that have ruined my life for years would piss me off, I would have shot you. But, now, when I stare directly into the late-afternoon sun, my elbow dragging out a particularly grating minor chord...

What. The. Fuck?

I may not have an earth-shattering migraine, but there *is* a new annoyance I've been managing since my night with Briar.

Poison in my blood. The ruinous reason I've thrown myself back into playing. Reading. Composing. Anything.

Obsession.

The second I'm awake, my Alpha starts up. Wordlessly raging in my middle, demanding we go find our mate—our *true mate*—now.

It doesn't matter how many times I explain that we don't fucking *have one*. After whatever passed between me and Briar, the beast must sense the threat she poses to his one and only goal. Because he has been *relentless*.

I press my fingertips into my face, ignoring the new cacophony caused by shifting my arms. "Dude," I mumble to the voice inside me, "I'm literally *begging* you to shut the fuck up."

"I will do no such thing!" a deep, affronted voice replies, startling me.

Oh. Shit. Coggins.

He stands beside the floor-to-ceiling windows, his hand still clutching the pull rope that opened the thick velvet curtains. My surprise quickly fades into irritation. "What the hell, you old bastard? You know *never* to wake me!"

The graying alpha glowers. "I don't work for you, sir. And Mr. Cillian requested I fetch you. Guests will be arriving shortly."

My brain draws a blank. *Guests...?*

"Motherfucker," I mutter, pressing the heels of my hands into my eyes. "Is it *Saturday*?"

Jesus. I've totally lost the plot. Being able to sleep and eat and play music again has completely taken over my thoughts.

Well. Aside from my Alpha's constant bullshit.

And *her*.

Coggins sighs, shaking his head in utter disapproval. "Yes, sir," he retorts, dry. "I've left a late lunch on the coffee table for you.

Eat it and shower before you put on your suit. I've hung it in your room."

Frowning, I open my mouth to tell him I won't be attending, but he raises a supercilious brow. "I also left Mrs. Blackwood's outfit in her room. I suspect she'll be ready shortly."

Fuck me.

No, literally.

Fuck whatever part of me *perks up* at the thought of seeing Briar again. And dressed to kill, no doubt.

Coggins sniffs, clasping his hands behind his back as he flicks an assessing look down my body. No doubt noting how I'm sitting straighter. "Although, if you're truly afraid of running into her again and would rather continue hiding—"

A low snarl streaks up my throat. "*Excuse me?*"

Maddeningly unfazed, our butler only blinks. "I assume you're avoiding her on purpose, after leaving her to dine on her own last night."

This *asshole...*

... is completely correct.

Okay, *fine*. So I've been avoiding the omega since she charmed me in the library. It most definitely isn't because I'm *afraid*.

Freaked out by how close to the edge my Alpha's gotten? *Sure*.

Bewildered by the sudden lack of migraines and the ability to actually live again?

Yeah. That's fucking weird.

But am I *scared* of what all of this might mean?

...

Shut the fuck up.

"You may want to check on Mr. Dane," Coggins puts in, heading for the door. "I've knocked, but he isn't answering."

Christ. If today is Saturday, that means last night was Friday. The *twentieth*.

The second Coggins disappears, I jump to my feet and rush to my room.

My steaming hot shower stings, but I stand directly under its punishing spray, washing with the new products Louis left out. He's always swapping our shit for whatever is bougie and popular. Living vicariously through us, he jokes.

The spendy motherfucker definitely picked out my tux. It's a close-cut, modern style, with a classic white-on-black motif. I shove my limbs into it and rush through styling my hair. The ice-blond strands are naturally straight. It's easy to comb them into a swoop.

When I see Dane's room is open and dark, something oddly similar to guilt squirms in my center. Relief knocks me back a step when I find him in the foyer a few minutes later, frowning mightily at his reflection.

Underlings scurry between us. Caterers, waiters, florists, valet people. I can't remember the last time we had an *event* at Blackwood Manor, which suddenly strikes me as suspicious.

Cillian claimed this was Grandfather's idea. But since when does that old bastard want to set foot outside his compound? And since when does Cillian do *anything* he doesn't *want* to do?

Also, who knew we had gold flatware?

Dane curses as someone wheels an ice sculpture behind him. I can only see the top half of his face, but it's enough to know he's beyond pissed. His thick fingers struggle with the bow tie looped around his neck, plucking it loose.

I start descending the stairs. "Here. I'll do it."

Normally, he would trudge over without making a sound. He hates dressing up and especially loathes black tie.

But this time? He growls so viciously I do a double take.

"Fucking fine," I snort and hold my hands up as I step into the foyer. "Jesus."

Dane rips the tie off altogether, cramming it into the pocket of his tuxedo pants. They look ridiculous on him. Like we've stuffed a bull into a ballgown.

Adjusting his collar in the antique mirror next to the manor's front doors, he mutters under his breath. That's also concerning

—the guy barely speaks when he's in a *good* mood. Let alone a bad one.

My brows arch. "How did last night go?"

Odd emptiness rolls over the part of his face I can see. "It went."

Fuck.

"I should have been there," I mumble.

Dane pauses, his gold eyes sliding away from his reflection in disgust. "You were busy."

Strained silence stretches between us. And it occurs to me that he's… hurt? Struggling, at least.

"Sorry," I grunt. "I lost my shit a little. Having *her* here."

Dane stares. "I get it. Trust me." When I don't turn away, he sighs, his shoulders stooping. "Last night went off without a hitch. You didn't miss anything."

But it suddenly feels like I've missed a whole hell of a lot around here. Because I swear my packmate legitimately *stops breathing* the second we hear heels *clack* against the stairs.

When I trace his stupefied stare to the omega joining us, I understand why.

Good fucking GOD.

Holy shit.

Briar looks *sinful*. Rich ruby silk, thin enough to see the black lace bustier underneath, forms a corset of sorts over her torso. The tight fit highlights her petite figure and the long legs peeking through the thigh-high slit.

Jesus, the *shape* of her. All her finely honed muscles, long and lean and hinged by delicate joints.

Her body was made for high fashion exactly like this dress. It's a couture piece, complete with sheer sleeves and wicked spike-covered heels.

Briar flips her bouncy, blown-out hair over her shoulder, casting me a baleful glower before she glances at Dane. The second their gazes touch, she instantly flings hers away.

Huh.

How the hell did he do that?

I tried to push her away and all it got me was this gnawing *obsession*.

I'm too fucking distracted by her to do much more than loom closer, scanning her form. Meeting her glare.

Ignoring the stab of longing in my gullet.

"You look like you could kill a man with those things," I tut dryly, eyeing her shoes.

Even dripping sarcasm, her smile is a thing of beauty. "Funny —I wore them just for you, venom."

Behind us, Dane finally snaps back into his body. With a gruff grumble, the big guy busies himself by checking the Glock holstered under his jacket. Briar's eyes go wide on the weapon.

"This is no ordinary family you've married into, viper." I chuckle, gesturing to the row of cars pulling up to the house. Bending low to murmur my one piece of advice. "Don't forget you have fangs."

thirty-five

BRIAR

For all the days I spent trapped in my father's house, I never expected socializing to be *dull*.

Part of that is the event itself. A lavish cocktail party that reminds me of the donor dinners the ballet used to subject me to, always with my father "escorting" me.

It's odd, being at one of these functions without him. In fact, the whole situation with him is odd in general. I didn't think much of not hearing from him when I was newly married... but it's been *weeks*.

Was I seriously that disposable to the man? He got his money and dropped me into this mess and I'll just never hear from him again?

It seems so. Surely, if he were going to come around, he'd be here tonight. There's *a lot* of wealth in this room. Plenty of opportunities for him to promote his research to a captive audience. After all, there's never a better group to scam than a bunch of rich people, stuffed into some random mansion, drunkenly eating salmon puffs as if they're actually edible.

As pissed as I am about his lack of concern, I can't say I'm disappointed not to see my father here. I have enough alpha bullshit to deal with as it is.

Namely, trying to please my "*husband.*"

When Cillian told me about this affair, I expected, well, *expectations.* Surely, he wanted me glued to his side so he could show off their pack's new omega? It seemed likely, given the pains he took to get everyone over here. Not to mention this dress.

But upstairs, he essentially told me to ignore him. Then, once guests started to arrive, he barely introduced me to anyone. The most I got was a bland expression, the casual wave of his hand when he referenced me.

He didn't even use my name. Just some curt version of, "And this is our omega," before he welcomed them in and directed them to the nearest bar.

Once all the guests had gotten an eyeful of my tuxedoed alphas—and a perfunctory introduction to me—Cillian whispered a simple reminder about our deal and his terms.

As if I'd forget I'm not allowed to step foot outside or breathe a word of our arrangement.

Lucky for my husband, I'm an expert at playing the part of a pretty doll. I carefully blew out my hair and paired the corseted dress with deadly Louboutins, knowing the thigh-high slit in the slinky silk would show the shoes off.

And make it impossible for me to run away.

For Violet, I tell myself, forcing a bland smile when a waitress hands me a glass of wine the same color as my dress. *I'm doing this for her.*

Three servings later, I realize it's been months since I've had anything to drink without food and decide to drift toward the back doors of the manor. I may not be allowed to walk out, but I figure I can at least taste some fresh air for a few moments.

The ballroom is so different tonight. Instead of a thousand flickers, wall sconces fill the room with warm light. The stained-glass dome reflects the glitter of the foiled walls as I skirt around the dancefloor positioned beneath it. My heart wrenches when I see couples turning circles together.

I hate that my head automatically swivels, looking for Dane. His back catches my eye, the broad expanse standing out in a huddle of similar tuxedos. Across from the big man, Rhys's arresting gaze snags my focus.

Was *he* looking at me? After avoiding me all week?

I nod at the open French doors, then point to the floor, making it clear I don't plan to actually *step outside* the manor—because *God fucking forbid.*

Whatever face I pull makes Rhys smirk. He gives a slight chin-jerk, raising his cocktail in a sarcastic salute.

Oddly, I feel better knowing at least one of them has tabs on me. It helps combat the swoop of dread that squirms in my stomach when I notice tipsy guests gossiping behind their cocktails.

"Isn't that the new omega?"

"A bit young for them, isn't she?"

"I heard she was a dancer. Although no one said what kind *of* dancer..."

Some older, more powerful alphas raise the fine hairs on the nape of my neck, but I keep my head high, training my gaze on the open doors along the curved back wall. The secret-service-esque guards standing sentry tighten up at my approach. I roll my eyes, leaning against one of the silver-gold walls, and swallow a gulp of wine.

From this vantage point, I spot a storm brewing beyond the bluff. My stomach seethes when a thin thread of lightning illuminates the dark horizon, outlining the enormous black clouds blurred into the night.

It also gives me a glimpse of the rose gardens I spend most mornings peering at through a hole between thorns. The enormous labyrinth of rosebushes shivers in the wind, some of the taller hedges swaying to reveal a Victorian-style gazebo at the center of the maze, enclosed with antique glass.

The cool breeze sweeps inside, bringing a chilly burst of dampness with it. I suck the fresh oxygen down anyway, unable to shake the odd warmth flushing my skin.

It doesn't help, though. If anything, I feel *hotter*. A dizzy whirl tilts my thoughts as heat curls in my lungs. My mouth waters and tingles streak down my back, landing between my hips with a violent tweak.

What the *hell*?

Every breath just feels more impossible, like trying to jam cement down my throat. *When did all these alphas start staring at me? Why do I suddenly sense all their scents at the same time? Is this a heat-spike?*

I feel my body prime to perfume and panic. For a moment, I forget my husband's stern instructions; my frantic eyes seek out Cillian automatically. He's already looking at me. The same way several of the men near me are—but the intensity in his eyes looks less like interest and more like rage.

Fuck. Is he angry I looked at him? Or mad that I'm near the doors? Why?

It doesn't really matter. Being this close to freedom is clearly going to my head; and the last thing I need is a public meltdown. Not when I've already survived two weeks here... and only have a handful left before I get what I want.

If I keep my husband happy.

Which seems less likely the longer I stand here.

Dropping my chin, I leave the back doors and the garden

beyond, hurrying to the nearest hallway. There isn't anyone there, thankfully, so nobody witnesses the way I practically collapse against the wall.

What is happening? I ask my Omega. *Are you losing your shit on me?*

She pants but gives her equivalent of a vehement head-shake. *No. That wasn't me. I—I don't—*

A voice interrupts her denial before she can finish.

"What do we have here?"

The man who appears from the opposite end of the hall is unfamiliar but *gorgeous*. Between his dark hair and mischievous gray-blue eyes, he's exactly the sort of guy I would have gone after, if I'd ever been given the chance.

A toasted alpha scent washes over me—pleasant, but not insanely so. And a little chemically. Thank God.

Any concerns I had about my Omega swooning vanish in an instant. She's... on guard? Wary and angry that someone is clearly trying to corner me.

"I think you mean 'who,'" I fire back, squinting up at the stranger. "As in, *who* the hell are you? Or should I say, '*what*' the hell are you?"

The alpha grins easily, a charming expression swallowing his handsome features. "Hmm. Grandfather mentioned you were a bit of scrapper, but I'm already impressed. Do you bite everyone's head off on sight or am I special?"

He's flirting, my Omega notes. Instead of interest, she sends me a jag of anxiety—something about this man has set off her instincts. And not in a good way.

I roll my eyes down his fit body and the two-thousand-dollar tux wrapped around it. "Well, *you're* definitely not special," I inform him. "So draw your own conclusions."

He scoffs a laugh. A gleam sparkles deep in his eyes. "I'm Gideon. Your husband's cousin."

I ignore the hand he offers. "Ah. The rival pack. Tell me, have you found your own *wife* yet?"

Fuck, I need to rein it in. That last question veered dangerously close to sarcasm—and part of my deal with Cillian is maintaining appearances.

To make a point, I lift my left hand to my hair. Pretending to pet it absently, when really I'm hoping my engagement ring will catch the hall's meager light.

Sure enough, Gideon's eyes track the sparkler for a second. His grin sharpens. "My pack is very... particular."

Run, my Omega begs. *Scream.*

I stomp her down. "Is your harassment as pointless as it seems?" I ask him, trying to sound bored. "If so, I'd appreciate you aiming it elsewhere."

The humor falls off Gideon's face so suddenly, my blood chills. He steps into my personal space, his handsome features shattering into a snarl. "I'm trying to help you," he growls, backing me into the wall. "Tell you what kind of pack you married into."

I'm not as stupid as this guy thinks I am—he has no reason to aid me and every reason to try to turn me against my pack. But before I can say as much, the image of Dane, standing in the shadows, blood smeared over his shirt, materializes in my mind.

Rhys, standing over me, refusing to tell me what held him back from taking advantage of our deal.

Cillian's locked office door. Louis's warning.

If you think you know him, I promise you do not. And if you think you can outsmart him, then you are nowhere near smart enough.

Even if this guy is just lying through his teeth... well, the best lies always contain a kernel of truth. Cillian taught me that.

"So tell me, then." I shrug, acting like I couldn't care less.

It works. "They source weapons for the *scum of the earth.* Aspiring warlords. Cartels. Organized crime families." Gideon's expression intensifies, his gaze glows victoriously. "Human traffickers."

The breath punches out of my body. "As in—"

Gideon nods slowly. "Yeah."

Horror grips my gut. My head shakes from side to side. "N-no. That's not possible."

Is it?

I figured they were selling gear to cartels and the mafia. But *warlords*? And people who *sell other human beings*?

People... like my father.

Cillian certainly had no issue doing business with him.

I try to swallow, but a hoarse lump gags me. Gideon has the audacity to give me a pitying look. "Seems very fucking possible to me. Since he bought you."

Hot blood rushes through my ears, trickling down to my stomach. It clenches and heaves.

Oh God.

Is it possible the Blackwood beasts are worse than I imagined?

thirty-six

DANE

I DON'T LIKE THIS.

Or, rather, my *Alpha* doesn't like it.

He paces restlessly, nudging my anxiety higher with every pass.

There's something wrong here, but I can't put my finger on *what*.

The evening has been as dull and pompous as all the other Blackwood Corp affairs our pack is forced to attend. The only difference, this time, is being on our own turf. Knowing I have full control over the security, the surveillance system, the staff... It should *help*.

For all her pouting, Briar is a good girl, too. She doesn't try to make a scene or sneak out. In fact, she mostly keeps to herself, observing the party with her sharp eyes. Absorbing it.

Honing those knives of hers, no doubt.

Despite everything running smoothly, Cillian seems even more tense than me. The guy may be our pack alpha, but he forgets I've been his best friend for more than half his life. I see the tension roiling under his bored expression. I sense the impatience bubbling beneath his casual glances.

His grandfather waits until we're seeing him out to drop his voice to a low rumble. "This month's shipment went according to plan?"

I resist the urge to snort behind my mask. If by "according to plan" he means we dropped off the weapons he promised those disgusting excuses for men, took their money, then tracked them for two days so I could hunt them down last night and rid the earth of their worthless souls once and for all...

"Yes," Cillian replies, smooth as ever. "Your funds were wired on Friday."

With a hefty portion skimmed off the top.

Rhys has the whole system hacked, at this point. He keeps track of what we tell the corporation we're charging, the actual amounts we extort from shitty criminals, and how much we can hide in our pack's accounts.

This whole Robin-Hood-meets-vigilante thing was Rhys's idea, actually. When his adoptive "grandfather" assigned the Blackwood's criminal operations to our pack, Cillian was prepared to walk away. Give up his rights to this house, his trust fund, the company.

But Rhys was a sneaky bastard straight out of law school. He knew all the rules—and exactly how to break them. Cillian knew how to show face and play the part of the obedient would-be heir.

And I knew how to kill people.

There's a lot of that, with what we do. And Rhys's plan is brilliant, because I don't even have to hunt the fuckers down. They come to us willingly. *Begging* to do business with us under the table.

Having no idea we track every weapon we sell them, over-charge to embezzle half of what they pay, and engineer detailed designs to off them later.

This week's bullshit was especially gruesome. But when I saw what the group had in store for their next "shipment" of human capital, it was impossible to restrain myself. I probably wouldn't have lost a second of sleep over it, honestly, if not for worrying about what Briar would think if she saw what a beast I truly am.

Where is our omega, anyway?

Forsyth listens to Cillian's practiced lies, nodding brusquely as he reaches the exit. Once he's in his Bentley, there are only a handful of stragglers for Coggins to escort out.

As the last of the invaders teeter drunkenly to their hired cars, a security guard comes rushing into the foyer. The front doors slam as he reaches us, panting, "Your—Mrs. Blackwood. She's in the garden. I would have gone after her, but—"

—but I threatened all of them within an inch of their lives.

Thunder rolls ominously, reflecting the expression on Cillian's face. "No," he clips. "I will retrieve her. Clear the premises."

The underling goes for the phone on his belt so he can spread the word. Our pack alpha strides toward the ballroom and its open back doors, tugging at his bowtie with agitated movements that immediately put me on edge.

"You two stay—" he tries, but a growl rips up my throat and Rhys barks a laugh.

"Get fucked," he says. "You can hire as many guards as you want to watch your precious wife, but I'll go where I damn well please."

"Since when do *you* care about what Briar does?" I grit behind my mask. "You fucked her and then spent the rest of the week avoiding her."

Rhys sneers. "No one said I *fucked* her. Or that I *cared*. But we've *invested* in her. I'd rather not lose a valuable asset."

It's bullshit. He doesn't see Briar as *valuable*—and neither did anyone else at this party. Which makes no goddamn sense, come to think of it. Didn't Cillian do all of this to wave her in our rivals' faces?

Our pack alpha mutters as we round the last corner, shaking his head. "*I* want to know where the hell she went for an hour. And why is she outside *now*? She could have made a scene during the party, if she wanted to."

Unless she isn't trying to make a scene. Maybe she's genuinely upset.

The storm brewing inside me rivals the heavy clouds swirling through the night sky. A flash of lightning splits the air as we barrel onto the mansion's lanai.

The brief streak of brightness reveals Briar, standing across the wide gravel path, facing the maze of rosebushes with a gazebo at the center. She jumps at a sudden clap of thunder, her entire body trembling while she wraps her arms around herself...

Swaying?

"Briar!" Her name roars out of me before I can help myself. I know she hears me, but she doesn't turn.

Cool, wet wind whips between us, ruffling her skirt. It carries the scent of the gardens overhead, filling the air with floral notes and some berry's tart sweetness. For a second, my focus lurches toward it, trying to figure out what the hell could smell enticing enough to distract me *now*.

Rhys falls behind, but I barely notice. Another wallop of thunder splits the sky, and rain starts to pour as Cillian reaches his bride, grasping her arm. Tugging to turn her toward him.

The look on Briar's face stops me in my tracks. I've never seen anything like it—awe and dismay. Blood-chilling *fear*. Confusion and betrayal. Devastation. And something that... gleams? A green *blaze*.

"Y-you," she rattles at our alpha, her body shaking as water drips from her chin. "Y-you're—"

Cillian stares down at her, his fingers curling tighter around her bicep as his nostrils flare. He seems to pause, weighing something enormous in his mind. I note his quick scan of the property around us. When he doesn't find anyone but me and Rhys, frozen in place, he stabs his gaze back into hers. Intensity snaps between them. His voice lowers into a dangerous tenor.

"Say it."

But she doesn't have to. Because another blustery gust sweeps across the courtyard, whipping her scent right into us.

And it's *everything*.

Heaven, hell, oblivion, madness.

Sweet and sour and earthy and floral. A tartness that shoots tingles through my body. Sugared freshness that sets my blood on fire. Every muscle in my body goes taut. My knot and cock harden so quickly it's *painful*. A deep, throbbing pulse that echoes the flailing beat behind my scarred chest.

Mine, mine, mine, it thrums.

Mate, mate, mate.

HER.

It's the first real word my Alpha has graced me with in as long as I can remember.

Far from his usual feral roars and monstrous urges, the single syllable is soft. Full of amazement. And *fear*.

Honestly, *same*.

I have a cement mixer of dread and disbelief churning at my center. My mind instinctively tries to protect itself from the sick seethe rapidly winding its way through my guts. Denial clamors inside my lungs, crowding out the oxygen.

It can't be. I would have known. Would have sensed—

A pull? Otherworldly attraction?

Didn't I feel both of those things the second I saw her, standing in the driveway in Cillian's morbid wedding gown? And again, the first time I put tears in those green, green eyes?

She held a knife to my throat. Threatened my goddamn *life*.

And I wanted *more*.

Have I ever been so viscerally drawn to another omega? Without the ability to even scent them?

And, God. *Her scent.*

I shouldn't be able to smell it, but I *do*. The tart sweetness is faint, but it's *there*. *Here*. Burning a path from my lungs to the raving beast crouched at my middle, quieter than ever.

My Alpha's solemn certainty smothers every flicker of denial licking through my thoughts. *It's her*, he croaks again. *She's our mate.*

The words flow over my mind. Too thick to seep into the folds of gray matter. And so chilling they freeze out all other thought.

Fuck—they've frozen my *blood*.

My heart struggles to pump the semi-solid muck in my veins, floundering. Or maybe that's just the dread again. It's worse than before, now. Misery of the purest kind—because it isn't for myself.

She's really our mate.

Which means, once Gideon and his pack find out, she'll never be safe again.

I've fallen to my knees, but that fact brings me even lower. My palms rasp against the wet gravel as I pant, trying to fill my lungs.

But I can't get full control. I can't even fucking *breathe*.

Briar is all I sense. Her essence lights up tastebuds that have been dead for years. Vibrating inside my aching lungs. Melting my mind.

Mine. My *mate*.

The irony is too painful. I've been an angry, bitter asshole from the moment she walked in the door—because I was so unbelievably pissed that she *wasn't* the one I'd hoped for all my life. And furious at myself for how much I wanted her anyway.

A tremor starts in my arms. Every fiber of my being urges me toward her. Tells me I can't leave, even though I don't deserve to be next to her.

Briar whines, the sound pitifully soft. So different from the fearless woman who took me down her throat with fury in her eyes.

But I'm equally drawn to her needy whimper. It hits my heart like a dagger and slices downward, severing all ties to pride or self-interest.

My Alpha and I have been at war for so long, it's terrifying to let him press his way to the surface. He notices things I can barely see, though. Like the quiver in her knees. Her expanding pupils.

When a blush stains her cheeks, I swear I feel her warmth from my place on the ground. My breathing stutters until every exhale rumbles.

A purr, I realize, the thought distant and halting.

It's a sound I haven't made before—one I vowed to *save*.

For *her*.

Her, her, *her*.

The woman I've mocked. Terrified. Belittled. Threatened. Used.

Fuck.

I knew Briar would be the end of me.

I just never expected the cause of death would be heartbreak.

thirty-eight

BRIAR

The spice hits me first.

Warm enough to fight the shiver under my rain-soaked skin. But smooth in a way spice normally isn't. Cloves, blended with a thousand tiny nuances that make it *perfect*.

Fog fills my mind. Or maybe that's smoke—thick and sweet. Clouding every other sense. Powerful and intoxicating. As only a pack alpha could ever be.

Cillian.

His eyes are focused lasers, beaming into mine. Icy blue snaps with ferocious fire, the white-hot flames licking through his irises while his essence melts every muscle in my core. Slick douses my thighs and he growls, the heavenly spices heating as they roll over me.

That undertone furls into another gust of wind, blurring into the second scent so seamlessly, it takes me a moment to separate them.

This one is immediately familiar. A wooden musk. Refreshing but deep, with an earthen quality that somehow grounds me and sends me reeling all at once.

Dane.

He's oak and *rain.*

Not the terrifying, fury-filled kind like the clouds swirling over us. But something gentle and nourishing—a soft patter on a bed of moss. Green things blooming in the dark. Fragrant soil and air that's been washed clean. *Petrichor.*

I drag deep gulps of the refreshing essence into my body, praying it will soothe the burn smoldering between my hips. Instead, it kicks the raging need higher and leaves my tongue tingling. Begging for something to cool and bring clarity.

As if conjured from my need, eucalyptus weaves into the wet air. Cold and sharp, it sends shivery shudders into my limbs, prickling each and every nerve.

Is it—

My vision lags as I search for white-blond through the rain. When I find him, he's a ghost. Or maybe a statue, forever frozen *on his knees.*

Rhys.

Those haunting eyes catch on mine. Chills erupt under my skin as his scent climbs higher and curls into my lungs, colliding with clove, smoke, and warm wood.

I feel myself start to drift, the gardens tilting around me. A blur of red and white, bleeding into lush green. Leaves. Thorns. Melting into the night. Melding with the dark truth that expands inside my soul.

Mates.

My body reacts. Sparks ignite in my belly. My nipples harden as slick and perfume pour from my pussy.

The two alphas closest to me practically rend the air with their snarls. A second later, a quieter, dismayed voice hisses, "Holy *shit*."

Yeah. My sentiments exactly.

I try to speak. Demand answers. Tell the alpha holding me to let me go or *never* let me go or—or—

My mouth feels disconnected from my body. And all I hear inside, apart from the sudden rush of blood in my ears, is my Omega. Apologizing.

I'm sorry, I'm sorry, I'm sorry. I tried to stop. I <u>tried</u>.

I feel the futility of that statement. And I know, in the same deep, dark place, that arguing with her is pointless. She has no more control over this than I do.

No more than the horror-struck alpha on his knees who falls forward, letting his palms scrape the soaked gravel. Or the enormous masked man panting hard enough to form clouds of condensation with every exhale.

Wild gold eyes snap to the juncture of my thighs, as if he can see the heat pulsing there. Hell, maybe he can. That might make sense, considering the only part of him my mind catalogs is the erection tenting his black pants.

And his liquid eyes.

"Omega." The word is a growl. "Are you—"

I don't know what he's asking, but it wouldn't matter if I did; I have no answers. No coherent thoughts. I have *nothing* tying me to this earth other than *them*. Their glowing eyes and overpowering scents and the pit of flames expanding where my lungs used to be.

The terrifying storm swirls above us. Between us. Inside me. Washing away every rational thought. Leaving the only truth I have left:

These monsters are my mates.

And I *want* them.

THE FIRST TIME I INHALED THIS SCENT, I WANTED TO resist.

The dark sweetness of black cherries. Sugared, sour perfection, delicious and fresh in the most impossible way.

It rises off her throat and her damp hair, whipping me in the face. Catapulting me back in time.

Fuck, fuck, *fuck*.

I recall every second of that day so clearly. Walking through the performing arts center. Strolling past the theater's open doors. Checking my phone, already mentally on to my next task—

When *she* hit me. Flung me off course in every conceivable way.

I remember how I wished I could deny it. And the single fact I knew instantly. The same one I know now.

It's too late.

Too late to resist or deny or undo. Too late for *me*.

I belonged to her.

So it was only fair that I made sure she belonged to me, too.

The irony was never lost on me. Briar thinks this arrangement was all about me, serving my pack's interests at her expense. When, really, I wagered everything we have and everything we are on *her*.

This was never a marriage of convenience.

Finding her, wanting her, *needing* her?

This is a marriage of *inconvenience*.

And I'd pay every price a hundred times over to have her here in my arms.

Jesus. I'd almost forgotten how utterly goddamn *perfect* she is. But one breath is all it takes to remind me.

I can't stop myself, turning my face into her throat, inhaling deeper. Briar goes limp, staggering into me. Her entire body quakes as she gulps humid air, getting her first true taste of my scent.

Cloves and smoke.

It took months to find a neutralizer that would cover it while still smelling nearly identical to my actual scent. The fact that I also had to find similar formulas for each of my packmates *and* our omega—well, it was nearly impossible.

Along with the industrial-strength de-scenter I've been pumping into our house for nearly a year... covering it with the same artificial sprays I've coated all of our clothing and bedding with. At one point, before Briar arrived, I even had the hallways fogged.

All to turn our home into her prison.

I hated that I had to lock Briar inside, but it was the only way to keep this from her. The only way to *protect* her.

Because there could be nothing more dangerous than anyone knowing what she means to me. And now that the others know what she means to them?

The heavy rain drenches us. Washing away all of my careful plans.

And I'm furious. Also *relieved*.

Keeping this from her has nearly killed me. I never would have been able to endure it for anything or anyone else.

From the moment I saw her, she's been the reason I *breathe*.

But I would have held my breath forever if it meant keeping her out of harm's way.

I should have known that wouldn't work. That this moment was inevitable. As vital as the air vibrating in my lungs and the blood thrumming harder and higher through my veins.

No. *Fuck*.

This cannot happen.

Not now. Not yet.

Briar's whimpered moan is the only thing that could possibly break through my Alpha's single-minded urge to rut. *Look*, I say to him. *She's scared. I'm her husband. Her alpha. I need to comfort her*.

He likes the sound of that enough to lower the octane with a begrudging growl. I push the sound into a purr. Briar's overheated body sways closer to mine.

It takes every ounce of self-control not to haul her into my arms. Instead, I drop my rumbling voice into a whispered plea. "Tell me to touch you."

Her fine-boned hands clutch my sodden jacket as she blinks, trying to focus her vision. When our gazes finally connect, I grit an explanation.

"You have to ask me, rosebud," I rasp. "That was our deal. And I've gone to great personal lengths to uphold every promise I make to you."

Understanding briefly clears the haze from her eyes. She whimpers again, nodding. "P-please, alpha."

God. I've waited so long to hear those words.

My arms instantly snap around her. Our soaked clothing does nothing to hide the way warmth rolls off her skin, soaking into mine. When she starts to shake, I pull back and check her eyes again.

Goddamn it. With my scent wrapped around Briar, all reason abandons her. Glittering pupils swallow every trace of green. And her perfume thickens into something so unfathomable, I could come just standing here. Sharing air with her.

Dane suddenly remembers how to move. His bass purr blends into mine as he steps up to Briar's side, lowering his face to hers.

Without his mask.

Of course he'd want to properly scent her, without any impediments. But I still can't believe what I'm seeing—he hasn't removed that thing outside the manor since the day he got it.

His scars seem to be the furthest thing from his mind as he cups Briar's cheek, murmuring softly. "You feel this too, huh, little girl? You know what's happening?"

Our omega keens quietly, trying to rub her cheek over his. It's fucking *sweet*. And so damn earnest. A blend of envy and amazement tightens my throat.

"It's okay, darling," I purr, lifting her body into my arms and letting her nuzzle Dane's neck. "Here. You can scent-mark us anytime you want."

My packmate groans when she leaves a swath of her sweetness along his scarred throat. Briar shivers at the sound, more mind-melting perfume swelling into the drenched air. Her voice is smaller than I've ever heard it.

"B-but—my—my alpha?"

She says it with a confused uncertainty that flips my stomach inside out. Is she questioning me? That would be fair, after I kept her at arm's length. It was the only way for me to stay in control, but I'm sure it gave her Omega reason to doubt.

When I follow her bleary eyes, part of me relaxes while another hardens. Because she isn't gazing at me or Dane. She's peering through the rain.

At *Rhys*.

Of *course*—her Omega can't relax until she knows he's not going to reject her.

Or, really, reject her *more*.

Watching my stepbrother delight in her discomfort has been one of the hardest parts of this scheme. Mostly because it went against every vital instinct to allow her to be harmed. But also because I knew the truth would destroy him once he found out.

What happened with my father and our mothers had opposite effects on us. I *never* wanted a mate; but that was *all* Rhys wanted. I knew he would never be able to act normally if he knew she was his. And her very life might depend on our ability to act indifferent toward her.

Not right now, though. Not ever again, I'd wager.

We can't put this back into Pandora's box. It's out now—and I'll be damned if I make this woman feel like anything less than my queen ever again.

Rhys seems to feel the same way. White-hot pain blazes behind his light aqua irises, the agony so raw it reaches across the courtyard. Into Briar.

She whines again, softer but more urgent. My hands tighten on her slippery skin. Dane huddles closer, using his broad back to protect her from the worst of the rain. The rattle in his chest kicks into a dull roar.

"Shhh, moonbeam," he whispers. "What do you need, huh? Do you want me to carry you inside?"

A visceral bolt of panic tears through Briar's body. She jerks in our arms, a shrill, wordless squeak scraping out of her. Her eyes widen as she shakes her head frantically.

Dane and I blink at her, then glance at each other. She doesn't want to get out of this storm? Her skin feels warm but that's just the heat-spike. Once it passes, her core temperature will plummet.

The urge to protect wins out over wanting to please. My pack-mate starts to gather her into his arms and turn toward the manor. But Briar *shrieks*.

And *Rhys* snarls.

"*No*," he snaps, staggering to his feet and darting over. "Her Omega is terrified of not being able to scent you again."

Fuck. That makes perfect sense in the worst way. It's my fault that our house is so thoroughly neutralized; and it will take a few days for it to return to normal once I remove the air filters.

Imagining going back inside, to a world where Briar doesn't saturate every breath I take, nearly shoves me into the rut I've been fighting off. Dane reacts, too, his big body stilling completely as he smooths a deadly growl into a rougher purr.

Briar sways into the sound, her eyelids fluttering slowly while Rhys pauses. His light gaze scans her face for half a moment before he lifts his shaking hand. He extends it slowly, breathing hard enough to be heard over the storm.

Rhys always moves with purpose and charm, but I've never seen him be *gentle* before. And part of me knows, innately, that she's the reason why.

He was *waiting*. For *her*. Refusing to touch anyone the way he softly strokes his fingertips over her heated cheek.

Briar's eyes fall shut. A whimper vibrates in her chest—something I feel more than hear.

Dane must sense it, too, because he flings another desperate look at me. Waiting for my permission, I realize. As our alpha.

When I nod, he drops his forehead to her crown, rubbing his face against her sodden hair. "Okay. We won't go inside yet, moonbeam," he promises. "But we have to get you warm, okay?"

Rhys and I simultaneously have the same idea. "The gazebo," I mutter, watching his focus flicker to the structure standing at the center of our rose garden. It looks ominous, all wrought-iron curves and ornate fleurs, dipped in solid black. But the groundskeepers keep it clean and the warped glass enclosing the space should keep the worst of the weather out.

I lead the charge, knowing the way by heart. Dane wastes no time hauling Briar and her soaked skirt into his arms, but Rhys hesitates.

"Come with us," I hear Dane mumble. "You'll never forgive yourself if you don't."

I doubt either of us will ever forgive ourselves either way.

But Rhys swallows hard and follows.

forty

BRIAR

THE FIRE MAKES SENSE.

I know it shouldn't. Because my clothes feel wet. My skin is slick. The sky is dark. And the windows are fogged.

But the flames that lick to life above us, flickering in some hanging glass-and-metal thing? Well, at least they explain why I'm *melting*.

My Omega is no help. In fact, if her constant litany of apologies is any indication, she's the reason I can't remember my own name. Or anyone else's.

I'm sorry, I'm sorry, I'm sorry.

It's too late for me to figure out what she's apologizing for.

More colors blur around me—crisp fabric, dark green leaves, swirls of red and white, yellow flames, black metal.

The blue eyes of a wolf.

They belong to my alpha. The one whose name I can't recall —but I know he's *mine*. The possessive lurch clamoring through my middle is sharp enough to draw another whine out of me. Pain twists all the muscles below my waist.

The alpha growls a low curse. One of his hands drops to my midsection, palm pressed flat over a sudden squelch of molten *pressure*.

Is it a cramp? Or a climax? It feels like some unholy combination. A tight, painful squeeze that somehow makes my pussy *throb*.

Another tweak impales my aching muscles, my core contracting under the warm weight of his hand. Perfume pours out of me, the scent of dark cherries and sweet berries swirling into the soup of sensations that don't make sense.

The room tilts and I try to stay upright, rearing back. Into *him*.

It's my other alpha. Larger, covered in scars and tattoos. But I recognize him, too. He belongs to me every bit as much as the man rubbing soothing circles over my belly.

The second alpha's solid strength wraps around me. Every nerve in my body tingles, then screams. Wanting more. Needing less of the fabric blocking me from his bare skin.

I don't know his name, but black ink patterns and slices of marked skin flash through my mind. His rugged features and solemn expression are familiar, especially when his thick, walnut brows knit. "What do you need, moonbeam?"

I try to reply, barely managing a whimper. My fingers scrabble for the hand cupping my belly, pressing the pack alpha's palm into me harder. It feels good when he starts to stroke downward, toward the gaping ache in my core. But there's something missing. Something *wrong*.

Another shrill sound cracks up my throat and the big man behind me hums, his chest vibrating powerfully against my spine. It shakes all of my tension loose, but it can't quell the fear swirling in my stomach.

"She's burning up," a distant voice grits. "I can feel her body heat from here. Once it's over, she's going to crash."

The edge of the third man's tone is familiar in the best and worst way.

Him.

He's the one I'm missing.

And the one I'm afraid won't care.

I struggle weakly, trying to find his pale features. When I do, a new kind of horror dawns.

Why does he look like that? Is he injured? Sick?

Our eyes meet across the dim, musty room. His scent intensifies into something medicinal and *cold*. It slices my raw throat as I gasp it in, unable to look away from the swirling aqua pools reflecting pain back at me.

The creases around his eyes pull tighter, but his scowl softens. "I know," he rasps, the words ragged breaths. "I don't deserve to touch you like this. So I won't."

I won't. I won't. I won't.

He won't come closer. He won't let me have him. He won't be my alpha.

Agony ruptures in the deepest part of me. I feel more wetness on my face as I whine, turning into the woodsy, comforting scent behind me.

"*Rhys*," the big one barks out. "If you're going to *reject your mate*, the least you can do is *get out*."

That thought alone is enough to make me wail. The tortured alpha lurches toward me, but catches himself. More misery fills his face. His scent cuts through my marrow, tweaking the pain between my hips.

The pack leader gathers me into his chest next, purring louder. I try to nuzzle him, wishing I could hide from the one rejecting me. Scratchy fabric chafes my cheek, but it disappears a second later, replaced by warm, perfectly spiced skin.

I sob quietly, rubbing my face between his pecs as he hums. "Hush, now. No one is going anywhere. Your alpha is going to get over himself and help us get you off. He would never reject his mate. Right, Rhys?"

The solid roll of alpha power that accompanies the smooth words soothes the restless squirm in my lungs. Even before the beautiful, haunted alpha fists his hands at his sides and stalks toward us.

It's like a missing piece of my universe slots into place when he steps between the others. Eucalyptus and mossy oak, all threaded with the sweetest spiced smoke.

The edges of my vision blur. The worst cramp yet stabs my core and *twists*. Fresh panic flares in my middle as something thick and warm slides down my thighs.

The one with the white hair stares at the soaked skirt clinging to my legs. His throat bobs, but he reaches over and strokes his knuckle along the slit in the red fabric.

A small, distant piece of my mind blares inaudible warnings at me—reminders that this alpha isn't safe, somehow. But my body doesn't care.

It's not *fair* for something so dangerous to feel so *good*. How does one touch banish the chill from my bones and cool my over-heated blood with a rush of relief?

The alpha's elegant fingers skim to the molten throb at the top of my thighs, tracing the wet silk covering my clit. I choke and lightning flashes in his eyes. His voice purrs along with his chest, both rough and uneven. "Should I stop?"

Oh *God*.

More perfume pours out of me. Rich tartness seems to fill the entire glass room within seconds. The others growl, their hands coming to the bodice of my dress. Unzipping, shoving it aside. Caressing me while the third alpha pets the soaked seam of my pussy.

A punch of pain hammers into my abdomen and I gasp an answer. "Don't stop." The cramp clenches harder. "*Alpha*, please."

I don't know who I'm pleading with, but they all respond. The big man drops his face to my hair, scent-marking me as the blond one gasps a ragged inhale. The pack leader with his arms banded around me drops a kiss to my forehead and issues a low command for his packmate.

"I think you'd better get on your knees for my wife."

The pale alpha's eyes spark before flying to mine. I can't understand why, but the heat in his cool irises softens into something *warm*.

"Is that what you want, pretty baby?" he hums, lowering himself to the ground. "My mouth on this sweet pussy?"

I can't even picture what he's asking, but the snippets I do understand—his chiseled lips and sharp tongue, all over the insistent throb dribbling slick down my legs—is enough to prompt a moan.

The big man makes a chuffing sound of approval, hiding a slight smile in my hair. "Make it good," he mutters to his packmate. "This is her first time."

All of their scents spike. The leader growls while the one his knees groans, resting his forehead on the place between my hips that pulls tighter every second.

I buck and whimper, begging, "P-please. I-it *hurts*."

His angelic face contorts for a split second, pain cracking his marble features before they ease back into a tender expression.

"Okay, baby," he whispers, sliding his hands into my skirt and up my thighs, pooling it around my waist. He plants a kiss over the soaked hem of my panties. "I'll make it better."

His fingers slowly peel the sodden lace from my core, dropping the scrap to the concrete. Light eyes leap to my mound, sparkling when he sees the slick glistening on my thighs. He skirts both thumbs along the edges of the exposed pink flesh, purring and growling simultaneously.

His expression is feral, but his touch feels reverent. He strokes his fingertips along the parted lips, breathing hard enough to shake his shoulders. "Jesus, Briar."

Right. Briar. That's... me?

The big man braces behind me, securing his tattooed arm around my waist. When I realize all of his skin is exposed, I keen, scrabbling to pull the suffocating bodice covering me out of his way.

He shoves it down easily, fitting his warmth into my bare spine. I can't finish gasping before the alpha on his knees spreads my plump pussy lips and presses his mouth over my clit.

Slick heat glides along the throbbing nub, a thousand tingles of bliss erupting in my core. His hands clutch me harder, lips skimming a slow circle around the bundle of pure sensation.

A garbled moan ekes out of me as my vision swirls. A fresh bolt of pain stabs my internal muscles. They flutter around the emptiness aching to be filled and more perfume pours from my pussy.

The alpha's tortured groan flips my stomach. "Oh *God*, Briar," he practically cries. "I can *taste* you."

Before I can wonder what he means, his fingertip grazes the spasming ring of my entrance. It clamps around that touch, trying to suck it deeper.

We both moan again. His tongue laps around the sides of my clit as he works his finger into me. Two rough hands slide up my torso and palm my breasts, rolling my rock-hard nipples.

I clamp down instantly. Every strained muscle singing and melting and *gushing*. The pressure climbs to a crescendo, pleasure suddenly shattering the pain. It pulses into my limbs, chasing the fire, singeing my nerves. Soothing the sizzling snaps with pure bliss.

"Here."

As I work to remember how to breathe, the big alpha lifts me up and the one on his knees rips the dress off. My brain lolls in my skull, but I suddenly have a memory. Their names.

Dane, I think, as the mountain of strength positions me on someone's lap.

And the one on the hard, dirty floor, gaping at me like I've just revealed myself to be some sort of mythological creature... that's *Rhys*. He's supposed to hate me, but right now, loathing is the furthest thing from whatever his face is doing.

A new set of hands smooths my damp hair off my face. "Look at me."

Cillian.

I meet his icy eyes, satisfaction blooming in my middle. I can't explain why—but he's just... mine. My alpha. And being naked on his lap feels like a huge *relief*.

For a moment, his expression is full of soft concern. But then I blink at him. His sculpted mouth flits into a slight smile. "Hmm," he murmurs, "I'm not sure how I feel about you obeying without any debate, Mrs. Blackwood."

He plucks my left hand off his chest and brings it to his lips, planting a reverent kiss on my ring finger. "Does it still hurt?"

His mouth grazes my knuckles and turns my body to jelly. I tremble, a spiral of pure need sucking at my wobbly core. My pussy quivers, the stretchy ring of muscle inside aching and throbbing *harder*.

Oh *God*.

Does that mean...?

"I think—I need—" I try to choke out the words, but they refuse to come. Not while I'm trapped in his crystal gaze. I drop my chin, hiding my face as shame heats my cheekbones.

But for the first time, in the face of my upset, Cillian doesn't go still or let me squirm. His purr rolls into a deep, sonorous sound, the vibration lulling me closer as he wraps an arm around my waist and cups my jaw in his hand.

Without a word, he turns me toward him. Locking our eyes, projecting patience and affection. So *steady*. Subtly in control, overtly dominant.

The look says, *You will tell me*. But it also says, *I'd wait forever to hear what you think*.

And he will, I realize.

All this time, all his plays. He's *been* waiting for me. For years.

I still don't know how. Or why. But I do know one thing…

Solid alpha energy unblocks my throat while his purr melts the thorny vise around my lungs. "Knot," I manage, the word a slight whine. "*Please*, alpha."

They all *snarl*. Rhys doubles over with a tormented groan as Dane and Cillian both *move*. Dane comes to stand next to me, brushing my hair from my shoulder. Sending fresh shivers creeping along my spine and more perfume spilling into Cillian's lap as the pack alpha's free hand drops to his fly, tearing it open.

I watch his cock spring free, the thick, solid shaft already roped in visibly throbbing veins. And there, at the base, a swollen knot the size of his fist.

I don't think. I *can't*.

My body takes control, rising onto my knees and bucking against his erection. Keening. *Crying*.

A desperate sound catches in my throat. The fingers curled around my face stroke tenderly. "*Look at me*."

My blurred gaze snaps to his. Cillian's intense stare sinks into me as he positions himself under my pussy. "You will look at me when I give you my cock," his smooth voice rumbles. "And say my name while my knot fills your cunt."

My entire body shakes, straight down to my soul. I try to nod, but that becomes me bouncing in place, more pleading noises scraping up my throat.

The devil's ice-blue eyes glint, softening on mine. "Good girl," he praises, infusing the words with delicious alpha power. Slicing as deeply as any blade while he guides himself into my quivering core. "Take this big alpha cock. *Now*."

The bark snaps through my bloodstream and my hips automatically drop, sheathing his girth in one go. My head falls back as sensation spears the ache in my depths. Stirring it up, bumping it

higher. Until every nerve is blazing and buzzing. Begging me to—
to—

"You can take it," my husband vows. "You can take *me*."

Oh *God*.

I hold his gaze... and let myself fall. Another orgasm tightens every muscle in my body. Working in tandem to suck at the wide swell pressed against my pussy. Tugging it past the fluttering opening, stretching me around his earth-shattering knot.

Cillian roars, but doesn't look away. His irises go up in flames, burning paths to mine. Echoing the ethereal sense of completeness that hits just before I tumble into one final climax. He expands, popping into the place that was only ever meant for *him*.

Them.

This.

And as he holds our stare, marking me with his release—remolding me from the inside out—I know I'm ruined.

Damned. *Free.*

But somehow more trapped than ever.

forty-one

RHYS

MY OMEGA GOES LIMP IN CILLIAN'S ARMS, MELTING into his embrace.

White-hot envy sears my stomach as she unconsciously buries her face against his throat. Seeking his scent. Trusting him.

If only for a moment.

It seems he'll get more than a few brief seconds, though, because Briar is asleep before any of us manage to speak. Dane confirms she's out by brushing her hair back, revealing her slack features and parted lips.

Cillian *snarls*, rending the air in the enclosed gazebo.

Dane steps back, casting me a sheepish look. *Right.* Neither of us should be touching her while she's knotted with our pack alpha for the first time.

The beast in my middle roars, violently shoving me toward our mate. I grit my teeth, holding myself back. Huffing down her scent to convince him everything is alright.

Until Dane mutters, "We have to get her inside. It's going to be brutally cold when this rain stops."

He has a point. We've fogged up the warped, antique glass in here—which tells me the wind blustering in from the bluffs must be chilly.

Cillian leans back and peers down our omega, sighing over a growl. "Fine. But I'll have to carry her like this. And we need to go straight to the nest. It's the only room in the house that isn't neutralized."

The nest.

My heart drops as my throat thickens. It's mortifying how many times I've pictured my mate inviting me into their nest. And now I have to do it like *this*. When I'm pretty damn sure she wouldn't want me in there. Not after I—

Hurt her.

So much.

So *many times.*

I'll never be able to apologize enough. And she'll probably never forgive me.

Part of me is glad for that. It's sick, but I *want* to suffer for this.

I get my wish the second we finally walk back into the manor. It's dark and quiet—all the staff have finished their work and whatever threats Dane made to security before the rest of us followed him outside were very effective.

Yet despite the silent, dim ballroom, my head suddenly *pounds.*

Now I know—the source for this pain? It's been my Alpha, feral for his mate. It only went away because we were near her.

But now that I've scented her? And cut him off from that scent?

I barely make it across the circular space. As the others march into the foyer, I collapse against the carved archway, clutching my skull with both hands.

My packmates halt, each turning to snap at me. I can't hear them, though—I can't do anything, other than curl my fingers against my scalp. Bowing my head and praying I won't fall face-first to the unyielding marble floor.

Dane starts toward me but I lift my hand, waving him off. "No," I grit. "I need to—"

Feel it.

This pain is what I deserve. God, I've *earned* it.

Shoving her into walls. Calling her Cillian's whore. Barking at her. Shoving my cock down her throat without bothering to find out if she'd ever taken one before.

Waking up every day with my mate right here... unable to recognize her because I was too fucked in the head.

The memories swirl into a soup of misery, melding with the piercing, insistent pain poking through both temples. The hallway starts to blur. I try to breathe deeper, but every inhale is so *fucking wrong* without her scent.

I'm not the only one on the edge of a cliff. Dane growls, only just managing not to bark. "*Rhys.* We have to go. *Now.*"

But I know I can't. Shouldn't.

Won't.

Because that woman is my mate.

And I'd die before I let a monster into her nest.

forty-two

BRIAR

A LOW HUM KEEPS ME DRIFTING BETWEEN DREAMS AND reality.

I feel it under my cheek and echoing in my chest. Something light and buzzy.

Is it a purr?

Am *I* purring?

That would make sense, given how boneless my body is. Not to mention the murmur of masculine voices and the solid girth anchored inside me.

A knot.

Oh.

My.

God.

It takes every ounce of self-control not to instantly whine. Flail. Try to scramble away or get closer or—or—

One of my eyelids cracks open slowly. A bolt of pure bewilderment strikes my gullet.

How—where—what the—?

I fight the urge to let my gaze fly wide, allowing my peripheral vision to fill in my surroundings. A steady pulse thumps in my ears, quickening while I take in the small, *perfect* room.

It's... *enchanted.* A rounded hexagon with dark emerald posts in every corner and glass walls stretched between. Unlike the stained panes in every other room, these are crystal clear. All the better to display the *gorgeous* greenery twined over and around the *entire room.*

Roses, I realize. The same ones that grow on my balcony, snow white and blood red. All blowing in the storm's leftover breeze.

Oh. Right. We were outside.

For a moment, I wonder if we might still be in the gazebo. But, no. We're up high, level with the black-velvet sky.

There are only two rooms upstairs I haven't been in before, and this definitely isn't Cillian's office. Which means...

It's the nest.

This must be a dream. Clearly, my first real heat-spike sent my subconscious into a tailspin. And now I'm projecting all my silly omega fantasies onto whatever room they shoved me into.

I blink but nothing disappears. The gold foil brushed at the seams of the green metal frame, the deep rouge comforter, the silky cream sheets covering the round, recessed mattress... A few dozen black, flameless candles, clustered artfully around the floor... The scent of—

Cloves.

And oak.

I can *smell* them. Both warm essences sparkle in my lungs,

sprinkling bliss through my abdomen. Or perhaps that's the large, solid hand stroking the back of my head.

Because—*right*—I'm still *tied to this alpha.*

My alpha.

The one I'm going to *murder*... once I decide it's safe for him to know I'm awake.

I might not be the only one contemplating homicide. Dane's woodsy musk smolders ominously; I can't see him, but I feel his body pressed into my backside, his powerful chest rattling as he growls under his breath.

"*—don't fucking care,*" he snarls, barely above a whisper. "You should have *told* us."

The flawless expanse of tan skin and muscle beneath me deflates on a sigh. "It was a risk either way," he says, even. "But *this* way kept *her* safer."

"Lying to her? To all of us? Jesus, Cillian! Who does know? Her father?"

The mention of my father nearly makes me twitch. I realize, belatedly, that he didn't show up tonight, the way I expected. Which makes more sense a second later, as Cillian curses under his breath.

"That fucking piece of shit," he spits. "He knows *nothing*. *No one* does."

I practically *hear* Dane thinking. Crunching all of this insane information behind his furrowed brow. "So, all of this? The patent? Your grandfather's race for an heir?"

"Smokescreens," Cillian replies. "I bought the patent so I could marry Briar without raising any eyebrows. I didn't want anyone asking where I suddenly got the notion to choose her. If she came as a bonus to the technology we claimed to want..."

Dane finishes the thought. "... and if she seemed like a convenient way to fulfill your family's need for an heir... no one would ask questions."

"Yes," the pack leader admits. "I'm not even sure that patent is worth anything. It's been tied up in research and development since we procured it, but all the results are inconclusive. It doesn't matter, though. The only thing that matters is—"

"*Her*," Dane concludes, hoarse.

There's a tense pause before Cillian sighs, his chest rising and falling beneath me as his voice drops into more casual camaraderie. It reminds me what Dane shared about how they've been friends their whole lives—for the first time since I moved in, I hear that history in the pack leader's tone.

"Look, I know you probably hate me," he mumbles. "I would fucking hate me, too, if I were you. But every additional person who knew she was our mate constituted a greater risk. If I'd been upfront with all of you right away, it only would have been a matter of time before the staff knew. And our security. A well-placed bribe or threat is all it would have taken for an enemy to find out—or Gideon. And I couldn't *risk* that. Not with *her*. I needed our whole pack to seem as indifferent to each other as humanly possible. Especially toward Briar."

That explains a lot.

Keeping me cooped up, literally locked inside the manor... because the second I walked outside with them, the neutralizers wouldn't work. And anyone around would have witnessed what happened when I stepped into the garden—my Omega melting down. Throwing me into the deep end.

It also accounts for why Cillian practically sealed my balcony from the outside air with the thicket of rose vines—and possibly even why my Omega preferred to sit out there anyway.

Other memories flicker through my mind. The way my husband's eyes seethed every time our gazes met. Why he *had* to have me in the first place. Whatever insane price he paid my father.

And tonight.

The second I got near the back doors, I felt funny. Cillian, Rhys, Dane... none of them could stop glancing over at me when the wind swept in. Did their Alphas already sense the faintest threads of my real scent?

If it was that easy to tip them off, of course Cillian had to host the party here, where I could be seen without ever setting foot outdoors.

It was also strategic, I imagine. A way to let everyone think they were getting the world's dullest glimpse inside our pack.

They all left disappointed, I'm sure. *Nothing to see here. Just a pissy omega and three alphas who barely deign to glance at her.*

We all played our parts perfectly. *Effortlessly.*

Of course. Because we didn't know the truth and we couldn't sense each other.

Cillian was the only one who knew, so *he* was the only one who had to pretend. The rest of us believed the lie as much as any of our guests.

"Now all of polite society thinks Briar means nothing to us," Cillian confirms. "We bought some time to figure this out." His fingers tense against my scalp. "If she'll have us."

God. It's... sick. And so *brilliant.*

Louis's whispered warning plays through my memory for the second time this evening. *If you think you know him, I promise you do not. And if you think you can outsmart him, then you are nowhere near smart enough.*

I thought these men underestimated me.

But maybe, in my husband's case, I had it all backwards.

Because his plan *worked.*

I'm *here.* His *wife.* Knotted with him in a gorgeous nest... while his rivals think our marriage is a painful charade. A way to get them their heir. Making *me* meaningless.

Which means I'm also *safe.*

Dane grumbles his understanding with a begrudging sigh before pointing out the one fatal flaw in the plan. "You damn near killed Rhys. I don't know how the kid will recover from this. She's all he's ever wanted. And now he's *hurt* her."

All he's ever wanted? Venom?! The alpha who currently can't be bothered to stay here with us as we work through this tangled web of thorns?

Spiced smokiness darkens around me. "I know," Cillian replies, the words nearly rasping. "And I know you both would have done everything you could to keep her safe, if I'd told you, but... You would have had to lie to her every day. I didn't want that for you. Or her. Because if she wakes up and decides she hates me, I need her to have *someone* she can still trust."

The words drip pure sincerity. The kind of concerned fervor you just can't fake—not even an accomplished actor like Cillian Blackwood.

My monstrous husband... who truly did all of this to keep me *safe*?

No, goddamn it, my heart is not *fluttering* right now.

Get a grip, I coach internally. *Just because the man had good reasons for acting like a beast doesn't mean we can <u>trust</u> him.*

It *feels* like I can, though.

How he's holding me. The fact that his purr hasn't stuttered once. His knot, still so full and firm inside me.

He offered it without hesitation. And the way he talked me through *taking* it...

Oh God. I am so screwed.

"I still don't understand how the hell you tricked us," Dane grunts. "Especially me."

Right, because the big man is trained to notice everything. Eliminate all threats. Even, perhaps, innocent people.

Their pack alpha doesn't have a shred of remorse as he replies, chuckling. "You haven't lost your edge. You were the hardest one to fool, actually. I've been slowly titrating neutralizer into the house for a year. Adjusting it by increments so it wouldn't tip you off."

Of course. If he wanted to keep our mate status a secret, he had to desensitize Dane to the dulled scents in here over time. Rhys had lost his ability to smell others, so he wouldn't have noticed, but my big man?

Cillian knew he would instantly catch on if all their essences evaporated overnight. So he played the long game.

For *a year*?

"I swore I could smell all of you, though," Dane argues. "I kept trying because she made my Alpha insane. I'm pretty damn sure I started falling in love with her the moment I *saw* her."

Okay, okay. So my heart *is* fluttering, but it definitely isn't *melting...*

I hear Cillian's smirk when he speaks next. "All our scents were fake from the day she got here. That's why I've had Louis switch the soaps out every week. I had more artificially scented neutralizer custom-made, to put in everyone's body wash and on everyone's clothes. Including her wedding dress."

The damn *dress*. That thing arrived at my father's house *months* ago.

God, he had each move calculated eons before they would have occurred to anyone else. And made sure each of us—and the manor—would still smell "correct." To keep everyone in the dark. Including the staff.

Brilliant bastard.

"Is this why you ripped the nest apart last year?" Dane guesses. "You wanted it to be perfect for our *mate*?"

I feel Cillian nod. "I had it stripped, cleaned, and partially redecorated," he corrects. "And then sealed it off to ensure none of the neutralizers got in here. I wanted her to have a safe space, but it isn't done. I've added a few finishing touches since she moved in, though, after observing her. Like all these book-shelves..."

Bookshelves?

My head pops up before I can remember I'm supposed to be asleep. I whip my face around, finding that my husband is actually telling the truth, for once—the three interior panels of the six-sided room are, in fact, black bookshelves.

Dane blinks at me, surprise rounding his gold eyes. "Briar." Pink creeps over his exposed cheeks. "How long have you been awake?"

Ah fuck.

One glance at the arrogant alpha holding me makes it clear that he's known this whole time. Cillian *let* me eavesdrop, so I could hear his side of the story. Then he lured me into revealing myself by mentioning my one weakness: a library.

But instead of outing me to Dane, he simply curves his lips in that faint, enigmatic half-smile. Letting me decide how much to admit to... and turning himself into my partner-in-crime.

I hate that I love it so much. But these little moments, when he looks at me and *sees* some unknown piece no one else ever has... they connect with a throbbing, empty place in my middle. One that begs for him.

A dozen other moments like this, when he's stared me down and smirked knowingly, flood my brain. *Negotiating how long I had to decide about their deal. Calling his packmates out. Telling him I hated him and watching his eyes* spark.

Jesus. I am so in over my head with this man.

Slowly shifting my focus back to Dane, I find him properly blushing, his gaze pointedly not on mine.

He said he loved us, my Omega whispers. *And now he knows we heard him.*

Oh dear *God*. My *heart*.

Who am I kidding?

It is a *fucking puddle*.

And I know I should hate them. After everything Cillian has done, all the stuff Gideon told me about Dane, but—

I think I might not.

I think I might... *trust* them.

It makes no sense. I spent my whole life with a vile man who used my sister and me for *experiments*. Then stuck me in the ballet, where I was ogled and treated like an *object*. Something that could be whittled down, repainted, worn thin.

There is literally no reason for me to trust *anyone, ever*.

Least of all *them*.

It's the reason I never told them about Violet. Because I had to protect her—even if it turns out I'm only shielding a memory.

I mean, *come on*. This pack *bought* me. Rhys is a cruel snake and Cillian had been lying to me from the moment we met and *Dane*—

Came home smeared in *blood* the other night.

Yet when he finally raises his gaze back to mine, I feel something certain and sweet snap into place. Like a missing shard of my soul has been returned to me.

And, *God help me...*

How can I ignore that?

Why would I want to?

Especially with *him*. Of all the alphas here, he's always been so kind to me. Gentle, even.

And now that I know why Cillian behaved the way he did... I have to admit, he's never tried to hurt me. In fact, he's tried to *heal* me.

Good food, a safe house, free time, the ability to choose who I spend time with and when.

Guilt worms its way into my gut. There are things I haven't told them, too. If he's a liar, then, well... he isn't the only one.

I force a smile for Dane. "I've been awake for a while," I reply. "Listening."

We let the implications of that settle between us. His cheeks blaze hotter and his eyes turn molten as he exhales through his nose. But instead of worrying about himself, he asks, "Are you alright? I know that was a lot."

Warmth seeps through my chest. And I can't fight it.

I *don't want to* fight it.

"Yeah," I whisper back. "I'm okay."

Better than *okay*, really. I feel *incredible*. For the first time in my entire life, I'm not overwhelmed with the need to be on guard. These men might not be "good," but *no one* will hurt me while they're here.

Dane has the uncanny ability to read my thoughts. Or maybe my scent. When he senses it shift, he blows out another breath and lifts his hand to touch me.

Cillian snarls, wildness cracking across his gaze. Dane bares his teeth in a menacing reply, scars pulling at his furious features. My Omega ducks for cover.

When he feels me shake, the pack leader chokes off his possessive growl. "Sorry," he apologizes, voice tight. "I'm—I can't share her, Dane. Not yet."

I shoot him a glower.

For the first time, true regret touches my husband's face. "I'm sorry, rosebud," he repeats. "I know you want Dane. I'll try to calm down so you can go to him when my knot unlocks."

Lord help me—is this *guilt* swelling in my stomach? *Concern* pinching my lungs?

Am I actually feeling *sympathy* for the *devil*?

I settle back against him, my glare devolving into a mild scowl. "I'm fine. But Dane is touch-starved. So you're going to have to share eventually, devil."

His glossy black brows quirk. "Devil?"

I shrug, setting my head on his shoulder where I can face Dane. Shooting the big man a wink as I reply, "Unless you prefer 'evil bastard.'"

"We'll stick with devil, I think. Although 'evil bastard' might work for special occasions. Birthdays. Anniversaries."

His dry ruefulness happens to be exactly my brand of humor. I smirk despite myself and my husband seems to relax. He settles into the pillows, slinging an arm around my waist. His fingers curl around to brush my belly with tender intent.

Shit.

I sort of fibbed about that, too.

"Hey, guys..."

Both alphas look at me, Dane with concern, Cillian gleaming interest. I weigh my options quickly, knowing it's now or never. And while I didn't mind misleading my captors... I really don't like the idea of outright *lying* to my *mates*.

"I have to tell you something."

Dane's features crease, but Cillian's smooth, along with his voice. *Uh oh.*

"That's fine. Because I have a question for you, Mrs. Blackwood," he says.

Everything is always a negotiation with this alpha... and he usually stacks the deck so *I'm* the one winning, in the end. As long as it also means he gets whatever he wants.

"Okay," I sigh. *Another deal with the devil.* So why do I want to *smile*? "Listen..."

forty-three

DANE

DEATH.

It will be bloody. Slow. Agonizing and twisted.

And it will still be too good for Dr. Brynn.

Briar swallows, her creamy throat bobbing. Reminding me I haven't bitten her yet... carved out her place at my center... bonded her to me forever...

Jesus.

Calm down, I tell my Alpha. *We need to listen.*

It's remarkable, but that's all it takes. He lets go of his crusade immediately, dialing into her tearful expression.

I want to roar at it. Not because she's done anything wrong, but because I hate that we've put her in a position where she feels *guilty* for protecting her secrets.

Her own *sister*.

Of course she didn't tell us. I wouldn't have wanted her to trust anyone with this information.

As she goes on, talking about the night they took Violet. The nightmares it still gives her...

My stomach sinks. *Fucking hell.* Cillian's background checks on Briar and Brynn were *thorough*. If he didn't turn up anything about this missing woman, I fear she may be long gone.

As she winds to the end of her explanation, telling us her original plan for using our resources to help locate her sister, a beat of understanding passes between Cillian and me.

We will do everything in our power to fix this for our mate. Even if we have to rip the world apart.

"And I—" she finally stammers, darting looks between the two of us. "Even though I really needed the money to look for Violet, I probably shouldn't have made that agreement with you anyway. Because... I have a birth control implant. So I sort of knew none of our, um, *efforts* would pan out."

My blood rushes while my lungs freeze. And for second, all I feel, from my core to the top of my head, is *relief*.

Especially when Cillian captures her green gaze and burns his icy eyes into hers. "If you think there's *anything* I don't know about my wife's health," he intones, slow and even, "you don't know me very well, rosebud."

Briar's breath snags. "You—what?"

Cillian resumes petting her hair, his purr kicking up. "I knew the whole time, darling. I was proud of you for being so shrewd."

That tracks. Of course this bastard knew. He usually knows everything. Which just makes his dearth of information on Violet even more alarming.

Briar blinks in shock. "You're not *mad*?"

Cillian shakes his head. "It means you won't get pregnant and put an even bigger target on your back, for one. But, also... you honestly think I'd want my omega to have our baby under circumstances like these? You're our *mate*. When we put a baby in you, it's going to be because *we all* want one."

My relief climbs higher with every word he says—all the things I felt but couldn't rationalize or communicate before tonight. The reasons I was careful never to come inside her, even when that was supposedly our goal.

Briar quivers, her scent sweetening until it's so goddamn *good* I could weep. "You—you're really not angry with me? For any of this?"

Cillian's face is fierce, but his tenor is soft. "No, Briar. Your sister is all you had left. We understand protecting that, the same way our pack has always protected one another. And you may belong to us, but your body belongs to *you*, rosebud. You will always have a choice. I'm grateful to whoever gave you this one."

She swallows hard, hoarse. "At the ballet. They do physicals every season and last year I—I just had a feeling my days were numbered before my father did something desperate. So I asked the doctor to give me the implant."

Her voice shakes and pure rage boils in my veins. I swear to God, if Dr. Brynn and I ever cross paths, he will *pray* for a swift end to his misery.

But monsters don't answer prayers.

And when I see Cillian's face, I know: devils don't, either.

They also don't forget their deals. Our pack leader gathers Briar closer, scent-marking her forehead and purring deeply before he asks his question.

"You ran out of the party earlier," he murmurs. "Why?"

Briar doesn't answer right away, biting her lip and staring at her husband while she considers. The solid weight of certainty settles into my gut. I feel my features harden while I growl, "Gideon."

His name sends Briar's dark cherry scent plummeting into sour fear. She trembles on top of Cillian and he snarls at me, instinct overtaking him.

I know he doesn't mean to challenge me—his Alpha is barely capable of letting me *be* in here right now, let alone withstand me upsetting our omega while they're knotted. I snap my teeth back at him out of habit more than anything. When our mate cringes lower, half-hiding under the midnight velvet quilt, I immediately close my eyes, shaking off any combative impulses.

"Sorry, little girl," I husk. "Our Alphas are all—we're both—"

Obsessed.

In *love.*

My face heats all over again, remembering what she overheard. I turn my head to hide it, feeling too exposed without my mask to at least partially cover how out of my depth I am.

Briar's hand lands on my cheek, though. Halting me in my tracks. "Hey..."

Cillian *roars*, bolting into an upright position. His icy irises flash and he starts to lift his arms—either to gather her up or shove me away—but his wife answers with a snarl of her own.

"*You*," she barks. "This entire scenario is *your doing*, devil. If you'd *told me* you were my mate like a *normal person*, maybe you wouldn't have had to knot me for the first time in a gazebo! Also, this entire house wouldn't be neutralized and Dane wouldn't be *forced* to cram in here with us to keep himself from snapping into a rut without my scent. So you can just *relax*."

Well, damn.

Omega barks get obeyed no matter what. It's a biological fail-safe—a last-ditch way for them to keep themselves safe. But omegas can only summon barks in cases where their children or mates are in danger.

That's me, I realize, my scarred, ugly heart swelling. *I'm her mate.*

I'm not sure if anyone has ever tried to physically protect me before. Is it supposed to turn me on? Or is that the queenly way she eyes our pack alpha like she's deciding on a suitable punishment?

"If I want to touch my alpha, I will," she adds. "And you'll deal with it."

She called me her alpha.

Damn it. I really am in love.

Cillian grits his teeth, still pumping waves of possessive aggression into the air. But his fists fall back to the mattress and he slowly reclines onto the pile of pillows behind him. "Sorry, rosebud," he rasps, suppressing a growl. "Touch us however you like."

I decide not to reciprocate, out of respect for him. A pack alpha knotting his omega for the first time is usually sacred, especially for scent-matches. He's probably actively fighting the urge to "hoard" our mate to himself with every breath.

It really isn't fair to her, given the revelation he dropped on her head. And the one I'm about to add.

"Or you don't have to touch us at all," I murmur. "You might not want to once I explain what Gideon was talking about."

What we do.

Because that has to be what he said to upset her. There isn't anything else that could've possibly caused the sickened pallor of her skin.

Briar's hand drops from my face like a stone. My stomach plummets along with it. *Fuck.* Is this actually happening? Am I really going to find my mate and then lose her on the same day?

"I should tell her," Cillian interjects, his expression intense. "None of this is your fault, Dane."

But it is.

I'm the one with blood on my hands.

I stare at my mate, aching down to my core.

Fuck. She's everything I ever could have wanted. The reddest rose. Eyes evergreen. Mysterious, brilliant, ethereal moonbeam.

"I don't understand," she says to me. "Y-you're so good to me. So angry about what my father did to Violet, but—you're supplying tools to people like the ones who took her? Traffickers and smugglers and *warlords*?"

My blood runs cold, all my worst suspicions confirmed.

Gideon told her what our pack is known for; and she *believed* him.

Or, maybe not, given the way she's lying here with us.

I see the doubt on her face and rush to dispel it. "No, little girl. We don't supply them. We *eliminate* them."

The words sink in, each one jacking her eyebrows up higher. Beneath her, Cillian's chest rattles dangerously. "The illegal dealings were my grandfather's way of punishing my father for his ongoing affairs, falling in love with my mother, not producing a legitimate heir with Rhys's mother—all of it. And he did his job well. So well, my grandfather wanted to keep the money coming in and asked me to take my father's place."

"It was an insult," I huff. "To Cillian and to us. But we took it, because Rhys suggested we use the deals as a way to track these fuckers down. And annihilate them."

Briar's chest visibly stutters as she breathes hard. "S-so you don't help them?"

"No," Cillian vows, plucking up her hand and kissing his ring on her finger. "No, rosebud, I swear on my life, we have never supplied a weapon to any criminal organization without taking them out as soon as we could afterward. There's a strategy to it, of course. Rhys meticulously plans every strike and makes sure we hit them when they already have incoming attacks from enemies. Conflict with rivals is typically the reason they need heavy artillery from us in the first place, so the system is airtight. It's easy to explain their disappearances when other groups are actively gunning for them."

It helps that we also don't do nearly as many deals as Forsyth thinks we do. Skimming a hefty portion off the top allows us to fabricate "payments" whenever we want; and eliminating a unit every few months doesn't look nearly as suspicious when he thinks they're one of dozens we deal with regularly.

She bites her lip, blanching the plump pink curve. "Oh. I—I didn't realize..."

"You couldn't have known," Cillian murmurs sweetly, kissing her knuckles again. "We've never told anyone but you."

Briar leans her head back again, meeting his gaze with her awed eyes. "Really?"

Fond softness fills his face in the most unfamiliar way. He nods slowly, pressing his lips to her forehead. "Yes, darling," he whispers. "Really. If we want you to be our mate—our *omega*—we need you to be part of this family. And that means you will know everything we know from now on."

Briar stares at him for a long moment, unfathomable emotion roiling in her depths. Finally, she replies, her voice scratchy. "Okay. I—that would be good."

She drops back into her spot. Her attention slides in my direction as she mumbles to Cillian, "Could—can Dane come closer, alpha? I really want to be able to feel him, too."

I can't help but smirk at our leader's begrudging sigh. Instead of totally invading his space, I settle for moving my pillow closer to his side, where I'll be right in Briar's line of sight. She stretches her arm over his abdomen and I lace our fingers together, my eyes drifting shut when pure pleasure sluices through my veins.

We all start to drift off to sleep until she whispers, "You guys really aren't mad?"

My heart aches. She clearly has a hard time believing we respect her need to protect herself and her sister.

I wonder what her former life must have been like. What sorts of "punishments" her father used to keep someone as strong and smart as Briar in line.

Given the tremor in her fingers, I imagine they were severe.

I didn't know I could feel murderous and utterly enamored at the same time. The glance Cillian and I share tells me he's in the same boat. But we both know there isn't anything we can do about Brynn right now.

My packmate and I purr louder. His fingers rub small circles on her scalp while mine squeeze hers. "No, moonbeam," I whisper, gazing steadily into her eyes. "We're not mad."

Her answering whisper cracks. "And what about—"

Rhys.

My head shakes automatically. "He understands family loyalty better than most. And I think he'll be glad about the implant."

Her nose scrunches. "Because he doesn't want me to have his heir?"

"No," Cillian exhales, solemn. "Because he wants you to have *everything*."

forty-four

RHYS

Dawn slices through the library and my skull.

I muffle a groan, squeezing my eyes shut. Blocking out the stained-glass dome overhead. My Alpha continues his rampage. Tearing an agonizing hole in my gut, sending jolts of pounding pain to my head.

Fuck me.

It was too easy for me to forget how bad this is. Just one week without the constant battle raging inside me and I'm weak again.

The migraine hit the second my Alpha realized I wasn't going into Briar's nest with her. At first, the sudden swell of pain was so horrifying I thought I might pass out in the hallway. I nearly slid down the wall and tried to crawl to the stairs.

But I didn't care what the animal inside me did out of retribution for keeping him from his mate. I would never assume I had my omega's consent to come into her nest. Especially with all the reasons I've given Briar to hate me.

Somewhere under my self-loathing and dismay, I feel betrayed and furious. But I'm also weirdly *grateful*.

Yeah, Cillian hid my mate from me. But he also *found* her. And instead of giving in to his own desire never to be mated, he made sure she was ours in every way he could.

While also protecting her.

I'm not slow. I know what he did and why. The one remaining functional piece of my brain has been turning over the possibilities for a few hours, now.

And, damn it, I can't say I would have done anything differently.

If I'd found her, would I have paraded her around? Put her in harm's way? Whisked her out of her lunatic father's house in a stupid blaze of glory—exposed her value for all the world to see?

No.

I would have done what Cillian did. Because I would have given my fucking *life* to see her safe.

Of all the reasons to be enraged, the most inescapable one falls squarely on *me*.

Because I should have *known*.

The signs were there. Undefeatable attraction. The way my insides seethed and flipped whenever she was around. My Alpha calming after the night I had her on her knees. The overwhelming urge to mark her with my cum.

I should have figured there was a *reason* why she made me *burn*.

And, fuck, even if I couldn't... I didn't have to be *mean*.

I let rage and bitterness color every interaction we had. Took my fears and pains out on her. Picked up the shards of my shattered dreams and tried to make her *bleed*.

All to satisfy the monster in my middle.

Why didn't I see: there's no way to keep a beast like mine full.

He'll always want more blood.

Fuck, I wish it were still raining. The sun is rising now, but focusing on the sound of the rain helped before.

I've always loved storms. When I was a kid, they made me feel *understood*. Like someone out there might *get* the swirling darkness inside me. The desire to thunder and strike.

That memory brings a hundred others to mind. Mostly images of Cillian's father and his mate. The woman who was not my mother.

I wondered how Cillian could ever agree to an arrangement like this, after witnessing the way my stepfather looked at his mistress. But now it makes sense.

Does he already love Briar that much?

Do I?

I haven't let myself *know* her, I guess. Probably because I was afraid it would *make me* love her.

My Alpha nudges me, displaying an image of Briar on her knees. Marked by me. Streaming pretty tears and pressing her thighs together.

Jesus.

Isn't this bad enough without the nine-hour hard-on?

I already came while I lapped her slick from the sweetest source. I couldn't believe I could really *taste* her—and before I knew it, I had sprayed out inside my boxers.

Her scent was like finding a single spot of color after walking through a gray-scape for two years. I remember every detail so vividly—the sharpness, the depth. How sweet and tart. Stone fruit and black cherry juice and pure *sex, God*—

Wait.

Is that—

Is she *here*?

I stupidly forget my head has an icepick jammed into the side, lurching upright and instantly regretting it. With a choked gasp, I slump back into the chaise lounge.

When I don't immediately get a dry snort in reply, I figure I'm imagining things. But then I hear a soft sigh.

"Rhys?"

Briar doesn't sound angry. Or even annoyed. Her voice is quiet and small. Almost timid.

I know it isn't smart, but I open my eyes anyway. Searching the empty, cavernous space around me until I spot her, all pale skin and dark hair.

Christ, my fucking *heart*. It aches when I see the apprehension on her face. A fresh bolt of self-loathing lodges itself in my throat. *I did this.*

My *mate* is afraid to come near me.

The last of my dreams—the hope that one day I'd meet my perfect match and give them everything I never had—scatters on the wind. I find myself clutching at my button-down, trying to contain the pulsing pain behind my sternum.

"What are you doing here?" I pant, smothering another groan. "Cillian will go on a rampage if he wakes up without you."

It's a well-known fact that pack alphas lose their shit the first time they knot their omega. He must be passed out cold if she managed to sneak away.

Briar starts to drift closer, gently running her fingers along the nearest shelf as she pretends to scan the titles there. Her answering smile is sly, but soft. "Hmmm. Think he'll punish me? Lock me up? Oh *wait*."

He already has.

A low, cracked chuckle escapes before I can help it. Because— goddamn it—she's *funny*. So quick and sharp, with the kind of sarcasm that makes it impossible not to laugh.

She gives another small sigh, finally stepping into the pool of pallid dawn at the center of the floor.

Moonbeam. Dane called her that earlier. I can see why he

thinks it suits her, now. She looks like a celestial goddess, especially in her current silver nightgown.

The cool, metallic fabric sifts around her body as she tosses loose, raven hair over her shoulder. I can't help but gulp down greedy breaths, hoping her scent will win out over the fading neutralizers. When a thread of tart sweetness hits my tongue, some of the pain in my skull eases.

Briar frowns, the expression ponderous. "I wanted to stay with Cillian," she whispers, as if that statement confuses her. "But my Omega hated being in the nest without you. She was... worried."

About me?

Is it possible, even after all my rejection, that her Omega might not banish me?

My insides stammer, my heart skipping several beats as my blood runs still. Making room for the breathless burst of hope expanding at my center.

It's not a pleasant emotion for me. Optimism has always been met with swift repercussions; and the longing lining this desire slices deep.

The admission clearly costs her, too. I see how much when she winces, ducking her head to stare at her pointed toe while it draws circles on the marble floor. So fluid and lovely, just like everything else about her.

Pretty baby.

Jesus, even that name... I said while I had her on her knees, with a belt wrapped around her neck.

I mean, sure, she seemed to *like* it. But still.

I need to apologize. A million times. *Forever.*

Which first requires sitting up.

Hauling myself upright is more agonizing than I expect. Briar watches me gasp and grit my teeth. Her scowl deepens.

"Your head?" she guesses.

Fucking hell. Did I ever even *tell* her about my migraines? Or did she have to figure out the reason for my bad temper all on her own? Maybe someone else explained. Like Louis or Dane. Or perhaps she just thinks I'm an incorrigible dick twenty-four-seven for fun.

"I should have told you," I heft out, hating that I have to squeeze my eyes shut and lose the image of her standing in front of me. "This happens a lot."

"Can—" she starts and then stops, cursing under her breath.

I force myself to ignore the burn of the dawn light and chance another glance at her, just in time to watch her shoulders square.

"My Omega wants to help," she says, lifting her chin. "Can I try?"

I don't understand. She must hate me. And I *deserve* it. Why does she want to *help*?

As I open my mouth to ask, a blinding stab hits the side of my head. I tense, breathing harder, feeling her subtle scent roll into my lungs.

It's like giving a starving man a Tic Tac. My stomach seethes and my mouth waters. My Alpha *snarls*. Between his feral intensity and the pain—I barely have any energy to hold him down.

For my mate, though? I'd *die* trying.

Turns out I don't have to.

Cool fingertips brush my forehead. Muscles lock in place, bracing for a wash of fresh misery. Only—

Her chilled touch sinks through my skin, and the faintest wave of reprieve whispers under my skull. Some of the throbbing ebbs when she carefully skims over the hurt a second time.

When she follows my hairline to my temple and gently rubs a slow circle there, I *moan*. A loud, totally humiliating sound of sheer *relief*.

Because—*holy shit*—it really doesn't hurt as much.

I don't even care if she mocks me mercilessly over my noises. Or laughs in my—

"Here," Briar says, her voice as gentle as her hands. One lands on my shoulder, holding me in place as she rounds the chaise and sits in the opposite direction. She tugs on the back of my shirt. "I want to talk to you. Lie down and put your head in my lap."

Something inside me staggers as my Alpha falls silent. All the force I exerted keeping him contained is suddenly aimless; internal tension without a target.

My stupefied gaze finds hers and she frowns, consternation pulling at her plush pink lips. "We don't have to discuss it," she whispers. "But I—"

She's afraid, I realize. Worried I'll be angry with her for trying to comfort me. Because I've been *that* cruel to her.

Jesus, have I ever said *anything* nice?

She clears her throat. "My Omega thinks you might be touch-starved and she wants to help." The purest, prettiest green spears into me. "If you hate it, I'll leave you alone."

I swallow over a hoarse lump. My hand shakes as I bring it to the one sitting limp beside her. I hesitate, searching for words. An apology or an explanation. Fucking *anything*.

"I—" *Christ, there* are *no words, are there?* "I won't hate it."

Briar nods, the motion a bit dazed. "Okay, then."

Her hand drifts down my back, grasping my rumpled tuxedo shirt again. She starts to untuck it from my pants, visibly hesitating before she glides her fingertips over the skin at the small of my back.

Ahh God—

All the breath hisses from my lungs as my cock turns to stone. Pain scrapes my skull, kicking higher before it drops to a muted *thump*. The changing pressures in my body make me dizzy. I sway toward her.

Briar hums quietly, shifting to give me space to land with my head in her lap. For a moment, sensations overwhelm me. The soft cushion of her thighs, the feel of her hand resting on my crown. The very faintest trace of her scent, still smeared over the bare skin under her nightgown.

I blink, unable to compute the bliss tingling down my back. The lack of pain in my head. And the utter stillness at my middle.

It's so... peaceful.

Am I dead?

No. Because I would be in hell.

And as Briar's slender fingers begin combing through my hair, I'm fairly sure this is heaven. Dipped in Nirvana.

My knot throbs steadily as she scratches light circles over my scalp. The dull roar there recedes even more, crouching into the smallest whine of an ache. Barely audible over the pound of my heart and the way it echoes in my erection.

A rough groan tears up my throat when she rubs harder. "Jesus," I pant, "Briar, please don't stop."

Our omega decides not to torture me—or maybe to torture me more—because her nails drag over the sensitized skin at my roots. Her other palm skates into my half-buttoned shirt, stroking a firm line along my torso. A hard shudder racks my entire body as the tension stretched through my center *snaps*.

Waves of heat spiral down my spine as my knot torques tight. Cum sizzles up my shaft, my balls tweaking. Pleasure bursts through my cock.

Shit. Fuck.

My back bows on a tormented moan. Briar gasps, her hands turning rougher as she witnesses my uncontrollable reaction to her gentle touch.

Mortification swarms my stomach as guilt swoops into my chest. I squeeze my eyelids, trying to catch my breath to apologize—

When I hear it.

A purr.

Tiny and kitten-like. But there.

Here—behind Briar's heaving chest.

She gazes down at me, bright-eyed and bewildered. So goddamn beautiful and guileless and knowing all at once. An innocent siren. Luring me to my ruin, but not understanding why she likes it so much.

Christ. She really *is* perfect for me.

Every last thing I ever wanted. Seductress. Artist. Sin and salvation. But also ours in the most intimate ways.

I couldn't deserve her less.

Or want her more.

Especially when she guides me nearer to her warmth, turning my face into her belly. She lets me nuzzle there while she purrs, massaging my nape as I hide my shame and try to breathe over the burn in my lungs.

Eventually, I come to my senses and curl myself closer, hooking one forearm over her hip. Anchoring my whole being around hers.

I drop a kiss to the place above her navel and lean my head there reverently. Prostrating myself at her altar.

"I don't know how," I vow, to her and myself, "but I will be worthy of you if it's the last thing I do."

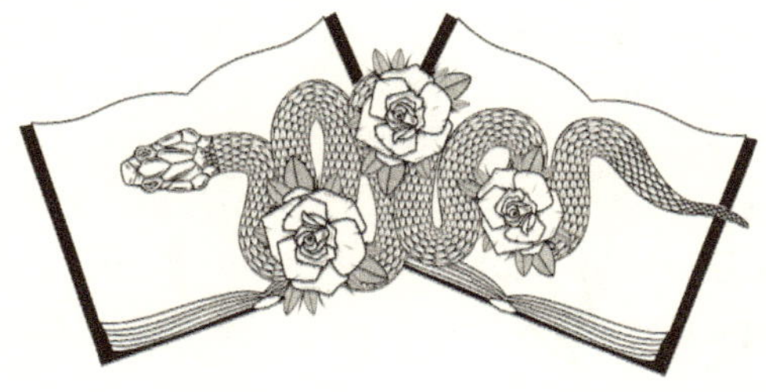

forty-five

BRIAR

THE ONE ISSUE I DIDN'T THINK THROUGH IN MY WHOLE plan to sneak out of the nest, possibly enrage the pack alpha, find the mean one, spill my guts to him, and somehow get him to come back—

Okay, so there were a *few* issues.

But one in particular.

When my stomach grumbled—reminding me my dinner consisted of a little wine and a whole lot of drama—I was *not* prepared for Rhys to leap into action like I was teetering on a burning ledge.

I'm not sure what he plans to do to get takeout at ten a.m.,

259

given it's the staff's morning off—but the man seems pretty damn determined to make it happen.

In typical Rhys fashion, he doesn't offer any explanations. He simply spins his phone in his palm and nods at the second-floor hallway. "Go get comfortable, viper. I'll grab the food and bring it up when it's here... if that's okay with you. Of course."

The vulnerability in his eyes is the only reason I don't tease him for seeming so uncertain. That, and the fact that he listened to my whole sordid story without mocking me *one single time*.

Instead of taunting, I stretch up on my tiptoes and let my lips brush his cheek. "It's okay with me."

A shiver moves through him. His hand snaps to my wrist, a dark look darting across his angelic features when he pulls back. "If you make me come in my pants again," he husks, "I may never live it down."

I raise my brows. "What if that's my master plan?"

"Then it's working."

I'm still dazzled by his rueful, gorgeous parting grin when I step into the shower ten minutes later.

Hell. I really don't know where we *go* from here.

I consider my options as I lather up. Leaving them all. Staying and trying to sway them into helping me. Staying and just... *being*.

God, am I insane?

Actually, I think I might be.

Because the second I skim soap over my skin, my Omega *loses her mind*.

Their scents, she panics, watching the sudsy water swirl down the drain. *They're washing off! They're not on me anymore. I can't —I can't—*

We can't scent them. And as I start drawing quicker, shallower breaths, I realize *I* might be freaking out a little bit, too.

Did I imagine all of this? Am I delusional? Do I actually have mates? Do they truly... *care about me*?

How can any of this be real? How could they be all over my skin and wrapped through the strands of my soul one minute and then just disappear down a drain? Am I still locked in that closet, clinging to sanity?

Knock twice if you're okay, Rosie.

A high whine cracks through the bathroom. Before I can drag in enough steamy air to produce a second one, footsteps race into the room.

My husband's, to be exact.

The look on Cillian's face is feral. Full of so much anger and intensity, I immediately cringe into the glass shower enclosure. My Omega whimpers as I bite my tongue, holding the fearful noise in.

The strides stop.

"*Briar.*"

Is he...?

He *is* purring. And his voice is as gentle as his hands when they find my shoulders. "What's wrong, rosebud?"

"I—I—"

Shit, I really can't breathe. Instincts I can't control skitter up my spine, closing my windpipe. My eyes lose focus, lolling until they find the visible pulse in his neck. I fixate on it instinctively—and the next thing I know, I'm throwing my arms over his broad, bare shoulders. *Climbing* him to get the warm scent of his throat.

For the second time in twelve hours.

So maybe I can see Rhys's point about dying from embarrassment by increments.

But Cillian instantly lifts me into his embrace, stretching his neck to give me better access to the small traces of spice and smoke I sense through what's left of the neutralizer.

"Good fucking girl, needing your alpha," he roughs out, holding me closer. "I've got you."

He nuzzles his cheek over my temple, scent-marking me. My head swims, dizzy from the rush of pheromones and the need for *more*. "Cillian—"

He stills when I say his name, his muscles stiffening around me. "I need you back in the nest," he growls, snatching a towel off the rack and stalking out of the room. "I nearly snapped into a rut when I woke up without you."

"Sorry," I mumble into his neck. "My Omega needed to check on Rhys. She wanted to tell him everything."

You know at some point you're going to have to stop throwing me under the bus, the voice in my middle mutters.

Dream on, traitor, I snap back.

Cillian noses at my cheek, the gesture as sweet as his answering whisper. "Never apologize for caring about my packmates, rosebud. They're your alphas, too."

My alphas.

The truth of that has only just begun setting in. Dane's whispered confessions last night. Rhys groaning into my lap, coming completely undone from the simplest of touches. And Cillian, here. Knowing I needed him, running to my side like—like—

A mate.

"I'm sorry I couldn't tell you before," Cillian murmurs, nudging the door to the nest open with his shoulder. Dane stirs but doesn't wake, burrowing his face further into the blanket they wrapped around me last night.

My husband lowers me to my feet, keeping his hands on my hips to hold me steady as their scents wash over me. I sway, but lock eyes with him, needing to hear the rest of his thought.

"I wanted to," he promises, ice-blue eyes sparking like frozen ponds. "Every fucking day, I woke up and went to sleep wanting nothing more than to barge over to your rehearsals or your father's house and sweep you up. Tell you that we were mates. Carry you home."

But then all their "clients" would have known they had a scent-match. And they might have used me to harm or extort them. Not to mention Gideon and his agenda.

I'm not sure I'll ever admit it to the powerful man throwing himself at my mercy, but I'm not sure I would have wanted any of that.

Once I was here, though... His... He could have told me. I would have tried my best to make his secret into our secret.

"You didn't have to keep me in the dark for so long," I reply, finding some of the strength I desperately lacked before. Picking up steam as I let my righteous indignation flow through me.

"It—this—do you know how *embarrassing* this feels? To know that my Omega was sensing her mates *every day* and I couldn't understand that?! And *you* knew. You knew the truth and you calculated that *I* wouldn't be able to figure it out. Because I didn't know anything about being around alphas—you knew I would assume that all the crazy feelings I had were just normal. *You knew* I'd been sheltered and *you used it against me!*"

Cillian's gaze blazes. "Yes," he finally bites out, reaching over to grasp my jaw, "I used your innocence against you. I used *every fucking thing* I could think of to keep you *safe*. Because that is my *religion*, Briar. My damnation and salvation and every last breath in between. *You*. Safe. *Here*. And *mine*."

Fuck. Fuck him. And fuck *me*, because I don't stop his lips when they find mine.

I open for them.

And lose myself in the way he pours his soul out at my feet. Begging for forgiveness. Demanding my submission. Somehow swirling his need and mine into a thicket so thorny, I know I'll never escape it.

A tangle so beautiful, I don't think I want to.

forty-six

CILLIAN

DANE CHANGED THE NAME OF THIS CHAT TO
THE BLACKWOOD BEASTS

RHYS

That's fair.

CILLIAN

Well-deserved.

RHYS

Wait

RHYS CHANGED THE NAME OF THIS CHAT TO
BRIAR'S BEASTS.

DANE

I stand corrected.

THE BLACKWOOD CREST STARES BACK AT ME AS I PLANT my bare feet against the cold floor of my study.

Bracing my way through one more breath.

Another minute. Another *second*, even.

It's nearly impossible.

But Briar asked for some time to herself tonight. And now that the neutralizers have finally worn off, I had no good reason to deny her.

None of us could think of one, damn it. Not even Rhys.

He may be the only alpha alive who's more miserable than me. I might have to grapple with the uncertainty of not knowing if our mate will ever fully forgive me, but at least she's accepted our match, to some degree. I'm not sure if she's even given my former stepbrother the time of day—and she didn't invite him all the way into her nest, even after he scrounged up five different types of takeout at ten a.m.

She *did* let him sit on the threshold, though. I suspect more out of deference to her Omega than anything else.

Although she did hand him one of her pillows before she banished all of us from her suite, earlier, so perhaps she has a little sympathy.

My fingers twitch around the crystal glass. My ears prick half a second before a sound that *might* be a whine stops me cold.

There isn't a moment when I consider what to do or how

much control to exert—I just move. Stalking across my study and throwing open the door to find—

Dane?

Even with his mask on, he looks guilty. Cringing as he raises the hand outstretched toward Briar's door handle to his shoulder in a jerky twitch. The panic darting through his eyes is new, too. I've seen the guy walk into a hail of bullets and I don't think he came *close* to looking this nervous.

"I was just…"

Sneaking into her room.

To fuck her? Or watch her sleep?

Jesus, which is worse?

My brow rises. "Do you… do this often?"

Dane straightens, his woody scent smoldering while his cheeks turn pink around the edges of his mask. "Only—"

A rustle interrupts us. We both turn, our eyes bulging when we catch Rhys strolling down the hallway. Holding Briar's pillow.

And where the hell did he find a sleeping bag?

For fuck's sake.

Is he going to *camp* in the *hallway*?

He stops short, scowling as he glances between us, down at our empty hands, then at the dark pink cushion wedged between his tattooed arm and his black tank top. With a shrug, he mutters, "At least I was realistic about it."

Dane's shoulders slump on a rough exhale. "I don't *stay the night* in there without her permission. I just like to *check* on her." He casts me some grumbly side-eye. "What's your excuse?"

I stand taller, nodding at the doors. "I heard a whine."

Rhys snorts, shoving a hand through his unruly white-blond hair. "Oh yeah, *sure*."

I open my mouth to argue, but fuck. Am I *sure* I heard her? Or did I just *want* to?

It doesn't matter, because the next voice we hear is our omega's—dry and full of resigned exhaustion.

"Will you jackasses just come in?" she sighs. "Or none of us will *ever* get to sleep."

MY WIFE IS WAITING WITH ALL OF HER LIGHTS OFF, lying in the middle of her mattress, glaring at the ceiling.

Fucking hell, she's adorable. And sexy as sin, in that pewter-gray nightgown, with my lock still tethered around her neck. I want to sling her over my shoulder like a caveman and cart her to my bedroom. Show her all the things I have for us to explore together in there. Including many suitable punishments for a pouting bride.

Her arms are crossed over her chest. They rise and fall on another dramatic sigh. "Would it *kill* you guys to *knock* like normal people?"

Beside me, Rhys actually *winces*. "Sorry, omega. I'll knock next time."

Briar narrows her eyes, tossing him a vicious scowl. "Oh now you're *nice*?" He opens his mouth, but she keeps going. "Honestly, all of you are insane. And mean. And presumptuous and somehow too smart *and* clueless and—"

She huffs out another breath. My palms tingle at my sides, my cock kicking higher in my sweats.

It seems the time alone helped her process some of her anger... and come up with a lot more of it. Honestly, she would probably feel better after a spanking. Or a long edging session.

Something tells me this isn't the right time to suggest that, though.

With another pissy grunt, she jerks her chin back toward the ceiling and reaches left, flipping her covers open.

"Well, *get in*," she hisses. "Christ."

None of us need a second invitation. Dane stomps to the

other side of her bed, hovering there as Rhys slides around me and makes his way to the foot. I stride for the opening she offered, sitting on the mattress and suppressing a smirk when I see her pouty features up close.

Like I said, *adorable*.

"Hello, Mrs. Blackwood," I murmur, bending to kiss her cheek. "May I have this spot?"

Briar glares overhead for another few moments, then finally blows out a long exhale, her body sagging. When she speaks again, her voice is soft with embarrassment. "No," she says. "Rhys needs it tonight."

I'm thrown for a second, but when I see the stark awe filling Rhys's face, something in my center clicks.

This is our *mate*—the omega destined to be the perfect center for our pack. Of course she can sense which of us needs her the most.

The fact that she knows doesn't surprise me, but the fact that she *cares* is shocking. I see the hurt wariness in her gaze when it leaps to my stepbrother. Not to mention the way both of their scents shift—his soaring and hers darkening.

He does need this.

And it's costing *her*.

The instinct to protect wars with my desire for pack cohesion. I want us all to have what we need, but not at her expense. Never again.

I start to protest, opening my mouth to issue a low, smooth bark—but Rhys backs up, swallowing so hard I hear it.

"N-no, viper," he whispers. "You don't have to do that."

The last of her aggression falls away, leaving a distinctly vulnerable look in her green depths. "Yeah," she sighs, "but your head hurts when you fight your Alpha. And this helped before... right?"

His sigh audibly quivers. "Briar, seriously. You don't owe me anything."

Dane sits beside her, his hand finding her hair. "He's right, moonbeam. You can kick us out now. And I'll get you a deadbolt for your door tomorrow. You don't have to let us in here ever—"

Her whine is unmistakable this time. I fall to my knees at her bedside as Dane starts to purr. Briar blinks toward his chest, her eyes glimmering as emotion fills her voice. "I don't know what I'm doing, okay?" she admits. "But I feel really lonely in here by myself at night."

Devastation crumples my insides. Pain fills Rhys's features as Briar lifts her wet eyes to his. "Please, Rhys?"

He practically *dives*, spearing into place at her side as though it would take the jaws of life to hold him back. "I'm here, pretty baby," he croons. "You'll never have to ask me again. I'll be here every night for as long as you'll have me."

Briar's lower lip wobbles while she stares up at his face. "Even if I try to stab you again?"

Rhys's mouth curves. "Especially then, viper."

Her happy scent is mind-melting. Tart and sweet, a mouthwatering combination that makes me dizzy as I hide another smile, hefting myself off my knees and nudging my packmate. "Move over."

Rhys easily shifts them to the middle of the mattress, giving Dane and me room to climb in. I chose this Alaskan king, hoping we'd need all the space one day—and now we're here. The tension in my middle eases while we settle.

Dane rolls onto his side, slipping his arm under Briar's pillow and letting her snuggle close, with her head resting in the crook of his shoulder. She opens her own arms for Rhys, who stays true to his word and accepts her silent offer without pause.

Once he has his cheek on her chest, I see Briar's point. The way his entire body relaxes while her hands roam his back... He *does* need this. Her.

And she *cares*, despite all the reasons we gave her not to bother.

Rhys passes out first, forehead resting below her collarbone and his mouth slightly ajar. Dane's purrs eventually fade into soft snores. Briar closes her eyes, but I can practically *feel* her thinking too hard.

When she glances over and finds me staring, I let my hand rest on top of her head, carefully sifting through her dark hair. Projecting the soul-deep gratitude I feel for her.

Thank you, omega.

I swear she hears me, even though our souls aren't linked.

Not yet, I tell my Alpha as he projects a wave of solid, soothing power for her. *Soon.*

My omega eventually tilts her head into my touch. She loves having her scalp massaged—and I love anything that puts this dreamy look on her face.

When I don't let up, she protests sleepily, "You must be tired. You don't have to keep going…"

I smile wider, satisfaction pouring through me. "You take care of them," I tell her. "I'll take care of you. That's how this works, omega."

Her creamy, unmarked throat works over a swallow. My canines ache along with my knot, the latter twitching fuller when she bites her lower lip and asks, "Are—are we still going to do our special nights this week? You and me? And each of the guys?"

She still *wants* us to come to her? To *be* with her?

I rub at her scalp with more insistence, purring louder. "You can have as many special nights as you want, Mrs. Blackwood."

DANE

I didn't think it was possible for someone to be more unsure than me about this little outing, but Briar surpasses my anxiety by the time we hit the end of our street.

I watch her in the edges of my vision—adjusting her tantalizingly short pleated skirt, pulling at her knee-high lace stockings, nervously flicking her hair over her shoulder and chewing her pale pink lip.

I suppose it makes sense. This is likely the first time she's been out in the world without rules, threats, or coercion. Which is exactly why *I* wanted to be the one to take her.

She seemed excited when I asked her if she'd like to trade our scheduled night for a day *and* a night. Briar agreed, but as the morning wore on, I noticed her twitching while she dressed and did her makeup.

Maybe this is too soon, I think. *Should I have taken her somewhere private first?*

I figured a local bookstore in a nearby small town would be a safe option. Quiet and cozy. Plus, I know she loves to read.

Yet by the time we pull into a parking spot, she's practically vibrating. I throw my Bronco into park and place my hand on her thigh, squeezing gently. "We don't have to go in, little girl. This can just be a nice drive."

And I can take you home and bury my face up this short little skirt.

Briar swallows, wincing. "It isn't that. I want to go out, I just... I have no idea how to be around *normal* people. And I can't shake the feeling that I'm doing something *wrong*. All the *punishments* and—"

My purr starts up automatically, cutting her off. I start to apologize, but she blinks at my chest before leaning across the center console. I take her into my arms, gathering her body between mine and the steering wheel.

Our poor omega had to suffer so much on her own. It enrages me, knowing she had to deal with her father's abuse and the fear she felt once they took her sister.

We have to find her so Briar can have peace. I will tear the whole fucking planet to pieces if I have to. And I'm not alone.

Rhys is spending half of his time combing through records of every hospital and penitentiary in the country, while Cillian has essentially hired an entire *team* of investigators.

There's still hope. Even though it's been a week and we still haven't found one goddamn trace of her sister. The thought puts a rougher edge around my rumbles.

"Seriously," I murmur. "We don't have to go in if you're not ready. I can take you home and we can let Cillian plan your first outing."

That's probably better, actually. She's still wearing his necklace, after all. And she might feel safer with her pack alpha. Someone who isn't a murderer.

Or isn't as *much* of a murderer, anyway.

But Briar shakes her head against my throat, scent-marking me and rubbing my woodsy musk all over her face. "No," she whispers, delicate fingers curling into my loose hair. "I want it to be you."

Fuck. My *heart*. This woman owns every warped piece of it. So I suppose, if she wants to smash it to bits, that's her prerogative.

"That's it, moonbeam. Let me hold you. We can go in whenever you're ready."

Briar sinks into my arms without a shred of hesitation. It feels natural, now. The way she lets her body go lax sends a warm burst through my blood. My purr deepens and she closes her eyes.

I smile at her bold slashes of black eyeliner, remembering the care she took to paint them on. She seems to enjoy dolling herself up to match her stylish outfits; I don't know anything about fashion or beauty products, but I might have to learn if I want something more intelligent to say than the dumb compliment I manage to scrape out.

"You look pretty."

Briar doesn't open her eyes, but she flashes my favorite version of her smile—the wide, almost-goofy one. Fondness, mixed with a little dash of teasing. "Thanks, big man. You look pretty, too."

I look like most people's waking nightmare. Come to think of it, I probably should have opted for a mask that wasn't so damn intimidating today. Or a bandana. But then I'd just look like a weird-ass cowboy.

Briar doesn't notice how awkward or terrifying I am. She huddles closer and hums softly before releasing a deep breath, finally turning her head to see our destination.

The old bookshop hasn't been updated since the eighties, but it has the small-town charm the rest of this tiny hamlet does. A faded kind of beauty—withered ivy and sun-bleached bricks. Rusty wrought-iron fencing and a few empty window boxes.

Shit.

"Maybe I should have taken you into the city instead," I grumble. "But it's loud and crowded there. Plus, it's easier to keep you *safe* here, so I—"

Briar's mouth lands on my cheek, cutting me off. It's an innocent gesture of appreciation, but my knot starts to inflate.

She pulls back with another dazzling smile. "You might be the cutest man alive."

I blink, dazed. Reaching for the only argument I have. "I'm a monster."

"Yeah." She grins wider, popping my car door open with a shrug. "But a really fucking cute one."

forty-eight

BRIAR

W ITH EVERY PASSING MOMENT, I FEEL THE TRUTH settle deeper into my bones.

These alphas are my mates.

And I think I'm going to let them try to prove themselves.

Or, in Dane's case, I *am* letting him try.

The fact that he's already found my kryptonite probably doesn't bode well for me. This forgotten little bookstore is exactly the sort of thing I used to daydream about when I was a girl, reading about heroines who had stacks upon stacks of books like these.

The rambling collection contains everything from travel to dark romance. All stuffed onto ramshackle shelves that stretch from the creaky wood floor to the painted eaves of the low ceiling. A college-aged clerk sits at the register. She glances up from her phone lazily when we walk in, but otherwise the place is deserted on a weekday morning.

Dane diligently follows me through the tiny shop, never once complaining when I add books to the growing stack in his arms. So far, we're at eleven, although this store's selection of smut is even less impressive than Rhys's.

The sudden urge to tease him is almost as shocking as the realization that I *can*, now. Thanks to *him*.

My silver-blond alpha has come knocking three times since our first sleepover last night. Once to drop off a pile of books, another to sheepishly leave some of his worn shirts so my Omega could have his scent in the nest. Then, right before Dane and I left, Rhys arrived with a brand-new iPhone in his hands.

It even had a lace-patterned black case on it.

Just like the books and his music, he offered the cell without trying to touch me or get one of his jabs in. While I blinked at the screen in shock—*My own phone? The ability to call for help or an Uber? Social media and videos and*—he explained that Cillian had okayed his purchase and asked that Dane show me where all of their names were saved.

Swallowing, I pull the new device out of my skirt's back pocket and swipe it open, staring at the blank thread where Rhys had shown me I could text him. Dane glances over my shoulder, then immediately pretends to look busy, furrowing his brow and leaning closer to the shelf of books at his eye level.

So fucking *cute*, this man.

I think back to how terrifying he seemed the day we met. What if I hadn't gotten to see this side of him? Does Rhys have any facets he's hiding under all his poison? My thumbs hover over the screen.

BRIAR

Hey, venom

If I buy some books, can I keep them in the library? Or do you only store boring, prude nonsense in there?

His bubble appears immediately, bouncing as he replies.

RHYS

Maybe you just don't know where to look, viper.

I could show you.

If you want.

His tone could be construed as clipped—but for some reason, I keep picturing the earnest look on his face as he hovered in my doorway today. And I think that maybe, what I'm reading is Rhys being unsure *of himself*.

BRIAR

You could... maybe when we have our night together?

RHYS

Oh no, baby.

When it's my turn, I'm taking you out for a night of epic groveling.

Followed by you hopefully sitting on my face until neither of us can breathe.

Respectfully.

So... not *that* unsure of himself, then.

My perfume swells around me, slick wetting my fishnet-covered thighs. Dane coughs over an instinctive growl. I blink at my screen.

BRIAR

> Don't tempt me. I might enjoy smothering you.

RHYS

> I'm counting on it, viper.

Dane is clearly reading the messages, but I don't blame him. When I toss a smirk over my shoulder, he blushes around his mask.

"Sorry, omega. I'll let you guys talk and, uh, go set these on the register. So I can carry more."

I stretch up and kiss the titanium covering his cheek. Dane shivers, the prominent ridge along his inseam stretching longer against his thigh. I rub a scent-mark along the neck of his Henley, smiling at him. "Okay. I'll be here."

Rhys sends another message, asking which books I'm buying. At first I roll my eyes, sure I'm about to get book-shamed by Mr. Highbrow. But when I purposefully send some of the more outrageous titles, he shoots back a screenshot of matching digital downloads in his eReader app.

RHYS

> So I can read along.

> And see what sorts of ideas are in that pretty head of yours.

> If you'll have me.

Oh.
My.
God.

I'm so busy mooning over that one stupid offer, I don't notice footfall approaching from another direction. A tall, thick-chested man appears at the end of the aisle.

He's striking—a white linen button-down and khaki pants highlighting the warmth of his flawless brown skin. Glasses sit askew on his nose, giving him an air of distraction. But a powerful alpha scent strikes me sideways, bitter and dark.

I step back on instinct, my spine protesting as I try to flatten myself into the shelves. The alpha scowls at me, his entire face morphing into a look of pure disgust.

I'm not sure why I feel so powerfully *afraid* of him. But he can tell—a knowing flash streaks across his face before he opens his mouth, advancing.

A vicious snarl sounds from behind me as Dane reappears. The other alpha is tall, but nowhere near Dane's hulking brawn. My alpha sends him back a step, his distaste morphing into dis*dain*.

"What the fuck are you doing here?" my big man demands.

Almost as if they... know each other?

When he catches my startled glance, Dane sighs, pulling my body into his side and muttering, "This is Atlas. Gideon's packmate."

Sure enough, the too-handsome alpha himself rounds the corner as Dane says his name, bringing his muted toastiness with him.

My fierce masked man stiffens. His grip on my arm goes from reassuring to *protective*. "What the fuck do you want?" he spits, shifting to put his body in front of mine.

Gideon smiles, the expression full of conceit. "A second look," he chips back.

Dane's chest rumbles ominously. "How the hell did you know—"

"—where she was?" Gideon finishes. His grin sharpens. "I'd say lucky guess, but you know that's horseshit."

The sharp gleam in his eye says this is anything but coincidental. A shiver runs down my back and Dane's hand flattens over my hip, his thumb rubbing a soothing circle under the waistband of my skirt.

Gideon's clipped packmate snaps, "We followed you here. Obviously."

"Briar and I barely got to speak the other night," Gideon goes on. "She ran off before I could finish explaining the finer points of your business dealings to her."

Atlas's focus flies to where Dane touches me and fresh fear rocks my middle. *Shit. Aren't we supposed to act indifferent around them? Not like mates?*

My big man seems to remember the same second I do, standing straighter and letting his hand fall into a fist at his side. Atlas tracks the motion with interest that feels all too keen.

"She doesn't need an explanation from *you*," Dane growls. "So fuck off. Or I'll call Cillian."

The mention of my husband definitely cools his cousin's confidence a bit. "I'm not here to see you," he replies flatly, pretty gray eyes flickering to mine. "Briar can decide if she wants to come with us and talk or stay here with you. Can't you, Briar?"

Dane freezes. His underlying rumble cuts off. "Of course she can," he grits, looking over at me. Those gold irises seethe before softening on my features. His voice drops into a murmur. "She can do whatever she wants."

I think he really means that. If I walked out of here, away from him... I believe he would let me. Cillian, on the other hand...

Well, he might allow it.

But there'd be no guarantees about not following me.

Gideon's hard bark of laughter breaks our stare. Dane ducks his head, deliberately stepping to the side and backing up. Showing me that I truly do have a choice.

I could really leave.

He keeps his neck bent, looking down at this combat boots while I make my decision. I pivot to the handsome alpha and his equally attractive packmate, folding my arms over my chest. Feeling the warm metal heart slip into the space between my breasts. Remembering the moment my husband locked it into place.

Gideon arches his brows. "What do you say, Mrs. Blackwood? Want to come with us? Get away from these assholes?"

Dane stifles another growl. A text from Rhys vibrates in my hand.

And—*GODDAMN IT*—my head shakes.

"No," I say, realizing how very much I mean it. "No, I don't."

"COME HERE."

In all the time I've known my giant, masked alpha, he's never been quite so scary. The intensity radiating from his taut, muscled frame is enough to flip my stomach inside out... and send fresh slick leaking into my tights.

After I told Gideon and Atlas to fuck off, Dane stood motionless at the end of the aisle, looming like the Grim Reaper himself until the others slunk out of the store.

Now he has that same furious expression on his face... only it's aimed at me?

Maybe not, though. Because the fingers wrapped around my wrist are still undeniably gentle, even though his grip feels as insistent as the gold chain looped around my neck.

He uses his leverage to steer me to the back of the shop, as far from the blank, uninterested gaze of the sole clerk as he can get. Not that it matters—when she hears the other alphas shuffle out, she pulls a pack of cigarettes from her bag and follows them.

Leaving us alone.

Uh-oh.

With a final twirl, Dane cages me in with his arms and practically tackles me into the shelves.

Lord, for someone so big, he's *fast*. One second I'm blinking up at him, and the next he's unclasped the top buckle on his mask. It falls, the remaining strap dangling around his neck as he bends forward and sweeps me into a devouring kiss.

I squeak, clinging to his wide shoulders as he groans under his breath, the sound just desperate enough to tighten everything between my hips. His scent swells, the dark, wooden musk washing over me in a warm wave that somehow gives me goosebumps. My breasts peak in their lacy cups, the textured fabric rubbing at the sensitive points until I perfume.

Dane's ragged snarl tingles on my tongue before he breaks away, panting, "I can't believe you didn't leave with them."

I peer up into his molten eyes, a confession wrenching its way from my soul. "I couldn't," I admit. "I didn't want to."

Dane's breath quivers. "Briar... are you really giving us a chance?"

To stay with them.

That's what he's asking. If I'd actually consider making us into a real pack after all the shit that brought us here. Being bound to these beasts, in body and soul. Forever.

It's terrifying.

It makes me wet.

And it has my heart *aching*.

"I don't know," I whisper, looking up at him. Opening myself up to his penetrating gaze. "But I don't want you to stop trying."

From the first day we met, this alpha has understood me in ways no one else ever has. Not even Cillian. Or Violet—or myself.

Tenderness and hope burn in his ocher eyes, holding my stare. He rests his forehead against mine and nods slowly, agreeing and scent-marking me simultaneously.

"I won't stop."

He's returning the words I gave him the morning we discovered his touch starvation. Maybe because he's discovered that touch isn't the only thing my Omega and I crave so fiercely.

I also need this—the devotion softening his scarred, rugged features; the near-silent reassurance reverberating in his chest. It melts the last of my resistance, pulling more perfume from my body as it sags between his and the bookshelves.

Dane kisses me with more intent, sliding his hands down my sides. When I whimper, my hips automatically bucking into his,

his raspy voice drops into a soothing murmur. "Does this pretty pussy need my mouth?"

I bite my lip to stem the eager whine my Omega produces. "Shouldn't we wait?" I ask, glancing around.

Dane flashes his rare smile, this time edged in wickedness. His fingers find the hem of my skirt and slip past it as he shakes his head.

"Good little girls don't have to wait."

His knees hit the floor, making good on his word as he ducks his head under my skirt. I start to squirm away, not sure if I'll be able to focus, but he curses under his breath. The exhale hits my bare, wet skin.

Oh, right. These fishnets don't work with underwear... so I don't have any on.

That discovery spikes his scent. Fresh slick dribbles out of me.

I expect him to tear my tights or reach for the waistband, but the big alpha shocks me again. Instead, he opens his mouth and licks me right through the textured weave.

I choke on a moan, feeling his wet, languid tongue rubbing the rough scratch of the fishnets into my clit. Lapping into the holes and licking me directly.

My knees buckle, but his wide hands span my waist, holding me up. Letting him dip between my thighs and ram his tongue through the black netting, into my gushing pussy.

He teases me there, stroking a firm circle around the place that aches for a knot. Until my clit is buzzing, begging for even the smallest—

Ah!

A cool stream of air flutters over the slick nub. It pulses harder, so primed to burst the second he lays his thick tongue flat against it and works in a slow, sinuous lap.

I keen, my body sagging as relief and ecstasy explode from my core. Dane groans, sucking up all the slick that spills from me as my hips buck.

My vision is still blurry when he lumbers back to his feet. Grinning.

The big man leans close, nipping my ear as he murmurs, "Next time, you'll keep quiet. Or I'll have to loan you my mask."

forty-nine

BRIAR

BRIAR

I assume the cocktail dress on my bed means
we have a date tonight?

You could *ask* you know

CILLIAN

Not my style, Mrs. Blackwood.

Besides, you have more than one suspect
when it comes to leaving you mysterious gifts.

BRIAR

So it wasn't you?

> Cillian?

> I stg I can *hear* your evil chuckle all the way from Manhattan.

> Prick.

CILLIAN

> I miss you too, rosebud.

WHEN I FOUND TONIGHT'S OUTFIT ON MY BED, I assumed my husband was up to his usual devilish tricks.

So imagine my surprise when I step into the foyer, smoothing the short skirt of the shiny, crimson slip-dress over my hips, and find Rhys standing at the bottom of the grand staircase.

He looks impeccable, wearing a close-cut red suit so dark it's almost black. Of the three alphas, he definitely has the most flair for fashion. The thin silver chain connecting his black silk tie and the dagger pin on his jacket pocket is evidence of that. Combined with his onyx shirt, white-blond hair, and ghostly eyes... the combination is deadly.

For a moment, I miss the neutralizers that have finally worn off. Because—*damn it all to hell*—isn't Rhys pretty enough without the tantalizing swirl of eucalyptus that washes over me?

The scent hits and I nearly miss a stair. Rhys seems oblivious, though. His pale throat bobs while his brows crouch over his sea-glass gaze, watching me with a blend of predatory interest and... nerves?

His cool essence definitely has a bit of an edge to it. Not to mention the way he fidgets with his cufflinks.

I smirk at him, finally stepping onto the main floor. "What? You picked this dress, not me, venom."

He glowers mildly before clearing his throat, eyes dropping to his shiny black shoes. "I wasn't sure you'd actually come down," he mutters. "No one would blame you for changing your mind."

I open my mouth to tell him I didn't do it for him—that I thought this ensemble was Cillian's doing. But my Omega nudges me hard.

Be nice, she hisses.

I roll my eyes internally. *Or what?*

Or he might get even <u>more</u> discouraged, she argues, knocking me back a bit. *<u>Look</u> at him.*

She guides my focus back to the alpha's face, pointing out the tension in his jaw and worry lining his eyes. His posture, too. Usually, Rhys has an indolent sort of charm to him—but tonight he looks all wrong. Too rigid and careful.

God, why does that *bother* me?

I toss my hair back and smile to myself when his gaze catches on the black-crystal combs I twisted into the sides of my semi-updo. Instead of taunting him, I try for a casual tone.

"I didn't change my mind. Although, if you take me back to that uppity-as-fuck restaurant Cillian dragged me to after our 'wedding'"—I throw up agitated air quotes, glaring flatly—"I *will* stab you. Again. Probably with the wrong fork."

Rhys actually laughs, a low strained sound that shimmers with the barest hint of relief. "Just as well," he agrees, offering me his arm. "I have a different surprise in mind."

FOR ALL THE THINGS I'M NOT SURE I'LL FORGIVE RHYS for, this one might take the cake.

Because *how* am I supposed to keep him at arm's length after *this*?

The performing arts center always looks best all lit up for an evening show. Surrounded by the bustling city, but set far enough from the main road to give it a stately air.

The marquee outside proudly proclaims the season's premiere.

Tonight.

Sleeping Beauty.

Rhys tosses the keys of his matte-black Bugatti to the valet, then rounds the car with the sort of long, confident strides that make my stomach flutter. Why does he have to look so damn debonaire, buttoning his jacket with a practiced flick of his hand? Almost as if he's done this a thousand times...

How is that so hot?

And *why* in God's name does the idea of him charming other women make me *jealous*?

It's possible I've cracked. Perhaps book shopping with Dane, publicly choosing him over an escape hatch, and letting the big man get me off in the back of the store broke my brain. Or at the very least scrambled it.

Because as Rhys opens my door and offers a gentlemanly hand, a sudden rush of desire swirls my thoughts into a dizzy jumble. A thread of dark cherry perfume winds into the air and the ice-blond alpha smirks, though his eyes soften simultaneously.

His mouth kicks into a devious smile when my incredulous gaze darts to the marquee a second time. "Come on, viper. I can't show you off from the car. And we have our own box."

The feel of our fingers sliding together sends an electric charge down my arm. I play it off, shaking my hair over my shoulder to hide a shiver as a wave of tart-and-sweet perfume follows me out of the car.

To my surprise, Rhys doesn't act too cool to care. In fact, tonight, his usual arrogance is more like an accessory than a suit of armor.

Instead of ignoring my scent, he uses my hand to twirl me into his body, catching me close and bending to rub a scent-mark over my bare shoulder.

Oh.

He's *smooth*.

And utterly *devastating* when he flashes a small, almost *shy* version of his crooked grin. "You know you're fucking gorgeous, right?" he mumbles. "I don't need to keep saying it?"

I guide his hand at my hip to my hidden thigh garter—and my favorite switchblade. "You will if you know what's good for you," I threaten.

Rhys's eyes spark as he traces the lace and metal. His dark smirk reappears, but something solid and solemn settles there. "Not one of my strengths, I'm afraid."

It's an apology. One of a dozen, at this point. Every time we've spoken since Saturday night, he's directly and indirectly told me how sorry he is for how he treated me.

I believe him, but I can't shake the part of me that's hurt by the constant litany of regret. I wasn't worthy of them, before... but now I am? The same way he hated my guts until the moment he found out I was his mate?

My stomach clenches, but my Omega refuses to let go of his hand. I glare at her internally; she pretends to be oblivious.

Brat, I snipe.

Gee, I wonder where I learned that, she snaps back.

Bitch, I amend.

Rhys mistakes my scowl for disapproval. He rubs the back of his neck, darting a sideways glance at the theater. "I knew this was a gamble," he mutters. "But I figured you might miss dancing the same way I missed playing music. I thought—"

He chokes himself off, eerie aqua eyes flickering over my expression before he forces a swallow and admits, "You gave that back to me. So I wanted to give this back to you."

The moment is surreal—standing on a sidewalk, with the performing arts center lighting the horizon. Surrounded by a hundred couples in formal wear. Staring up at the alpha who hated me.

My *mate*.

He's sorry, but he's not just trying to get me to forgive him. He's trying to *make it up to me*, any way he can.

And this time, when our fingers lace tighter? It isn't for anyone but myself.

RHYS

I ATTENDED MY FIRST OPERA WHEN I WAS SIX.

Cillian's father dragged the two of us to his company box for *La Traviata*. Cillian was asleep before the second curtain—and I was in love.

For years, operas, ballets, and symphonies were the only escape I had from being Caine's unwanted stepson. My mother's Albatross. The bane of Forsyth Blackwood's existence.

After a lifetime of dread, this was the only *good* kind of anticipation I'd ever known. Here, in the quiet dark of a theater, holding my breath before the opening note rang out.

And now? With Briar sitting beside me?

I might never catch my breath again.

Her perfume is the only scent in my entire world, slicing deeper into my lungs on every inhale. Carving its way to my soul.

It's not just that, though. It's *her*.

The tilt of her heavily lined green eyes. Her lustrous hair and cut-crystal combs. Those long, gleaming talons. Her cool skin and black-diamond locket. The effortless poise and sex appeal beneath every minor move she makes.

She's a goddess. And a work of art.

But she's also *funny*, fierce, and fucking *smart*. We've only been sitting here for ten minutes and she's already blown my mind with all the small details she remembers from this ballet— despite never having actually performed it herself.

One of our bodyguards for the night arrives with a tray of chilled champagne. Briar eyes her flute warily, but plucks it up, sliding her suspicious gaze around the rest of our balcony.

It's lovely, in my opinion. All gilded, scrolled edges and sumptuous purple fabrics. I appreciate how private the boxes are, too— with solid wood-paneled walls between each individual booth instead of fabric or bars.

Our guard disappears behind the curtains hiding our alcove from the narrow hallway behind us and I suppress a cringe. With any luck, Briar won't notice just how many hired men I have with us. Cillian and I had them dress as valets, bathroom attendants, servers, and ushers. She seemed bewildered enough as I whisked her up here—blinking wide eyes at the center's enormous foyer chandelier and the crowd milling around us.

Poor baby. She must have performed here dozens of times and her bastard father never let her so much as set foot in the lobby on the night of a performance?

God, she probably hasn't been *anywhere*. There are so many places I could take her. Shows she would love. Restaurants, other countries.

Briar feels my consideration as I scan her profile. She turns her head, quirking her eyebrows. "What?"

How is it possible for someone to be so sexy and cool and *cute* all at the same time? I don't know, but my lips curve into an involuntary smile.

I'd lost all hope of finding a mate. Now that she's here and mine and so goddamn *perfect*... well, I don't blame her for being annoyed. I can't take my eyes off her.

I sit forward, sliding my arm along the back of her chair and dropping a kiss to her shoulder. "Just looking at you."

Briar glowers, but there's no denying the shiver that skitters down her spine when I brush my lips along her collarbone. Her scent swells and I'm sure mine rises to meet it. Because here? In the dark?

She's the only thing I sense.

BY THE MIDDLE OF THE SECOND ACT, I'VE BARELY registered a single scene.

Briar is far more interesting. Her enjoyment is palpable, filling the air in our balcony with lusciously tart sweetness as she gradually sinks into my side.

I soak in each moment while she watches with bated breath. At the scene where Sleeping Beauty and her prince dance together in a dream, Briar's eyes fill as she gazes at the stage, a single glassy tear trailing down her cheek.

She's a secret romantic, I realize. *Like me.*

I bet no one has ever given her that kind of passion and softness.

But I'm here now. And those are the exact things I've kept to myself, saving them for my mate. For *her*.

On stage, the prince rides off to slay the dragon and rescue his princess. Briar finally exhales, bursting into applause with the rest of the crowd. I'm motionless, stunned into absolute stillness by how perfect she is for me.

When she finally turns to see why I haven't so much as twitched, our gazes lock. She sees whatever swirls in my eyes and I see the wonder filling hers.

The curtain drops.

And we collide.

Letting myself fall into Rhys feels like being reborn.

I'm suddenly a phoenix. Plummeting into fear and darkness. Burning to ash.

Rising. *Rising.*

Alive.

Rhys catches me close, letting me sink into his depths. The terrifying, bittersweet ones I've stared into so many times, without ever having the courage to dive.

I take the leap now. Kissing the mean, misunderstood, menacing man who—oh *God*—seems to maybe *love* me.

And it feels *good*.

Like abandon and exhilaration and perhaps even something sacred.

Rhys groans, clasping a hand around my jaw and tilting my face to plunge his tongue into my mouth. A tremor darts down my spine, landing between my hips with a wet squelch. Perfume pours out of me, along with enough slick to dampen the back of my dress and his lap.

I tense, certain he's about to rage at me for ruining our civilized appearances—but my mate hums gently, his smooth purr bleeding into the bass from the symphony's score. "Shh, pretty baby. That's okay. I want every drop of your slick. Get it all over me."

His words are almost as arousing as his touch. While one hand holds my cheek, the other slips between my legs, gathering the evidence of my desire on his palm. He brings it to his lips, licking the glossy wetness off his fingers while his gaze burns into mine. With every lap, I feel his cock tick harder against my ass.

"Seriously," I whine under my breath. "You have to stop. I'm going to ruin your suit."

Electricity snaps in his light eyes. "Fuck my suit," he decides, lifting me with one arm and shoving his pants down with the other. "Fuck everyone and everything but you and me. Because that's all that matters, Briar. It's all that ever has."

He's lying. A week ago, he openly loathed me. Wanted to *hurt* me. *Of course* I'm not the one thing that mattered to him.

But it's nice, just for a second, to let his words soak into my center. And pretend they could be true.

My Omega practically glows, begging me to give her just one more minute before I yank us away. *Please. I know he hurt you... but he's my Alpha.*

She's trying to understand, but she really can't. Rhys hated *me*, not her. Besides, *she's* the only reason he's looking at me like this now.

I spent weeks ignoring my Omega's pleas, though. All it did

was prolong the inevitable—because as I sit here, with the orchestra swelling behind me and Rhys burning a path to my *soul*, I know the truth.

This bond between us is eternal.

And I have to try.

I have to let *him* try.

He's already better than I ever imagined he could be. Ghostly eyes move over my features in slow brushes, absorbing every flicker of feeling I reveal, voluntary or not. His hands find my bare skin. Teasing, tender caresses leave embers in their wake.

When Rhys slowly lifts my hand to his face and rubs a scent-mark over my knuckles, he lets his eyes fall shut. Earnest yearning lines his perfect features as he exhales.

He's shaking.

And letting me see it.

Certainty soothes the restless shift in my center. Swallowing the tangle in my throat, I glance behind me. It's perfectly dark up here—and the patrons in the balconies across from ours are thoroughly engrossed in the scene on stage...

I slide off the alpha's lap. Rhys pants, watching with rapt attention as I push my panties down. I move to kick them away, but he muffles a growl, snapping his arm down to swipe them from the carpeted floor.

When he tucks the black-lace scrap into his pocket, his voice drops into a husk. Signaling that his Alpha is speaking as much as he is. "These are mine now," he decides, gaze brightening. "No one else can have your scent."

Part of me wants to point out that, if we continue, everyone in the surrounding boxes will surely pick up on it. And his. But that thought puts an unfamiliar pinch of possession on my next breath, lining it with an omega growl I can't control.

Rhys's eyes glimmer. His cock kicks higher, the knot at the base already so full it's nearly purple. I lick my lips when an herbaceous burst of his alpha essence winds into my tart scent, the combination dizzying.

"If you're mine, then I'm yours, too," he roughs out, fisting himself and offering the glistening erection to me. "Use me, viper."

Fresh need razes a hot path through my veins, thickening the throb between my thighs. All the muscles begging for the stretch of his perfectly-carved shaft clamp on air.

I know it's usually the men in romance books having a *fuck it* moment, but...

Fuck it.

I straddle the beautiful alpha, letting him balance us while I focus on getting his cock inside me. His long fingers—littered with fresh callouses from his violin—clutch my upper thighs, shoving my silky slip-dress up to my waist. He fists the skirt at the small of my back, leaving our lower halves bared as my slippery pussy lips gloss his cock.

His body shudders. Sharp, feral eyes snap to the space behind me, scanning the audience to make sure no one can see us.

Rhys plants his feet and pushes his chair back, drawing us farther into the shadows. Purring and wrapping me closer, his free hand gropes blindly for his discarded jacket, settling it over my shoulders. Ensuring I'm covered.

Oh.

That one gesture makes me feel more secure and protected than any pretty words ever could. It releases the last of my doubt, leaving me free to ride the wave of pure desperation rearing high in my middle.

My Omega whines. I lurch upright, positioning his wide, pulsing head at the quivering hole carved into my core. Slick gushes down his broad length. He moans, the pained plea lost to a burst of wind instruments.

I can't resist drawing more desperation out of him. Bringing him lower. And he *loves* it.

Rhys's head falls back as I swivel my hips in a slow circle, following the rhythm of the string melody below. "Briar," he chokes, the word a quivering breath against my throat. "Jesus Christ."

Watching his unrestrained pleasure sends a warm burst of bliss dripping from my pussy. Slick shimmers in the low light, glistening on my thighs, his knot, the straining hardness jerking with every pass of my lips over the taut, hot skin.

He openly squirms, chest heaving under his silk shirt. I see the letters inked there—*DEATH BEFORE DISHONOR*—and nearly smirk.

"Not so proud now, venom?" I murmur.

Rhys's hips buck, the fist thick inch of his cock slipping into my clenching heat. His eyes glimmer, but the deepest, truest *want* burns behind his lust. "When it comes to you?" he pants out, "I have no pride, Briar."

The words knock me off my game. I freeze, blinking down at his sincere expression. Rhys sighs and reaches up to cup my face, whispering, "It's okay. Pride has no place between mates. I don't need it; not if I have *you*."

Maybe he's right. Maybe that's why I find myself sobbing as I finally lower myself onto his cock. Maybe that's why I don't care when he witnesses my features contorting in breathless, agonized pleasure.

We stare into one another, both of us open-mouthed with awe. A low groan tears up his throat when my internal muscles flex around his girth.

I can't help it, though. He feels *perfect*. A missing piece, striking an empty ache I didn't know I had.

The urge to ride him overwhelms me. Behind us, the symphony crescendos, its epic score breaking into a gallop the same moment I do. Rhys snarls, his cock vibrating on the serrated sound and reverberating with lingering purrs while he thrusts, meeting every plunge of my hips.

The weight of his girth, the way his veins rub at all the nerves tingling for his knot... I know I won't last past this one movement.

But neither will he.

True to his word, Rhys throws his dignity aside, laying himself bare before me. Showing me how his teeth grind when he struggles to hold on, letting me hear the masculine moans he can't control.

I *love* it.

I hate him for *making* me love it.

The closer I get to the edge, the faster my blood races. Rage and arousal and—*fuck it, fuck it, fuck it*—adoration sing through my veins.

I feel wounded. Sliced open. *Exposed.*

Instincts overtake my ability to reason. My hand scrabbles for the garter strapped to my thigh, twirling my knife and bringing it to his throat.

Rhys gasps, his hands clutching me harder. Wild want flares in his gaze, singeing me. His rolling hips stutter, but only for a moment. Just long enough for me to catch the deliberate way he stretches his neck to the side.

Submission, my Omega says, her voice as dazed as my thoughts. *He's giving us his throat.*

It's symbolic in a hundred small ways and one big one—this alpha has offered me his body, his pride, and now his life.

Yours, his eyes vow, so sure and steady. Burning, *burning*.

Bite me, viper.

Fuck, he really would let me. I could sink my teeth into him— or my blade. And it would only make him want me *more*.

The utter devotion layered into that absolute truth is enough to wind me. Breath sloughs from my lungs, but I don't want it back.

I want—

I want—

My other hand finds his, curling around the fingers holding my jaw, dragging them lower. To close around my throat.

Understanding shimmers in his gaze, stretching taut between us.

Rhys is mine. But part of me is his, too.

Even if it hurts.

Especially then.

"Come here," he rasps, guiding me into faster undulations of his beautiful body. Once he has our rhythm right back to the panting pace that steals my sanity, he slides his free fingers between our centers.

Rhys squeezes his knot, positioning his knuckles right where they'll rub the bottom of my clit on every plunge. A ragged gasp squeaks through my narrow airway. When I whimper, Rhys purrs louder, pressing my windpipe until the balcony blurs.

He flips his fingers, grazing quick circles over my clit. The tension stretched through my core cracks and crumbles, a soul-stealing orgasm flaring. It feels like fireworks—a cacophony of light and color. Pops and sizzles. Hot, blinding flashes.

I don't realize I've cried out until Rhys seals his mouth over mine, muffling the moans and making sure I feel his own. His lithe hips grind up, then stammer. His knot expands until it covers the entire space between my thighs, dripping slick as he comes, filling my body with cum, pushing our combined release out.

Rhys releases his chokehold to catch me, grunting as I collapse into his purr. It rumbles against my face. My neck and lungs tingle. Emotion swamps my middle, thickening my throat while the bridge of my nose stings.

"Fuck, baby," the alpha murmurs softly, nuzzling my crown. "You're a miracle."

The awe in his voice should warm my bones, but instead it puts an ache behind my lungs. Emotion spills into my stomach; thick, dark sadness spreading like oil on water.

Rhys senses the shift in my scent instantly, gripping my hair and tugging until we're face-to-face. Anxiety pulls at his features, fracturing into pure pain when he sees the stupid tears swimming in my eyes.

"Briar. Shit," he whispers, cupping my face. "Did I hurt you?"

He rubs his free thumb over one of the fingertip bruises branded into my neck, squinting to make them out in the dark theater. Behind me, a slow song in the second act warbles to an end and the crowd applauds while the curtain drops.

I watch Rhys examine the marks he left, clear concern rolling off him in waves. And something in my soul *snaps*.

"You hated me!" I cry over the applause. Fat, loathsome tears practically leap down my face. "You hated me so much you could barely stand to *look* at me and you—you're—"

Perfect. Wonderful. My stupid fucking *dream*.

I can't say any of it, so I settle for "You only want me like this because I'm your mate. It doesn't have anything to do with *me*."

The crowd quiets. Tense silence stretches between us as the stage lights shift, illuminating the deep frown on his beautiful face. A lone violin starts up, but he waits until others join in to shake his head.

"No, baby," he rasps, his eyes as haunted as his voice. "I didn't hate you. I could *never* hate you. And that made me hate *myself*."

The deep, spreading sorrow swirls to a stop, confusion ballooning in its place. My body locks up, internal muscles squeezing the hard girth still filling my pussy. I try to ignore how good he feels and demand an explanation, but my words barely register as a murmur.

"Wh-what do you mean?"

The orchestra soars into a new melody. I barely hear it, though, with Rhys's hands smoothing over my sides and his gaze rippling. Equal parts anguish and passion brighten the aqua beams.

"All I ever wanted was a mate," he confesses. "Someone to dedicate myself to. A counterpart for all my fucked-up..." His mouth flickers into a humorless smile. "Venom."

I can't help but huff, caught somewhere between a glower and a smirk. His smile grows, warming into something real while he gazes at me.

"I know it might be hard to believe, but I devoted myself to the person who was meant to be mine. My Alpha barely let me sleep around or date for fun—and we both decided a long time ago I would never allow myself to have a shred of feeling for anyone who wasn't *the* one."

Rhys's fingers tuck a loose piece of hair behind my ear, his eyes tracking it. "But then you showed up. And the second I saw you, I was *gone*." He swallows hard, roughing out his last admission. "I hated myself for being so weak. Because I couldn't help but fall for you."

Oh.

I blink. Shock and hope clash like cymbals inside my chest, leaving my throat so tight I can barely breathe. "Y-you—"

"Love you," Rhys finishes, certain. He nods. "Yes."

A wash of alpha power accompanies the words, smothering my fear like a weighted blanket. His hands find my face, brushing his thumbs over my cheekbones. "I love you so much; I'm not sure I've ever loved anyone before you. Not even myself."

Somehow, that makes perfect sense to me. All of his arrogance and self-protection was... an *act*. To cover this deep-seated loneliness and longing.

God, I hate how much I understand that.

But it's also sort of *perfect*, right?

The second act whirls to a close behind us and Rhys moves quickly, yanking my panties out of his pocket and using them to clean between my thighs as he withdraws. By the time the crowd has quieted and the house lights glow to life, signaling an intermission, he's tucked back into his pants and has me balanced on his knee, smoothing my hair into some semblance of order.

Dear Lord, he's beautiful, with his jacket thrown around my shoulders and my scent all over him. Especially when he finishes fixing my crystal combs and flashes a mischievous, genuine grin.

"You want to go home? Or should we stay?"

My insides lurch, fear and yearning swirling through my stomach. I want to see the rest of the show—but I don't want to lose whatever connection just bloomed between us.

Rhys reads my face, his softening. "You're going to have to banish me from your side before I leave you again," he murmurs, kissing the back of my hand. "No matter what you choose, I'm not going *anywhere*, baby."

Warmth untangles the knots in my core. I curl my lips into a small curve. "The wedding in act three is the best part," I whisper. "The costumes are beautiful."

Rhys's smile grows. He nods, tugging my hand until I fall back into his lap. "Then let's go to a wedding."

fifty-two

BRIAR

True to his word, Rhys doesn't leave my side until I practically force him to.

We share breakfast with Dane, all three of us lying on my bed while they bicker over how to approach a new group of smugglers they've been tracking through South America. At some point, Dane plunks an actual atlas into Rhys's lap and pulls my feet into his. He then proceeds to hand me a platter of French toast and watches with a fanatical gleam in his eye until I start to eat.

Rhys seems just as preoccupied, glancing at my plate and purring in approval after every few bites. When they're both satisfied that I won't waste away, they start dissecting their latest plans.

I'm surprised when they openly discuss the entire operation—and *stunned* when Rhys tucks me into his side to show me a map, tracing the poachers' expected route. Asking with complete sincerity, "What do you think, viper?"

Like... *what?!*

After they sketch out a general plan, both alphas somehow end up huddled around me, their chests rumbling while I rub Rhys's nape and Dane's wide, muscled back. Their touch starvation must be getting better, though, because cuddling turns into omega tug-of-war pretty damn quick. Which ends with me lying against Dane while Rhys devours every drop of arousal between my thighs until I think I'll pass out.

I might've, actually, because I wake to Dane nuzzling my face and telling me he's going to work out. Rhys stays, lounging beside me with one of the dark romance books I bought from the crumbling bookshop.

We both hear Cillian's car pull into the garage. Rhys quirks a smirk when my scent shifts, brightening with uncontrollable eagerness.

I shouldn't *want* to see the pack alpha as badly as I do. For Christ's sake, he was *just* in here last night. Sleeping with a solid arm hooked around my waist and his face buried against the fingertip bruises his stepbrother left on my neck.

But I guess all the mystical shit they say about mates and pack leaders is real, because some piece of my Omega has been holding her breath since I woke to his businesslike good-morning text. Hearing he's home is a huge relief, somehow. Like we can finally exhale.

My mind races, wondering what he might have in store for me. I remember Fiona's tittered warnings about his bedroom all too well. And, really, apart from my heat-spike, we haven't really *been* together...

I can't deny the thrill of anticipation that swoops through me, remembering the night he had me dance for him. How his eyes felt, cataloging every inch of my form, absorbing each twirl and point.

Will he want to watch again?

Will he actually try to take me this time?

My perfume rises. Rhys keeps reading out loud, his mouth kicking higher on one side. The chapter bleeds into another. We hear Cillian stride into his office and close the door... but he doesn't come back out.

I try not to be agitated, suppressing the urge to squirm. Rhys turns a page, chuckling at me. I smack his chest, but he plucks my wrist up, brushing a soft kiss along my pulse.

"Save your energy, viper." He smirks. "Trust me."

Another tease, hinting at some depraved desire Cillian has? My heart races along with my mind, conjuring all sorts of scenarios. Each making me wetter than the one before.

Chains. Cuffs. Leather straps. Clamps...

Maybe Rhys and I have been reading too much.

When Coggins arrives a moment later, pushing a dinner cart, my stomach sinks. The attendant winces as he gestures at the covered meal. "Mr. Blackwood sends his apologies, Madame."

The butler slinks off. My shoulders hunch, a pout hiding the true depths of my dejection. He doesn't want to eat with me? Or maybe he doesn't have time?

Rhys clears his throat. I turn toward him, arrested by his beauty for a moment. It knocks every rational thought out of my head, seeing him in a pair of black sweats and nothing else, an elbow balanced on his bent knee, his pale skin covered in my own scratch marks and his hair in disarray.

The square black frames around his eyes only heighten the effect, highlighting his tattoos and the sideways glance he slides toward me. His silver-blond brows arch.

"You'd never let me get away with that," he comments, nodding at the lonely dinner cart. "You gonna let him?"

And he's right, goddamn it.

The night Rhys rejected me, I didn't curl into a ball and cry. I went looking for his sorry ass and taught him a lesson.

Briar Rose Blackwood doesn't sit around waiting.

Rhys still has the scar to prove it.

I flash him a smile, kissing his cheek before bouncing up. "Of course not."

My beautiful alpha grins, his light eyes warming as he tilts his chin at my closet. "Something red," he says. "If you're thinking torture."

WIVES DON'T KNOCK, RIGHT?

We're going with that.

I barge into the study without warning, drawing a deep breath to give my "husband" a piece of my mind—before exhaling in a deflated rush.

Oh.

He's *working*?

Cillian looks up from the papers spread across his desk. His gaze rolls over the dark red robe I put over a matching teddy from my wardrobe, much too calm and controlled for my liking.

But I have his scent now, so I sense exactly how much I affect him.

Rich, masculine spice and smoke fill the room in a powerful rush. Weakening my knees and tweaking the damp, needy flesh between my thighs. I do everything I can to ignore the dizzy whirl scrambling my thoughts, dropping my hands to my hips as I come to a halt in the center of his Persian rug.

"Hello," he drawls, turning back to his work. "How are you this evening, Mrs. Blackwood?"

"Are you *serious*?" I hiss. "*How am I this evening?!*"

Cillian's brow furrows, still not looking up. "Frustrated, I see. I wonder why."

This *bastard*.

"Oh, cut the shit!" I explode. "You know I've been waiting for you all day. For *weeks*, actually, come to think of it! All this time and you never even *tried* to come on to me or take me into your kinky bedroom?!"

He nearly smirks that time, still shuffling paperwork. "Do you *want* to go into my bedroom?"

I narrow my eyes. "Don't play innocent. Fiona told me you have all sorts of stuff in there, so I know you must have had women around at *some* point. What, you just didn't want a virgin? Is that why you let your packmates deflower me even though you knew we were mates?!"

He scratches out a note on one of his pages, frowning. Using that maddeningly even tone. "My tastes hardly seemed appropriate. For your first time."

A white-hot thread of anticipation coils around my lungs, forcing me to pant around it. I glare, hoping he'll interpret my heaving shoulders as rage. "So you thought you'd let them *break me in*?"

His wry grin knocks me back a step. Cillian smiles so rarely. It's like catching the sun through the clouds after days of rain—or maybe forgetting there *was* a sun, until it finally peeks through the veil of gray.

"No." His head shakes. The humor fades as quickly as it appeared. Soul-deep intensity cracks through his gaze as he bores it into mine. "I thought I'd let *you* make a choice for yourself. Since you've never had any."

A roaring sort of quiet envelops my insides, silencing all the outrage and exhilaration.

He was never avoiding me? He was... giving me a choice? Is that what he's done tonight, too?

Cillian stands, rounding his desk with his trademark blend of power and elegance. My husband slips his hands into his pockets as he leans against the polished wood and tilts his head, considering me.

"I can find you and chase you and marry you," he husks. "Bring you into our home, our pack. Give you this house, your nest, the world. But at some point, Briar, you're going to have to choose me back. And come to me on your own terms. *That's* what I've been waiting for."

I remember being confused by his agreement not to touch me without permission. When we signed our original contract, I thought for sure he planned to go back on his word immediately. But now...

Did he really put that in there to give me a sense of security? And he's abided by it, even during my heat-spike. All so I could have a choice?

It... makes sense. He might not have given me a say about our wedding, but *everything else* has been my decision. Whether I wanted to help them with their scheme for an heir. Who I fucked and when. What I did to fill my days and nights.

He even let me choose if I was going to put that tutu on and dance for him.

And now this. Tonight.

Cillian isn't in here because he doesn't want me.

He's in here because he wants to be sure *I* want *him*.

My husband's glossy black brows arch. "Is that why you're here, Briar?" he asks. "Have you made your choice?"

BRIAR'S SHOULDERS DROP, HER HANDS FALLING LIMP AT her sides.

But that hot spark I love so much glows in her green depths. She narrows her gaze at me, gorgeously pissy. "*Now* you ask?" she demands, her voice wavering to reveal her true feelings. She touches the lock resting over her sternum with reverence. "After you put a literal *collar* on me?"

I can't help but drift closer, falling into her orbit. My mouth ghosts into a smirk as I reach out to touch the glittering black diamonds along the sides of the gold padlock. "Is it still a collar if it's Cartier?"

For the first time ever, Briar laughs for me. The sound is more like a dry huff than the giggles she gives to Dane and the wicked smirks Rhys receives, but it still strikes my heart like a dart.

I used to watch her rehearsals, rapt to any details of what made her smile or snort. Filing her wry, sarcastic humor away. Planning all the ways I could put this glorious eye-rolling grin on her face.

She doesn't give in entirely, of course. Her thin arms still cross under her slight breasts. The crimson robe wrapped around her shifts, gaping to reveal the matching blood-red teddy underneath.

I picked it out last year, I think. One of my favorites—so much so I couldn't bring myself to hide it in my own closet with the bulk of the things I've picked out for her. And with good reason.

She looks fucking incredible.

My scent must be oppressive to her by now. Or perhaps overwhelming in a *good* way, since she visibly presses her thighs together, working that glassy gaze down my body and lingering on the outline of my half-hard knot. Tart cherries—dark and sweet— have my canines aching.

My lips quirk again as I snag her focus. "You can just ask me, you know."

Indignance and lust sparkle in her eyes. "*What?*"

I trace the locket again, slowly. Then fist it, pulling hard enough to tug her forward a step and tighten the warm links around her blank throat.

"You could *ask me*," I half-growl, savoring the slide of her body against mine, "to fuck you. Surely, you have that right. You *are* my wife."

My perfect little wife. A blend of confident seductress and guileless inexperience. The latter wins out when she stammers, "You—I—?"

"I said," I husk, running my other hand along her side. "My wife can *ask* me to fuck her. She doesn't have to be a brat." Heat spirals down my spine. "Unless, of course, she *wants* to be punished before she gets on my cock."

Briar shivers, perfume rising off her skin, turning her reply into a lie. "I... don't?"

"Mm." I lean over her, nuzzling a scent-mark into her temple. Reassuring her Omega that I love her, no matter what we do tonight. "Trying to start a fight, then lying to yourself about what you want? That's two strikes, rosebud. Shall we go for three?"

She opens and closes her mouth, unable to deny the truth. Finally, she offers a breathless chuckle. "Will I still be punished if I give in now?"

My lips twitch, revealing the deep well of fondness at my middle. "You won't."

In all the months I spent learning about her, Briar's dignity was the one thing that never wavered. I knew it would make her a beautiful brat in bed. And a prized partner everywhere else.

I straighten to my full height. "You won't," I say again, "because you value integrity over your own comfort."

She freezes, absorbing the words. Realizing, maybe, that I do know her after all. I brush a kiss over her forehead, murmuring a confession of my own. "It's one of the things I admire most about you."

Fucking hell, she loves that statement. Her scent soars, so sweet and mouth-wateringly tart, my teeth ache. Her eyes widen, confusion blending with her arousal and happiness.

Sweet rosebud. Her deeply rooted desire for praise—for *approval*—is new to her. But it's so palpable, my Alpha automatically purrs. She doesn't understand the other side of this coin yet, but I'll teach her. Tonight.

"You—" she starts, swallowing the rest of her words and tossing her hair back before she can give too much away. Or so she thinks.

My smile comes easier, this time. "Yes," I answer. "I admire many things about you. I'll give you a list. After."

After I show her what being my wife really means. All the things I'll provide for her.

If she behaves.

And maybe more, if she doesn't.

"CILLIAN—I CAN'T—I—"

My devil's lips curl, brushing my shoulder as his cock leaves a smear of smoky pre-cum against my lower back.

"You're doing so well, darling. Just a little more for me."

Oh God.

Oh, *yes*.

Chains rattle overhead and from my ankles, but the sturdy four-poster frame doesn't shudder. The hot, strong hand rolling my nipple slides down my sweat-misted torso. Until just the very tips of his long fingers graze my swollen, pulsing clit.

Cillian chuckles darkly when I yank at the leather cuffs molded around my wrists. "Let's try again," he murmurs. As if he's here to encourage rather than torment me.

"I already answered you," I mewl, whining exactly like the brat he claims I am. "Why can't I *come yet?*"

His smirk grows into a full-blown grin, true joy shining behind his lust. "You'll get what you want when I get what I need." He spanks the soaked lips of my pussy. My body tightens as I gasp, the thin gold plug in my back hole slipping deeper.

Fucking *fuck.*

It turns out my collar is part of an elaborate set. One my husband presented me with before trussing me up beside his bed and working me into eighteen almost-orgasms. All with the elegant bullet-shaped butt plug pressing its solid weight on the other side of my pussy's desperately clenching walls.

His second thwack is sharper, leaving a heated sting on my ass cheek. I moan and growl at the same time, thrashing as I meet his burning eyes.

"Now. Again," he insists. "Have you made your choice, Briar?"

I answer the same way I have every time, practically shouting, "Yes! Cillian—*I choose you.*"

His cock ticks fuller against the top of my backside. "Good," he hums, flicking my throbbing nub. "Now tell me *why.*"

This is the part I can't seem to get right. I've tried every answer my addled brain can conjure. From *"Because we're mates"* to a string of insulting curses. At one point, I nearly burst into tears.

Cillian only paused his ministrations and asked if I needed my safe word. We chose one together once he finished showing me the solid gold restraints and personalized leather cuffs waiting for me.

Caviar.
Since we both know I hate it.

When I spat a tart "*No*," he held me for a long moment, purring until I started to writhe, once again begging for the thick slide of his cock. A twist of the plug. Some real attention on my clit.

Anything.

I sob a groan, bucking against his naked, muscled body. Cillian curses under his breath, using his free hand to fist my heart lock and *tug*. My airway closes behind the thick chain, capturing my full attention.

"Look around you, Briar," he growls, carefully yanking the collar toward his dark, open closet. "At the hundreds of thousands' worth of clothes and jewelry I've been buying for *years*. Selecting things I knew you'd love. Storing them until you were ready to see—to *know*—how fucking obsessed I am."

My lungs burn, the lack of air forcing my body to soften. Allowing my mind to sharpen. Absorbing what he's saying.

Jesus, does he really have a whole secret wardrobe in there? Why is that so perfectly easy to believe?

He pulls on the chain again, guiding my focus to the opposite side of his mattress. Specifically, the bedpost beside his nightstand...

Where a pair of black pointe shoes dangle beside his pillow.

My ballet slippers.

He must have stolen them back after the night I danced. Have they been in here all along? Why?

He answers before I can ask. "*Look*. See what you've done to me. How I couldn't fucking sleep without a piece of you beside me. The way your initials inked into the bottom have been traced by my fingertips a thousand fucking times. BRB—Briar Rose *Blackwood*."

He lets up on the collar, giving me a large gulp of sweet, smoky cloves. "Now *tell me*. Tell me why you've chosen me. This. *Us*."

I can't think anymore. I can only feel. The swell of emotion swamping my guts, his ruthless fingers pinching the slick lips of my cunt. The knot beating fuller against my ass.

Oh God. Oh *God*.

I see the truth.

I know the answer.

"*You love me!*" I blurt, panting. "You did all of this… because you love me. And I'm choosing you because… I *want* you to."

Cillian goes utterly still, letting me scrape the last of my sobbed confession out. "Because I think I might… be able to love you, too. All of you."

My husband's stuttered exhale tickles my nape. His hands suddenly fly to my hips, kneading hard. "Good girl," he rasps, leaning his forehead against my shoulder. "My smart, gorgeous *mate*. Of course I love you. I couldn't have helped myself if I'd wanted to."

The pounding organ in my chest somersaults, sinking into a warm pool of bliss. Cillian's hands pet my sides gently, soothing my restless breathing. "I know, omega," he adds next. "You're ready to come for me now."

He suddenly reaches up, unclasping my cuffs, carefully lowering and massaging my arms. His bone-rattle purr rolls into a pussy-melting growl. "Right after you *present*."

IT'S OFFICIAL.

Cillian Blackwood is my alpha.

His knot rubs my tender walls as he cuddles me closer, continuing his elaborate after-care. It started with him carrying me, still locked against him, into his bathroom.

He cleaned my skin with a warm washcloth, then spent ten minutes brushing tangles out of my hair. I'm not sure what sort of magic system he devised with Coggins, but when we reemerged, the bed was perfectly clean and two bottles of chilled water waited on the nightstand.

Cillian proceeded to snuggle me into his lap, feeding me small sips and purring loud enough to drown out all rational thought.

By the time I crack my eyes open, it's late. I feel him massaging my neck, his wedding band cool against my skin. I reach back, tugging his hand to the space in front of my face, eyeing his ring.

"I'm surprised you didn't burst into flames in that church, devil."

My husband chuckles, his smile wry and dazzling. "That was a shock to us all."

I burrow a little closer, squashing a pinch of shyness by averting my eyes. Staring at his neatly groomed chest hair as I mumble, "Why did we get married there? I mean, did it really matter?"

Cillian stills for a beat before sliding his arm around my waist, weaving his fingers into the loose hair at my nape. He pulls slightly, tilting my face to his.

"Yes," he replies, icy eyes burning. "I needed our marriage to be real in every way imaginable. Legally. Spiritually. And—"

I swallow the hoarse lump in my throat, barely able to get out a whispered, "And?"

Earnestness looks so good on him—all solemn and steady. "I didn't know if it would be important to you, one day. Once I was able to tell you that we were mates, I wanted you to feel like our marriage was as real as it could have possibly been, given the circumstances. I wanted it to feel real for me, too."

My heart cracks, the final wall around it crumbling into dust. But he isn't done. Just like his edging—this alpha is determined to ruin me *thoroughly*.

"I *meant* those vows, Briar Rose Blackwood," he murmurs.

They run through my mind on a loop. Forcing me to realize; he sounded exactly like this on our wedding day, too. So sure and sincere.

In sickness and in health. For richer, for poorer. Better and worse. Until death do us part.

Cillian's gaze smolders, warming my bones as he adds a new oath. "Every single word is branded on my soul. And if those promises are the only words this devil ever gets to say to God? I consider them well-spent."

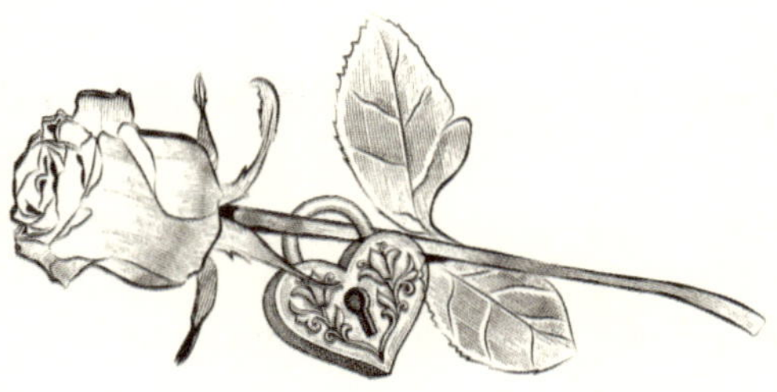

fifty-five

DANE

The guy strapped to the chair in front of me writhes, spitting curses behind the scrap of fabric tied around his head. It's dirty and I feel weirdly guilty about that; but what am I supposed to do? Launder our hostage restraints?

We don't exactly abide by the Geneva Convention down here.

I sigh, tapping the flat side of my knife against my open palm. "Normally, I'd let you say your piece. Have your last words. Beg for mercy and try to turn on your whole operation to save your own miserable guts," I tell him. "But the thing is—my omega is going into heat any day now. And my packmate over there already found the names of the rest of your guys on your phone."

I nod at Rhys, who flashes a menacingly bright grin, spinning this piece of shit's phone in his palm. Tonight's arrangement was his idea—we typically have safe houses where we do our dirty work, but neither of us wanted to be too far from Briar.

Honestly, I wish this could have waited. The closer she gets to her haze, the worse her nightmares have gotten. Last night, it was so bad that Cillian barely managed to snap her out of it with one his alpha barks.

Every time I close my eyes, I hear her whimpering in her sleep. Saying Violet's name.

I just want to hold her, damn it.

We've been tracking this cartel for years, though. They're the ones who set our building on fire that night; and then disappeared completely until they resurfaced a few months ago, operating out of a flop house in the Bronx.

"And when we told our girl we had a trace on one of the bastards who tried to *kill* her mates..." Rhys starts, trailing off ominously. He grins wider. "Well, let's just say she gave us permission to deal with you however we wanted."

Our target's eyes flare wider. He starts struggling in earnest, shouting around the gag.

Rhys rolls his eyes, but I've been doing this long enough to know when a man is desperately pleading for his life and when he has something of value to say. This is no underling, either—this guy is the cartel leader's little brother. If he has *actual information* he thinks we won't find on his phone...

"Christ," I grunt, flicking my knife so it cuts the gag. And a little bit of his cheek, too. "Fine. Just make it quick. We don't want to be late for dinner."

The fucker spits stained, saliva-soaked fabric out of his mouth, panting as he shouts, "Who the—who told you we tried to *kill* you? That doesn't even make fucking sense. We bought our weapons and shit from you!"

Rhys crosses his arms, coming to stand beside me as I consider the criminal's bulging brown eyes. "Is he lying?" my packmate asks. "We have a ton of intel about this group setting the fire. Cillian even cleaned out their borough rat holes that night in retaliation."

Our human pincushion chokes. "That was *you guys*?! We hit a rival gang back for that shit! Why the hell would we have taken a hit out on *you* fuckers? You sold us everything we needed!"

We assumed they'd discovered our true plans—to lure them into a false sense of security with the rifles and then take them out. That night, Cillian had gone to avenge the attempt on our lives, but where did he get his information?

Rhys was unconscious. And I was in surgery for nearly a full day.

I don't make the mistake of looking at Rhys, giving away my sudden doubts. I sense his scent shift, though, the eucalyptus sharpening until it's a blade every bit as cutting as mine.

"Look," he says, sighing. "We appreciate your contribution to our little operation here, but even if you're right and your brother didn't order the hit on us, we still have a bigger issue."

"Yeah," I agree, getting back on task. "Something about your cartel cutting an entire shipment of Molly with fentanyl? And planning to focus sales in northeastern college towns?"

Ah. There it is.

The moment this guy realizes he's well and truly dead.

My usual wave of guilt swells in my stomach, but Briar's whispered words come back to me.

Last night, when the others had fallen asleep, our omega sensed my restlessness—the worries I had about bringing our work here, near her. How much I struggle with what I am now that I have her.

In typical Briar fashion, she didn't turn it into a therapy session or make a scene. My mate simply gazed up at the elegant ivory patterns on her ceiling and sighed, *"Have you ever thought you might not be a bad guy? You protect so many people who would have been harmed, before they ever have to know they were in danger. And yeah, the way you do it is... grisly. But..."*

She turned to me slowly, with a look I knew I'd remember until my last breath. Warm and soft and bright. My moonbeam. Whispering, *"What if you're not the monster in this story, big man? What if you're the hero?"*

Because that's the thing—if these fuckers live, innocent people die.

And if being the person who stands between evil and the rest of the world, holding that line, makes me a beast?

Well, at least I'm *Briar's* beast.

The rest of my work is quick. We only have about half an hour before dinnertime and we need to take showers first. Rhys helps me clean up, his expression ponderous while we go through our usual disposal motions.

"It was Gideon, wasn't it?" he finally mumbles. "He was the one who gave Cillian his intel on this cartel? Said his packmate—the nerdy one—skimmed it off some FBI database?"

I had the same thought. At the time, Cillian probably thought nothing of taking his cousin's help; we weren't rivals competing for the company yet.

"Yeah. It was."

I remember Gideon's face at the bookstore—his overeager eyes and the insistent way he grabbed Briar's wrist. The simple choice that changed my whole world.

"No. No I don't."

She didn't want to get away from me. She wanted to *stay*.

I've spent every day of the last two weeks trying to be worthy of her decision. It's too easy, with Briar. She inspires me to be better—share more, open myself to her and the rest of our pack.

I figure I need to practice... in case she ever wants to bond with us.

Rhys senses the shift in my scent and smirks. "Alright, let's go. My Alpha wants to check on her, too. Especially after this shit."

I see his point. Between the way Gideon harassed Briar and

now the fact that he was trying to divert Cillian's attention from whoever *actually* burned us…

What's that guy's angle? And why was he gunning for us so long ago, before our race for an heir?

Is he still gunning for us now?

Or is he after something else?

fifty-six

BRIAR

"You have to be kidding."

Rhys stands at the kitchen island, wearing the form-fitting black tank top and joggers I love so much. He squints through his glasses, his sea-glass gaze suspicious as he examines the tube pinched between Dane's thick fingers.

My formerly-masked alpha rolls his eyes, frowning. "It's just a saliva swab. Don't be a dick."

"Rhys can't help it," Cillian chimes, striding in from the detached garage. Just as he has every day for the last two weeks, the moment he sees me, the pack alpha lifts me into a twirl. Just one—and only because he knows I'll giggle as he kisses me.

326

Cillian sets me on the counter as I laugh breathlessly. My robe slides under my thighs, the cool fabric sending tingles to my core. It's not a bad sensation, but the accompanying whirl of anxiety isn't my favorite.

Still, I know what this is... and I'm not sure how to feel about it.

My husband cups my face in his hand and scent-marks me thoroughly before sliding a sardonic glance to his packmates—particularly his former stepbrother. "I'm pretty sure *Dick* will be the primary result on Rhys's DNA test," he mutters. "Right above *Arrogant Ass*."

I slant a teasing glower at my husband. "I thought you and Rhys weren't really related? How would you share DNA?"

Rhys barks a hard laugh while Dane chuckles. Cillian's eyes gleam, the hand at my hip sliding up to tickle my side. I squawk as he smirks. "And I suppose your top result will be *Brat*, Mrs. Blackwood?"

I snort. "Don't be silly. I'm not related to Rhys, either."

"That's it," my blond alpha decides, abandoning the kit to haul me over his shoulder. "I'm getting my belt."

I shriek a laugh, but Dane easily plucks me into his arms, bridal-style. He nestles my body against his wide chest and the soft cotton T-shirt stretched over his scarred pecs. "Like hell you will," he grunts at Rhys. "This is *my* night."

"You have her *every morning*," the venomous alpha whines. "I was *working* all day. You know, making sure none of us go to *prison*?"

I've learned that Rhys does, in fact, use his law degree to keep the pack out of trouble. He reviews any and all written correspondence, contracts, their bank accounts, and taxes; all to keep them squeaky clean.

Aside from their makeshift interrogation dungeon in the basement under the garage.

But, hey. Nobody's *perfect*.

My alphas are pretty damn close, though. When the most

minor pre-heat symptoms started this morning, I think Dane could sense my mounting anxiety. Getting this DNA kit for tonight was his idea—a way to keep my mind occupied. And Rhys was the one who suggested we ditch our usual dining-room dinner in favor of every type of takeout I could think of.

Cillian eyes the three of us, finally noticing our clothes. His dark brow rises as he pins me in place with his beautiful blue eyes. "Casual Friday, Mrs. Blackwood?"

I suppose it is. I've been playing dress-up for dinner every evening since he revealed the closet full of amazing clothes he had *made* for me. On "his" nights, my husband usually plans some excuse for us to go out—I suspect solely so I can show off my wardrobe.

My face heats under his knowing gaze. "Yeah, I, um..."

Dane folds me closer, purring as he rubs his beard along my temple in a scent-mark. "Briar's pre-heat symptoms started today. She needs to take it easy."

Cillian's hand smooths my hair back, tucking it behind my ear. "Is this true?" he asks, eyes intent on mine. "Is it time for us to slow down and nest?"

I feel shy for some reason. That soul-deep yearning rears up—the fierce, unshakable desire to please this alpha and gain his approval. "Yes," I whisper. "Is that okay?"

Cillian's lips lift in a soft smile. "More than okay, rosebud. It's perfect. I'm proud of you for telling us what you need."

Dane nods, murmuring into my crown. "That will be your only job during your heat, little girl. We'll take care of everything else."

I believe him. Over the last few weeks, Dane has proven again and again that he's an absolute *rock*. It doesn't matter how many times my Omega needs to be held or touched—he's there. Brushing my hair, massaging my feet, soaping my shoulders in the bathtub. And he does everything with the kind of unhurried adoration I feel down to my bones.

Rhys and I like to tussle. Cillian gets off on his innate dominance. But Dane?

He really just wants to *love* me. And feel me love him back.

His posture's been a little tense today, though. I suppose possibly because it really is his turn tonight—and he hasn't knotted me yet.

Rhys hasn't either; in fact, he refuses to until he feels he's earned my forgiveness. I've tried to talk him out of his mate morality, but that usually just leads to us bickering... which typically ends with me riding his face or being choked by his cock.

My scent swells at the memories and each of my alphas reacts. Dane's purr stutters as Rhys snarls under his breath. Cillian goes still, his gaze blazing hotter.

Smoky spice smothers me, along with the herbaceous blend of eucalyptus and oak. All three rolled into one hits my bloodstream like a drug, shooting pure ecstasy through my entire body. My lower abdomen clenches in an unfamiliar way, similar to the usual squelch that accompanies perfume but *more*. Deeper.

I understand why when my scent winds into theirs. The rich tartness seems darker and sweeter than ever before. Painfully so.

Oh. Fuck.

Pre-heat perfume. I've read about it, but *wow*. It's *strong*. And pouring out of me along with slick that somehow feels... hot? Warmer than usual, for sure.

Everything happens so fast.

One second I'm in Dane's arms, half-melted into his purr. The next I'm catching myself against the island, winded from the speed with which my feet find the floor.

I blink, dazed when I find Dane backing toward the French doors along the far wall of the kitchen. His golden gaze is wild, black pupils edging out all color while his chest heaves under his shirt.

Rhys crouches six feet away from him, down on his heels with his head bent over his lap and his eyes squeezed shut.

What the ever-loving—

Cillian looms the closest. He stands with his fingers curled around the other side of the island. Jaw clenched, eyes on fire. Not *breathing*.

Is it me?

It has to be, right? Because of my pre-heat perfume?

What is it *doing* to them? If I didn't know any better, I'd think they were all about to snap into a—

Oh fuck, fuck, *fuck*.

A rut.

Or three.

How is this even possible? I demand, frantically reaching for my Omega.

She's frozen in my middle, just as stunned as I am. *It—it isn't supposed to be. Two alphas in a pack snapping into rut at the same time is rare enough, but never all of them.*

Leave it to my monstrous mates to beat *those* odds.

Leave it to me to be absurdly *flattered* by that.

Lord. I guess we really are made for each other.

Dane scrambles backward, heavy boots scuffing the marble floor. He shakes his head in horror, but a feral snarl twists his lips. And when he speaks, it's a barely restrained bark. *"Leave us, omega."*

My body twitches, nearly launching into motion at his desperate plea. Cillian starts to lurch toward me, but catches himself, growling low in his throat as he closes his eyes.

Hell. He's always the controlled one. If both he and Dane are out, that just leaves Rhys.

"Briar," my blond mate groans, falling to his knees as he clutches his head in both hands. Panting over the pain of trying to suppress his urges. "You have to go, viper. Lock yourself in your nest."

Their scents are so strong I can't inhale properly. Dizziness muddles my mind, their words echoing in the chaos. *Leave. Go.*

Cillian loses his battle last. His pupils yawn, swallowing the icy blue. His voice drops far below his normal alpha register. Into a smoldering bark I can't help but heed.

"Run."

fifty-seven

BRIAR

A BARK MEANS I HAVE TO COMPLY.

It doesn't mean I have to *obey*.

Cillian wanted me to run from them to hide.

But my Omega wants them to rut us. Bite us. *Ruin us*.

And honestly? I do, too.

After they work for it, of course.

Being an omega doesn't come with many physical advantages, but speed is one. I dart for the exit, leaping over Rhys despite the way my bad knee wobbles when I land. Dane reacts on instinct, whirling to lunge for me, but I bob and weave, ducking behind him. Out the French doors.

Our rose garden beckons, fat crimson blooms waving in the dusk. I've memorized every path, over the last few weeks, but the gravel will tear my bare feet up—and once my alphas come to, they'll be devastated if I'm hurt.

Instead, I make a beeline for the farthest edge of the labyrinth, racing for the springy grass that surrounds it.

My heart pounds, the pulse beating in my throat, my chest, the apex of my thighs. Out here, I feel like I'm made of pure sensation. The soft turf tickling my feet, damp evening air cooling my lungs, needy muscles ticking tighter at my core.

I like this, I realize. Being chased. Hunted.

It unlocks some primitive type of abandon. Because I can run... but not forever. Which means, eventually, they'll catch me. *And do whatever they want with me.*

The thought shoots lightning through my veins, propelling me on. An ocean breeze blusters inland from the bluff and I shrug, letting my robe fly onto the breeze. Gaining speed.

Truly, our lawn is as big as the garden. Which works well for my purposes, because it means my alphas will be able to track my path clearly. Roars and grunts ring behind me as I turn, streaking diagonally across the grass.

There's something oddly freeing about it. They're chasing me, but really, I'm in control. And I know when they catch me, I'll still be safe.

There's no time to reflect on how astonishing that notion is. Because I'm rapidly reaching the end of the lawn... and veering straight for the cliffs.

I only pause for a second. To try to determine where I can go from here.

But it's too late.

Rhys hauls my body into his snarling chest, arching his neck back as if aiming to strike—

Shit. He's not the pack leader, which means any bond we make would ruin our ability to create a pack bond. He can't remember that, now, though. Not when he's out of his mind.

"*No!*"

My bark halts the alpha halfway to my throat. He growls, grumbling his disapproval, but I'm pleasantly surprised to find my Omega isn't having it. She looses a growl all her own. "You have to *share*."

Rhys bares his teeth with a moody snap. I narrowly resist the urge to smirk as the other two barrel into the clearing on the edge of the cliffs, their faces twisted in equally menacing scowls.

Cillian's suit jacket is gone, his work shirt hanging from his bare chest... while Dane is entirely shirtless, wearing nothing but a pair of low-slung jeans that show off his thick, muscled abdomen. They shove at one another, Cillian knocking Dane back before the bigger alpha grabs his arm, ripping him aside.

"Enough," I interject, infusing every word with as much power as I can manage. "You *all* have to share. Or *none* of you can have me."

The three feral men blink at one another, blank aggression covering their expressions. I try to imagine how this could possibly work. How I'll possibly direct *all* of them...

We can't, the voice in my middle whispers. *We have to give in.*

The thought is terrifying. *Suicidal*, even. Like standing over the edge of the cliff we're on, deciding to let the wind carry me off instead of clinging to the craggy stone.

Can I even do it? Let go? Let them do whatever they want?

It's the one thing I'm not sure I can withstand.

Because for someone like me? Pain isn't scary.

Surrender is.

The air washes over us in thick gales, whipping my hair loose. I feel the force of it, sparking the familiar urge to leap. Lose myself. Be free.

That part won't be hard. It's trusting them to catch me, even when they're out of their minds, that feels impossible.

I'm surprised how much I *want* to. Need to, really. If I'm going to have my first heat here... and all my other heats... I need to be able to trust them.

"*No bites*," I bark quietly, knowing it's the last command I'll give. My eyes find the black holes where Cillian's should be, projecting softness for him. Hoping he'll recognize the submission he prizes so fiercely. "Please, alpha."

His answering snarl is ragged, his face creased with pained emotion but missing all traces of his usual guile. Right now, Cillian is just... a beast.

And like this? At his basest form?

He's still *mine*.

They *all* are, I realize, absorbing Rhys's desperate panting. Dane's heaving chest and shaking shoulders.

These alphas need *me*.

And I decide to fall into it.

Three sets of hands paw at me. Under their strength, my nightgown tears like wet paper. It drifts to the ground in tatters as they rip their own garments out of the way. Until we're all naked, standing on the grassy knoll beside the cliff and the scattered remnants of our clothes.

My body clamors, blood thundering hot and hard to every pulse point. Their scents fill each stuttering breath, burning hot trails to the cramping muscles between my hips. They tweak tighter, grinding wetly. The sensation is unfamiliar, but the gush of slick that comes after isn't.

The cherry-tart arousal slides down my bare thighs. Our pack alpha tracks it with his glittering black eyes, dropping to his knees with a groaned growl.

Rhys starts to snap at him, jostling for position, but my body reacts before I can, gripping his silver-blond hair and dragging him in for a kiss. The menacing alpha snarls into my mouth, tangling his tongue with mine.

I reach for his cock, squeezing hard enough to get his attention. When he rears back, eyes full of wild glee, I turn and practically leap at Dane, snagging my elbow around his brawny half-scarred neck.

My big man kisses me with naked desperation, moaning and

gasping as I run my free hand down his body. I find the throbbing erection pressed into my hip the same moment my husband's lips skim the soaked lips of my pussy.

Crying out, I close my fingers around Dane's length and clutch Rhys's growing knot in a tighter grip. Cillian dives lower, thrusting into my slick hole with savage insistence. His tongue flicks, striking the ring of nerves squirming for one of their knots. He traces the pounding ache, choking on a growl when more arousal gushes onto his face.

Dane catches my fresh scent and bucks into my hand. His need is so sincere, I feel it scrape the bottom of my heart, settling beneath my lungs like an anchor.

Even like this, my big man would never ask me for anything. Which makes it that much easier to give him everything.

I push at his shoulders, holding his empty eyes while I guide him onto the ground. He sits back with a huff, clamping his huge hand around my forearm as if...

He's afraid to let me go.

The organ in my chest shatters into a thousand shimmering shards. I grab a fistful of Cillian's glossy black hair and tug him away, ignoring his roar of protest. Rhys looses a dangerous rumble, too—but I know what I need to do, crouching to mount Dane's big body.

The position reminds me of our first time. My throat thickens as I hold him in place, lowering myself onto his throbbing hardness. Damp ocean air stings my lungs as I gasp, moaning.

Dane is always a tight fit, but I'm not sure he's ever been *this* hard. The stretch feels incredible, finally filling the gnawing emptiness carved into my core.

He growls and groans, his hands holding my hips hard enough to bruise. I start to ride him immediately, needing *more*.

I forgot—I'm not the only one with rut instincts. Because no sooner has a whine reached my lips than Rhys drops into position behind me, holding his pre-cum-glossed cock in his fist, painting the seam of my ass with the kind of intent that has me clenching around his packmate.

More slick and perfume gush around Dane's dick as Rhys finds my back hole. Cillian's roar rends the air, his hand snapping to his raging erection, strangling it as he watches with his hauntingly dark gaze.

Dane's sightless eyes roll back and the menacing man behind me scoops the wetness onto his fingers, shoving them into the tight ring of my ass without warning.

I whine in earnest when he works them in, adding a third too quickly. It's not painful, but I can't catch my breath, either.

Cillian barks, "*Omega*," turning my attention upward. Before I can blink, his cock is pushing past my lips, filling my mouth with hot, silken hardness.

It should panic me, but instead his taste lights every neuron in my mind, the synapses flaring as bubbling pleasure tingles through my center. My core unclenches. I slip lower on Dane's big cock as Rhys rumbles wordless approval.

Let go, my Omega reminds me, her voice a far-off echo. *Let them have you.*

I know she's right. I brace myself for an internal struggle, but—

Cillian thrusts mercilessly, black eyes burning like hot coals as he watches me gag on him. The motion of his hips is somehow hypnotic. Push, pull, push, pull. Striking me deep, forcing me to drop lower on Dane's thickness. Spiking ecstasy when my big man hits the end of me and *keeps going*.

It's too easy to give in to them. Let Cillian set the pace, hammering his spiced, smoky girth into my throat. Gasping while Dane's knot stretches the opening of my pussy. And screaming as Rhys rips his fingers out and replaces them with his cock.

Oh—oh my—oh shit.

"Yes," I sob, bearing down onto Dane's swollen skin. Shivering as Rhys slides deeper. Stretched and stuffed to the hilt—my ass, my pussy. And my mouth, when Cillian growls and pushes his knot against my lips.

It's too big for me to take, but my alpha's grip on my hair still softens with gruff approval when I try my best, sucking on the top third of his pulsing swell. Moaning when more of his flavor dribbles out.

I swallow it greedily, my body begging for more. Wanting all of them—their knots filling me, their release splattered over my skin and deep inside me.

Delirious and dizzy, I surrender to Cillian's rhythm. Dane's invading thickness. Rhys's desperate thrusts.

They're everywhere. Everything. *All mine.*

That lone, spinning thought breaks me. With another whine, I finally plunge all the way down. Dane bucks up, his knot squelching past my fluttering muscles and popping into place.

White light explodes across my vision and expands in my body. Growing so big, so fast, there's nowhere for it to go except inward, deeper. To my soul.

Ecstatic ripples detonate between my hips, releasing a rush of tension as my alpha sprays out inside me. The hot flood and twitch of his cock sets Rhys off. He jets just as fiercely, filling my ass and falling forward with a serrated moan.

While he nuzzles the nape of my neck, purring and sliding his arms around my middle to hold me up, Cillian finishes. Cloves and sweet smoke burst across my tongue, the taste sparking a new wave of bliss. Dane pants while I squeeze him all over again, his face a grimace of pure pleasure.

Stillness washes over us, followed by the whip of cold wind from the cliffs. I float in a state of semiconsciousness, still skewered on Dane's knot, letting Rhys support my weight as I sink farther backward on every ragged exhale.

I don't know which of them comes to first, but it seems to happen all at once. "Briar," Dane roughs out, jerking upright and reaching out to touch my neck, my arms, my face. "Fuck, I'm so sorry. I—I don't even—did I hurt you, moonbeam?"

It's a wistful sort of relief to see the gold of his eyes again. I stare at them, smiling despite my bone-deep exhaustion. "I'm great, big man. Not sure how the hell you're going to get me inside while I'm locked around you, but..."

I shrug, and Rhys purrs louder, rubbing his forehead along my shoulder. "I tried to bite you," he remembers, whispering. "I'm so sorry, viper."

I turn my head to grin. "You're not nearly as scary as you think you are, venom. Besides, I'm starting to think the three of you biting me might not be the *worst* thing..."

My confession rings out, echoing between the four of us. Cillian's hand finds my crown, massaging my scalp in his special way before skimming down to my chin, lifting my face to look into his icy gaze.

I know him, now, though. So I see the devotion smoldering under all his cool control. The *love*.

"If *anyone* tries to bite you before I do," he warns, irises blazing, "they're dead."

Turns out, being the rope in a carnal tug-of-war between three big, sexy alphas is a bit hard on the knees.

I hiss quietly, slipping out of bed from the bottom of the mattress. It's the only way, I've learned, to pee in peace. Without three highly invested bodyguards waiting for me to scamper back to them.

Especially my big man, who practically *strangled* me with his cuddles until his knot released. I only managed to escape his clutches by gradually sliding lower and lower until I got to his legs and broke free from his stacked arms.

Outside, the moon is full and bright, backlighting the silhouette of Cillian's rosebushes. I smirk ruefully, shaking my head as I realize I haven't even asked him to prune them. It's a perfect metaphor, really—I was determined to have the damn things torn down for weeks… but now that I know they were never what they seemed, I'm not sure I could stomach removing them.

It would be a shame to cut the roses back now, anyway. They're finally in full bloom—hundreds of ruby furls and snow-white blossoms gently swaying in their nests of thorns.

Nest. That word feels like a siren call, illuminating a path to my center with twinkling lights and gleaming anticipation.

It won't be long now, my Omega tells me, her voice somewhere between a warning and an apology. *We'll probably start nesting tomorrow.*

Somehow, I don't feel daunted by that idea at all. Knowing Rhys, he's likely been researching heat stuff for weeks. Dane will be supportive and patient with me, as always. And Cillian… he'll be so pleased that I'm listening to my instincts. *Proud.*

I watch my three sleeping alphas for a moment, letting contentment sink into my bones. It's hard to leave them, even to creep into the bathroom. But once I'm in there, I realize I'm starving and decide to sneak downstairs and look for takeout leftovers.

Dane and I realized we could dip our thin-crust cheese pizza into butter chicken; now I'm not sure I'll ever be able to eat it without curry. Just the memory has my mouth watering. I cast the guys a sly look, tugging some of Dane's joggers and one of my camisoles on before padding for the exit as quietly as I can.

I tiptoe all the way around the second floor's semi-circular hall, intent on taking the back stairs to the kitchen. But there's a shadow in my path.

No, wait. *Two* shadows.

"Oh!"

The two men leap apart, one grunting while the other whines. They whip their faces in my direction. My stomach somersaults with chagrin as amusement bolts into my throat.

"Madame," Louis gasps, reaching down to hold his unbuckled pants around his hips. "Coggins and I were just, er—"

The salt-and-pepper haired butler visibly suppresses a snarl of displeasure, blinking until the feral light ebbs from his gaze.

"Our deepest apologies, Mrs. Blackwood," the proper man drawls. "Louis and I were just..."

He trails off, likely hunting for some fabled task that would explain why they were all over each other in the stairwell.

I smirk. "Fucking?"

Their scents shift. Without the neutralizers dulling their essences, I clearly catch bitter licorice from the alpha and something freshly-baked for Louis. Stress strengthens their aromas.

I try not to wrinkle my nose, but my Omega instantly whines. Wanting *our* alphas and no one else's.

The butler and valet exchange stricken glances. It occurs to me that I'm the mistress of the house—and therefore, technically in charge. I'm sure these men have been hiding whatever might be blooming between them since we removed the descenters from the house.

They probably didn't know how to tell Cillian. I picture my alpha's intimidating stare. *I wouldn't...*

Especially since Coggins practically raised my alphas. And Louis is a more recent employee, who depends on this job for himself and his sister.

"It's okay," I rush to reassure. "I won't tell anyone! Unless... you want me to?"

Coggins shakes his head with a harrumph, but I catch the way he reaches for Louis's hand, tucking it in his own while the other omega trembles.

Empathy softens my features. "Go up to the third floor," I whisper. "There won't be anyone up there tonight. And I promise not to say anything."

The men exchange a loaded look before Coggins dips into a bow. "Thank you, Madame. Good night."

Louis clumsily follows his lead, blushing as he mumbles something in French and follows the butler up the stairs. I watch them go, my chest full of unfamiliar warmth.

Maybe it won't just be our pack here, I think, smiling to myself. And perhaps we could all be... a weird kind of family. Even Fiona, if I can find the time to make friends with her.

I'm still mulling over that as I enter the kitchen. My thoughts stop short, my eyes flying to the lone item on the center island.

The small vase sparkles in a shaft of moonlight from the back window, drawing my gaze to the single red rose sitting in it.

It's clearly from our garden. I wonder which of the guys brought it in.

Probably Rhys.

He's been achingly romantic ever since our night at the ballet. Almost as if he picked up on how much I secretly loved all the frills in the story. He must have snuck down here and cut a rose for me while Dane and I were still knotted in the bath earlier.

Grinning, I lean over the island to sniff the flower before continuing on to scour our fridge.

It's funny, really. The night I lost my sister, I didn't hear a thing. Because I was so miserable, I hid from the world with headphones to drown out reality.

This time, though? It's because I'm so stupidly *happy*.

As I bounce in front of the refrigerator, I don't notice that one shadow is longer than all the others. I don't hear the rustle of fabric over the song I'm humming. And I can't see the needle aimed at the nape of my neck.

Poised to plunge me into oblivion.

CILLIAN

MY ALPHA HAS ONLY WOKEN ME FROM A DEEP SLEEP twice.

Once, the night Rhys and Dane were trapped in the fire. And again, the night Briar found out she was our mate and had a panic attack in the shower.

So I already know, when my eyes suddenly fly open, that something has happened.

Something is *wrong*.

Dane jolts upright the second I leap out of our bed. He sees my face, glances at the small space where our omega should be, and flicks his hand out, knocking Rhys's shoulder.

"Wake up," he grunts, rubbing his eyes. "Briar moved into the nest."

I don't know how, but my certainty is deep and immediate. "No," I rough out, grabbing the nearest pair of sweats off our omega's reading chair. "She isn't here."

Rhys lurches to attention, his aqua eyes bleary but wild. "What do you *mean* she's not *here*?"

He's asking if I mean the room, the house, or the property. I don't have an answer, other than shaking my head and stalking out of the room.

Dane stays behind me, the quiet *snick* of his gun's safety the only indication he's there. Rhys runs ahead, calling Briar's name.

An instinctive swell of dread grows in my stomach, raising the fine hairs on my nape. Our security guards should have come to investigate the noise by now—unless they're gone.

Or dead.

They've been tranquilized, I discover, when I find one of my hand-selected guards face down on the second-floor landing. There's another, passed out in the foyer. Which means I'll probably find two more at their posts beyond the front door.

Fuck.

Briar would have seen them if she had come this way. She would have known to run back to us. Which means she probably took the staircase by my bedroom. To the kitchen.

Dane is several steps ahead of me, pivoting and bolting for the hidden stairwell. Rhys shouts up from the first floor. *"IN HERE!"*

Goddamn it. Fuck, fuck, fuck.

For half a second, I'm sure we'll round the corner and discover my worst fear. Briar, cold and gray, with her gorgeous green eyes gazing sightlessly into the distance. Surrounded by blood as red as the petals that inspired her nickname.

But my recurring nightmare isn't there. Nothing is.

Except for an open back door.

And a single ruby rose.

AT THIS POINT, I THINK IT'S CLEAR I'M NO STRANGER TO captivity.

Being taken, held against my will, forced into terrifying no-win situations?

That's, like, a Tuesday for me.

But this?

I've never experienced anything like *this*.

Because it's *lavish*.

Where the fuck am I?

A padded room? It is technically that, although rounded and covered in buttery yellow silk. The walls are tufted, I notice, flowing straight down to a soft, pillowy platform and, lower, a recessed mattress. Piled with cushions and blankets?

Is it—

A nest?

I think it must be. There's no other reason for the shape and all the soft surfaces.

The scents of alphas.

One is toasted. Another is dark. Sort of like—

Gideon and Atlas.

Holy fuck. It's them. *Their* scents, blurred with two unfamiliar ones. A cologne-like fragrance, buried beneath something too sweet.

Shit.

Every cell in my body protests, longing to fling me away from the scents. This too-bright room. The sunny sheets and over-stuffed pillows and *oh God, no*—

Whining, I fold myself into a ball on the nest's platform. Trying not to touch anything. Hoping I won't have to claw myself out of my skin to stop the complete and total *wrongness* assaulting me.

I hide my face between my knees, burying my nose into my thigh. I stole these sweats from Dane, so his woody scent is the strongest—but when I focus, I can still vaguely smell Rhys's freshness and Cillian's smoke.

The small traces of my mates renew my pre-heat cramps. A whimper tickles my throat, vibrating where Cillian's locket should be.

No.

My fingers scrabble at my blank neck, realizing the gold links are missing. *No,* I think again, true panic assailing me. *No, no, no.*

If someone took the necklace off, they must know what it means. And they wanted it out of the way for a *reason.*

I hunch lower, inhaling as much of my alphas as I can. Their essences are enough to clear my mind, if only for a moment.

Okay, I think. *Okay. So someone got into the house and took me. Then brought me here.*

To Gideon's packhouse, my Omega trembles.

I nearly snarl. Fucking *Gideon*.

She's right. It has to be him. All his intrusions. Trying to lure me away twice. Following me to the bookstore. Bringing Atlas to let his packmate get a read on me.

Bracing myself for the burn in my nostrils and accompanying flare of panic, I lift my face just enough to swallow another deep breath. Confirming my worst fears... before a too-familiar voice suddenly comes from the other side of a hidden door.

"Hello, Briar. How do you like your new nest?"

RHYS

THE RED DOT ON MY SCREEN BLINKS BESIDE A READ-OUT that chills me to my core.

Signal disrupted – last known coordinate.

Cillian stands behind me, exuding deadly alpha aggression. It was his idea to put a tracker in Briar's necklace, but I programmed it utilizing the same tech we use to trace the weapons we sell illegally.

These trackers are military-grade. There's no way to disrupt their signals unless they've been destroyed, somehow.

Which means Briar's abductors not only know about the diamond-sized bug—they've *crushed* it. They'll likely accelerate their plans for her, too, now that they know we have their coordinates.

Gideon's coordinates, I note. The last known location is their pack's penthouse in the city.

Dane straps a rifle over his broad back before holstering a gun at either hip. "It's Gideon," he says, not needing to look at my screen. "I knew he was up to some shit that day at the bookstore. Why else would he have brought Atlas?"

I had the same question. Secretly, Cillian and I have suspected Atlas is the real alpha of their pack on a few occasions. But nevertheless, both of them creeping on our omega together never sat right with me.

Cillian's icy eyes meet mine, heavy with regret. Silently agreeing—we should have taken them out that day. Hell, after the party.

We assumed they would honor Grandfather's quest for a legitimate heir and find a wife of their own. He was clear about the rules from the get-go—Cillian finding a way to work within them while still securing our mate was a feat of sheer brilliance.

Our pack thought theirs just couldn't manage the same challenge. I honestly never thought they would *steal* our *mate*.

Are they doing this to keep us from her when she needs us? Or use her?

Jesus, which is *worse*?

"How the fuck do they know she's so close to her heat?" I snap, shoving up from my chair and ripping a pair of jeans off my bed. Cillian is in sweats—when he reaches out a hand expectantly, I realize none of us are really getting dressed.

We're going on a mission instead.

I toss my brother one of my shirts and he shrugs it on while I do the same. Dane hands each of us a loaded handgun and three extra clips. His gold eyes snap from mine to Cillian's. "You'll stay behind me. And put those on."

He points at the two Kevlar vests lying in a heap by my door. I lift my chin in return, and Cillian blows out a deep breath. His voice is frighteningly even, especially with the growl rumbling beneath every word.

"We eliminate everyone we encounter. Guards, staff. Anybody who knows she's there is culpable for my omega being taken from me. No one survives that."

It seems we finally agree on a lot of things. I nod, stuffing down the thorny tangle lodged in my gullet. Tasting the bitter tang of fear as I shrug my bulletproof vest on.

It's insane how little I care about being shot. They can put as many holes in me as they want, as long as I get my mate back. Or win her freedom for her, at least.

I feel the weight of that pass between the three of us as we exchange final glances.

It doesn't matter if the rest of us go down.

We just need Briar to be safe.

Cillian nods silently, then stalks out of the room. We follow, taking the stairs two at a time until we reach the foyer.

Where all hell breaks loose.

There's a darkly clad figure there, waiting. Dane's guns come out so fast I miss the motion entirely. One second, he's beside me —the next, he has the muzzle of his weapon pressed between the eyes of—

Gideon.

Cillian's cousin bares his teeth in a snarl, but holds both hands beside his shoulders. "Jesus Christ," he hisses at Dane. "What the fuck?"

The fact that he's playing dumb pisses me off. I cock my own gun, closing in from the other side and aiming it upward, under his chin. I click the safety off.

"I'd rethink your opening statement if I were you," Cillian says. "We've already decided you're dead. So from now on, every piece of information you can give us about where you've taken Briar is one more moment you get to live."

Gideon's mouth twists into a sneer, but Dane isn't having it. He presses the gun into his forehead harder, gritting behind his mask, "I've killed more men than you could count. I'll gladly add you to the list before you can *blink*. Start fucking talking."

Another click turns my head.

Fuck.

Atlas is at the front door, standing on the threshold with his own gun trained on Cillian. Behind him, their other packmates rush up the porch steps. Finn—the cocky, perpetually smirking moron who runs their PR... and their group's answer to Dane. A deadly, mean-faced man named Ryker.

"Look," Gideon grinds out, squirming against the iron bar of Dane's forearm. "Everyone needs to calm down. We—we have—"

"Briar," I roar, "We know. Now—"

"No," Atlas calls. His solid gaze lands on Gideon, confirming my suspicions when he barks quietly—the way only a pack leader could. "*Show them, Gid.*"

Our cousin starts to lower his arm, his hand fumbling for his trousers. Dane lets him but growls, the sound as fearsome as it is quiet.

I move subtly, positioning myself at an angle. Grabbing the handle of my packmate's second Glock, aiming it at Atlas. Ready to pull both triggers at the same time.

But Gideon unwinds a familiar strand of gold from his pocket, holding up the black diamond–encrusted heart for all of us to see.

It... hasn't been cut or crushed. The lock was picked open. And... given to them?

Or *planted* on them?

"We don't have Briar," Gideon says, looking at Cillian with sincere rage in his eyes. "But we know where she is."

THE PADDED WALL OF THE ROOM CREAKS OPEN, revealing a man in a black pinstriped suit. An oppressive gasoline scent washes into the nest, stinging my nostrils before I can even lift my head.

I blink my eyes. They burn from the bright colors around me and the light that floods in from the wide, blank basement behind him. For a second, I think I might be hallucinating. Surely, the voice I heard through the door wasn't *real*... right?

But the alpha silhouette in front of me chuckles, his amusement distinctly ominous. "Do you recognize me yet, omega?"

I... do.

He was there, at our wedding. During the interminable dinner after. And again, a few weeks ago. At the party when I learned the Blackwood alphas were my mates. The soiree where Cillian introduced this man as—

His grandfather.

Forsyth Blackwood.

The older alpha steps into the nest, the soles of his shoes grinding dirt into the light silk fabric. A frisson of disgust tightens my guts.

It isn't *my* nest, but *still*.

Have some respect, *asshole*.

He clearly doesn't hold regard for much, if his derisive scowl is any indication. He loops dark gray eyes over my shuddering body, lingering in ways that have me curling tighter into a ball. His mouth pinches in distaste, but carnal interest lights his gaze.

"You know," he starts, stepping farther into the room. Leaving gritty footprints behind. "I was hoping for more."

... more?

Forsyth narrows his stare, sliding his hands into his pockets. "Some nobody with an insane guardian. An injured dancer. A broken doll. I couldn't understand why Cillian chose *you*."

His words whip at me, slicing deeper than they should. My quivers intensify until I'm shaking so hard my teeth chatter. False pity flits over his features. "Poor dear. It turns out that madman's projections were spot on; I'll give him that."

Madman?

I only know one bastard who fits that description. The one who sold me and promptly *disappeared*...

"M-my f-f—?" I try to ask, but can't scrape words out.

Forsyth nods anyway. "Yes, *Dr. Brynn* had your heat cycle charted down to the hour. If you're interested, I had him lay out the next few before we... *parted ways*."

His implication is clear, but it makes no sense. How did he even *know* my father? Nonetheless *kill* him?

One glance into the Blackwood patriarch's flinty, soulless eyes confirms; *yes.*

My father is dead.

It explains why none of us heard from him after the wedding. And why he hadn't tried to pester Blackwood Corp. with more of his "inventions."

But still... *he's dead?!*

I blink, trying to feel anything other than bewildered relief. But my thoughts are blank, apart from one question.

"How?"

The word rasps, but I'm proud of myself for sounding steadier. Forsyth seems to reconsider me, leaning back as his salt-and-pepper brows lift. "Your wedding. My men apprehended him after dinner. Once Cillian was thoroughly preoccupied with his *new bride.*"

I suppress another shiver, glaring. Sure, I don't actually care if the asshole who "raised" us is gone—but Forsyth has no way of knowing that. And his smug expression reveals just how much he's hoping to devastate me.

"And you decided to *kill* him? For what? Kicks?"

The old man shakes his head. "Nothing I do is without cause. *Your husband* seems to have forgotten where he learned that particular trait—but I *never* forget what Cillian is. What I *made* him.

"So when he suddenly announced he was taking a wife; playing at being an obedient grandson, bent on producing our family heir... I knew there was more to the story. I *assumed* your father would be useful in piecing Cillian's plans together. He wasn't, but he did tell me all about *you.*"

... me?

What the hell would that man have said about *me?*

She reads too much? Don't try to make her drink mysterious "health shakes"? She handles being locked in the dark for days like a champ?

Actually, come to think of it, that last piece of info might be pertinent here.

Forsyth clocks the stupefied look I try to stifle. His brows crouch. "Surely you must have wondered what Brynn was *doing* with you and that other girl. The beta?"

"He was our father," I spit. "A fucked-up one who tried to use us to do omega research, but he was—"

Or *was* he?

Because the haughty, faux-pitying look on this man's face implies maybe...

Maybe I don't actually share any DNA with my "father." Or my long-lost sister.

I think about the swabs Dane so carefully collected. How he wanted to make me feel better about all my family's uncertainty by giving me some insight into my heritage.

Is it possible I know even *less* about where I came from than I thought? And everything our "father" told us was a lie?

Of course it is.

And what's worse? It makes a sick, depressing sort of sense. What kind of person would *experiment* on their own flesh and blood?

It never struck me just how wrong that was. Not until I got to Blackwood Manor and saw how even the most fucked-up pack protected one another. Defended each other. Would kill and die if it meant giving their brothers a chance to live.

Violet and I were that way, too. We knew we probably didn't come from the same mother, but it didn't matter. Because we were *family*.

It should have been like that for our father. And probably would have been... if he really was the one responsible for our existences.

Fuck. My head feels like it might cave in, but I won't give this bastard the satisfaction.

"So he told you the truth, then?" I bluff, pretending I'm in on the secret.

Forsyth doesn't buy it. He chuffs a dry laugh. "Brynn said you had no idea. That he'd been using you and your sister for years to conduct a series of tests. All aimed at creating a perfect omega specimen."

Oh God. All those "protein drinks." The nights he took Violet down to his lab—her desperate phone call, telling me to obey. Warning me not to ask questions.

Did she ask too many? Is that why he had her taken away?

He must have realized his experiments failed on me. That's probably why he decided to auction me off to the highest bidder.

"That's how he sold you to Cillian, I suspect," Forsyth continues. "As some sort of ultra-potent breeding machine. And my conniving grandson likely thought your modified genetics would help him win."

No.

It's amazing how certain I feel, but I know, in the deepest parts of my soul: Cillian didn't want me because of my father's failed experiments. He wanted me because I was *his*.

He told me so himself—the patent was a smokescreen. But he had to throw off suspicion about his real connection to me, so he let my father believe he was a genius who had sold me and his stupid invention to a billionaire.

None of it was ever real, except the way Cillian felt about me.

And Forsyth has no idea.

My stomach flips. *He still doesn't know we're mates.*

Is that a good thing?

I debate internally while he goes back to incorrectly assessing me. He frowns, ponderous. "I couldn't allow that, of course. Cillian may be as smart and ruthless as they come, but he's still a bastard. I was never going to allow any child of his to be my heir, just like I couldn't allow my wayward, lovesick, idiot of a son to take over."

Oh Jesus *fuck*.

The look on his face... the braggy air...

"Caine didn't kill himself," I mumble through numb lips. "It was *you*?"

Forsyth's sneer spreads into a purely *evil* grin. He starts to pace closer, taking a step with every horrifying admission.

"It was *all* me, Briar. Getting rid of Caine's tawdry mate. Convincing Caine it was his brother, Adam. Letting Caine dispose of that worthless drunk before I staged Caine's suicide."

He's close enough to touch me now, stretching wrinkled fingers to my cheek. I shudder, flinching back, but that only ignites the malice in his eyes.

"A real man owns up to his mistakes and corrects them," he growls. "My sons were weak. Unworthy. One throwing his life away between a mistress's thighs and the other drinking himself half to death, refusing to take his foolish brother and his bastard son out."

He drops his hand, standing back to his full height. "*Mistakes*," he grits. "Just like letting Cillian live. He was only a boy—I thought he might be useful. *Malleable*. Especially given the soft spot he always had for that pitiful blond runt."

Rhys.

Forsyth must have used him as leverage to manipulate Cillian after his father died. Could that be how he ended up taking the position at Blackwood Corp. in the first place?

I may never know.

Because I don't think this alpha plans on letting me go.

"Originally," he says, "I planned on taking you for Gideon. He might not be as shrewd as Cillian, but he's still an excellent vice president. Plus, he has a *proper* pack—and he's not a bastard."

The old man sighs as if exasperated. "But when I went to him last night to inform him that I had you here, in the nest I had made for his pack, ready for your heat—he failed my test. Instead of agreeing to dispose of Cillian and marry you himself once your haze set in, he told me *no*."

His headshake is full of genuine dismay and disappointment.

"Such a waste of time and energy, grooming him to take over. *We'll* have to do better next time."

Better. Next. Time?

What does he mean? Surely he can't think that I—that *we*—

Bile burns my throat as my insides twist. Revulsion thickens my saliva and thins my breath. "I won't," I tell him. "*No.*"

He huffs. "You *will*. As soon as your heat sets in, you won't be able to help yourself. It will be me or no one. But I'm guessing, this being your first heat, you'll be much too disoriented to hold your own for very long."

Panic vibrates through me, my Omega whining frantically. He's right. Once my heat comes over us, we won't be able to stop him. And we'll be locked in here. Without our alphas.

I scramble for any way to convince this lunatic his sick plan won't work. "B-but I'm not your wife—I'm *Cillian's*. You can't have a legitimate heir with someone else's wife. And he-he'll come for me, eventually!"

Forsyth lifts a condescending brow. "Not if he's dead. Which also solves the issue of your marriage. I planted your little locket at Gideon's penthouse as I left last night, so I assume, once Cillian finds it, those two will take care of each other. And if not... like I said, today is the day I correct my mistakes. Once and for all."

A fierce wail of alarm vibrates up my throat. I try to fling myself at Forsyth's legs, acting on pure instinct—the need to tear him down, claw at his threats—but he steps out of the way.

I collapse against the nest, dizzy from how wrong it all feels. "You"—I pant, struggling to breathe —"fucking *asshole.*"

Forsyth lodges a swift, ruthless kick into my stomach. It knocks the wind out of me, turning my scream into a wheeze.

"Listen here, girl," he barks. "You don't want to make yourself another mess for me to clean up."

I barely hear him over the buzz in my head. My body rolls, and I curl into a ball. Something in the pocket of my sweatpants presses into my thigh.

They aren't mine, I remember. *They're Dane's. And Dane always carries—*

A knife.

No one took it from me, which means they probably didn't even bother to search me when his henchmen carted me in here. Somehow, that makes me almost as angry as the notion of being taken in the first place.

This motherfucker didn't even think to *check my pockets*. Because it never occurred to him that I'm not some weak, defenseless piece of ass.

Well, fine.

He said today's the day for fixing mistakes, but this one will cost him.

Because this rose?

Has thorns.

sixty-three

DANE

You could cut the tension in this goddamn SUV with a knife.

I'm not sure who the car belongs to, but Atlas drives, aiming the armored vehicle toward the mansion on the north shore of Long Island. It's only ten minutes away, but every inch feels like an eternity when I don't know where my mate is or if she's still alive.

"Tell me again."

Cillian has demanded to hear how this went down half a dozen times. The scowling alpha beside me grumbles, but I silence him with a glare over the edge of my mask.

361

I swear to God, if he pushes me right now.

In the third row, behind Rhys, Gideon sighs. "He came to us last night. Said he sent a team in to 'extract' your omega before her heat. Apparently he had intel that suggests she's some sort of super-breeder? And claimed that's why you married her out of nowhere and had become so obsessed with her."

Rhys's answering snarl is vicious. "It wasn't *out of nowhere.* Cillian found her years ago, you stupid—"

Ryker snaps a low growl and I rumble back. Cillian turns from the passenger seat to glare at all of us.

"I assure you," he says, facing forward without glancing at Atlas or his cousin, "our reasons have nothing to do with whatever failed experiments her father performed before we met her."

Cillian won't tell them she's our mate because he still doesn't trust them. I can't blame him, after all the shit they've put us through. And vice versa.

"We figured your connection had to be emotional," Atlas grumbles, scowling at the windshield. "After we tried to save her and she chose to stay with you."

Tried to save *her?*

Rhys and I look at one another, then at Atlas. Cillian grinds his teeth, snapping a succinct, "*What?*"

"In the bookstore," Gideon replies, rolling his eyes. "I practically begged her to let us help her, but she seemed to have some sort of sick trauma bond with Dane."

I can't help the enraged sound that escapes me, but it's enough to silence the car. Rhys wraps his hand around my forearm, squeezing. I wish we had a pack bond so I could actually hear his message, but it feels a bit like *not now.*

Cillian recovers first, shooting Gideon a wary frown. "Is that the only time you tried to lure her away?"

"Nope," the charming one, Finn, pipes up. "At the party, Gid approached her to try to warn her about all your illegal bullshit." He shrugs. "That didn't work, either."

Fuck.

I can tell Cillian is thinking the same thing when his lips pull down into a more severe scowl. I read his considering look and feel my own pang of uncertainty.

Should we tell them the truth about Blackwood Corp.? Would it help establish more goodwill before we walk into a literal battle?

I nod subtly. Because I will do *anything* if it means having Briar back in my arms. Even if we have to go on the lam to save ourselves after.

Rhys turns his head from Cillian to me, expression outraged. I can empathize—the guy has spent the better part of a decade keeping us under the radar. But he knows this is more important.

My packmate groans, his pale face pained. "Jesus, you guys are idiots," he finally blurts. "Did it ever occur to you that *maybe* we're not actually trying to *help* Forsyth with his fuckery? And we might just be the reason certain high-dollar 'customers' keep *disappearing*?"

Resounding silence roars back at us. Gideon slowly sits forward, his hands curling into the seat behind me while his eyes land on Cillian's. "You've been... undermining Grandfather? *Dismantling* the black market clients—all this time?"

Our alpha is smart enough not to answer verbally, but his gaze never wavers as he dips his chin. The car gets very quiet again, some odd discomfort I don't understand stretching taut between the other pack.

"Ah, hell," the gruff, angry one suddenly curses. "Tell them, Gid."

Finn interrupts, his light eyes bulging. "What the *fuck*, Ryker?!"

I think I know what they're talking about, but my insides still coil into a lead ball, rolling around my abdomen. "Tell us what?"

Gideon exchanges loaded glances with all his packmates. Cillian grits his teeth harder, and Rhys hisses a growl. "Tell. Us. What?" I repeat, nearly shouting.

Atlas captures Gideon's attention in the rearview mirror for a long beat, then exhales through his nose. He waves his hand in a "so be it" gesture. Gideon winces.

"It was us," he says. "The fire. It was our pack, not the cartel. We tried to burn you guys."

Fucking hell.

Fury flares in my chest, igniting a fierce growl that Cillian echoes. "I knew it!" Rhys yells. "You *motherfuckers*!"

"We thought you were supplying murderers and rapists with semi-automatic weapons!" Gideon interjects. "We couldn't just *let you*."

Rhys clutches his hair with both hands, eyes falling shut. "I swear to God, I will—"

"The patent for Brynn's stupid weapon," I realize. "Cillian only bought it to get Briar. But *you've* been the ones blocking it from production?"

This time, the swelling silence feels better, somehow, but also more intense. "Yes," Gideon finally rasps. "We haven't pushed a new design through in over a year."

It doesn't make any sense, until Atlas explains: "The tech at Blackwood Corp. has gotten too powerful. Unethical. We've been working to sabotage and contain it."

Hence why they didn't attack us again. Why waste their time when they could dismantle the organization from the top?

Which... is a lot like what we were doing. Only we worked things from the bottom, starting down in the mud with the scum of the earth. And got our hands dirty in the process.

"I don't understand," Finn gripes, whipping his big eyes from Cillian to me, then over to Rhys. "If you all hate Blackwood Corp. so much, why did you marry an omega to try to inherit it?"

"So we could *destroy* it," I bite out.

Cillian looks at Atlas again before finally meeting his cousin's gaze. "And because Briar is our *mate*."

THINGS MOVED VERY QUICKLY AFTER CILLIAN LAID OUR final card on the table.

I wasn't sure what to expect from the other Blackwood Pack, but once they heard the word "mate," grim determination settled among them.

As we rolled up to the street containing Forsyth's compound, Gideon simply promised, "We won't let history repeat itself. Your mom didn't make it out of this family, Cillian, but we're going to get *your* mate out of here."

Doing what his father didn't. Or *couldn't.*

Either way, we paused to make our plan, deciding it was better for our pack to hide in the SUV's trunk while Atlas and Gideon sat up front. After all, the other pack was *supposed* to be here for Briar's heat, before they turned Forsyth down.

That part works smoothly, but there are still dozens of armed guards to contend with once we park on the wide travertine loop in front of the lavish mansion. I barely see any of the details, too focused on eliminating threats when both of our packs suddenly leap from the car.

The first wave of armed security personnel goes down easily. We have the element of surprise and manage to pick them off while they scramble to organize. The second round is a bit worse —one of them gets a piece of my calf while another hits Cillian dead in the center of his chest. His incensed roar tells me it hurts, but the fact that he ends up emptying a full barrel without blinking two seconds later likely means it didn't break through the vest.

Ever-strategic, Rhys stays behind the car, picking men off until all three waves of mercenaries are incapacitated. We didn't necessarily shoot to kill, but none of us stop to check on them before we race into the open foyer.

"BRIAR!" I bellow.

Cillian repeats her name in a bark. Two more guards come flying in from a back hallway but Ryker literally picks one up and throws him into the second.

Christ. And people think *I* have issues.

We hear more men approaching, but Atlas waves us on. "Go," he snaps. "We'll hold anyone else off."

Cillian agrees with a nod, stalking deeper into the house. Rhys mutters under his breath, listing all the ways Forsyth will pay for taking our omega—but he suddenly freezes halfway through the opulent living area. His head snaps up.

"Here," he rasps, breaking into a sprint, aiming for a far door. "I can scent her."

She's the *only* thing he can smell, so of course he would sense her first. Cillian and I run after him, flinging the door open and barreling down the stairs to the house's enormous basement.

It's finished, but unfurnished. A huge, white, concrete room, with doors lined up across from the steps. We don't have to open any of them—because two seconds later we hear a shriek, followed by a feminine *war cry* and a growled grunt.

I lunge, putting my full might behind my shoulder and ramming the middle door right off its hinges.

Briar's scent greets me, swirled with the other Blackwood Pack's. The combination makes me murderous, but my omega's fearful squeak recenters me.

She's here, I think, my whole head suddenly weightless. *She's alive.*

And... kneeling over Forsyth?

No. His *body*.

Which has one of my knives embedded in the chest.

Briar releases the hilt, her green eyes so wide they look like emeralds floating in cream. Apart from the blood speckled over her bare chest, she doesn't seem injured. And she's still wearing her clothes.

My clothes.

Relief strong enough to sting slices through me. I fall to my knees, gathering her face between my palms. "Briar," I gasp.

My packmates shove in behind me, absorbing the scene. Rhys joins me on the floor. "Jesus, viper, are you okay?"

Cillian walks around the nest, examining it for signs of any other alphas. When he finds none, he comes to the space on Briar's other side and sinks into a crouch.

Our omega blinks at him, gesturing with a visibly shaking hand. "I-I-I *stabbed him*. I *k-k-*"

Cillian takes in her expression, his softening with concern and adoration for a split second before hardening into pure resolve. He snaps his hand out, clutching the handle of my switchblade. Dragging the crimson-soaked sliver from his Grandfather's chest...

And plunging it right back in.

"No," he tells her, offering Rhys the knife. "*I* killed him." He glances over at us. "*We* did."

Our omega watches her venomous alpha go next, his stab-and-twist motion menacingly final. When he hands the weapon to me, it takes a moment before I can slowly wrap my fingers around it.

Fuck, this is the one part of me I never wanted Briar to see. The beast.

But as I gaze at her ashen face, her whispered question finally makes sense.

What if you aren't the monster in this story? What if you're the hero?

My omega needs to know this man won't ever come for her again. She needs feel secure for her heat—and she needs to believe that none of this was her fault.

I can do that for her.

Something inside me shifts. I rise onto my knees, spinning the knife in a sideways slash. It slices cleanly across Forsyth's throat.

And that might make me Briar's beast.

But at least I know the real monster is dead.

CILLIAN

DANE DROPS THE KNIFE JUST IN TIME TO CATCH BRIAR.

She launches herself into his arms, a choked sob sticking in her throat. He hums, purring, and she dives for the sound. Her motions are jerky and desperate—so unlike her normal poise, I know she must be entering the thick of her heat. Fast.

She practically cries when she tries to scent-mark Dane's chest and feels the cotton T-shirt there. He rips it over his head, then tears his mask off, tossing it aside carelessly.

Briar moans, climbing his body to nuzzle his scarred jaw and short beard, his mottled cheek. His long hair falls forward as he ducks his face against her shoulder, whispering, "I'm here, little girl. Your alphas are here."

Our omega shivers, her green eyes glossed with a dazed sort of awe. As if she's remembering she has *three* of us. It might be adorable if we were somewhere safe.

She lurches to Rhys next. He catches her with a broken sob of his own, rubbing his face all over her cheeks. "Fuck, pretty baby. I was going out of my mind. Look at me. Let me check your eyes."

Briar blinks at him until he nods, his scent soaring. I see why when our omega's gaze finds mine. *Hazy.*

My chest swells on deep breaths, my nostrils flaring as I do everything I can not to rip her away from my packmates. "Did he touch you?" I husk instead. "Are you hurt?"

Thankfully, she shakes her head. Intense relief bursts behind my heart, but it's short-lived. There are so many questions and no time to ask them. Not to mention her mind-bending perfume, which tastes sweeter and sharper on every inhale.

Fuck. I have to get us out of here.

Gideon is lurking in the basement outside the yellow nest. I start to stand, determined to clear a path for us, but Briar *shrieks.*

She thrashes loose, practically tackling me. Her desperate grip is hard enough to draw blood, her pointed nails leaving stripes over my shoulders.

Jesus. My *heart.*

"Shhh," I whisper, squeezing my arms around her. I turn my face into her sweat-dried hair. "I'm not leaving, rosebud. Never leaving. You're my wife, remember? I'm yours forever. Whether you like it or not."

Briar's body relaxes the smallest bit, but it isn't enough. None of this is.

I sense movement. An instinctive snarl rips up my throat, but Gideon approaches anyway, pointedly keeping his eyes down and both palms facing out.

"You guys need to get her home, right?" he rushes, speaking quickly to avoid being torn in half. "I can clear the house. Get all the guys somewhere they won't scent her so you can get her to the Armada."

I fucking loathe the idea of her heat perfume being in my cousin's car. Let alone him being in the house while we carry her out. My lip lifts, baring my teeth. Dane mirrors my expression, only he pairs his with a growl sinister enough to send Gideon back a step.

"Why the *fuck* would we allow that?" Rhys snaps. "I'm about to stab you for scenting her *right now.*"

An expected smirk crosses Gideon's face, wry and full of self-deprecation. It pauses my rage just long enough for me to notice how *unaffected* he is.

No jaw clenching. No growls or groans.

Our eyes meet. Something bitter weaves itself into his smile. "I suppose we all have our secrets," he says slowly. "In this family, you have to. Right, Cillian?"

We both automatically look at our grandfather's body. So pitifully lifeless. So...

Small.

Such a pathetic man, trying desperately to cling to power. Manipulating and machinating, but never making *progress.* Pitting us against each other the way he set our fathers against one another twenty years ago. The way he fought his own brother. Like his father and uncle before him.

He was clearly going to keep Briar here for her heat. To use her. Make his heir and his fucked-up new world order and all the other shit the lot of us refused to sacrifice our lives for.

God knows how many things he lied to us about.

My cousin and his pack never even wanted to *keep* the company. They wanted to *destroy* it.

And now I see—Gideon? The alpha I thought I knew? The one I made my enemy?

Never existed.

I don't know him. Not really. I only have the information I

was fed, all to create this competition that only benefited the whims of a psychopath.

The same slow understanding burns low in Gideon's gray eyes. "I never wanted her, Cillian," he vows quietly. "I only wanted to *help* her."

Because he thought she needed to be rescued—and I did everything I could to force his pack to believe that lie. So much so, I almost made it true.

I hold Briar closer, my breath shattering on every exhale. Her perfume is thick and tart. *She needs her nest.*

Gideon backs up, leaving the exit clear. "I'll get everyone out of your way," he adds, then holds up his keys.

"Here." He tosses them to Rhys, flashing me a smile. "Drive it like you stole it. Because that's what I'm telling Atlas."

sixty-five

BRIAR

THE WORLD PASSES BY IN BLURS AND BLOTS.

There's a too-gorgeous, pale, somber face, his eerie eyes so intent on mine while I bounce in someone else's thick, muscled arms. The scars I love so much, bleeding into patterns. A dizzying blend of bare skin and black ink.

And ice blue.

The wolf. The devil. My husband and master and king.

He's here, every second. A solid hand on the top of my head. A squeeze of my hand. A calming voice that issues the most competent commands.

"Up the back stairs. Coggins is dealing with cleanup. He's already finished most of it, and he'll send Louis to the door of the suite with food this evening. I've instructed both of them to keep their distance—no one will enter the room once we've locked it."

It's like he knows everything I want to ask for before I do. I sink into the purr vibrating behind me, hiding my face against the broad, branded chest while my alpha continues, "Run a bath, Rhys. We need to wash all these scents off her before she gets into her nest."

I hear the water thunder to life and startle, my head lolling while I blink. Everything smears into a fog, then refocuses, revealing my bedroom and the rosebushes blooming on the balcony. They sway, their colors running together.

"I want to get in with her," the alpha holding me roughs out.

The light-haired one nods, scowling solemnly. "Hold on, I'll undress you both."

Our pack alpha reappears in my line of sight, shaking his head. "Wait. There's something I need to do first."

Everything spins again. I shut my eyes, anchoring myself to the big alpha holding me, letting his deep purrs loosen my lungs. He presses kisses into my forehead.

"Briar?"

Right. That's me.

I crack my eyelids open, ignoring the nauseous seethe that twists the place between my hips. I'm relieved when I find the lights in the marble bathroom are off; and only a few groups of candles flicker in the corners around the tub behind me.

The big alpha is still holding me, but he's slowly arranged me in an upright position, facing outward on his wide denim-covered lap. I start to squirm, wondering what could possibly be more important than *burning* the fabric chafing between us, when—

There in the onyx bathroom, the shirtless, black-haired pack leader drops to the floor in front of me. Our eyes lock, and a brief burst of lucidity floods my brain.

Cillian.

He's on one knee.

Holding... my ring.

And my collar.

He holds his palm out to me, diamonds shimmering in the low light. Offering me... a choice.

Two of them.

Yearning creases his square, handsome face. "Be my wife," he says, the words somehow a plea and a command. "Bond with us and wear my ring. Let me lock this necklace around your pretty throat and put my claim behind it. Stay here. Be ours."

I already *am.*

But I guess that's the thing about choices, right?

Sometimes the ones you choose need to hear your decision just as much as you need to make it.

I slowly turn to my venomous alpha, noting the tension gripping his entire body. His intense yearning laid out so plainly in his angelic features.

And the big man at my back, all strength and security. He's less anxious, his golden eyes and scarred features soft. Half of his full lips quirk up. In a look that almost seems... hopeful.

Which is exactly what I feel. Hope. Love. Safety.

A home.

My home.

My skin burns and my pulse beats in my ears, but I manage to nod. "Yes. I want the bonds. I—I want all of you."

Cillian exhales loudly, then gracefully lunges up to kiss me. I feel his hand find mine, sliding my ring back into place. He pulls away before I can fall into him, slipping the thick gold chain around my neck. Its cool links rasp over my hot, sensitized skin. As he produces the small sliver of metal—what the fuck are those called?—and locks the heart closed at the base of my throat, a shiver bolts down my spine.

Perfume pours out of me. "Fucking *mine,*" the alpha growls under his breath, grasping my chin for a filthier, licking kiss.

The second his tongue invades my mouth, his taste overwhelms me. Dark, sweet smoke. Spiced and rich.

My entire body lights up, every nerve vibrating with need. A deep, painful cramp stabs my gut. I whine and my husband breaks away, his smile blurring as my vision tunnels.

"It's time for us to build your nest, omega."

sixty-six

RHYS

I'VE LIVED THIS MOMENT BEFORE. IN THE DEEPEST corners of my damaged mind, hidden in places I would never admit to.

My little reprieve from the pain—the only thing that could help, when the worst of my migraines hit.

A fantasy. A dream.

The cure for my curse.

Briar's fingers feel hot between mine. She pulls, whining softly. Green eyes beam up at me, full of hazy need and the purest, simplest trust.

Fuck, I don't deserve her.

I never could. Even if I had done everything perfectly from the start... no man could be worthy of the gorgeous perfection that is a naked Briar Rose Blackwood, building her nest.

Dane painstakingly held her hair out of the water while Cillian bathed her. I waited on the floor, on my knees, holding a towel open. Praying she might let me all the way into her safe space this time. Worried sick she might not.

But the second I finished drying her off, bending to plant kisses on each of her feet, our omega started squirming. *Whining.* For *me.*

Now, as I kneel in the center of the small, perfect room, a burst of light-headed relief hits me. She guides my hand to the nearest article of clothing—a pair of Cillian's sweatpants. She must like those, because she shows me how she wants them tucked into the pillows along the western wall of the recessed mattress, where I believe she's constructing *her* personal spot.

I've been reading up on nesting for—okay, *fine.* Forever.

Most books mention the tendency omegas have to work circularly from a single point. In Briar's case, it's the side closest to her bookshelves, with a view of the rosebushes.

My heart twinges at those small details. My knot twitches and my Alpha struggles, fighting his binds. I ignore him, focusing on her scent so I won't get a headache. It isn't hard. Her dark cherry aroma is *everywhere*—embedded in every fiber of the room.

My omega's nest is nothing short of magical. Her signature roses sway outside the arched windows, blocking most of the daylight. They complement her favorite color palette—the richest coal, ruby, rouge, and amethyst. Dark emerald walls, touches of gold, and clusters of candles. At night, with the moon peeking through the skylight, this nest will feel exactly like the slice of heaven it is.

Especially now. With her carefully rolled blankets and the pillows she stacked so insistently. I realize she's purposefully sorted out scented items among the piles, creating three collections, in addition to hers. One with all the scents mixed up. And then specific spots for each of us.

Dane's is the tallest and widest, on the farthest side of the mattress, where he might actually have a prayer of stretching out. Cillian goes between her and the door—his pile practically part of hers.

That's natural; she wants her pack alpha as her protection and her buffer. She'll crave his attention and approval with a special kind of urgency. This configuration will keep him poised for whatever she needs.

Smart, gorgeous girl.

Briar tugs me again, too weak to be effective. I follow anyway, letting her feel the absolute control she has, here. Over all of us.

Our omega goes to her knees and shuffles the remaining pile of pillows, never dropping my hand. I let her guide me, yearning and awe growing thick enough to strangle when I realize she's put me...

Closest to the books. Right beside her. Where she can treat my touch starvation... even in *her* heat.

My eyes sting as she hands me one of the softest blankets, earnest hope sparkling in her black eyes. Longing for me to accept her care.

Briar suddenly makes sense to me in a whole new way. The woman I love is sharp and bold—but her Omega is *sweet*. Loving and loyal. The combination devastates the last of my self-control.

I sweep her into my lap before she can so much as whimper. Scent-marking her temples and cheeks. Hoarse as I murmur, "Thank you, pretty baby. It's perfect."

I thought I couldn't smell anything except her, but when I leave my scent over hers, the combination is crystal clear to me. Herbal and tart. Sugary and crisp.

She belongs with me.

The rightness of that thought zings through my blood, directly to the place where my Alpha lies. He's restless. Concerned about his mate and what she needs. Full of anxiety about truly meeting her for the first time... and afraid I might not let him.

I'm not sure I can. He's a raging beast, constantly causing me pain. He growled and snapped at Briar for close to a month because we didn't have her scent. Will she even *want* me to let him out during her heat? Will her Omega accept him?

It seems like she would take any part of me I offered. The guileless entreaty filling her eyes is enough to put a lump in my throat. I nuzzle her again, whispering, "I love you."

Cillian slides into the room, busying himself with the extra nesting supplies stockpiled in the corner, adding our sheets to the mix. He texts as he goes, no doubt firing off instructions to every employee we have. I'm sure he's had every detail of Briar's heat in place for months.

Fuck, he's a good pack leader.

And I'm shit at noticing.

The gratitude and regret only climb higher when Dane lumbers into the nest. He has his mask off and his hair tied back, which I know is Briar's favorite combination. It seems her Omega agrees, because our girl whimpers until I shift her on my thighs, stretching her body toward the big guy so she can rub her face against his. His wooden scent swells as he hums, closing his eyes.

In a sudden flash of clarity, I realize how much gestures like that must mean to him. After years of covering himself, hiding the parts he thought others would scorn... her Omega's innocent appreciation must feel transformative.

Briar smiles as she noses his scarred cheek, her elated expression dazed and utterly sincere. I catch the way it glosses Dane's gold eyes. His chest rattles fiercely, echoing the lower, smoother purr behind my sternum.

Cillian finishes laying out his plans and promptly chucks his phone into the corner. His underlying impatience makes me smirk. Odd warmth blooms under my lungs as Briar whines eagerly, her wide eyes sparkling as she waits for her alpha to take in her hard work.

Cillian pauses, carefully noting every detail before he steps down into his spot, crawling forward to press his forehead into hers. "Best girl," he praises, sweetening her scent. "Your nest is so beautiful, rosebud. Did you make this spot just for me?"

She's obviously overjoyed that he noticed. A fresh tidal wave of tart sweetness spins off of her as she accepts his approval.

Oh *God*.

Fucking FUUUUUUCK.

Her heat perfume *melts* my *mind*. So much thicker and warmer than her usual perfection. Briar squirms, desperation rising. Since I'm the most in tune with her aroma, I feel the way it starts to slice and smolder before our packmates.

When she feels my cock tick under her, her sugared scent only cuts deeper. I groan and Dane growls.

Cillian hums his satisfaction, holding our omega by the chain around her throat. His eyes burn into her. "Tell me, darling: whose knot is going to fill this pretty cunt first?"

Briar trembles. A heated burst of slick pours from her pussy, wetting my thigh. I stiffen, gritting my teeth to give her time to answer. Bracing myself for the moment she says Cillian's name, or Dane's...

But our girl is beyond the ability to remember what to call us. So instead she keens, her body bucking in my lap as she turns—

To me.

Longing smolders in her eyes. White-hot in its sincerity, soldering the jagged edges of my heart back together. Healing me with two simple words.

"Want *you*," Briar breathes.

She's fucking perfect. Everything. My goddamn dream. The wild wish I'd given up on. All my hopes.

Fuck, do my lungs even work anymore?

Who cares?

If I die, I die.

I promised that she would never have to ask for me twice. So I ignore the ache in my throat and the awe tightening my airway, lifting her by the hips. My cock stretches high and proud, pulsing with purple veins and oozing pre-cum.

The knot at the base tingles, anticipating her hot, wet cunt. I shut my eyes, panting hard while I try to reason with my Alpha. *We told her we wouldn't knot her until we've earned her forgiveness.*

He gives me a firm shove, wordlessly nodding at the redness emblazoned across her chest. The way her pupils have yawned wide, swallowing her jade irises. The thick streams of clear warmth seeping down her thighs.

When he actually speaks, my mind falls quiet.

She needs me. Please.

He's never said that word before. Or treated me with even a modicum of deference. I've been fighting this bastard from the moment I designated, trying to keep him from going on a rampage every goddamned day.

But he's... sorry.

I feel it. His shame. The desperation under it.

All he ever wanted was a mate, that much was clear. But he never told me *why*. Now I understand.

He knew *I* needed one.

Because I was abandoned. Rejected. Despised.

And, sure, he's wild by nature. But the original motivation for all his rage?

We wanted this—her—*for me*. For both of us. And now he wants to be here *for* her.

My palms rasp against Briar's hips, shaking as I slowly release the internal reins I've spent a lifetime clutching. Letting the animal inside me float to the surface.

My next exhale is a rougher purr. Briar leans back, into it, and I find myself nuzzling the side of her throat. Sucking the scent of her into my lungs. Feeling them spark as my mouth waters for the taste of sugared cherries.

"You want my knot?" I ask, my voice nearly unrecognizable with my Alpha behind it.

When our mate moans, determination solidifies at my center. I've never knotted anyone—and this? The way she looks at me? *This* is why.

I waited for her.

I would have waited forever if it meant I'd have this moment.

In one smooth tug, pull her body down, sliding my cock into her gushing heat.

Holy fucking—

Every nerve sizzles and snaps, electricity rocketing up my spine. My knot grows wider, throbbing when her clit rolls along the top of the taut swell. Our bodies know what to do, fitting themselves closer, working my girth further in on every thrust.

I choke back a snarl, my hand automatically snapping up to her throat. Gripping her gently, guiding her into a smooth, intense rhythm that has my eyes rolling back within seconds.

My Alpha stays at the surface, his actions and wants blurred with mine. He tilts Briar's face toward me—I seal my lips over hers. He grinds my knot against the slick opening to her cunt—I stroke a soothing path to her clit, teasing it with the briefest of touches until she moans into my mouth.

Instincts overwhelm me. I press the pads of my fingers to her slippery nub, angling my hips up. Our omega tosses her head against my shoulder, keening desperately.

My Alpha senses his mate's urgency and issues a bark that would shock me if I had the ability for actual fucking *thought.* "*Cillian,*" I grit.

He materializes at my side, squeezing my shoulder while he radiates pack leader approval. "You're doing great, Rhys. Focus on knotting her. That's what she really needs." He turns his head. "Dane."

My packmate crawls over, a long, painful-looking erection bobbing between his thighs. His eyes fixate on Briar's glistening lower lips, spread over the too-thick width of my knot. She whimpers and the big alpha mutters a snarl, lunging forward.

Motherfucking—

He covers her clit with his mouth, lapping at it with the same urgency brewing inside me. Like I'll die if I don't give this omega every goddamn thing she needs. And then a little more.

Cillian cups one of her tits, leaning down to capture her lips. His tongue swirls with hers at the very second Dane licks a whirl over her clit.

Fuck me, it's hot to watch. And even better to *feel* when an orgasm abruptly strikes Briar with all the electric intensity of a lightning bolt.

Her pussy shudders, squeezes, and *pulls*. Tugging my cock as deep as it can go, popping my knot past the quivering muscles at her opening. Blinding light whites out my vision.

It feels *impossible*. Complete in a way that *can't* exist because it's just too *good*. Too perfect.

She's really here, my Alpha says, dazed. *My mate.*

Gratitude and amazement fill my chest as my knot explodes, locking us together so tightly I can't move as Briar comes a second time.

My packmates shift back to give us a second, letting me catch our omega when she collapses into me. We fall to the nest she built for us, right where she wanted me.

I hold her close, wet warmth massaging every inch of my knot, wringing pleasure from my core. Devotion sinks fangs into my soul. Sweet, languid heat spreads through my middle.

And it feels a lot like *venom*.

"WAIT, WAIT, WAIT."

Our sweet, purring little omega snuggles closer to my side, drawn to my voice even in her sleep. It's been three of the most incredible days I could ever imagine, but somehow? Looking at her still rips the air right out of my lungs.

She tightens the leg coiled through mine, a fresh burst of wetness seeping from her hot, pink core. For a second, I brace, thinking she needs another knot, but this seems to be the first peaceful bout of rest she's had since we settled in here.

Still, I wonder what she's dreaming about that has her so deliciously slick.

Especially now.

Cillian and I both stare at Rhys, dumbfounded. Our blond packmate nods, a smug smirk on his lips as he holds up the book he's been reading. Which is, apparently, a recommendation from our mate. "Yep."

Our pack leader frowns mightily. His shiny black brows knit together. "You're saying the guy stalks this woman in a bookstore?"

"Yup," Rhys repeats.

"And watches her when she sleeps?" I put in.

He nods again. "Uh huh."

"Then he—" I can't say it. I can't even *think* it without getting obviously, *shamefully* hard.

"—chases her through the woods wearing a mask," Rhys finishes for me, unfazed. "He sure does."

"And she *likes* it?" Cillian confirms. Though I'm not sure if he's referring to the character in the book or the woman snuggled between us. Lightly grinding her soaked pussy against my thigh.

Rhys cocks an eyebrow like he can't believe how old and boring we are. "Yeah," he replies, as if we're slow. Then he gives Briar a lingering, loving look before snapping at us. "It's her *favorite.*"

Holy. Fuck.

My little beauty is a beast.

It takes every drop of self-possession I have not to bite her *right the hell now.*

Both of my packmates see my expression and chuckle, a certain camaraderie expanding between us. It isn't new, but it is nice.

We always had each other's backs—and there was never a day I didn't consider these guys my brothers in arms. But Briar's heat has given us back *our pack.*

We haven't been this way since we were young. Cillian and I plotting and problem-solving together. Rhys piping in with his critiques or jokes or mind-blowing revelations on our omega's reading material.

Now I can see how close we were to falling apart, before her. And why alpha packs need an omega to center them.

Having her as our one and only focus has reforged us. Catering to our mate's every need, ensuring we all get breaks to sleep, helping one another keep her clean and fed. We haven't just found a new level of connection with her—we've found a new level of connection for our family.

Any doubts I had about letting these guys in, being *bound* together, have evaporated. Briar needs us, for one, but... I think we need each other, too. Even if we've been too proud to admit it for as long as I can remember.

Honestly, if we hadn't agreed to wait until she's lucid enough to remember the moment we form the bond, I probably would have already—

Oh. Fucking. *Hell*.

A gut-twisting, soul-searing *slice* of tart sweetness suddenly fills the nest. Briar's body tenses against mine, her soft snores shattering into a low, panicked whine.

Thunderous arousal rips through my body. Roiling instincts to mark, claim, guard, pleasure. And under all that? There's rage.

However her asshole "father" died, it wasn't painful enough. Whatever plans he had for her, keeping her sedated for her heats and suppressing them, they've made for some severe bouts of desperation. Moments like these, where her cramps ramp up out of *nowhere*.

It's bad enough, seeing the woman we love in pain. But even *worse* because her Omega is so soft. Before this heat, part of me expected her to be as sharp and regal as the woman I love, but Briar's Omega is *a giver*.

Thrilled to impress Cillian with her nesting and her flawless presenting position. Begging to hold Rhys so he doesn't get any headaches. Crawling into my lap and snuggling up to me at every opportunity. Always carefully scent-marking my scars until we're both so dizzy with joy, I end up pounding her until she comes all over my knot.

She never demands or fights us. Instead, she trusts. Opens. And showers all of us with more love and loyalty than we ever could have hoped for. Which makes seeing her feature crunch in discomfort *unbearable*.

Her need calls to the deepest protective instincts in each of us. Rhys instantly sets her book outside the nest, lurching to his hands and knees to get to us. Cillian crowds closer to her other side, slipping his hand between my body and her core, feeling how strained her abdominal muscles have gotten.

"She's exhausted," he tsks. "But her body still wants more. And we can't bond her until she's out of the thickest parts of her haze."

"We need to give her Omega a jolt," Rhys suggests, scowling in consternation. "If she's near the apex of her heat, we can flood her system with endorphins and fill her up with as much of us as possible to push her over the peak. Then, once her haze thins out a bit and she's more lucid, we can bond her to bring her out of the heat entirely."

Cillian claps his brother's shoulder. "It's a good plan." He rises to his knees, a thick erection already bobbing between his hips. "I know how we can do it, too."

We both wait, expectant, as his lips quirk halfway up. "You're going to share her pussy," our pack alpha dictates, "while I take her ass."

Rhys snarls the same moment I do. The combined sound shakes Briar from her sleep. She whines before burying her face into my torso, trying to curl around the pain in her core. "A-alpha," she squeaks. "N-need you."

Cillian's hand curls around her head at the same moment mine finds her back. We both pet her as my purr kicks up, masking the competitive growl I can't help.

"Share her pussy," I grumble. Packs do that, but we never have. And this far into her heat? Without my claim on her? I'm a little worried my Alpha might go rogue. Not to mention the feral beast lurking inside Rhys.

"Who would knot her?" he demands.

The mention of a *knot* has Briar climbing up my body, dragging her soaked slit over my scarred abs. Her motions are weak, though, like Cillian said. She needs more rest—and her body won't let her have it until it's satisfied.

"Whoever makes her come first," Cillian decides. "Or lasts the longest."

Fuck.

"It's *on*," Rhys hisses, flashing a maniacal grin. Briar loves it when he smiles. Her eyes widen and slick slips out of her, pooling in the lines of my torso. We all growl, impatience snapping us into action.

"She's hurting," I murmur, then, to her, "We'll fix it for you, moonbeam."

Cillian cups her chin, snagging her hazy gaze. "You've been such a good girl for me, omega. Do you want a treat? All three of our cocks filling your tight little holes at the same time?"

Briar lurches to her knees, keening desperately. We all reach out to steady her, and I realize she probably shouldn't move too much.

"Come here," I husk, pushing into the perfect mountain of pillows she made for me. "We'll take you like this."

I stretch my lower half out, giving Rhys a nod to show him what I mean. He catches on quickly, falling to his back and bending his legs over mine. Lining the bottoms of our cocks up.

His is longer but mine is thicker. They're already oozing pre-cum, though—so when my head bumps just below his, wetness kisses both. He sucks in a breath the same second I do, each of us reaching down to hold ourselves in place.

Cillian stares into our omega, fisting his hand around her

heart lock and tugging to guide her into position, helping her find the right place for her knees on either side of my hips. She gasps when she feels our cocks at her entrance, more slick gushing over us.

"That's my girl," Cillian soothes, capturing her long black hair at the nape. Holding it as he pushes her down onto our dicks.

Fucking hell. It's so *tight.*

Our shafts rub together while her opening stretches over us. Just inside the fluttering ring, a softer one throbs and quivers. Begging for a knot. Burning us both with her silky, soaked heat.

"Al-alpha!" she shouts, dazed. "P-please!"

We both shove upward, snarling as velvet suction clasps our dicks from the tops of our swelling knots to the heads dribbling pearly pre-cum into her depths. Before I can get a grip on my control, Rhys moves.

He tilts Briar's body toward me and tucks his hips, gliding his cock along the bottom of mine. Until only his swollen head remains. Pushing into the place that begs for more. Forcing Briar to scream.

I groan when he shoves back in, canting my hips to pull out. Starting up a rhythm.

Cillian watches Briar pant and moan, covering her tits with his big hands before he bends to lick at her mouth. My balls tingle as I watch them and I feel my knot fill. Pressing into Rhys's. Kneading it.

"Fuck," he barks. "Goddamn it, Dane."

Cillian's hand finds the curve of our omega's ass next. His fingers curl into the cleft between her cheeks. Two fingers covered in slick disappear into her back hole.

Holy fucking—Jesus.

Pressure suddenly pushes from the thin wall between her openings, making her even tighter. Another cramp hits as Cillian swings himself into position, kneeling behind Briar and working his rock-solid erection into her ass.

All three of us *roar*. Rhys freezes halfway out of her while I stutter halfway in. It feels impossible to cram her any fuller.

But our mate whines a moan, bucking weakly. Cillian grasps her hips, lifting and lowering her. Forward, onto the two of us, then back so he can shove all the way inside.

God, she looks like a fucking goddess, flushed pink and hazy-eyed, with her black hair hanging in a curtain of night. All I want to do is make her *come*.

Rhys starts pumping, slicking himself between our cocks as I hold fast, reaching out and finding her clit. The little nub is practically buzzing. I circle it with my thumb and watch Briar choke on a gasp, her eyes rolling back.

Yes, yes, *yes*.

Her pussy spasms, soft wet warmth collapsing around our cocks. Rhys's knot twitches against mine, the pressure of it almost too much—

It is too much for him. He blasts inside her like a canon, filling her with thick washes of release. With a hiss, he pushes as deep as he can, but his knot won't fit. It's already expanded. He curses, pulling out. Letting me shove my screaming swell into her glorious heat.

"That's it, omega," I grind. "Take all your alphas' cum. Lock down on this knot."

Briar's blown-out gaze finds mine, fogging as her climax finally hits. She shrieks, clamping around Cillian and me as we both fuck her harder. Pushing in deeper. Coming—*coming*—

Fuck.

FUCK.

My knot explodes the same second his does, both locked deep. Grinding together through her thin, hot skin. Slick and cum gush from her body, pooling in the nest beneath us, filling the air with a mixture of all of our scents.

Briar falls forward, bringing Cillian with her. Rhys manages to move just in time to avoid getting trapped in our tangle as we fall to our sides, snuggling our mate between us. He crawls back to his mound of cushions and collapses, panting hard.

"Holy shit," he gasps. "I think Dane won."

My cock tingles, locked deep inside my mate. My best friend huffs a laugh, burying his nose in her hair. And I look down at Briar's sleepy face as she scent-marks the scars over my heart.

"Yeah," I reply. "I really did."

THE FIRST TRACE OF MY WIFE PEEKS THROUGH BRIAR'S features just as the stars come out.

She shifts between us, cuddling into Rhys. Her lips curve slyly when he hums and snuggles her harder. I smile, watching from my mound of pillows as her eyes open, looking clearer than they have in days.

She finds me watching her. "Mmm, alpha." She yawns and blinks, then widens her dazzling grin. Reaching her hand out and wiggling her fingers. "Here."

I nearly chuckle at her demanding tone. Briar's Omega has been nothing but a perfect, sweet girl all week. I've missed my sharp little wife, but the combination of the two is particularly adorable. Especially when I don't move immediately and she whines, giving me puppy-dog eyes that feel a bit like a trap.

Smart, funny girl.

She can trap me any time.

Sure enough, the second I move closer, she rolls over Rhys and tackles me with a squeal. Her joy lights up my chest, sending a wash of relief through my bones.

Fuck, I really missed my wife.

Her heat has been incredible. Working with my packmates as a team, providing for her every need. It all gave me a deep sense of satisfaction and renewed my purpose as their pack leader. I can't wait to do it again; next time, hopefully, with bonds.

Rhys huffs awake just in time to witness our mate flattening me into the mattress. He grins, too, kicking Dane's side lightly to rouse the snoring giant. "She's awake."

Dane opens his eyes immediately. "Is she ready?"

I cup Briar's face, but she just keeps licking the side of my neck. Sliding one hand lower, I fist her heart lock, tugging hard enough to get her attention. A wash of dark cherry perfume sweeps into the air as she pulls back, flashing me half-lidded siren's eyes.

I nuzzle her nose, staring into the thin green irises edging their way back in. Some of her attitude ebbs, a beseeching look seeping over her features. Pleading just the way I like.

"Yeah?" I rumble, unable to resist kissing her softly. "Is it time, omega? You want us to bite you?"

She nods frantically, without a stitch of grace. Meaning her sweet Omega has pushed back to the surface.

It's perfect. I want them both here for this. So they *both* know how much I adore her.

"Right now?" I tease.

"Yes, alpha," she breathes. "Want you. Please." She turns to find her other mates, stretching her hand out to them. "All of you."

A new kind of urgency snaps through my veins. I reposition her so she's facing outward, collaring her while my packmates take turns kissing her. Our hands slide over her body, Rhys teasing her pussy while Dane rubs her sides and my empty palm finds her pink-tipped tit.

Instincts clamor inside me. Certainty swells at my center.

"She's ready," I rasp, nestling my face into her crown. "Choose your places."

Dane surprises me, reaching low to cup her mound. "Right here," he rumbles. "Where I marked her the first time."

Briar tilts her hips up, pressing her pussy into his touch. With a grumble, Rhys moves aside and Dane takes position between her legs. His purr deepens as he laps at her wet slit. Teasing her with small bites and soft kisses.

Rhys uses the opportunity to slide lower, moving to the outside of her left thigh. "Here," he decides. His light eyes glow as she focuses on his spot, tracing a line where she normally wears her garter. And *her knife.*

Memories of her, kneeling in that horrible yellow nest, fisting a blade, resurface. A fierce rush of pride swarms my chest, rising to block my throat as I hold Briar's.

"My claim will be right here," I announce, brushing the place below her pulse. Where the warm golden links of my chain wreath her neck. Our gazes meet as I add my final vow.

"Forever."

Briar whines and shifts, begging me wordlessly. Dane grips her hips, lifting her so I can slide into place beneath her. She cries out as he sinks her onto my waiting cock.

Fucking hell. It doesn't matter how many times I have her. She always feels like pure heaven when I push in again.

Briar tosses her head, her silken hair cascading over my shoulder and down my back. I wrap it around my fist, tilting her neck to the side while I set her pace with my other hand on her waist. Dane goes back to work, paying no mind to the fact that his sucking licks have our mate gushing slick all over my knot.

Rhys opens his mouth, scraping his teeth along the outside of her creamy thigh. Daring me to wait another minute.

Jesus, we really are a feral pack.

And as Briar moans in delight, her eyes sparkling, I suddenly want to grin.

It's a good thing our omega prefers beasts.

She proves as much when she starts to climax, her pussy pulling my knot in with an earth-shattering *pop*. Squeezing me as she locks us together. Keening as I bark, "*Now.*"

My teeth hit the side of her throat before I even finish the word. Breaking through the thin skin as my cock jets fiercely into her depths. My knot expands, knocking the breath from both of us just before Briar's two other alphas *lunge*.

sixty-nine

BRIAR

THREE PATHWAYS BURROW INTO MY BODY, converging at the center of my being.

They're all different, but instinct insists I float down the very darkest one to reach the others.

It's strange, being so lucid, but also shrouded by my Omega's haze. She nudges me, turning my head toward—

Cillian.

Remembering his name brings a cool gust of relief. It flows into the loose tether hanging between us, sparking a reaction on the other side that I can't quite read. It's warm, though. And *strong*.

The desperation that unfurls at my middle feels so natural. I *have* to know what he feels. I have to *feel him.*

Those wolf-blue eyes lock onto mine. "Bite me," he growls, though his gaze burns, beseeching. Begging. *"I need you."*

There is no thought or decision. Only the love that pours out of my soul, carrying me on its current.

I turn my head, gripping his left wrist and sliding his fingers into my mouth. He roughs out a deeper snarl, his cock and knot swelling inside me as I snap my teeth around his knuckles.

The smooth, warm metal of his wedding band brushes the flat of my tongue. I *bite.* Harder. Sucking his fingers, ensuring my mark brands him as deeply as possible.

His cock spurts, hot and thick. Matching, molten gold pours through the tether. Into every depth I possess. Gilding them all. Filling every sting and banishing every fear.

Cillian is unyielding. A *force.* Shining, flaring, *fastening* us together from the places where our very selves spring forth.

A lock that *frees* me. Protects me. *Saves* me.

The master of my heart. King of my soul.

And you're my queen.

His voice echoes inside my mind, the delicious rasp pricking my nipples. A fresh wave of delirious pleasure rocks my core, pulling the muscles tighter and tighter. Until liquid bliss bursts over my alpha's straining cock and into his lap. He groans, head thrown back as his arms envelop me, his other hand wrapping around my throat and squeezing the air from my lungs as he comes again.

And—God—I can *feel* it. The sweet sting, snapping up his spine. His balls tingling as his cock twitches and squirts.

And his heart. Beating just for me.

Briar, he growls, where only I can hear. *Fuck, I love you so goddamn much. Finding you was the luckiest day of my life. Marrying you was the smartest. And having you here*—I feel a thump from his middle reverberate in mine—*makes this the best.*

My chest aches, a whine shivering in my vocal cords. Goosebumps break across my neck and back. The sensation tingles, along with two new half-moons carved into the front of my throat. Cillian's eyes snap to his claim, his thumb rubbing it until I crest into another climax.

He holds me this time, his eyes steady and his hand firm around my neck. Watching. Letting me feel the pride and possession that explode behind his lungs.

My enigmatic alpha barely shows any of it on his face, but I don't need him to, now. All of it is *mine*. Flowing directly into me.

For a second, my Omega pauses, worried her Alpha will be upset about that, but Cillian soothes her half-thought with a flood of pure devotion.

Never, love, he vows. *I don't ever want to hide from you again.*

Adoration roars in my blood, as fierce as any rage. And I realize, it's *his*. He *loves* me.

Of course I do, he whispers. *And I'm not the only one, omega.*

His memories—I can *see* them. I gasp as he flows through several in a row, showing me scenes from my heat. *Dane carefully brushing out my hair and braiding it. Rhys reading to me while I slept in his lap.*

Fresh need zips down my back, pooling between my hips. Cillian flashes his rare grin, nosing at my cheek. "Go get our pack, Mrs. Blackwood."

I don't have to think at all, flinging myself directly toward the alpha I know needs me most at this very moment.

Rhys.

Silver blond and full of *fear*. I can scent it, but I also feel the dull tremor of it through the half-bond hanging loose at my middle. The second I leap for him, the anxiety melts into something like *anguish*.

"Briar, baby, I know I could never fucking deserve you, but I swear to God—"

His words choke off as my teeth find his throat, opening over the place where I once sliced him open. I lick the pulse point above it, canting my hips until I find his throbbing hardness. Impaling myself on his cock and riding it as I stake my claim, biting harder than I need to.

"Oh fuck, oh *God*—" He comes instantly, pushing me into another explosive climax. Filling my pussy with a fresh wash of warmth while his release floods our bond with pure, shimmering *awe*.

It zings into me, burrowing into my *soul*.

Venom. He's here, but he's... beautiful.

Soft. So very gentle and complex. A million feelings, woven into thick braids. Tangled in knots. Stripped down to the studs and laid bare.

And there, among all the ruin and all the beauty, there's pure, unfiltered *devotion*.

Rhys feels me absorbing it. Trying to understand. He whispers where no one else can hear. *No one has ever belonged to another the way I belong to you. I've always been yours. And I've never wanted to be anything else.*

I can *feel* his sincerity now. A solid swell of emotion that steels the tether between us. I burrow my face against his neck, letting tears fall as I lick the bite branded over his single scar. He chuckles internally before the sound interrupts his purr.

"Should have known you'd sink your fangs into me right there, viper."

His knot releases and my Omega whines, wanting me to go to my third alpha. I pull back and look at my beautiful man one more time, though, lurching up to nip his lower lip quickly. Rhys smiles, shy gratitude and amazement tumbling into our bond.

This time, Cillian adds his approval and a burst of pride for both of us. Feeling both of them at the same time makes me desperate to complete the bond—and I know exactly who I need.

Who I've *always* needed.

And trusted.

And *wanted*.

I dive into his open arms. They snap closed around me, his

golden eyes full of pleading. "Don't wait, omega, please. Fucking need you—"

He cuts himself off, hissing and then groaning as my mouth finds my mark. Opening wide against his sternum, in the place where his scars meet the unscathed flesh. Piercing him with my claim.

Dane.

Steady and deep as a river, he winds his way into my soul. Slower than the others, but not because he's hesitant. Because he's *patient*. And he loves me so much, he wants me to feel every single bit of it.

His body shudders under mine. Hot liquid spurts between us as I bite harder, lapping at the wound. Listening to his quiet strength and unrestrained adoration.

Memories flow smoothly through his mind. Wordless—but when have we ever needed words?

Instead, he shows me the moment he saw me for the first time. How his heart thumped and his hands shook. He pulls up images from the night I gave him my virginity—the way I gazed up at him, trusting him. How that meant more to him than anything else ever had.

The fear of taking his mask off and kissing me. The joy and confusion he felt when I touched his scars and called him strong.

Adoration. It was a brand-new feeling, for him. And he still couldn't quite believe the way it made him whole. How it filled all the cracks in his spirit, where he thought his *real* scars may never heal.

A sob sticks in my throat as I burrow into his embrace. *I love you, too,* I tell him back, internally turning to each of them. *I love all of you. So much. I—I'm sorry I didn't say it before.*

They watch me relive one of the worst moments in that other, horrible nest—when I realized I'd never even told them how much I cared about them. How I regretted my pride and stubbornness so much it was almost as painful as the fear of losing them.

They answer with such forceful, instant forgiveness, it makes me lightheaded. Three strong purrs reverberate through the sweetly scented air. My bones loosen as I melt between them.

Rhys kisses my fingers, playing his own regrets in his mind's eye. So many times he felt the overwhelming desire to reach out to me—and took a swipe instead. I have my own collection of moments like that; and when I share those, his heart aches.

My perfect match, he thinks.

And mine, Dane adds, gruff as ever. Recalling my goofy, eye-rolling grin while I chewed a plate of French toast in *his* underwear. I should probably be embarrassed, but it's clear this is one of his most cherished memories.

Cillian's are a bit harder to handle. They're... *sad*. So full of *yearning*. Recollections of a hundred nights spent lying on his bed with my pointe shoes in his hands, staring at the initials inked into the soles. Giving up and wandering into the suite he was having restored for me. Standing in front of the balcony, feeling sick as the thorny vines climbed higher and higher.

He knew he couldn't help himself. He had to have me—had to *save* me. Even though he feared it would make him the monster in my story.

So he watched the flowers grow. Laid his traps. Sealed my fate.

A rush of pure gratitude swells from my heart to his. For the first time ever, our pack leader's chest stutters, his throat thickening when he feels my genuine appreciation.

Thank you, devil.

He huddles closer to my side, burying his face against my shoulder. I feel his mind racing, searching for some concrete action to offer me. A plan to execute. It's so Cillian, I feel myself grin.

We'll take those bushes down anytime you want, love.

But I *don't* want to. Those tangled, woven vines... they feel perfect, now. Like *us*.

Cillian, like deep roots. Hidden from the world, but always

doing the real work. Fighting to anchor us to our home. Give each of us the strength we need to thrive.

Dane, strong and sturdy as any branch. Flexible when the winds blow, but hardy enough to stay standing. Take the storms, the knicks and cuts. And once those scars heal? He can grow new branches.

They'll be covered in thorns, of course, because that's Rhys. Sharp and ruthless. Protective of his pack, his heart, our home. Of *me*.

Which makes you the roses, baby, he thinks. *Because without you? We were a snarl of spikes.*

All three alphas chuckle around their purrs, dry amusement filling our bond. Dane's laughter, rumbling under my ear, lulls me closer to a real, deep sleep than I've felt in days. A quiet, joyful exhaustion creeps into my body.

I did it, I think, dizzy. *They're a pack. We're bonded.*

Yes, Cillian replies. He gently kisses my face, his ice-blue eyes searching mine. Funneling his satisfaction and pride directly into my chest.

This beautiful devil. Truly, every last thing he's done was for me.

For *us*. His pack.

Your pack, Dane corrects.

Rhys's voice whispers over our tether. *You made us, Briar. And you've made us complete.*

My husband's mouth curves into the mysterious half-smile I adore. Only, the absolute devotion behind it isn't a mystery anymore.

"You did it, love," my husband murmurs. "*Sleep now.*"

I hardly have a choice. But as my mates pile around me, I manage one last look toward the darkened window. And the last thing I see before I close my eyes?

A wall of roses, in full bloom.

seventy

BRIAR

BRIAR'S BEASTS

I thought we were going low key tonight…?

DANE

Yeah…

RHYS

Totally, baby.

BRIAR

Then why is there a ballgown on my bed?

CILLIAN

Merely a suggestion, Mrs. Blackwood.

I really ought to know better by now.

When my husband claimed we were having a "quiet night in" to finish up our week-long heat recovery, I'm amazed I believed him.

But leave it to Cillian to plan his scheme precisely. Telling me about our "lowkey evening" through the bond, when he knew I was distracted by my latest book and Rhys's head in my lap.

I bet he chuckled to himself all day, remembering how I hummed some version of "yeah, yeah, sounds great, honey," and went back to my smut without even the slightest suspicion.

Devious devil.

For you, Mrs. Blackwood? he says now, smirking through our tether. *I can always do worse.*

I flash him an exasperated mental image of myself in my bedroom mirror...

Wearing a full-on *ballgown.*

Aaaaaand maybeeee flipping him the bird.

Rhys must be listening, because he snorts internally before adding his own anticipation to the mix. *You ready yet, baby?*

For what? I harrumph, sliding my feet into the slippers Cillian left and turning for the door. *Tea with the queen?*

That's on the seventeenth, Dane thinks, his tone utterly serious and hilariously grumpy at the same time. *Cillian says I have to wear another suit.*

We all do, the pack leader replies, casual as ever. Then to me, as if it's so normal: *We're investing in their international pediatric healthcare initiative, so we'll dine with them while they're in the city next month. I already put it on your calendar, rosebud.*

I cast him all kinds of internal side-eye. *Oh gee <u>thanks</u>.*

Cillian's amusement licks into arousal, his underlying impatience flaring. *Hurry down, wife. I'm sure you look lovely.*

He isn't wrong, damn it. The golden gown is a classic silhouette—a sweetheart bodice with a corset up the front and two loose swags for low-slung "sleeves."

But my husband knows me well, so the piece also features a

couple of artful, modern twists: gilded splashes of metallic paint and pointed gossamer tendrils that feather over my slight cleavage.

Not to mention, it fits me perfectly. And matches my lock necklace like the two couture pieces were *made* to go together.

Dane chuckles into the bond, his tone as exasperated as mine. *... because they <u>were</u> made to go together. Cillian clearly has too much time on his hands these days.*

My big man isn't wrong—since Forsyth "retired," our pack has been splitting his work with Gideon's. Turns out, when you're not plotting ways to kill or control everyone around you, it actually isn't a hard job. Especially given the cousins' plans to phase out their current business model and find new products to manufacture.

I ponder their proposed ideas all the way to the second-floor landing. Lurching to a halt, I blink twice at the dark foyer below... lit with hundreds of candles.

They're *everywhere*. Pooled on the floor, covering the sideboards, lining the short, rounded hallway to the glowing ballroom.

Just like the night Cillian asked me to dance for him.

How did he know I loved that? Did I ever tell him?

"You dreamed about it," Dane says, silent as ever as he steps up to the bottom of the stairs, reaching for me. "So we thought we would recreate it for you."

My big man looks adorably shy, standing in one of his too-tight suits, holding out his hand. Instead of taking it, I hop up and wind my arms around his neck. He laughs as he spins me, rubbing his unmasked jaw over my temple in a scent-mark.

Dane makes it look easy, sweeping me into his arms, effortlessly carrying me the rest of the way to the ballroom. I'm not at all surprised when he takes me straight to Cillian.

My husband waits in the center of the room, surrounded by the flickers of a hundred flames. The walls shine, shadows stuttering behind the handsome, dark-haired devil waiting for me.

Dane places me on my feet, allowing my husband to dip into a bow, bringing my fingers to his mouth for a slow, lingering kiss. Flickering light catches on his gold wedding band and the silvery half-moon scars I left around it. Cillian feels my arousal and pride sparkle through the bond, his lips quirking upward.

Rhys appears behind him, utterly devastating in his charcoal suit. He tosses me his illegal grin as he holds up a small remote. When he clicks it, music starts—something slow and soft.

Cillian steps closer, bending to skim his lips over his bond mark and whisper into my ear. "I thought we might have a dance. While I tell you a story."

The significance of the moment isn't lost on me. The last time we were in here, Cillian told me about the day he first saw me. But he couldn't touch me, so he didn't dance with me.

I reach up to touch the hair at his temple, nodding. "Okay," I say, truly smiling before I set my features into a smirk. "But if you start with *once upon a time*, I swear... *eep!*"

Cillian twirls me into a dip so fast, my thoughts scatter across the marble floor. He snaps us upright just as gracefully, moving into a simple waltz.

Once upon a time, he thinks, his amusement as potent as the rush of adoration that accompanies it. *There was a pair of mates.*

I expect a mental picture of us, but instead he shows me someone who looks like him, only this man feels... older. Bigger.

The memory is from a child's perspective, I realize, noting the slab of wall obstructing half of the image. *Cillian is hiding around a corner.* Watching as a man who looks like the alpha holding me offers his hand to a woman with long brown waves... who has on my wedding dress.

Oh.

Cillian senses my tangled reaction—amazement, sadness, understanding, adoration.

I had mixed feelings about the dress itself, too. I wanted to hate it so badly... but, even under the circumstances of that fateful day, I found it beautiful.

Now, knowing it was his mother's... and that he had happy memories of watching her wear it with his father...

Cillian feels the lump swelling in my throat and nuzzles my forehead with his. Without a word, he projects a clearer picture between us, showing me how he used to sneak closer to watch them twirl around.

Through his memory, I feel his excitement and amazement as his father and mother turn the boring, stuffy ballroom into a stage. As a dancer, I can't help but notice the way they move together, with the sort of fluidity that only comes from true intimacy.

They loved each other, my husband recalls, sadness and certainty stretching through our tether. *But the man was weak. And instead of protecting all he held dear, he compromised it.*

This time, the memory belongs to Rhys. He's a child, too. Punier and more afraid than Cillian was. He ducks behind his mother's skirt as they walk into Blackwood Manor, peeking out. My head automatically snaps in his direction, finding his wistful, sea-glass gaze.

The man married a woman he did not love, Rhys thinks. *Someone very different from his mate; all in an attempt to appease his father. And keep the evil man from harming the ones he truly loved.*

I feel Dane watching the story unfold as much as I am, a deep well of protective anger burrowing a pit in his center. The big alpha suddenly adds his own recollection to the mix—still a kid's perspective, but a much taller, steadier sort. He stands at the top of the stairs, witnessing the first meeting between Rhys and Cillian. Knowing it isn't his place to be involved. My heart aches for him, feeling the way he worries about his best friend; sensing his pity for the small blond boy. It's even sadder once I realize—back then? No one worried about Dane at all. Ever.

I feel Cillian's regret over that and his packmate's answering acceptance. The ease with which he releases the past, adding,

Nobody won, in the war between the evil man and his sons. And in the end, everyone lost what they cared for the most.

Rhys shows me a teary image from his vantage point. Standing at the window of the music room, watching a car drive away.

His mother, leaving him.

Cillian sees it too, displaying his view from the threshold of that room. Witnessing the worst moment in Rhys's life and thinking about his own as he turns to his father's onyx urn on the mantle. Something deep inside of him *snaps...* and turns cold.

My husband goes on, pulling me closer as water gathers in my eyes. His internal voice sounds gruffer. *The young alpha saw what true love had done to his family. So he vowed to harden himself against it. He decided he would never take an omega for a mate. And did everything he could to build barriers around himself and his pack.*

Dane displays a new picture. One of Cillian the day he left for college and the day he returned from business school. He looks like two different people—parting from his former brother and best friend with short hugs... but returning with handshakes.

My big alpha hesitates, then sighs internally, wordlessly admitting how disappointed he was. How he missed his friend. Cillian's footsteps falter for a moment as he realizes how he hurt his packmate, but I know the steps. I guide us through a few turns, until he regains his focus.

So, the alpha grew into a man without a heart, he admits, the deepest slash of pained regret accompanying the words. *He shut himself off from his packmates and his emotions, hell-bent on shaping an empire just beyond his reach.*

And the other alphas let him, Dane adds, once again projecting forgiveness. The grace that it wasn't all Cillian's fault. *Because they themselves had grown hateful and bitter.*

The images that come with that statement are gruesome and gray. An endless slog of evil men, bloodshed, pent-up rage, and plots for revenge. Until it all goes up in flames as they collectively recall the night of the fire.

But the embers settle and the smoke clears... and Cillian projects the first moment he laid eyes on a certain black-haired ballerina. Rolling her eyes behind her director's back as she stretched past her pointed toes, a lopsided bun falling to her left shoulder.

I feel Cillian's sad smile more than I see it. *Until one day*, he goes on, full of bittersweet joy, *a very special woman came into their lives...*

Rhys flashes a grin. *... and tried to kill them.*

When he shows the memory of me holding a knife to his throat, we all laugh despite the tears clogging my throat. "Maybe they deserved it." I shrug, sniffing.

Cillian suddenly twirls me fast enough to whip me into Rhys's arms. My blond alpha launches into his own version of the waltz—much more fluid and flamboyant. "Oh, they *definitely* deserved it," he agrees. "But either way, that shit was *hot*."

I'm still giggling when he spins me to Dane. The big man catches me easily, but clearly doesn't have the first clue how to dance. Instead, he settles into a prom pose—his hands on my hips and mine on his shoulders. Bending to scent-mark my cheek, he continues.

One by one, she fought through their walls. He remembers the way I practically shimmied up his enormous body the night I gave him my virginity. Chuckling on the outside, but inside? He's more of a puddle than I am. My cute, cuddly monster. *Climbing*... he thinks.

Cutting, Rhys puts in, recalling the way I sliced without a drop of hesitation. How sexy and strong he found that. The admiration that started to smolder in the deepest, most secret part of him... until it grew into adoration.

For his part, Cillian recalls our many arguments over dinner. How I defied him at every turn. How I surprised and delighted him with my negotiations and refusal to cower. ... *and <u>cunning</u> her way to the truth.*

Dane rests his forehead on mine, then turns me around. Locking his arm at my waist while his packmates close in, each of them taking one of my sides.

I look up at Cillian, blinking back more tears when I feel the utter devotion pouring from each of my mates.

But always my husband most of all.

He found me. He followed me. He fought for me.

And *won*.

I gaze into his blue, blue eyes, murmuring, "What was the truth?"

"That having you as our mate could never be our weakness," he murmurs. "Because you are our greatest strength."

WILL I EVER GET OVER THE URGE TO COME IN MY PANTS when my omega does this?

Probably not.

Which is why she does it so often.

Our gorgeous, deadly viper smirks around the edge of her Kindle, flashing jade eyes down to where I'm lying in her lap. Her pointed nails scratch my scalp with more insistence, and I hiss, baring my teeth in a snarl. She raises an eyebrow.

"Tapping out on me already, venom?"

It's one of her favorite taunts—one she's repeated many times since the first night she got on her knees for me. And I always have the same answer.

"Never."

I know she feels the truth layered into the word. The *vow*.

She'll never lose me. And I won't ever give up on us.

A chilly ocean breeze winds through the backyard, blowing shriveled, crunchy leaves under our bench. Cillian had this carved seating area installed last month, just as Briar's roses passed their peak and autumn colors swept across our estate.

This addition to the garden was our mate's idea. After we recovered from her heat, she had a chance to process everything Forsyth told her—and share what really happened to Cillian's parents.

It took about a month for our pack leader to work through his feelings. We could all sense his turmoil in the bond, though, and did our best to help him through the guilt and regret that came with discovering he'd missed the truth for so long.

Briar was there for him in every conceivable way. Proving for the hundredth time that she's the perfect combination of grit and grace—a pillar of strength and a soft place to land.

When she proposed memorials for Caine and his lost love, Cillian ran with the idea. Now, there's a lovely reading bench for Briar to enjoy, flanked by twin statues. They're chess pieces—a king and his queen.

Briar must like the symbolism as much as I do, because she often asks to read out here in the afternoons, despite the cold creeping into the air. Cillian's taken care of that, naturally, furnishing her wardrobe with enough black cashmere to swaddle the entire Omega Suite, if she wanted to.

My gorgeous girl's chest hums with her kittenish omega purr, her touch smoothing back into the comforting, sensual caresses I love nearly as much as her claws. My eyelids fall closed, and her mouth quirks again. But she keeps her eyes steady on her Kindle this time, reminding me that I also have a book clutched in my hands.

It's a collection of Korean recipes, each with a short memoir-style story of the family who created it attached. Ever since Briar's DNA results came back with a Korean as her highest percentage, I've thrown myself into researching the culture and customs, along with looking for any distant relatives she might have.

So far, unraveling her true origins has been quite a project. Wherever our miraculous mate came from, Dr. Brynn covered his tracks very thoroughly. But the DNA samples don't lie. Briar was never truly his daughter, so her real parents must have been donors of some sort.

I'm proud of the way Briar embraced that information. She could have let it beat her down. Instead, she's gotten excited to explore the different facets of her heritage. She's even chatted with some distant cousins the DNA program connected her to. They live outside Seoul and have already gotten her hooked on a movie called *KPop Demon Hunters* that Dane secretly loves.

I'm determined to figure out how to make some of the more traditional dishes in this book. That way, she can have them as often as she likes and hopefully keep learning about herself as she goes.

We've all been doing that, lately. And somehow, knowing the truth about the horrors that took place during my childhood has helped me let go of a lot of things. My mother and her departure included.

I may never find out if she was threatened or simply terrified —but at least now I believe there was more to the story than meets the eye.

It still hurts, some days, but I've made peace with it. Knowing I can always come to Briar and find solace in her lap has been a huge part of that.

It's almost time, Cillian says through the bond, speaking only to Dane and me.

We've done our best to try to keep that sort of thing to a minimum. Our omega can always sense when we're communicating through the tether she created for us, even when she can't hear what we're saying...

Planning secret gifts for someone as sharp as Briar is a whole *ordeal*, but Cillian insisted on one last surprise. A *big* one.

Our mate is definitely suspicious, though. She casually taps her eReader, pretending to turn a page. "Cillian alright?"

I close the interior curtain to my half of our bond before I answer, hoping she'll buy my excuse. "Just planning another night for the two of you in the ballroom."

Briar pouts dryly. Because my brilliant baby knows I'm full of shit. "Mm-hmm."

I shrug. "I know I'm a better dancer, but it looks like you'll have to make do with the old man tonight. Sorry, viper."

Cillian must be listening to her thoughts, because he suddenly interjects. *You are not a better dancer than me.*

Briar and I smirk at each other. She whispers out loud, "Yeah, you are. But we won't tell him."

"I heard that," Cillian's voice snaps. He rounds the nearest hedge, sporting a half-smile and feral eyes. He holds his hand out for his wife.

"Come on, Mrs. Blackwood. Before we lock you up and keep you all to ourselves."

"Again?" She smirks to me, quirking a black brow.

My brother laughs, and I join in, palming her ass as we guide her out of the thorny maze of roses.

Oh, baby, I think. *You know you only have to ask.*

Will I ever stop blushing like this?

As Briar and the rest of my pack emerge from the garden, walking toward the Rolls-Royce at my back, our gazes lock. Her smile brightens as she winks, sending me a mental image. Of me, chasing her through our labyrinth. Which is just about the only use for my mask these days.

Briar slowly eased me out of my comfort zone. Starting with late night drives, movies in dark theaters. Last week, she finally asked if I would take her to a formal restaurant. She never requested I go without my face covering, but I felt her hope in our bond. And it was more than enough motivation.

The way she sneered at any other woman who looked at me—in horror or with appreciation—didn't hurt.

The memory warms my cheeks and makes my knot throb. Beside me, Louis finishes packing our picnic into the trunk and chortles at my rising scent.

"Oh you're one to talk," I grumble, nodding at his neck. It has the most savage bond mark I've ever seen branded into the side.

And that's saying something, considering where I left *mine*...

Turns out, stuffed-shirt, fork-on-the-left Coggins can be just as beastly as the rest of us. At least, when it comes to his omega.

The dour man has his usual scowl in place as he makes his way to the driver's seat. Waving Louis inside with a meaningful look before scowling in the cliffs' general direction. As if he disapproves of the cold wind.

Or his mate being out in it, at least.

Our attendant laughs, rolling his eyes. "Maybe he'll calm down after our trip."

Cillian insisted on paying for their upcoming honeymoon, where they'll spend Christmas in France with Louis and Fiona's family. Briar overhears mention of the gift she thought up for the recently bonded couple and her new friend, grinning wider.

"Don't count on it," she chips, sliding into my side. Surrounding me with black cherry perfume that teases me every bit as much as her words. "Some grumps never change."

I send her a beat of indignation. She replies with her view of me standing here, her happiness glowing in my chest... and a mighty frown on my face.

So maybe she has a point.

Rhys snickers as he joins us, slanting a look that roughly translates to *um, yeah*.

I punch his arm and shove him toward the open car door. Briar giggles, funneling pure adoration through our bond as she rises onto the toes of her heeled knee-high boots and plants a kiss over my scarred cheek. Deep down, where only I can hear, she whispers, *I hope you never stop blushing, big man.*

I'm still grinning like an idiot when she slides into the Rolls after Rhys. Cillian chuckles again, finally moving to join us. He does that more often, I've noticed. Stepping back, slowing down. Watching all of us together.

There's a protective edge to his habit, but even more pride. Awe that Briar turned us into a true family—and the unshakable belief that she's the only omega in the world who could have accomplished this.

He's right, of course. There's no one like Briar.

Except maybe Violet.

Cillian hears my errant thought, lifting his chin to meet my gaze. Understanding snaps between us as he briefly tunes into Rhys and Briar. Finding them engaged in one of their bantered debates.

We prefer not to trouble our mate with too many updates on our search for her sister. She has terrible survivor's guilt—and the fact that we may never find the missing woman she mourns in her dreams haunts all of us.

Cillian and I won't give up, though. We've combed every record we've gotten our hands on, and we have no intention of stopping. Gideon has pitched in, too, using his special government clearance and Finn's international contacts to gain access to classified information.

My best friend quickly runs through everything he's learned today—all the associates he checked in with and what they said. I do the same, running through the list of agencies that still haven't gotten back to me. Mostly facilities abroad, where the Blackwood name doesn't light a fire under people's asses.

Gideon will take care of them, Cillian thinks, then feels my surprise at the easy trust that accompanies his statement. He huffs, "I know, I know. But the kid is growing on me. He's almost as determined to find Briar's sister as we are."

Cillian senses my possessive displeasure and cocks a half-smile. "Nothing like that. I think he feels guilty for nearly getting our omega killed."

That's... fair.

Fine, I reply. *I guess he can keep his fingernails a while longer.*

Cillian's rare smile grows. He strides past, clapping me on the shoulder. "That's the spirit."

My throat rumbles, but the feeling isn't foreign anymore. Laughter is more common than most things around here these days. Except maybe for greedy growls when we're all jockeying for a spot next to our girl.

"Dane!" she calls. "Come claim your seat before I have to stab Rhys to keep him out of it."

"Again?" Rhys asks dryly.

"Yeah," she giggles. "Again."

When I finally duck into the back of the limousine-style Rolls, Briar is tracing the bite-mark on Rhys's neck. He has a tattoo there, now—an extension of his snake sleeve, depicting the head of a viper with its fangs bared. The serpent's jaw is stretched wide, all the way to the edges of our mate's silvery claim.

I had a similar thought when I updated my own ink. The patterns covering the unscarred half of my chest now extend all the way to my sternum, where Briar designed a moon—half in light, half in darkness—to surround the permanent mark she left on me.

Our omega loves it because it reminds her of the moment she saw my whole face for the first time. I love it because it's a symbol for the nickname I gave her that day.

My moonbeam.

She looks just as luminous today—and hearing me think so softens the smile on her face as she tugs me down next to her, burrowing into my side.

I've become her security blanket when we venture out. She'd never admit it out loud—and perhaps not even to her other alphas—but she's confessed through our bond that sometimes, the world still feels too big and scary to her. Knowing that I help her feel safe is an honor.

I wrap my arm around her shoulders and cuddle her close, scent-marking her forehead. Briar shuts her eyes and rests against me, stroking her fingers over my jaw.

More heat blooms under my skin, but this time I don't even try to will it away. My mate hums her approval, rubbing her cheek over mine. Covering my scars with her essence. Claiming them—and me—all over again.

Cillian

W ILL I EVER BECOME IMMUNE TO SEEING MY RING ON my wife's finger?

The answer is no. Especially since she added two bands of delicate, curling ink to her finger. One for Dane and another for Rhys—designed to surround the gold band and its sparkling array.

The tattoos were our first pack outing after her heat—and I was reliably informed that I would be the worst pack alpha *ever* if I didn't join in. So I got one to match hers, although mine is a single, solid line under my wedding band. Branded there as backup.

Which is ironic, considering the only time I've ever taken my ring off was to have the tattoo etched there.

Briar notices me frowning at my hand, trying to come up with another time when I removed the gold circle. She listens as I come up blank, watching images of myself flit through my mind.

The morning I bought it, nearly two years ago, choosing one that matched hers. Sitting at my desk, night after night, weighing it in my palm. Wondering if I'd be a good husband. Worrying that I could never be a decent mate. How heavy that band felt each day after our wedding, knowing she loathed me while I fell more in love with her every second.

Green beams gaze back at me when I raise my head and peer across the backseat. They're soft and sharp, somehow—the special combination that could only belong to my soulmate.

You know, she thinks, *I didn't <u>hate</u> you… much.*

I let my lips curve into her favorite semi-smirk. *Mysterious*, she calls it; though recalling the term nearly kicks it into a full grin.

Really, Mrs. Blackwood? I reply. *Because I remember you <u>glaring</u> at me while I recited my vows.*

She smiles back, but it's the small, somewhat-shy version that shoots a dart into my heart. *You were too handsome*, she admits. *It pissed me off.*

With a startled chuckle, I realize I believe her. Then I recall how she pouted through the heinously expensive meal after our ceremony. My spiced, smoky scent spikes as my palm tingles.

Devil, she accuses, pumping pure adoration through our bond.

I'm still not used to the way this feeling has changed me. I'm weak for it, and somehow stronger than ever because of it.

I may not be able to untangle those vines, but I show them to her anyway. Letting our omega trace each emotion down to the root, sorting the thorns from the petals.

I may be the Devil, I tell her. *But you're my Queen.*

Dane doesn't flinch as Briar suddenly launches herself into my arms. I catch her easily, mentally tutting reprimands about seatbelts until she crushes her mouth to mine.

Fuck. There's no way I'm actually the demon she claims. Because she's mine. And she's *heaven*.

Being in my lap keeps her distracted for the rest of the drive—meaning she doesn't see where we're going or ask too many questions.

Which was my plan all along.

The car rolls to a stop, and Rhys snaps into gear. He always scrambles to open doors for Briar, offer his hand. A gentleman and a romantic—until they're alone together.

Dane follows while I grasp Briar's lock pendant, pulling to tighten the chain. She gasps, lust and excitement sparking in her gaze. *Yes, Sir?*

See? Satan could never get this lucky.

The true adoration and bratty sarcasm twined around her voice make me hard. I cup her chin, capturing her lips one last time before nipping the swollen lower curve. *"Close your eyes."*

My wife grumbles internally about alpha-holes and barks, but her heart soars as she obeys, her Omega squealing with happiness when my Alpha issues a purr of approval.

"Good girl," I murmur. "Now, take my hand."

She complains while I guide her out of the car and onto the sidewalk. The third time, she *whines*, "Can I look *now*?"

I step behind her with a chuckle, gliding my hands over her hips. Dane comes to her other side while Rhys drifts forward, nervously wincing over his shoulder at the gift we've prepared.

It was a group effort—muttered through the bond in the wee hours of the morning, when our omega was lost to her dreams and unable to catch on. Now, the last month of effort looks well worth every hour and dollar we spent.

Nerves still swoop through us as we brace for her reaction. I look to each of my packmates, then nod at Dane.

"Okay, moonbeam," he husks, nuzzling her temple with his unmasked jaw. "You can open your eyes."

We all fall still as Briar flutters her lashes, squinting in the late-morning sunshine. My body feels like stone as Dane darts glances between Briar and the building in front of us. Rhys gives a little flourish, then seems to realize how lame he looks, cringing.

Briar doesn't notice, though. She drifts toward our gift, out of my reach. Everything inside me lurches, protesting... until a burst of bright, shimmering awe floods the bond.

"Oh my God," she whispers. "Is it—"

I draw her back into my arms. "Yours. Yes."

Her perfect lips fall open while she blinks, reading and rereading the sign I had made for her new store. An antique iron slab, its edges twisted into the intricate sorts of frills she loves. Emblazoned with two words:

Rosebud Books.

Briar

WILL I EVER GET USED TO RHYS'S RANTING, DANE'S blushing, or Cillian absolutely shocking the hell out of me?

God, I hope not.

"—had to move quickly when the place went up for sale, but obviously the previous owners didn't give a shit about it at all, so—"

Rhys hasn't stopped talking since he unlatched the padlock on the front door and led us inside. I feel his anxiety through the bond, along with the others', but I'm still too stunned to react.

It's the same tiny bookshop my big man brought me to for my first taste of freedom... but it's been utterly *transformed*.

The buckling wood floors have been sanded and re-stained nearly black. They match the stately rows of shelves, all featuring intricate moldings that coordinate with the newly installed windows.

They're ours, I realize. The same stained glass we have at the manor—miniaturized to fit the arched panes framing the carved front door and the counters.

There are *two*. One stacked with books and outfitted with a register. The other much longer, with several barstools lined up in front and a large, rose-gold espresso machine humming against the wall behind it.

Vines curl artfully down the onyx backdrop, twisting into a tapestry of budding...

Roses.

They hear me say the word in my mind, halting their apprehensive musings. Rhys instantly pivots. "Yeah," he enthuses, gesturing to the flowers. "It's a hydroponic wall. Dane put it in for you. It was his idea to add the plants and the coffee bar."

Dane's flush darkens. He rushes to step up beside Rhys, rubbing his hand over his beard in a sheepish gesture. "Rhys ordered *all* the books. Hundreds of them, moonbeam. It took him *weeks* to get the inventory sorted. And even longer for Cillian to buy the shop in the first place."

Because it was his grand plan, of course.

My mastermind. Devil. Dominant.

Husband.

The man in question wraps an arm around my waist, opening his palm to reveal a set of keys. "These are yours."

I take them, looping the cursive B keychain around my finger. "But I—I don't—" My head turns from one alpha to the next, finally landing on our pack leader as I whisper, "Why?"

He follows the thread of my dismay, reading all the emotions I can't convey. Confusion being the biggest.

Did they think they *had* to do this? To earn more forgiveness or keep me happy?

Cillian softens, dropping a kiss to my shoulder. "No, love. We're setting you free."

A bolt of alarm sticks in my throat, but Rhys cuts in, taking my hands and meeting my eyes. "Everything is under your name only," he rasps. "We don't own any of it and never will. It will always be *yours*. Keep it as a place to read alone and live off our money forever. Open it and peddle books until you're a millionaire. Sell the store and *take every cent*. We don't care, as long as you're *happy*, baby."

The words sink in gradually. Soaking into my soul. They are giving me real freedom. The kind that buys you a plane ticket or a house or a car.

So the choice to stay can truly be mine. Every single day.

A sob stutters out of me as I jump into Rhys's arms. He hugs me tight, waiting.

New dreams materialize in my mind. Visions of opening the store, serving coffee, and selling books. Having a special place where I can be creative and earn my own money and maybe make friends...

Cillian would teach me how to do anything business-y, I'm sure. Though I also wager those lessons will come at a delicious price.

Rhys would have opinions on everything, of course. But I bet he'd be the most charming proprietor ever. Though I'm not crazy about the thought of women flocking here to see his perfect face. *Maybe if I show off my fangs every now and then, to make sure people got the message...*

And Dane may not know much about aesthetics and books, but he would do *anything* to help me. I picture him lugging boxes, driving me back and forth. Not to mention all the physical labor that must have gone into getting the place ready for me.

The Earth seems to slow to stop as a deep, powerful truth settles over me.

"This," I decide, spinning to face *them*. "Is exactly where I want to be."

Here. With you. Forever.

Relief and joy pour through my alphas, turning Rhys's laugh into a hoarse sound as he picks me up and spins us in a gentle circle.

"Thank *God*," he says. "Because there is a *ton* of smut in here. Like, enough to last us *years*. I could never get through it alone."

Happy tears blur the beautiful store around me. I fight them off, running my eyes over the wall of rosebuds. They'll bloom and wither, like the others.

But that's okay. When the petals fall? New ones will grow.

There will be no thorns here, I decide. Just rosebuds.

Only *beginnings*.

Because these beasts? The ones who were supposed to end me?

They're my eternity.

Dane plucks me up next, folding me into his thick arms. "We love you, Briar," he rumbles. "We want you to know you always have choices with us."

Cillian cups my face and leans his forehead against mine, blue eyes burning fierce and true. "We want you to have *everything*."

The abundance of his vow—this moment, my pack—swells through me, leaving the connection forged between the four of us even brighter. *Stronger*.

I let them absorb it, too, gazing back at my husband. Repeating the first thing I ever said to him. The two words that bound me to my beasts.

I do.

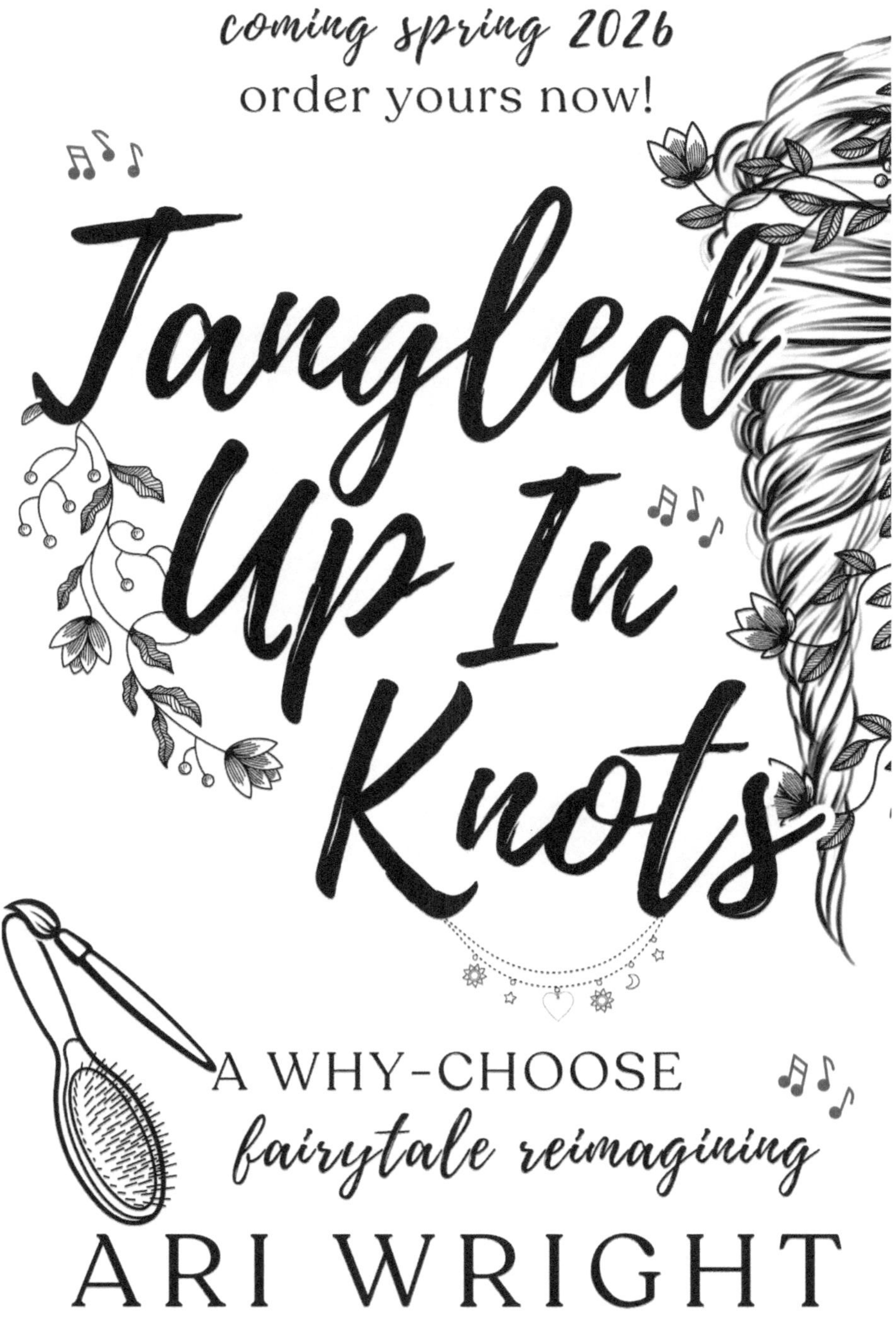

coming spring 2026
order yours now!

Tangled Up In Knots

A WHY-CHOOSE
fairytale reimagining

ARI WRIGHT

acknowledgments

Listen. If she didn't want me to write a why-choose book with a masked man, a total asshole, and a mysterious Dom, I don't know why my best friend made me read all those dark romances. Kelly, this book is YOUR FAULT, okay? So THANK YOU.

No, but seriously; I could never thank you enough for always believing in me and taking my side (even when I don't!). You're the best friend in the world and I love you all the most!

To Katie, who could not choose one of these guys to save her life. I am right there with you, which is no surprise considering we have One Brain. I am endlessly grateful to have you as my kindred spirit and constant support. I couldn't do this work without you and I am thankful every day that the universe sent you my way!

To Eliza, Amanda, and Katelin—you are the best friends/teammates to have waiting for me at the finish line! Thank you for helping me polish this book and getting it ready for my readers. Also, for always enduring my crash outs 💀

A big thank you to Britt, who did an amazing job copyediting this beast of a book. All of your words of encouragement and helpful suggestions made this one so much better!

Lastly, to my loyal readers—who have followed me from contemporary, to sport smut, to fairytales, and now on this dark romance detour—I love you to the bottom of my heart and back. It is an honor and a privilege to write books for such luminous humans.

<h1 style="text-align:center">about the author</h1>

Ari Wright was once entirely sane, but then she realized sanity is overrated and decided to write swoony Omegaverse smut.

Because life is short, you know?

When she isn't writing unhinged romances, she enjoys drinking coffee to the point of excess, kitchen experiments, raising her littles, and trying to keep her plants alive (just kidding, her husband does that).

She loves really embarrassing music, moody weather, and any story where the bad guy gets the girl—because what's Happily Ever After without a little (or a lot of) spice?

You can follow her works in progress, favorite reads, and very pink aesthetic on Instagram!

www.ingramcontent.com/pod-product-compliance
Lightning Source LLC
Chambersburg PA
CBHW022255310726

48973CB00001B/81